The I

By James Berardinelli

© 2017 James Berardinelli

Cover art by Jacob Atienza
Map by Jack O. Gibson

Table of Contents

Chapter One: Awakening
Chapter Two: A Stalking
Chapter Three: The Verdant Blight
Chapter Four: The Headache
Chapter Five: Aeris
Chapter Six: Father Backus' Catechism
Chapter Seven: The Summoner's Test
Chapter Eight: The Missing
Chapter Nine: By the Pricking of My Thumb
Chapter Ten: Something Wicked This Way Comes
Chapter Eleven: The Consequences of Breathing
Chapter Twelve: Fragments of a Life that Was
Chapter Thirteen: The One-Handed Tinker
Chapter Fourteen: The Long Road Beckons
Chapter Fifteen: Ill Wind
Chapter Sixteen: Pyre
Chapter Seventeen: West Fork
Chapter Eighteen: The Princess and the Guide
Chapter Nineteen: The Westerlands
Chapter Twenty: The Presence in the Rank
Chapter Twenty-One: The First Day of Fading
Chapter Twenty-Two: Stricken
Chapter Twenty-Three: Smoke Signals
Chapter Twenty-Four: The Man in the Mountain
Chapter Twenty-Five: The Mysteries of the Mind
Chapter Twenty-Six: Hobson's Choice
Chapter Twenty-Seven: Summoner's Gambit
Epilogue: Alone Again

LINGERING HAZE
by James Berardinelli

Chapter One: Awakening

In a life suddenly gone mad, Janelle - my name - was the only thing I had left. It came to me forcefully, like a lightning bolt in the dead of night, and I clung to it like the drowning girl I was, repeating it in my mind and with my lips like a mantra. Perhaps if I said it enough times, the reality - my reality - would replace the one momentarily glimpsed by my eyes when they had fluttered open moments ago.

It was a strange and frightening thing to be marooned in the present with the past evaporating like a mist in the face of a hurricane. My memories had been shredded by whatever force had brought me to this state. It was impossible to find stability with everything around me shifting. The human experience is a sum of memories and when those are no longer reliable or accessible, existence becomes tenuous at best.

At least I knew who I was. True, my identity had fragmented along with my remembrances but my core essence remained firm. I was Janelle. It was more than a name, more than the two entwined syllables people used to identify me. Now, it defined me. With past and future equally nebulous, it provided the anchor I needed.

When a person wakes from a dream, the sum and substance of the mind's nocturnal wanderings fade quickly and permanently, leaving behind only impressions: fear, longing, desire, joy, despair. For me, in this fragile, fleeting state of being, memories had become like dreams. But there was one image that lingered, perhaps the last one: a flash of blinding light rending the sky and slashing toward me. Then white-hot pain and the surcease of darkness.

Now was not the time to grapple with what I had lost. If the present was the only thing remaining to me then I needed to live in the present until I could build new memories or recover the ones I had lost. As terrifying as my current circumstances were, I needed to face them squarely. So, steeling myself for what I might observe, I allowed my eyelids to lift.

Vegetation surrounded me - plants like none I had ever before seen. Big-leafed shrubs and squat, thick-trunked trees. The air was clear and pure, the sky high above incredibly blue. Instinct told me I was somewhere far from what I called familiar. Evanescent memories teased me - of paved lanes and meticulously groomed lawns, of pruned bushes and air thick with the haze of pollution. That was home. This was *not*.

I took a deep breath - old training asserting itself, reminding me that the first step in facing a new situation was to calm myself. Some part of me wondered if this might all be a dream but deep down I knew that whatever it was, I wasn't going to awaken any time soon. *Something* had happened but figuring out the *what*s and *why*s of the situation weren't paramount. Survival was my concern. The more my mind stabilized in the wake of the panic-inducing dispersal of my past and the physical transference of my body, the more certain I was that the continuation of my existence depended on decisions I was about to make. If I died now, it wouldn't matter what I could remember or where I was.

Reach out with your senses when you're in a new place. Not just one or two of them. You have five; use them all. I don't know whether I had been told that or read it in a book but it applied to this situation. There was only so much my eyes could tell me about my current circumstances.

My physical state was impossible to ignore. Without clothing or jewelry for my body or polish for my nails, I was stark naked, stripped bare of any and all protection and adornments. My nose sniffed the scent of something burnt and a quick check revealed that every strand of hair, whether on my head, eyebrows, or elsewhere, was singed, almost as if I had passed through a fire. My skin had reddened as if from an all-over sunburn - uncomfortable but not painful. I wouldn't have minded some lotion but that was so far down my list of concerns that it didn't merit a second thought.

At least for the moment, the temperature was mild so I didn't have to worry about freezing to death. The ground beneath my feet was damp, as if from a recent rain. I could hear the drip-drip-dripping of water as droplets slipped off overburdened leaves. As my eyes adjusted to the bright light, I noticed that everything glistened. Had my nostrils not been burdened by the perfume of scorched follicles, I suspected I might have discerned the distinct odor that followed a summer thunderstorm. The taste in my mouth was thick and metallic, unlike anything I had previously sampled. What that portended, I couldn't guess.

I strained my ears to determine whether there was anything around me beyond the verdant growth, the gentle carpet of moss and decaying leaves, and the bequest of the rain storm. It was eerily quiet: no buzzing insects, no cawing birds, no sounds of small animals rustling through the undergrowth. Aside from the vegetation, I might be the only thing alive for miles. It wasn't a comforting thought. Whatever my strengths might be, wilderness survival wasn't among them. Procuring water wouldn't be a problem, but what about food and shelter? Without matches or a lighter, I doubted I'd be able to start a fire. Rubbing two sticks together…? At the moment, the need to encounter another person outweighed the awkwardness of being seen unclothed by him or her.

Janelle, you've got a great body. You shouldn't hide it so much. The voice sang out in my mind almost as if the person speaking was standing next to me. But she wasn't. I didn't know who she was or why she had said it. Was she a friend? A sister? A mother?

A great body, though? Hardly. My chest was too flat, my hips not round enough. I had the appearance of an athlete although I lacked memories of doing anything sporty. I didn't need a mirror to know what my features were like; my face was, for lack of a better word, "cute." (That's what everyone said about me - not "beautiful" or "attractive" or even "pretty" - just "cute.") My shoulder-length hair was the color of a ripe acorn - or it had been before my ordeal. Now, it felt as stiff as straw. God knew what it looked like.

I tried to get up and found my legs to be as weak as rubber under me, their strength sapped. To stand, I had to rely on the support of a nearby tree. The smoothness of the bark, as slippery as glass or ice, was unfamiliar. Or maybe I knew of it but couldn't remember. That was the problem with holes in the memory: you couldn't be sure what you might have forgotten.

Leaning against the tree in a standing position, my breath streamed from me like I had run a marathon. Why did simple actions demand such exertion? Why was the mere act of rising foreign? What had happened to me? Denying the actuality of the situation was pointless. This was far too *tangible* to be a dream. But what was it? Had I gone insane and slipped into a self-created world, trapped somewhere in the deepest recesses of my mind? Or perhaps I was dead. This didn't seem much like the afterlife my pastor had droned on about Sunday after Sunday but what other explanation could there be?

After a short rest, my legs stopped trembling and I was able to stand without aid. I took a tentative step or two and felt like a toddler learning to walk. The ground, which was soft and warm, felt good beneath my feet until my left sole was pierced by a razor-sharp thorn buried in the upper layer of loam. The pain did two things: it caused me to let out a yelp followed by a string of profanity and it jogged free a memory from the haze behind which so many of my remembrances had retreated.

I had been perhaps eight years old, so the event had occurred a decade ago. Running barefoot along the sidewalk near my house, I had misstepped as children of that age sometimes do and fallen forward, barely raising my left arm in time to protect my face from smacking the concrete. In the immediate aftermath of the fall, I had hurt in so many places that it had been hard to determine which was worse: my twisted ankle, my bloody knees, or my shattered wrist. I had been crying - wailing and screaming, actually - but no one had heard me. Then, as now, I had been all alone. Except at eight years old, I had been able to make my way home, hobbled and bleeding and cradling my injured hand, where my parents had been waiting. This time, something told me home and my parents were far, far away.

The wave of isolation and loneliness was so unexpected that my knees nearly buckled. It wasn't good to think hard about my situation. Precarious didn't begin to describe it. I had a pretty good idea of who I was at the moment but only the vaguest notion of who I had been. As for my whereabouts… I was as lost as I was at a loss. Answers were for later. Now I had to start moving and thinking about the basics of living in these circumstances. Just because I wasn't a survivalist didn't mean I couldn't survive. The weather was warm although there was no guarantee the temperate conditions would last, especially after nightfall. If there were other people in the vicinity, I needed to find them. If not, I would probably either starve to death or poison myself eating a berry that wasn't meant for a person to ingest.

I sat cross-legged on the ground and gently extracted the thorn from my foot. A half-inch in length and curved like a talon, it awakened me to the hidden dangers I faced: cuts, punctures, infections. Once the offending object had been plucked out, I resumed my journey, stepping gingerly, using my toes to probe the mud where I couldn't see. My eyes were attentive, darting everywhere, and my ears were no less active. This wasn't like any forest I was familiar with. The trees *looked* different. They were shorter and stubbier with a sparse leaf canopy that allowed sunlight to filter to the ground. There wasn't much color - everything was shades of green and brown without small wildflowers or multi-hued leaves to break the monotony. The more I studied my surroundings, the more alien they appeared.

Time moved differently here. The sun's traversal of the daytime sky was slower than I was accustomed to. Without a clock, it was impossible to tell the passage of hours with any degree of accuracy, but it felt like I had been walking for hours while the sun had barely moved. By the time it reached its zenith, the air temperature had become unpleasantly warm. When I decided to rest for a while to ease the ache in my calves, I found a shaded spot under a large tree and practically collapsed. My skin was slick with perspiration.

As I sat with my back against the velvety bark, I contemplated my situation - something I had been trying not to do as I traveled lest it impede my intensity of focus. It would be easy to give in to despair. It took only a moment's consideration to recognize how desperate things were. I had been lost before but never this completely. It was as if some unseen hand had plucked me from a safe, familiar place and dropped me *here*. Not only didn't I know where I was but I didn't know where I was supposed to be going. I had always been decisive and goals-oriented. I remembered that much about myself. But how was I supposed to achieve an objective when I had no idea what it might be?

If I continued in the direction I had been walking, essentially following the path of least resistance through what appeared to be uninhabited terrain, where would it lead me? Was I headed deeper into the wilderness? I rejected the possibility that this place, wherever or whatever it might be, was devoid of people. Someone had brought me here and that implied intelligence and purpose. That belief kept me from sinking into dejection. I recognized that maintaining a hopeful attitude was one of the most important survival tools at my disposal.

After a short nap, I backtracked to a small running brook I had passed earlier. I slaked my thirst there, cleaned the wound on my foot, and took a quick bath with the cool water washing away the grime and the residual smell of burnt hair. Somewhat refreshed, I was ready to resume my journey. The long afternoon passed lazily, with the ground drying even as the air became pregnant with moisture. Other than the plants, there was no sign of anything living - not even the tiniest ant or mosquito and certainly nothing larger. By the time I stopped again, the sun was beginning to dip in the sky. Night would soon be here and, based on my rudimentary understanding of celestial mechanics, it would be as long as the day. At some point, I would need to establish some kind of shelter (or at least identify a place where I could spend the night).

Once the sun was closer to the horizon than its zenith, the air had cooled enough so sweat was no longer dripping off me. I located a clearing that I thought might make a passable spot to wait out the dark hours. Not having to worry about bugs or animals meant that the only real concerns were temperature and physical discomfort. The ground here was carpeted with moss. It felt soft enough at the moment but I knew that wouldn't be the case after lying on it for several hours. I wasn't sure how to keep warm. I lacked the materials to create a makeshift blanket - the best I could do was strip leaves off trees and sleep under a pile of them. I didn't think that would be effective but it was the best I could do.

My stomach grumbled, reminding me that, although finding water hadn't been a problem, I hadn't eaten anything since my arrival. Based on what I'd seen thus far, my only option seemed to be munching on leaves. Taste considerations aside (maybe I could convince myself I was eating a salad without dressing), I didn't know whether they were edible. Exchanging hunger cramps for a bout of vomiting wasn't an equitable trade-off. I decided to wait for as long as I could before sampling them. I recall reading about people who had lived weeks without eating. I doubted my stomach would welcome something that extreme but, at the moment, not eating anything was more appealing than eating what might worsen my situation.

Twilight was a long, lingering experience. In other circumstances, I might have enjoyed it. As the day's light dimmed with the sun sliding beneath the horizon, the forest became a strange and otherworldly place. It took forever for true dusk to descend. For what seemed like hours after sunset, I could still see my surroundings. Darkness came with such a gentle gradualness that it was with some surprise that, at one point, I realized I could no longer see. Even a hand placed an inch from my face was invisible.

I tried to sleep. I was sore and exhausted, my body unused to the deprivations and exertions it had been put through today. But my bed was too uncomfortable to allow me to doze even fitfully and my mind remained active. No amount of thinking, however, could resolve my situation. The *why*s and *how*s of what had happened were unknowable. Was this a physical place to which I had been unaccountably transported or was it a state of mind? The flash of light - had it been lightning? Had I been electrocuted? Perhaps… but all this seemed too real to be a figment of a broken or confused brain. The best I could do for the moment was to accept the facts of my condition: I was alive but marooned in a place very far from home.

I wasn't the kind of person who cried often or easily but, in the lonely blackness of the first night in a strange land, I wept like I hadn't since I was a little girl. Great, wracking sobs shook my body and tears bled from my eyes until they were puffy and my nose was clogged with snot. I was tired, hungry, scared, and naked. I wanted to go home. I wanted to be surrounded by family and friends. I whispered a prayer even though I didn't believe in God. It was said there were no atheists in foxholes. This was my foxhole.

The silence was more terrifying than rustling in the bushes or even distant howls would have been. The only sounds were when a breeze stirred the leaves. Maybe it should have been reassuring that I wouldn't become a meal for a nighttime predator but the sense of total isolation was so disconcerting that my mind shied from ruminating about it.

I considered making plans for tomorrow, but what was there to consider beyond walking and resting and hoping I would encounter something other than trees and bushes? In terms of choosing a direction, the only thing I had to be careful about was not to go in circles. The only thing worse than traveling to an unknown destination was going *nowhere*. I decided that, once dawn came, I'd start thinking aloud. I needed to hear a voice, even if it was my own. Otherwise, I would surely go mad. (Assuming I hadn't already.)

The impenetrable darkness didn't last as long as I expected it to. Only a few hours after the last rays of the evening twilight had vanished, a faint, silvery light began to filter through the forest canopy. I became aware of it when I saw the outline of my hand as I reached up to brush a lock of hair away from my forehead. A little patience revealed that this wasn't an indicator of an early dawn but the arrival of a gibbous moon.

As it rose into the sky, I became aware that this wasn't like *my* moon. Even though part of it lay in the planet's shadow, I could tell it was irregularly shaped. It also seemed smaller and closer. I took notice of the stars as well, silently cursing myself for not having shown more interest in the night sky. But I could detect none of the few constellations I was familiar with. Strange that I could remember such a minor detail with clarity while so much of my past was a hazy jumble. I knew the Big Dipper but I couldn't remember my mother's face or name. What had happened to me?

By the light of the celestial interloper, the forest became ghostly. The lack of noise made it unnerving. Even though the temperatures remained moderate - a fact for which I was grateful - my flesh broke out in goose pimples and I shivered involuntarily. Was this *normal* for wherever I was, or was there something wrong here? Answering that question might go a long way toward determining my prognosis for long-term survival.

At some point, despite my physical discomfort, I dozed off. When I opened my eyes, the moon had ascended to a point nearly directly overhead and another orb was cresting the horizon. The second source of illumination made it easier to see my surroundings - less like night and more like a dark, overcast day. If motivated, I could have resumed my travels, but I was still too tired and sore to start off and, being unfamiliar with the terrain, I felt it was best to wait until daylight. The moonlight was weak enough that it would be easy to misstep. If I became injured, especially if it was serious, I would stand no chance. No companions, no doctors, no food, no clothes, no help... that was the reality of my situation. The best way to combat it was to exercise an overabundance of caution. Not necessarily a strong suit for someone as impulsive as me but I had no choice.

Sleep eventually returned but it was neither restful nor revitalizing – just a way to pass the long, dead minutes and hours. When I awoke in the eerie, quasi-twilight provided by the twin moons, I was bathed in sweat and shivering. Dimly recalled horrific images from a nightmare flitted through my consciousness - ugly things fueled by a malignant power that sought to pull me under the ground and devour me. When I started into wakefulness with a cry, those imaginings vanished but the fear and revulsion remained. Somehow, even unremembered, that nightmare had been more substantial than my memories of my other life, as if the dream had emerged not from the depths of my subconscious but from something altogether more concrete.

Then, out of the corner of one eye, I saw it… movement. No more than a half-glimpse and, when I turned to look at the spot, there was nothing. I blinked several times in rapid succession to clear my vision but, no matter how hard I strained, everything was still as if in a frozen tableau. No breeze to rustle branches or tease leaves along the ground. It must have been a trick of the faint, fickle light or an afterimage of the nightmare. And yet… those explanations sounded like rationalizations. Part of my mind was sure I had seen movement, and movement meant I wasn't alone.

After that, sleep proved elusive. Every time I closed my eyes, I sensed something out there, watching me - silent and still in its vigilance. It could have been my imagination - the things I had experienced in the past day were enough to drive even the most sane, stable person past the point of breaking. Or it could be that my new land wasn't as empty as I had previously suspected - except, in this case, there was reason to believe that isolation might be preferable. How I knew this, I don't know. But whatever was out there, if there was anything, it wasn't merely aloof, it was malign. Survival might have just gotten more complicated.

Chapter Two: A Stalking

It took forever for morning to arrive. The night crawled by at a pace I could only describe as painful and my inability to shut down my thinking made it more torturous. I found myself wishing I had learned the skill of meditation at some point during my 18 years but I'd viewed that capability, like other "useless proficiencies" (mathematics, for example), as better left to those with an inclination. Why bother, after all, with something boring that I'd never use in "the real world?"

The real world. In my circumstances, what did that even mean? Stop thinking, start acting - that would have to be my catechism going forward. One decision I had made during the long night was to choose life. I'm not sure what that meant but I wasn't going to lie down, close my eyes, and give up. I didn't understand my situation but I could forge ahead. I could be in the moment. Maybe everything else would eventually be made clear. Maybe I'd wake up in a hospital bed somewhere. Or maybe, body and soul, I was *here*. Acting like it was the latter wouldn't adversely affect me if it was the former.

Struggling to my feet, I took stock of how I felt this morning. My body ached from having spent the night lying on a patch of cold, slightly damp moss and, although my skin's redness had abated, I still felt a little sunburned. Thanks to my nearly all-day trek yesterday, my leg muscles hurt. No doubt doctors would claim I had overexerted myself but it's not as if I had much choice in the matter. My foot was sore around the thorn's entry wound and there was some redness. It was probably infected but, like the gnawing in the pit of my stomach, I had to push it aside. I would likely die of something else before sepsis killed me. Time to get moving.

The terrors of the night - the sense of being watched, the phantom movement half-seen in the moonlight - abated with the sun's rising.

By the light of day, I felt almost ashamed of my fear. Here I was, 18 years of age, and afraid of the dark. People normally didn't like the night because of what it hid. Here, there was nothing to hide except trees and shrubs, and those didn't change from hour to hour regardless of whether the sun was in the sky or not.

It hadn't gotten as cool during the darkness as I had expected - I guess the humidity had helped to hold the heat - and it was already warming up by the time I re-started my journey. The sky wasn't the cerulean it had been yesterday. White clouds dotted a washed-out blue. I didn't see signs of imminent bad weather, but what did I know? Even in my "old" life, I hadn't paid attention to the forecasts. And if a storm came, there wasn't much I could do except hunker down and ride it out. One benefit of being naked was that it didn't matter if I got wet. In fact, as dirty as I felt, I might welcome it.

I had been traveling less than an hour when the feeling came back. It wasn't as strong as it had been during the night, but it was unmistakable. I was being observed. No matter how closely I scanned the nearby terrain, I couldn't see anything untoward. The air was becalmed so nothing was moving. Silence ruled the day as completely as it had ruled the night; I was the only source of noise. Now I knew what people meant when they referred to a "sixth sense." This was something I hadn't experienced before arriving here but it was as if I *knew* something was out there without seeing it. And it didn't feel friendly. If there was a malignant entity out there, was it too much to hope there might also be a benign one?

I resisted the impulse to increase my pace. Unless I could see it, unless I knew its precise location, there was no point in running. To do so would tire me out and expose me to possible injury. Better to continue at a slow, steady pace, paying more attention to the ground ahead than looking for phantoms in the trees.

I searched around until I found a smooth, thick stick. Its primary utility would be to help with walking over rough terrain but it could double as a weapon if necessary. It bolstered my confidence to have something stout in my hands. At five feet long and perhaps two inches in diameter (my height but not my width), it was a good size. Bigger and smaller options abounded - the forest floor was littered with twigs and branches - but this one was "just right." I thought of the Goldilocks fairy tale and, as I did, a memory awakened of me as a little girl lying in a warm, plush bed while someone read it to me.

The next hour or so of my hike was fraught with tension. None of my regular senses detected anything unusual - no movement, no sound, no strange smells. I was on constant edge, however. A part of me recognized how irrational my fear was but I couldn't shake the perception that I was under scrutiny, at best being studied, at worst being stalked. Several times, I stopped suddenly, crouched down, and waited in complete stillness for many minutes, scanning around me and straining my ears. Nothing. Then came the throbbing.

It happened during one of these quick pauses. The ground here was muddy with the shade of an unusually large tree having prevented the sun from baking it. My toes sank just beneath the surface, relishing the cool mushiness and, although my eyes and ears were treated to the same nothingness that had greeted them at every previous attempt to surprise a lurker, my feet detected a thrumming - a brief but undeniable vibration that was almost painful in its intensity. I started and, in a moment of panic, considered whether I could climb the tree, but the feeling was gone as suddenly as it had come. I had no idea whether it was connected with whatever was out there but it had been sufficiently unsettling to cause me to worry about the safety of the ground. Maybe this was how people who lived in earthquake-prone areas felt - a thing that should be immutable suddenly lost its solidity. If you couldn't trust the earth, what could you trust?

The rest of the morning - or at least the period it took for the sun to reach its highest point in the sky - passed without incident. I was tired, hot, and drained when I stopped for a "noon" rest. I was also desperately thirsty but, although water had been plentiful yesterday in the wake of the storm that had preceded my arrival, today was a different matter. My lips were parched and my throat sore. It was difficult manufacturing enough spit to keep the inside of my mouth moist. My pee came out in yellow dribbles instead of clear streams. My stomach continued to rumble its unhappiness with the lack of anything solid.

While I was sitting at the base of a tree wondering whether I was more likely to die of hunger, thirst, or an infected foot, I heard the noise. At first, I thought it was a breeze rustling the leaves... except the air was as still as it had been all morning and the sound didn't abate after a few seconds. It remained constant - a gentle whisper that promised *something*. I didn't know what it represented but was enough to pique my curiosity and compel me back to my feet. My energy level might have been low - the byproduct of too little to eat, a restless night's sleep, and a hot day without water - but hope lived in my breast.

I followed the sound, or at least wandered in the direction from which it seemed to be coming. My wariness of my surroundings was momentarily forgotten, set aside by my excitement at the possibility of something new. Based on directions determined by the sun's position, I was headed toward the southeast - a change from my previous course, which had been northeasterly. It didn't matter. One direction was as good as any other as long as it took me somewhere.

I figured out what it was before I saw it. What had sounded at first like a distant droning resolved itself into the rush of water as I drew nearer. The forest thinned just short of the river, giving way to a rock-strewn, gently sloping bank. This was no mere stream or brook like I had previously encountered. This was a raging torrent - at least a hundred feet from side to side with a swiftly flowing current. It was impossible to determine how deep it was at the center and I wasn't eager to find out. I didn't have a particular fear of drowning but it was far too dangerous to attempt a crossing, especially without a partner. Still, the water was shallow and gentle close to the edge. That offered the possibility not only of slaking my thirst but allowing me to wash away some of the dirt and sweat that had accumulated since my last "bath."

After spending several long minutes cooling in the shallows, I decided to follow the river upstream. My shaky understanding of geography indicated that the best chance of finding a settlement would be close to water. A river like this would provide not only sustenance for people and animals but a means to irrigate crops and a method of transportation. Like my recollection of "Goldilocks", these were shards of knowledge gleaned from a memory that had less difficulty summoning up facts and trivia than personal remembrances. I wondered why that was. How could I know that Columbus had sailed the Atlantic in 1492 yet not recall the name of the street where I lived or, for that matter, what my house looked like? How could I know that the first president of the United States had been George Washington yet not know whether I had brothers or sisters and, if I did, what *their* names were? It was beyond frustrating.

For a while, as I ambled alongside the river on the thin strip of beach separating the bank from the forest, I was able to put aside my misgivings about this place. The roar of the current, engorged by recent rainfall, was as pleasant to my ears as the sweetest music. It not only drove back the silence but caused me to wonder how much of my fear was borne of paranoia and loneliness. After all, who wouldn't be unbalanced after enduring an experience like mine?

The respite wasn't destined to last, however. Even the river's reassuring primal power couldn't hold back the sense of being watched. It crept up on me as I followed the waterway's northern progression, taking little time to reassert itself with the same force it had earlier exerted. It emanated from the forest; my right side, the side bordered by the river, was unthreatening. Could I escape it by crossing? Was it worth the risk? Gazing across the hundred feet of water, I saw only more trees. But what lay on the other side wasn't a source of great concern; the churning maelstrom in the middle of the channel was what worried me. Was I a strong enough swimmer to avoid being caught up in that?

After walking for another hour, I decided to rest. Although I didn't feel comfortable in the forest, I temporarily left the beach area because it was cooler under the trees. Although my thirst had been assuaged, not having eaten was keeping my energy level low. I was sleepy, weary, achy, and stretched thin with anxiety. I didn't know how much longer I was going to be able to keep up this pace. Right now, all I wanted to do was lie down and go to sleep. But the ground here was too rough and I didn't want to waste the light. Although, once darkness fell, I wasn't sure I'd be able to sleep - not with some invisible presence out there biding its time.

I sat under a tree with my back against its smooth exterior. It felt like glass - a sensation foreign to my experience of bark. I gazed unblinkingly at the greenery around me, willing my eyes to catch a glimpse of what I thought I had seen during the night, but there was nothing. I no longer doubted that there was something out there but I didn't know whether or not it was corporeal. It could have been a ghost or spirit of the forest. Could something with no body do more than unnerve me? I wasn't sure I wanted to find out.

Closing my eyes offered a non-visual perspective of my surroundings. It was almost as if I could reach out with my other senses to the nearby environs. I heard and felt the potency of the river, rushing along less than a hundred feet away. The stolid silence of the forest was equally forceful, a testimony to the enduring power of nature. And the watcher was there as well, more easily detected with my vision removed. It observed me but didn't desire that I reciprocate.

Tentatively, without understanding what I was doing, I reached out for it with my mind. It flinched away and, for the briefest of moments, it was gone. It soon returned, however, but this time I sensed that it was more reticent, almost as if it hadn't expected me to do what I had done and was wary that I might try again. I might have if I had understood what I had done but the instinct that had led me to act was no longer there and I couldn't replicate the deed.

I think I may have dozed off - not for a long while but long enough for me to feel groggy and sluggish when I stumbled to my feet. A quick dip in the shallows refreshed me enough to resume my trek. When twilight approached, I faced the unenviable decision of where to camp for the night. I could stay on the beach but I doubted I'd get any shut-eye lying naked on a bed of uneven, sometimes jagged rocks. The forest provided softer ground but moving under the canopy multiplied my unease. Eventually, acknowledging the necessity of getting some sleep, I opted to establish my resting place on the forest's fringes.

The closer the sun drew to disappearing beneath the horizon, the higher my dread climbed. As best I remembered, darkness wasn't one of my phobias. Night had always been a soothing time, a winding down of the day. The absence of light wasn't something to be feared. Sure, some animals slept during the day and prowled at night but I didn't live in a place where that was a concern. But here, where there were no flashlights or lanterns, and something was out there…I had never been more scared.

The period between sunset and moonrise was agonizing. With no light or way of making it, I was blind. This time of absolute blackness lasted only a couple of hours but it seemed to take forever. My ability to hear noise from the forest was defeated by the gurgling and churning of the river. I didn't even try to sleep. I sat with my back against a tree and my stick clutched in white-knuckled hands. The presence was all around me but it wasn't growing in strength. Something was holding it back. The more attuned I became to it, the more I could read things about it. I couldn't pinpoint its location but it was in the forest, not on the beach, and it wasn't dangerously close. It reeked of carrion and wrongness - not to my physical nose but to some analogous sense in my mind.

Once again, I recognized the influence of a "sixth sense." That elusive and contested quality, often mentioned in books about the paranormal in the world I came from, might be tangible here. I didn't understand it but like seeing, hearing, feeling, tasting, and smelling, some of its applications came naturally to me. Without it, I probably wouldn't be aware that I wasn't alone. I wondered if that might be better.

Moonrise made the forest more eerie but less frightening. Exhaustion-fueled sleep eventually claimed me and, in its bosom, I suffered through a string of nightmares. Visions of twisted, inhuman creatures troubled my mind and I woke frequently, crying and whimpering. By the late middle of the night, with both moons overhead, I gave up and rose to a sitting position, wincing against the protests of an aching body. It didn't take long for even an apparently smooth patch of ground to feel like a bed of nails.

Midway through the process of changing my position, I froze. There it was, not twenty feet away from me, regarding me with baleful eyes from its position behind a bush. In the ghostly, washed-out light, it was hard to discern clearly; it was squat and misshapen, perhaps the size of a large dog. Its body seemed to…undulate. The thing that captured my attention was the eyes - their darkness reflected the moon's light, making them glow white. The force of its presence was as powerful as it had ever been. The instant it realized it had been seen, it scuttled away into the forest, moving so fast that it seemingly vanished. But, although I could no longer see it, my mind told me it hadn't retreated far. It was still watching me, only from a distance.

Needless to say, any chance of additional sleep was dashed. With my heart pounding, I spent the rest of the night in terror, my only comfort derived from the solidity of the stick in my hands. I had no idea whether it would be effective against that creature - some inner instinct told me it wouldn't be - but it felt good to know that I wasn't completely defenseless.

Morning found me shaken, weary to the bone, and fully convinced I wouldn't survive another night in this strange world. The tension of being stalked was taking as much of toll as my physical deprivations.

The survival instinct that had driven me since my arrival - was it only two long days ago? - was dwindling. But the alternative to soldiering on was to curl up and die. That no longer seemed as unthinkable as it once had. When I had first come here, I had wanted answers. Now, all I wanted was peace.

An inhuman half-growl/half-scream from not far away in the forest ensured that peace was the last thing this day had in store for me.

Chapter Three: The Verdant Blight

I hoped a long, slow soak in the chilly river waters would at least partially revive me. Although my weakness was caused by a combination of hunger and sleep deprivation, I needed some sort of physical stimulus to sharpen my focus. I also realized I couldn't put off a decision about food for much longer. The idea of chewing leaves wasn't more appealing today than it had been yesterday or the day before but, since I hadn't seen an alternative - not even a berry or flower - the choice might soon be taken from me. Survival demanded food but it didn't require that the food taste good.

Being in the water helped clear my mind. It also brought back a memory - me, as a teenager, in a pool with a boy. Not that many years ago. I had been crushing on him for a while and that warm summer day was the first time he had approached me. In school, he had never noticed me but the daring bikini I was wearing caught his attention. He smiled at me and then one of my friends dunked me under the water. Thinking about that day brought a smile to my face even as it triggered a pang of longing. Gone. The boy. His smile. All gone. *Why??*

I surfaced from my underwater dive, pushed back the wet hair from my face, and froze. In that first moment, I couldn't accept what my eyes were seeing. But blinking didn't chase the vision away. It was real, or as real as anything in these circumstances could be. Across the river, one hundred feet away, were two people.

By the way they were acting, walking briskly along the bank toward the south and talking animatedly to one another, they hadn't seen me. They were close enough to be recognizable as a boy and a girl. They were oddly dressed in ill-fitting, homespun clothing but they were unmistakably human, the boy being around my age (or a little older) and the girl a few years younger. At this distance, the blondness of their hair was their most arresting characteristic.

My astonishment lasted only a few seconds. Then I began jumping up and down, splashing, and yelling. "Hey! Over here! Help!" The river's sound was loud but I was louder. They turned toward me as one and, when their eyes identified the source of the commotion, their surprise matched my own.

Without pausing to think, I plunged into the water and made for the opposite bank, the need to reach the newcomers overcoming my fear of getting pulled under or swept away. After about ten feet, the river bottom dropped away and I was forced to swim. I kept my eyes on the strangers as I paddled directly toward them but, as I got close to the middle of the river, I realized I'd never be able to maintain this trajectory. As I had feared, the current was too strong. It grabbed hold of me and began pulling me downstream. The more I fought it, the more tired I became, and I was already weak.

Another stroke and I went under, caught in an eddy that sucked me down. Moments later, coughing and sputtering, I popped back up like a cork only to be slapped in the face by a swell. Gasping, I strove to force air through the water that had invaded my nose and mouth. My waterlogged vision couldn't latch onto anything familiar. Disorientation gripped me in a vise's grasp. The current, more powerful than I had anticipated, was sending me spinning downstream like a top. I was no longer thinking about the people. Now it was just about surviving this ordeal. I went under again, came up, hit my arm and shoulder against something unyielding, probably a log or a tree branch. My breath was coming in great heaves. Tiredness and fear had transformed my confidant crawl stroke into a desperate doggie paddle.

I was dead. I knew it as surely as I had ever known anything. So close to salvation but done in by one rash decision…

Then I felt a strong, supporting arm close around my waist. Words were shouted into my left ear: "Come with me." Shaking my head to clear the water from my eyes, I allowed him to guide me toward the opposite bank. It was closer than I had suspected but we were far, far downstream from where I had entered. The girl was tracking us from the shore, jogging to keep up. "Hurry," pressed my companion, a note of urgency in his voice. "Swim as hard as you can. I'll help you. There are rapids near and if we don't get out of the river quickly, we never will."

I summoned my fading strength and stroked. Twenty-five feet: his arm, locked above my hips, was keeping me afloat. I couldn't do this on my own. Twenty feet: I choked as a crest of water overwhelmed me. I faltered but he didn't. Fifteen feet: my strength was spent. I fought the current but it was a losing battle. If not for his grip, I would have been pulled toward the rapids, a roar that was growing louder by the second. Ten feet: I caught a glimpse of the girl's face. She was alarmed. The boy gave up all pretense of helping me and manhandled me toward the bank. Five feet: the girl entered the water and grabbed me. Together they got me to land. Before I passed out, I caught a glimpse of the rapids. We were at their edge. Another ten feet and the blow of a rock would have rendered all my questions and trepidations moot.

I wasn't unconscious for long - perhaps no more than a minute. When I came to, they were both squatting next to my supine form, watching me with a mixture of concern and fascination. I noticed a familial resemblance - with features that similar, they had to be brother and sister. They had the same high cheekbones, upswept ears, snub noses, emerald eyes, and shaggy white-blond hair. They were fit with sun-darkened skin and lean, muscular bodies.

I could only imagine how I looked to them - a bedraggled waif with stringy hair and sunburned skin. The fact that I was naked, which might under different circumstances have caused me considerable embarrassment, was well down my list of concerns. I groaned, turned my head to the side, and vomited a considerable amount of water. I felt like I had swallowed half the river.

"Are you all right?" the boy asked. His features were etched with worry. It was a grave, serious face. A good face. Then again, in these circumstances, anything might be a good face.

Only then did it occur to me that I could understand what he was saying. I only knew one language: English. (In high school, I had dabbled in French but, other than *oui* and *non*, it hadn't stuck. Now where did that memory come from?) Was he speaking English? Somehow, I didn't think so. But I was hearing and comprehending him. Would he understand me when I replied in my native tongue?

"I shouldn't have tried to cross the river," I sputtered. My voice was shockingly weak. It sounded strange to my ears. Despite my resolve to sing and talk as I walked, I hadn't said a word out loud in two days (except for a few choice profane expressions when I had stubbed a toe or tripped).

"No, you shouldn't have," said the girl. I turned toward her. Her brother was on my left and she was by my feet. The seeming harshness of her words was belied by the caring evident in her gaze. More handsome than pretty, she was at that awkward age between adolescence and adulthood. Her body was as robust as her brother's although with a more feminine shape.

They obviously understood me. Another mystery. Not that I wasn't grateful. The absence of a language barrier would make things easier. Or at least I hoped it would. Maybe they were speaking English. Maybe I was overthinking this.

At that moment, I realized another thing: my stalker was still watching. It was on the other side of the river and I intuitively knew it couldn't cross. At least not here.

"Can you sit up?" asked the boy, ignoring his sister's comment. His eyes never left me, although his gaze wasn't fixed on my face. It made sense, I suppose. After all, I was naked.

With a little effort and some help from the girl, who was more willing than her brother to touch me, I got to a sitting position. I resisted the urge to use my arms to cover my breasts. By now, I was past that. It's not like they hadn't already seen everything. No sense in getting shy now, especially when protecting my modesty wasn't near the top of my list of things to do.

It was, however, apparently high on theirs. Without a word, the boy stripped off his muslin shirt and held it out to me. I took it and slipped it over my head. It smelled of sweat and dirt and felt considerably rougher than clothing I was used to wearing, but it was long enough to cover not only my chest but everything down to just above my knees.

Stripped bare from the waist up, he revealed a well-sculpted, almost hairless chest. His skin was as dark under the shirt as on his arms, an indication that he probably didn't cover his chest often.

"Who are you?" The girl and boy spoke in unison, their words and inflection identical.

"My name is Janelle. I…" How to explain? How to begin when I didn't know myself? If I spoke the truth, I was going to sound like a gibbering idiot. But if I didn't… I had never been good at lying. White lies, black lies, little lies, big ones… I was always found out. And the stakes were too important here for me to begin with a prevarication. "I'm not sure where I'm from or why I'm here. Or even where *here* is."

They didn't laugh. They didn't look at me like I was a moron. Puzzlement creased their features but it was a kind, sympathetic puzzlement not a disbelieving sort.

"I'm Samell," said the boy. "And this is my sister, Esme. You're in The Verdant Blight, south of the village of Aeris."

My blank expression told them that the places they had mentioned meant nothing to me. The Verdant Blight? Aeris? Every bit of evidence I was presented with pointed to my being far, far from home.

"I…I'm not sure how to say this. It's going to sound insane. But I'm not from *here*. I mean, I'm not from this world. At least I don't think I am. There was a flash of light and I woke up in this forest. My memories are all messed up. And I've been walking for days without seeing another person until you two came along." I was right when I said *it's going to sound insane*. Even to me, that's how it sounded and I was living it.

Samell and Esme exchanged a look before he spoke. His voice held no trace of skepticism or condescension. It was as if he had accepted what I said without question. "You need to speak with our village elders. If you're willing, we can take you to Aeris."

My stomach chose that particular moment to grumble aloud.

"Are you hungry?" asked Samell.

I offered him a wan smile. "I haven't eaten in days. I was thinking about chewing on some leaves since there doesn't seem to be anything better to eat around here."

Looks of horror crossed my new companions' features. "Whatever you do, don't do that!" warned Esme. "Thank the gods we found you before you ate!" I was taken aback by the vehemence of her tone.

"The trees are poison," explained Samell. "Not to touch but to eat. Since you've been here for a while, I'm sure you've noticed there's nothing alive in the forest. It takes care of its own. Anything that eats a tree, whether an insect or a bird or an animal, dies. This is the only forest of its kind on the continent and it's growing."

I suppose that explained a few things, although it made my heart flutter when I thought how close I had come to joining the ranks of all the dead creatures poisoned by the trees. But maybe there was something immune to the poison. Something with black eyes that scuttled around hiding behind bushes and watching.

Esme handed Samell a short sword and small leather satchel she had been holding for him - items he had divested himself of before entering the water. I noticed she had a similar pouch slung over her shoulder in addition to a bow and quiver of arrows strapped to her back. Surely I was safe in the company of a swordsman and archer?

Samell reached inside the bag and withdrew a crust of bread and a twisted, sinewy strip of cured meat that looked like beef jerky. Neither was appetizing but I was so famished that I made short work of the "meal." The bread was stale but the meat - whatever animal it was taken from - was surprisingly tasty, having been flavored with a variety of spices I had never before tasted. I would have liked more but thought it would be rude to ask for it.

"I think we'd better get you to the village. There's more - and better - food there. Esme and I were only provisioned for a day so we can't offer you a full meal. Besides, the sooner you talk to the elders, the sooner you'll figure out what's happened to you." Samell rubbed his clean-shaven chin between a thumb and forefinger, giving him the appearance of being deep in thought. As if to himself, he muttered, "There's something strange going on here."

"Can you walk?" asked Esme.

In addition to battering my body - I was going to be one giant bruise tomorrow - the experience had drained my already low reserves of stamina. There was only so much energy a small portion of bread and jerky could renew. But I didn't have much choice. This was survival not a camp-out. "How far is it?"

"About two cycles," said Samell, not realizing I had no idea what a *cycle* was. "We left before dawn on our patrol. We could get there faster if we set an aggressive pace but I don't think you'd be able to keep up. Esme could go on ahead and I could stay with you."

"There's something else," I said. "In the forest, there's a…*thing*…that's been following me for more than a day. I've only caught a few glimpses of it but I can feel its presence. It hasn't approached me yet but there's something about it…" I struggled to put into words what my mind had discerned about the stalker. "It's not clean. There's something ugly and twisted about it. I haven't felt comfortable with it nearby."

"What does it look like?"

I described the stalker as best I could. "I only really saw it once, and then only briefly. It wasn't like anything I've ever seen before." Of course, the same could be said about the trees and bushes, the night sky, and almost everything around me. Samell and Esme were the closest things I had encountered to *familiar* and they looked and dressed like they'd walked out of a Medieval history book. Based on the simple, homespun clothing they wore, the rough-hewn nature of Esme's bow, and the inelegance of Samell's blade, I didn't expect their village to be wealthy or modern. How deep into a time warp had I wandered? During my period of isolation, I hadn't considered that this world might have people but no Internet, no computers, and perhaps no electricity.

"I don't think we should split up," said Esme. "If it attacks, one of us won't be enough. Even both of us might not be enough."

"I agree." Turning to me, Samell added, "We know they're out here in The Verdant Blight, but we didn't expect any this close to Aeris. They usually stay to the far west or up to the north. I've never heard of any coming close to the road or the river. This isn't good."

"What are *they*?" I asked. My companions were obviously familiar with my stalker. Their reaction didn't fill me with confidence but at least it wasn't a mystery or a figment of my tortured imagination.

"I can't be certain without having seen it myself but it sounds like you're being hunted by an earth reaver." Samell's voice was grave.

"A *what*?" I'm not sure what I expected him to say but it wasn't that.

"An earth reaver," replied Esme with less patience than her brother. Implicit in her tone was: *Don't you know anything?*

Samell shot her a warning look. "An earth reaver is a physical manifestation of earth magic."

Say what???

"Normally they're very rare and stay away from inhabited areas but since this forest became The Blight, there have been sightings and even a few attacks. But the elders can answer all your questions. They know more about this than I do. Workers like Esme and me... things like magic aren't our concerns. We're farmers and hunters, not greybeards."

They might not be Samell's concern but they were mine... or would be until I could shake the one that had my scent. The sick feeling in the pit of my stomach wasn't caused by the bread or jerky.

"Do you know where it is? Right now?" Samell asked.

It took only an instant's concentration to answer the question. The presence was still on the edge of my awareness, just as it had been for more than a day and a night. "It hasn't crossed the river but it's not far. I can't pinpoint it exactly. Can you feel it?"

Samell was scanning the far bank. "I don't have any special talents like that. But I'm not stupid enough to say that if I can't see it or hear it, it's not there. There's been strange things going on of late and this might be another."

"No stranger than your being here," added Esme.

"If it's there, we'd better move out. The river might slow it down but it won't stop it. It might not be able to cross but it can burrow under it. The thing about earth reavers is that they're relentless. If it's got your trail, we might not be able to shake it. And, if it comes to a fight, I'm not sure we'll be able to kill it. Things born of magic can't always be stopped by physical force."

"We haven't fought one before." Esme's features were grim. She looked more like a seasoned warrior than a 16-year old girl. At her age, I had been planning for my junior prom - choosing a dress and deciding how to style my hair - not wandering through a place like The Verdant Blight with a bow and arrows.

"You ready?" Samell's question was directed at me. I nodded. None of my body's aches and pains were going to get better by waiting.

"Wait a moment, Sam," said Esme, reaching down to slip off her moccasins. She offered them to me. "Rough ground don't bother me. I've spent my share of days running around barefoot. More clothes on top than you, though." She smiled, the crooked grin lighting up her features and making her seem more her age. "Anyway, you look like you could use them." Unexpectedly touched, I accepted her gift.

Although most of her body was of a size with mine, her feet were smaller. The soft shoes pinched my toes but I was grateful for the protection they provided.

We moved slowly, heading upstream in the direction I had been traveling while on the opposite bank. I wondered whether I might have reached Aeris on my own if I hadn't encountered my companions. I sensed Samell and Esme were walking more slowly than their usual pace, although whether that was for my benefit or because they were being cautious, I couldn't say. They were alert with an intensity I couldn't match, especially not with weariness clouding my focus. But I was more aware of the earth reaver (if that's what it was) than they were. Their constantly roving eyes couldn't spot it, but I knew that it moved as we did. At one point, we paused so Esme could scamper up a tree but the higher vantage didn't uncover any signs of movement on the far bank. I envied her athleticism and she was right about being comfortable barefoot. The lack of footwear didn't slow her down.

The sun rose patiently into the washed out sky. Its slow crawl was maddening. I was used to shorter days and shadows that changed their positions more rapidly. The heat built steadily but the prospect of cooling off in the river had lost its appeal. A near-death experience had that effect. The farther upstream we went, the stronger the current became.

Samell followed the direction of my gaze. "It's not normally so wild. In fact, most of the year we use it for bathing and recreation. But there was a series of storms tenday ago that swelled the river. If'n we don't get more rain, it'll go back to its normal level soon. There's actually a ford near here but it's not safe in this current. Not that you'd want to be on the other side, especially after working so hard to get over here."

We progressed in silence for a while, picking up a thin trail I never would have noticed on my own that angled a little to the east of the river, although we were still close enough to hear its dull roar. Esme scampered ahead, scouting the way. I wasn't sure it was necessary but there might be dangers other than the earth reaver. This was their world, not mine; I wasn't in a position to gainsay their precautions.

I was sweating under the thin material of the shirt which, although it protected my modesty, chafed my reddened skin. The morning dragged on interminably and I was finding it increasingly difficult to put one foot in front of the other. If I had assumed a "cycle" might be close to an "hour", I was wrong. At least two hours had passed since we had started the journey to Aeris when Samell mentioned we were less than halfway there.

"I need to rest," I said. I hated having to admit weakness but I couldn't maintain this pace for much longer. Had I been healthier, I might have been able to but the deprivations of the last two days coupled with my bruising swim this morning were taking their toll on me. I wondered if I looked as whipped as I felt.

"Of course," said Samell. He dug into his leather satchel, took out two slices of jerky, and handed one to me. Esme disappeared momentarily then returned with a skin full of water. She passed it around and I drank greedily when it was my turn. The rest was more necessary than relaxing and I dreaded the moment when I would have to rise and set off again. That came much sooner than I would have liked.

Then, just as we started moving again, it happened. Somewhere deep inside of me, I felt a lurch, almost as if a fragment of my mind had been suddenly dislocated, and I knew we were in trouble. Something had changed. For the earth reaver, the period of waiting and observing was at an end. I spoke, my voice low and urgent. "I can feel it - stronger and more forceful than before. It's on this side of the river and it's coming for me."

Chapter Four: The Headache

"Let's move!" So saying, Esme broke into a run.

I watched her in dismay. As frightened as I was by the creature, I lacked the energy to do more than stumble along. Jogging, never mind running, was out of the question. Fortunately, Samell recognized this.

"Esme, wait. Can't you see Janelle's got nothing left?"

"Carry her," suggested Esme. It wasn't an unreasonable recommendation - he was strong and fit and I was light.

"No. I could do it but it would tire me out. Better that we move as quickly as she can. That way, I'll be at full strength if it comes to a fight."

So we headed along the path as rapidly as my wobbly legs would carry me. I could feel the earth reaver gaining. It was closing the gap with ease and would be on us in a matter of minutes.

"It's coming too fast," I said. "We can't get away from it."

Samell halted, nodding grimly. He unsheathed his short sword from the scabbard across his back and adopted a ready stance. "Get behind me," he said, motioning for me to stand eight to ten feet up the trail from his position. Esme, readying her bow, moved to his left and slightly behind him.

"Just like we've practiced, big brother," she said with a tight smile.

"Janelle, if this goes bad for us, don't wait for it to be over. This trail will take you out to the road and the road goes north to Aeris. Run as fast as you can. Don't stop and don't look back." Samell's advice was sound but we both knew that, if the earth reaver killed them, there wouldn't be any escape for me. I wished I had my stick, if only for the confidence it would give me, but I had lost it in the river and hadn't thought to find another one. Too late now.

"I can hear it," whispered Esme. Her ears were keener than mine but my mind agreed that it was very close. Perhaps close enough to hear. Or see…

It burst through the undergrowth twenty feet away, a squat shape. It reminded me of a giant, hairless rat or an oversized armadillo with scales all across its back and sides. Although its overall movement was forward, it undulated from side to side. If it had feet, they were small and hidden by its body. It almost looked as if it was moving like a snake, slithering on its belly. Its eyes were as black as coal. Its teeth - brown, rotten splinters of bone, were bared beneath a pointed snout. As it charged, it made the same half-growl/half-scream I had heard back in the forest.

Esme let fly with an arrow. It bounced harmlessly off the creature's tough shell. She reloaded quickly and shot again, this time aiming for the head. It struck somewhere in the face between an eye and the mouth, sinking into the soft flesh almost to the fletching. The creature didn't acknowledge the injury, neither wavering in its forward progress nor changing the timber of its cries.

Samell moved toward the earth reaver, his footwork as sure and precise as that of a dancer. His lunge was controlled and struck home as he moved to the creature's side, sliding past it to the right. Although the blade bit, there was no evidence of a wound and the reaver spun to face its attacker, springing at Samell like a coiled serpent striking.

He dodged but not quickly enough. A whip-like tongue, sharp as any blade, extended from between its teeth to lash Samell across the chest, leaving a bloody welt. At the same time, its teeth attempted to latch onto his leg but he was able to backpedal so all they shredded was his pants leg. The creature's aggressiveness gave him an opening and he used it, driving his sword into a soft spot between its eyes. The blade, when withdrawn, was coated with a dark ichor but the earth reaver appeared unfazed.

Thwang! Thwang! Two arrows in quick succession found their way into the back of the creature's head but it neither hesitated nor turned aside from its relentless pursuit of the now-retreating Samell.

"Janelle, run!" he shouted, apparently having decided that he wasn't going to be able to overcome the creature. "Esme, go with her!"

"No chance, Sam!"

I wasn't about to leave either but I couldn't just stand there like a lump in the path, doing nothing.

Samell used his sword to parry another thrust of the creature's tongue but its aggressive approach and unconcern about injury had put him on the defensive, giving ground as he stumbled backward down the trail in the direction from which we had come. He was deliberately leading the earth reaver away from his sister and me. By now, Esme had emptied her quiver into the creature's neck and head. Discarding her bow, she drew a knife out of a leg sheath and advanced on it from behind.

Before joining her brother in the close-quarters fray, she spared me a look. "Go! Now! Warn the village!"

I couldn't. Even if I had been fresher and stronger, I wouldn't have been able to outrun it. My situation was hopeless. If two athletic hunters proficient with weapons couldn't turn the creature aside, what hope did I have?

Then I felt it again - the same thrumming of the earth that had assailed me in the forest when I had first become aware of the earth reaver. If either of my companions noticed it, they gave no indication. Their concentration on the task at hand didn't falter, even if its success was in doubt. But, brief as the attack was, it was painful enough to drive me nearly to my knees. And that's when a possibility occurred to me.

Seeing his sister's approach, Samell abandoned his methodical swordsmanship and charged the creature, swinging wildly, hoping to keep it unaware of Esme's proximity. He wasn't successful. The earth reaver lashed at him with its tongue, tearing open his chest from left collarbone to right nipple, then spun to attack her.

Remembering how I had contacted it in the forest, I concentrated on the earth reaver, extending my senses toward it, activating *something* deep inside of it. In that moment, it was as aware of me as I was of it, and I perceived a sudden surge of… fear? It was more injured than it appeared to be but it didn't feel pain and, as a result, it could continue fighting until its body failed. Without understanding what I was doing, I impelled my consciousness along the link between us, imposing my will on it and dissolving the bonds that held it together. It screamed - a loud, primal cry unlike the other sounds it had been making - and a bolt of pain in my head knocked me to the ground and sent me tumbling into blackness.

I awoke to a splitting headache and the taste of vomit in my mouth. I was lying on my back with my head slightly elevated by a pillow of leaves. I heard whispered voices before opening my eyes to see Esme and Samell sitting nearby, the latter with a crudely bandaged chest. It was impossible to determine how much time had passed, although the sun's position directly overhead indicated it had at least been several hours (or however many "cycles" that translated into).

I needed a Tylenol but, obviously, I wasn't going to get one. This felt worse than the migraines that had plagued me as a child. Another fleeting memory - someone holding a cold compress to my forehead as I lay in bed weeping with pain.

"What happened?" I managed to croak. My companions turned at the sound of my voice.

"I guess she's not going to die," said Esme. I think she was trying for levity but, in my current condition, the humor was lost on me.

"We told you to run while we defended you. Instead, you saved us. I don't know how you did it but you killed it."

If the price for dispatching the earth reaver was this headache, I might have been better off dying.

Samell explained, "Just as it was about to attack me, it froze and…fell apart. Turned to dirt and tar. An ugly, stinking mess of soil and clay. You collapsed at the same time and we were afraid you might be dead as well. But your breathing was regular and we figured you'd come to eventually. Took nearly two cycles."

"What did you do?" asked Esme.

I wished I knew but I was paying a price now. "I'm not sure. It's like I pushed my mind toward it and forced it to disintegrate. But now my head hurts so badly." I squeezed my eyes closed, hoping the elimination of the harsh light would help. It did…a little.

"I don't have head-pain herbs with me and there aren't any in The Verdant Blight. We'll have to wait until you're able to travel," said Samell. "In different circumstances, I'd stay with you while Esme went for help but if there was one earth reaver there could be more. Our best chance at survival is to stay together. If we're gone long enough, someone will come looking for us."

"The creature was injured," I said, believing they needed to know this information. "But it doesn't feel pain the way we do so it just kept fighting. You can kill it if you do enough damage." The open question was: how much constituted "enough"?

"Can you tell if we're alone?" asked Esme.

"I can't, at least not right now," I said. The thought of casting out my senses made me want to retch.

"Let her lie there and recover," said Samell, motioning for his sister to join him a short distance away. They spoke in whispers while I drifted into and out of an uneasy sleep. It was late afternoon, verging on evening, before I was well enough to resume the journey. My head still throbbed but the pain was bearable. My "sixth sense" abilities hadn't returned. If there was another earth reaver out there, I wouldn't be able to sense it…at least not now.

"Are you alright to travel?" asked Samell for the third time. Were all boys in this world so solicitous and courteous?

I nodded my assent. It was time to move from this place. The dead earth reaver was beginning to stink like a swamp. My fragile stomach did a somersault when a random breeze brought a strong whiff to my nostrils.

"We're probably going to have to stop at nightfall since we can't risk lighting torches inside The Blight. We can start up again during Ire-light if the sky remains clear. Otherwise, we'll have to wait until the morn. The augurs predicted rain on the morrow but they didn't say whether it would come in early or late."

"How far away are we?" I asked. I felt like a child on a car on a long trip. *Are we there yet? How much farther?* And the answer wouldn't be meaningful because I hadn't yet been able to determine how long a cycle was.

Samell, however, grasped my situation. "Earlier, we walked for nearly a cycle to travel from where we met to this place. We're close to halfway back to Aeris. But the sun is low and it'll take less than a full cycle before its last rays have left the land. Normally, traveling by torchlight wouldn't be considered risky, especially so close to the village. But if earth reavers are roaming, who knows whether there might also be fire reavers? None of those creatures has ever been seen in this part of the land but it's not something I'd like to chance, not after what we just went through. And a lit torch on a lonely stretch of road would call out to a fire reaver."

We walked in silence, our pace painfully slow, as the late afternoon transitioned into twilight. We had moved from the side trail to the main road, a dirt passage through the trees wide enough for a narrow wagon led by a team of two horses. I noticed that the trees here were taller than to the south, possibly evidence that this part of the forest was more mature. There were no signs of other travelers.

When I remarked about this, Samell explained. "Even during the height of the day, we might not meet anyone on this road. There's not much casual travel between Aeris and our neighbor to the south, NewTown. It's a fourday journey and undertaken only for a purpose, usually trade. Wagons frequently go back and forth during Fading season as the villages prepare for Ice, but not at this time of the year. There are patrols all year round, even on the coldest days, but that's us for today."

The passage of time reduced the headache and I was able to focus less on my own misery. As my alertness returned, I became aware of my companions' injuries. Esme's were superficial - a few cuts and bruises and one nasty welt on her arm where the creature's tongue had brushed her. Samell, on the other hand, had suffered significant wounds, including a deep, ragged incision that split half his chest. It was bandaged but the blood was soaking through and it obviously needed re-dressing.

"It stings," admitted Samell when I mentioned it. "The healers will be able to care for it when we get to Aeris. They have poultices and potions they can apply that will stop the blood, knit the flesh, and ward showing early signs of infection. Before wearing Esme's moccasins, keeping it clean had been a problem.

"If your medicines can do all that, they're better than the ones where I come from." Regardless, I'd still kill for a Tylenol or an aspirin. The headache was down to a dull soreness between my temples but it was a distraction. My high tolerance for pain didn't extend to my brain.

"It's one of the benefits of The Verdant Blight. As pernicious as some things about it can be, it offers advantages as well. The magic that makes the leaves poisonous to eat also gives them unusual properties when correctly prepared - as a healing ointment, for example. You don't have to be a Summoner to use them."

Although Samell appeared to be speaking English, there was still a communication barrier. I didn't understand some of the things he said. A *Summoner*?

Once twilight had deepened to the point where visibility was rapidly diminishing, Samell called a halt. "We can continue once Ire has risen but this is as good a place as any to rest for a cycle. Although no one is likely to be using the road by night, we should move off to the side in case. It wouldn't do for us to be trampled by horses after surviving an earth reaver attack."

I spent a few minutes searching for a suitable replacement for my lost stick. The new one, a solid club of four feet from end-to-end, wasn't as long as its predecessor but it was thicker and smoother.

"Do you know how to use that?" asked Esme, looking at me as I tried different grips on my new tool.

"For fighting? Not really. Truth is, I'm not much of a fighter with anything." Except cutting remarks, and I didn't suppose those would be useful in these circumstances.

"When we get to Aeris, I'll teach you a few things. I used a stave before I graduated to a bow and I'm still better with it than a knife."

"Don't let her fool you," said Samell. "She's better than most in the village with a knife. In fact, the only weapon she's not good with is a sword and that's only because she hasn't practiced. Give her a few weeks and she'd be standing toe-to-toe with Blademaster Ulas. When it comes to combat, my sister is a natural."

It was too dark to be sure but I thought Esme was blushing. She was also trying to hide a smile. "The offer stands," she said. "I'll teach you how to use that stick if you want. If you're staying around, that is."

Would I be staying around? I had no idea. I hadn't thought beyond getting to Aeris, eating a full meal, sleeping on something softer than the ground, and learning answers to a few questions. I wasn't prepared to address the "what now?" question. Since I had arrived in this place, everything had been about survival. The mandate hadn't changed.

We continued to converse - words slipping into the darkness, three disembodied voices breaking a wall of silence. The river was too far away to be heard and the effects of The Verdant Blight extinguished other potential sources of sound - no animals, no insects, no things that went bump in the night. I tried to reach out with my "sixth sense" the way I had prior to the fight but the ability wasn't there. Even though the headache was nearly gone, it was as if what I had done to destroy the earth reaver had…limited…me in some way. I felt inexplicably diminished. On a more practical level, I couldn't warn my companions if there was another creature in the area. Without light, we were at our most vulnerable now.

"Tell me something about Aeris," I asked, partly because I was curious and partly because I wanted to keep the silence at bay.

"What would you like to know?" I could tell from the sound of his voice that Samell had moved closer to me in the darkness.

"Anything, really. I'm a stranger here. All I know about Aeris is from things you've said and that hasn't been much."

There was a brief pause as Samell considered where to begin. "It's a small community even compared to the nearest two villages, NewTown and West Fork. I've never seen the great cities to the east but they dwarf Aeris in ways I could only imagine. We were founded only a few generations ago as a small outpost to farm and cultivate leaves and plants from The Greenswood and The Verdant Blight. In those years, the magic part of the forest was much smaller and no one had seen an earth reaver. Several families from West Fork came up here and established what would become Aeris.

"In the beginning, there were maybe twenty or thirty settlers. Now, we have three-hundred people. We're mostly farmers, hunters, and trappers with a few craftsmen. There aren't any shops - we don't have enough people for that, although we have a tavern. The village is ruled by a group of elders - all direct descendants of the original settlers - grandsons and granddaughters, mostly. We marry among our own although there are occasional weddings with outsiders. Old Nat married a second cousin from West Fork a while back and brought her to Aeris to live."

I decided it was pointless to ask about electricity. It was obvious from his description that technology here wasn't that advanced. Maybe in the cities he had mentioned. Three-hundred souls wasn't a lot. At five people to a house, that was only 60 houses. Even a small development in my world's suburbs had twice that many. I wondered what the houses would look like. Images of wooden cabins with wood-burning stoves came to mind. Probably something like that. Still, it would be safer and more comfortable than in the forest.

"How do you spend your days?" I asked.

"Depends on the rotation. I'm a good farmer, so I'm in the fields most days except when I'm on patrol, once every fiveday or sixday. Esme and I are always paired for that. I do a little trapping and hunting but I'm not as good at those things as some others are. That's where Esme shines. Our younger brother Brin takes after her and she's giving him lessons."

"Any other brothers or sisters?"

"No. Just me, Esme, and Brin. When I was younger, after Brin was born, Ma and Pa talked about having more but the gods didn't bless them."

Samell's mention of the "gods" got me thinking about religion. Having been raised in a monotheistic society, although I'd never been much of an adherent to any organized faith, it was strange to hear someone refer to multiple deities. Perhaps the question of import was whether they were *real*. Ancient cultures in my world had often worshipped gods with complex, colorful mythologies but the nature of their theologies had been debunked over time, replaced by more "sophisticated" creeds. Understanding the beliefs of Samell and his people might be important to my being accepted.

"Which gods do you believe in?" It was impossible to tell in the darkness whether he was surprised by the question and whether my asking it branded me as an ignorant heathen.

"Don't you honor The Four where you come from?"

My response was carefully worded. Atheism and agnosticism might be accepted where I came from, but here…? I didn't know and didn't want to make assumptions. "My people believe in many different gods. They may be the same ones you worship but with different names."

Samell chuckled. "'Worship' may be too strong a term. We venerate the gods but not in any obvious or public way. We acknowledge their primacy and offer the appropriate prayers but only the priests lead truly devout lives. If an intercession is needed, we go to a priest.

"The Four are Sovereign the sun, his two consorts Ire and Concord the moons, and Vasto the void of darkness. If you're interested in a deeper understanding, you can speak to Father Backus in Aeris. He'll be more than happy to lecture you for hours on end about the gods, their history, and our obligations to them." There was a smile in those last words as he spoke them.

"Father Backus is a good man," added Esme. "But he is so boooooooring!"

The darkness passed more quickly with two others to share it. Even when we weren't talking, just knowing that Samell and Esme were with me, even if it was only by hearing their breathing, made the night less intimidating. Then, after about two hours, the faint light of the first moon's rising started to bathe the land.

"That's Ire," said Esme. "Concord rises later. During the period when they're both up, the farmers call it 'moonslight' and, especially during the planting and harvesting seasons, they work. As long as clouds don't hide Ire, it's safe to walk the road."

We moved carefully. There was enough of the ethereal illumination to ensure that we didn't blunder into a tree but the road wasn't smooth and we had to be vigilant not to turn an ankle in a rut. I could tell by the way he was walking that Samell's injuries were causing him pain. My left sole was on fire. I used the stick to avoid having to place full pressure on it. I sincerely hoped the medication Samell had spoken about would help. At least the headache was gone, although my mind's sense hadn't returned. Gone forever? Perhaps. Would that be a bad thing?

Two or three hours later - or what constituted a "cycle" as time was measured here - I saw the first of many squat, ramshackle buildings ahead. We had reached Aeris.

Chapter Five: Aeris

Walking quickly through the benighted streets of Aeris, I was reminded of a ghost town. The houses were all small and crudely made, constructed (as I had assumed they would be) out of logs. Most had a window or two and all of those were dark. There were no torches on poles or other artificial means to light the way. If there was a reason for reassurance, however, it came in the form of a faint chirping. For the first time since arriving here, I could hear an insect. The Verdant Blight might be nearby but its life-extinguishing influence hadn't spread this far.

Samell and Esme led me to a cottage on the far side of the village. Unlike most of its carbon-copy fellows, there was a faint illumination coming from inside, peeking out around curtains and through the gap under the door. Samell motioned for me to join him and his sister as they went in. I absently noticed that there was no lock on the door and therefore no need to produce a key.

"Thank Ire and Concord!" exclaimed a woman's voice as Samell entered. It belonged to one of the three people gathered in the cramped room beyond the threshold. The kinship among Samell, Esme, Brin, and their mother was immediately apparent - all had the same light blond hair and delicate features. Brin looked like a younger version of his brother, having just crossed over to the masculine side of puberty. The father had a darker, more rugged appearance and it took some looking to find evidence of his paternity in the children. I decided they had inherited his nose, if little else.

Expressions of relief turned to surprise as they saw me with concern following in quick succession as they noticed Samell's injuries. His mother, who scarcely looked old enough to have given birth to someone of his age, ignored me for the moment and rushed over to examine his bandages, now hardened and brown with crusted blood.

"How did this happen? And who's she?" Samell's father hadn't moved from the chair where he was sitting near the unlit fireplace. His eyes, exhibiting unconcealed suspicion, bored into mine. I became self-conscious about my clothing. Aside from Samell's threadbare shirt, which at least covered me from neck to mid-thigh, and Esme's moccasins, I was naked. I had grown comfortable about my garments around my companions but embarrassment was asserting itself now that others were seeing me.

Having been reassured that her son wasn't in imminent danger from his wounds, Samell's mother regarded me critically. "You look dead on your feet, dear. Sit down. I suspect there's a tale to tell and it won't serve anyone if you collapse in the middle of it."

I smiled wanly and lowered myself to the hard-packed dirt floor. She was right. Even standing took an effort I no longer possessed.

"Janelle, these are my parents, Rikard and Lissa, and my younger brother, Brin." Samell said by way of introduction. Neither he nor Esme sat. Brin's eyes were fixed on me as if I was some kind of space alien. I supposed perhaps I was (but without the bulbous head).

Samell summed up the situation as succinctly as possible, with Esme jumping in occasionally when he missed a detail she deemed to be important. I said little, in part because there wasn't much to add and in part because I was too weak for speech. Rikard, Lissa, and Brin listened attentively. Brin's eyes lit up with wonder as the story unfolded but it was difficult to ascertain what Rikard and Lissa were thinking.

When Samell was done, the first thing Lissa did was turn to her daughter. "Supper's gone but you know where the vittles are. Get some for yourself and your brother and a double helping for Janelle. She looks like she's starving. Brin," she added, "Run to the healer's and tell him your brother has come back with an injury that needs immediate tending."

Without a word, Brin dashed outside and Esme disappeared into another room. I wondered how many chambers the house had. It wasn't large, so I assumed no more than three. In addition to a quartet of crude chairs and an equally rudimentary table, there were two sleeping pallets in this room, so it served multiple purposes. I doubted people in Aeris used their houses as more than shelters. The concept of a home as a place of recreation would be foreign in a society like this.

"You don't know where you're from?" probed Lissa. Her eyes were as gentle as her words. There was no skepticism there; she believed my story, at least insofar as her son had related it.

"I have memories of another place but they're fragments. It's much different than here. Many more people." How to explain the concept of *technology*? "They can do things here that you can't… like make light without fire. Make a house warm in the cold weather and cool when it's warm."

"You come from a place of magic," said Rikard, as if that explained everything. "Are you a Summoner?"

Samell has used that word during our journey but I was ignorant of its meaning. "I don't know what a Summoner is. All I know is that I was doing something in the other world, there was a flash of light then I was in the forest, naked and with sunburned skin. I wish I could tell you more but that's all I remember."

"Magic," said Rikard again. "Has to be. No other explanation."

I might have agreed but I also recognized that, in a society like this, any sort of advanced technology would be indistinguishable from magic. A flashlight would be seen as a magical wand. Was there *true* magic involved here? Did such a thing exist?

"She warned us of the earth reaver's approach and dealt the final blow without touching it. She must be a Summoner," said Samell.

"You might think so. And I might agree. But it's up to the elders to make the determination."

Conversation halted as Esme returned carrying a plate heaped with nuts, grains, dried berries, bread, and jerky. She also brought an earthen mug of a darkish liquid. I gratefully accepted the food and ate it with a gusto that might have been considered unseemly in other circumstances. The beverage was an ale or beer of some sort - slightly bitter and stronger than I was accustomed to. I can't say I liked the taste - it was definitely foreign - but that didn't stop me from downing the entire cup and looking around for a refill. At that moment, another memory came to me: an old man with a well-trimmed beard and kind eyes handing me a small glass half-full of an amber liquid. With a wink and a smile, he said, "We won't tell your mother. This can be our secret." My past, replacing itself shard by shard.

By the time Brin arrived with the healer in tow, I was dressed appropriately. Esme gave me clothing from her limited wardrobe: a shirt similar in style and material to Samell's (although several sizes smaller and cut better around the bust), loose pants made from a stronger material that were too short at the ankles, and a simple rope to tie around my waist. I was encouraged to keep the moccasins. I didn't remark that they were too small since I didn't want to appear ungrateful, although I recognized that, if circumstances required me to do a lot of walking, I'd have to acquire footwear that fit better.

Healer Drabek was a no-nonsense middle-aged man with long graying hair and a fine mustache and goatee to match. He looked decidedly unhappy to have been dragged out of bed in the middle of the night although his interest perked up considerably when he saw me. He flashed a smile, introduced himself in an officious manner then examined Samell's injuries.

The interview with the healer didn't last long but it provided a preview of what likely awaited when our story was told to the rest of the town's population: a mixture of skepticism, anxiety, and open disbelief. I'm not sure which was the least credible portion of the tale - my mysterious arrival, the earth reaver's attack, or the manner in which it had been beaten. Although it wasn't clear how much of the account Drabek accepted, he acknowledged that Samell's wounds were unlike any he had previously treated.

Using water and a sprinkling of the dried leaves he carried in a satchel, he made an ointment to rub along the gash on Samell's chest. He then had me remove my left moccasin and, after examining my foot with many "hmms", he dabbed a little of the same substance on the reddened area surrounding the thorn's puncture. The result was immediate. A warm, tingling sensation flooded through my foot and, in its wake, even the vestigial traces of soreness were gone. The red vanished like paint scrubbed off by soap and water. It was truly amazing.

After the healer departed, there were still many things to discuss but, now that my stomach was full and my foot no longer felt like there was a needle embedded in it, the weariness washed over me like the tide over an unbroken beach. I was offered one of the pallets and Esme curled up on the floor next to me. I was asleep in minutes and didn't wake up until the hustle and bustle of the early morning household's activities pulled me out of my slumber.

It was surprising how restorative a meal and a halfway decent night's sleep could be. For the first time since I had arrived here - wherever *here* was - I felt ready to at least ask the salient questions. It was time to face the future and, to do that, I suspected I would need to rediscover the past. I knew a little bit about who Janelle was...but not nearly enough.

And, this morning, *it* was back - the mind-sense that had alerted me to the presence of the earth reaver. I couldn't say exactly how I knew it was there, but I did. There weren't any earth reavers nearby but I could feel things in a peculiar way that I hadn't been able to in the hours following the attack. I wondered if this was something I should mention but decided not to. These people, as helpful as they had been, didn't need to know all my secrets. Maybe if they committed to helping me... but what did I want from them in the first place? What were my goals? Until I figured that out, I would remain adrift.

"Sleep well?" asked Samell, crouching on his haunches next to where I was stretching like a cat.

"Better than out in the middle of the forest, that's for sure." I was hungry and thirsty but, by the noises and smells coming from the room next-door, some sort of meal was being prepared. "What's next?"

"Time for you to meet the elders. Brin and Esme are off on their duties but my parents and I will go with you. This isn't just about you, although you're a big part. Our being attacked by an earth reaver is unprecedented in recent memory. The elders will know whether there's anything written about this in the prophesies or whether there's been chatter in the other villages about strange, portentous occurrences."

At least I'm not the only one unsettled by my arrival.

After eating a tasty breakfast of spiced grains and cooked meat (I didn't ask what kind of animal it was because I wasn't sure it would taste as good if I knew) and washing my face in a basin of cool, clear water, I felt ready to face just about anything, even a bunch of grouchy old men. A glimpse of my reflection in the water showed a ragged, strained face. All I needed to resemble my old self were shampoo, conditioner, and makeup - three things I might never again see. So I'd have to make do with the limp, lifeless hair, the bruises under my eyes, and the chapped lips.

The trip to the elders' hall required that I traverse the main route through the village for almost its entire length. Many of the townspeople were out and about doing their normal chores and numerous pairs of eyes observed my journey. I didn't know whether there were rumors about me already or whether strangers were simply rare in Aeris. Either way, my appearance incited interest. I couldn't decide whether that was good or bad. Any hopes I might have harbored about anonymity were dashed but a little notoriety might not be a bad thing.

"No doubt Esme has told anyone who would listen about the 'pretty, foreign girl' who saved us from the earth reaver," said Samell, noticing all the interest in our passage.

The pretty, foreign girl... I liked the sound of that. It made me sound exotic. And what girl doesn't like being thought of as attractive?

The eyes continued to follow me as we entered the elders' hall, which was really just a big, two-room cottage. Samell, Lissa, and I remained in the outer chamber along with a few other men and women while Rickard entered the main room to request an audience. We waited patiently as the minutes ticked by. Lissa and Samell engaged in small talk with the others while I stood off to the side. In a community this size, I guess everyone knew everyone else. As the stranger, I was apart - an enigma. With a flash, I recognized that assimilation into this community, if that was my eventual desire, wouldn't be easy. If they closed ranks, I would be on the outside, looking in.

Another memory: me, as a child, waiting outside a classroom while the principal went in to inform the teacher that she had a new student. Only then was I ushered in. As I stood at the front of the classroom, the teacher - Mrs. Stewart was her name - wrote my name on the blackboard and greeted me with a warm smile. In contrast to her friendly reception, the stares of twenty fourth-graders were harsh, mocking, or bored. I had never felt more alone in my young life than at that moment. All my friends were many miles away and here I was, looking at the people who would be around me for six hours a day five days a week, and there wasn't a single welcoming face among them.

Rickard emerged. "They'll see us. I told them what happened but they'll have questions for you and your friend." He directed the words to his son, only glancing briefly at me. I felt a flush of irritation at the snub.

The six elders - three men and three women - sat in high-backed chairs in front of a thin table. After bowing, we took seats opposite them. I could understand why they were called "elders." The youngest couldn't have been less than sixty. Five of the six had gray or white hair; the sixth had none at all. One of the men looked like Ebenezer Scrooge in the old black-and-white movie of *A Christmas Carol*, another reminded me of the dead actor Yul Brynner, and the third was a dead ringer for a mall Santa. The three women were alike enough that they could have been sisters - stout, solid matriarchs who would be more at home stacking firewood than sitting by the resultant blaze and knitting something.

"Felicitations, Rickard, Lissa, and Samell. We don't know the fourth member of your party." These words of welcome were spoken by a woman with stern features and pursed lips. She looked like she had spent too much time sucking on a lemon.

Rickard, who had nominated himself as the spokesman for our party, introduced me. "This is Janelle, the stranger I mentioned. Samell and Esme met her near the river off the south road during their patrol yesterday."

The six elders turned toward me as one. Three of the faces - Santa and the two other women - wore welcoming smiles. Ebenezer and Yul, however, mirrored the speaker's unfriendliness.

"Felicitations, Janelle." There was no warmth in the speaker's greeting. "Perhaps you could enlighten us about how you came to be in The Verdant Blight - alone and, by Rickard's earlier account, unclothed - yesterday morn?"

I suppressed a sigh. It was going to one of *those* interviews, where I would be forced into a position of defending myself even though I had done nothing wrong. I had no idea why I was here, how I was here, or (in the overall scheme of things) where "here" was. Yet I was going to be pressed with questions I wouldn't be able to answer. I had come to Aeris hoping to learn about my circumstances. With every passing moment, that seemed less likely.

I answered as best I could, offering an account of what I remembered about my arrival, my period alone in the forest, the river-crossing to meet Samell and Esme, and the struggle with the earth reaver. When I was done speaking, the elders regarded me somberly -

six stoic expressions. At least no one seemed incredulous. Maybe that was a positive sign. If these people believed my story, perhaps they would take me seriously.

Finally, Ebenezer spoke. "Surely you must realize, young lady, that you tell an incredible story, although the audacity of such a tale may be said to vouch for its truthfulness. No sane person would make the assertions you have made if they weren't true. Tell me, do you claim to be a Summoner? Or perhaps one of The Summoned?"

This was the third time I had heard that word and I still had no idea what it meant. Oh, I knew what the verb "summon" meant but, in this context, it had a specific meaning beyond Webster's. "I can't make any claims, Sir, when I don't know what I'm being asked. Who or what are 'Summoners' and 'The Summoned?'"

"If you don't know that," said one of the women, "Then you truly are a stranger."

"A Summoner is one who can manipulate magic, tap into its vast resources to transform, negate, and create. One of the greatest abilities of a Summoner is to use those powers to summon another. It is a powerful spell, rarely used except in dire circumstances, because of the impact it has on its caster. The Summoned is one who comes in answer to the call. History tells us that a summons almost always brings a great hero - a mighty warrior or, more likely, another Summoner. So I ask again, do you claim to be a Summoner or one of The Summoned?"

Or both? There was a frightening logic to it and, if true, it brought clarity to my situation. Snatched from another life and pulled here by magic. Able to sense things no one else could and destroy a creature with a thought. "I don't know," I said honestly. "But it would make sense of many of the things that have happened to me over the past several days."

The three men and three women nodded as if they were one person, as if my simple answer had resolved everything for them.

Perhaps it had. But it left me with a great many questions. I wondered if they had answers.

"And in your *possible* role as a Summoner did you call the earth reaver to you? Did it hear your call and answer you? Did you orchestrate the attack that nearly killed your companions then relent at the last minute and dispel your creature?"

I was shocked at the allegation but probably shouldn't have been. Looking at it from their perspective, it wasn't unreasonable. After all, I was a stranger. There was no argument for them to trust me. They would accept Samell and Esme's testimony without question but not mine. Recognizing those things didn't soften the accusation, especially since it might be true. Had I unwittingly done something to call the earth reaver to me? After all, it had followed me without attacking for more than a day. Only with Samell and Esme's arrival had its latent malice turned into naked hostility.

"I didn't summon anything. It approached me of its own volition, stalked me for a night, a day, and another night before attacking me. It would have killed me as surely as it would have killed Samell and Esme. Yes, I did something to it. I used my will against it in a way I don't understand - may never understand - but it wasn't my creature."

"I see," said Ebenezer. I didn't think he did but that was something adults said all the time when they wanted to stop a discussion.

"What are you plans now, young lady?" asked the woman who had greeted us.

That was a good question and another one I couldn't answer. What were my plans? Finding a way to go home? Was there a way? Seeking out one of the cities? How could I be expected to answer that *now* with so little clarity about my situation?

"I don't know. I have to understand things better before I can decide how to proceed. If I'm a Summoner or one of The Summoned, I need to figure out what that means for me both now and in the future."

Yul spoke for the first time. "I recognize your dilemma, Janelle." He was the first one to use my name. "You're a stranger here and we're not welcoming you with open arms. On the one hand, that doesn't speak well of our hospitality. On the other hand, we don't know what's in your heart. It's possible that you come to us with the best of intentions but things are not always what they seem. Our duty is to safeguard the people of Aeris, so we must be cautious. Your situation bears consideration. If you are true, you could be a great asset to the village but it is premature for us to proceed without some degree of skepticism.

"To that end, if Rickard and his family are willing to vouchsafe for your conduct, we can allow you to remain in Aeris with two conditions. The first is that you must partake in activities to advance our society as would be expected of any young person of your age. The second is that you must study under Father Backus to learn about our culture. If these stipulations are acceptable and if Rickard is willing to guarantee your good behavior, we can invite you to join the community on a probationary basis."

Samell's father was unenthused about the responsibility placed on him by the elders but, recognizing that his family owed me a debt, he reluctantly agreed. Thus was I welcomed into the population of Aeris and given an island of stability in this new, frightening world.

Chapter Six: Father Backus' Catechism

Father Backus was an old man. And by old, I mean *really* old. His wrinkles had wrinkles. Actually, it was difficult to see any wrinkles because nearly every inch of his face was covered with white hair. His bushy mustache got lost on either side in his equally bushy beard, which stretched from ear to ear and hung down to his bellybutton. His eyebrows had never been trimmed; the same could be said about the tendrils of hair crawling out of his ears and nostrils. His blue eyes were those of a much younger man - clear and lively. At one point, he had probably been tall but age had shrunk him and given him a stoop so now the top of his head was just an inch or two above mine.

He was kind to me - an attitude that surprised me since, if there was one thing everyone in Aeris agreed on when it came to the priest, it was that he was a humorless disciplinarian. That wasn't my experience of the man. I found many of his lectures to be informative and entertaining, flavored as they were with anecdotes that had a first-person, "been there" quality. He would have made an excellent storyteller but he had little patience with writing. He preferred reading and his study was a trove of literature with shelves piled high with scrolls and tomes. The first time I saw it, I was plunged into a bout of depression. Not only hadn't this world entered the computer age, it hadn't even discovered the printing press. Every one of Backus' books had been hand-copied. This was more proof, as if any was necessary, that I had to adjust my expectations regarding the state of technology here. People lived simply but, for the most part, they seemed content with their lot in life.

Perhaps because I had been born elsewhere and had grown up in a different environment, I doubted I would be able to adopt the basic lifestyle that defined Aeris' residents - getting up early, spending the day doing their assigned chores, gathering together for an evening meal followed by an hour or two of leisure before bed. I needed *more*. And that meant, of necessity, my time here would be limited. Aeris was the starting point of a longer journey. Father Backus knew (or at least suspected) as much. And, aside from Esme, Samell, Brin, and a few of their friends, he was the only one who didn't demonstrate signs of suspicion and mistrust where I was concerned.

In less than a "fiveday" period (as time was measured here), the priest had taught me most of the basics about the gods, the seasons, and the other minutia necessary to living life in Aeris. Now our lessons were moving on to history and geology, two subjects that interested me greatly.

"What do you think of me? Do you think I'm special?" I asked him on the morning of our sixth day together. We were in his study, him sitting in a chair, me cross-legged on his hard-packed dirt floor. I absently brushed aside an ant-like insect that had decided to use one of my legs as a shortcut. Aware of how rare bugs were in Aeris due to the growing exterminating power of The Verdant Blight, I didn't kill it. It paused, perhaps annoyed at having been diverted from its route, then continued on its way. Father Backus, noting my restraint, smiled, or at least I think that's what the twitching of all the hair around his mouth meant.

"I think everyone is special. As a priest, I can hardly believe differently and minister to them all. More to the point, however, is what you think of yourself."

In my old world, Backus would have been a fair-to-middling psychologist. "I wish I knew. I remember being self-confident but that was a different reality. Here…it's all so strange and new. It's like a dream and I keep wondering when I'm going to wake up."

"I can't say whether all this is real or not" - he spread his arms wide to encompass the room and its contents - "but until you figure it out, the wisest course is to treat it as such. If it's a dream, then no harm is done. If not, the worst thing you could do is while away your time waiting for an awakening that never comes."

"Do you think I'm a Summoner?"

He didn't hesitate. "Yes. And I also think you're one of The Summoned. The elders aren't sure. In fact, they're evenly divided for and against. But I've read first-hand accounts given by other Summoned and they match yours closely. Of course, you could have read them as well and simply be parroting the words but I don't sense that level guile in you, and I'm a good judge of character.

"In recent generations, Summoners have always been Summoned and vice versa. It wasn't always so. History tells us that when there were more Summoners, some would call great warriors rather than replacements for themselves. Alas, today there are so few that it would be irresponsible for a Summoner to send for anyone but another Summoner."

"How many are there?" I asked.

"No one knows. Fewer than a dozen have declared themselves but there may be more - recluses who have decided to keep to themselves or who are ignorant of their power. Once, there were hundreds but attrition has taken its toll over the generations. And one other thing to keep in mind - the spell of Summoning is the most powerful spell any Summoner can use and it is invariably fatal. It requires the fullness of the Summoner's life energy to execute. If you were summoned as I believe you were, the Summoner who called you is dead, and he had good reason to sacrifice his life to bring you here. It may be that your first duty in this new land will be to discover what that is."

"Can you help me?"

Backus shook his head in the negative. "I know more about Summoners than anyone else in Aeris and possibly more than anyone in NewTown or West Fork as well. But I don't have the kinds of answers you'll eventually need. For those, you will have to seek out a Summoner."

"If there are fewer than twelve Summoners and one died bringing me here, that limits my options, doesn't it?"

"It does indeed. Remember, though, I said a dozen *known* Summoners."

"Are all priests as knowledgeable as you are when it comes to magic?"

"I daresay they would be if they had lived as long as I have."

"How long is that?" He looked as if he was about 80 years old, although an age in excess of 90 wouldn't have surprised me. Of course, time didn't pass in this world the way it did on Earth. I had already learned that each year comprised two-hundred days - fifty per season for each of the four seasons. A day here, however, was considerably longer than a day where I came from. That made it difficult to equate periods of time in this world with those I was familiar with.

Understanding these difficulties, Backus spoke in generalities that bridged the differences. "If we assume that a person has had a good, long life if he lives two or two and one-half generations, then a very old man or woman would be someone who has seen three or more generations. I have seen ten."

It took a moment for that to sink in. If Backus' definition of a "generation" was 25 years, that meant he was saying he had lived for in excess of 250 years. I didn't dispute it. I could tell when the old man was joking and, in this, he was in earnest. The only response I could think of was: "You look very good for your age."

"Not the response I expected but I suppose I do. I haven't aged a day in seven generations."

"How?"

"Before I tell you, Janelle, let me impress on you the necessity that this remain a secret between us. If I didn't believe you to be a Summoner, I wouldn't reveal this. No one in the village knows the truth of my age. Oh, they all know I'm old and the elders know there's something strange about me because I was old when they were young.

But no one knows what I have just told you. And they don't know what I'm about to reveal. I need your promise that you won't speak a word of this unless it's to another Summoner."

I was so afire with curiosity that I would have agreed to much more. I readily assented.

"Magic. An experiment that might easily have killed me instead prolonged my life beyond any reasonable measure. I was among the original settlers of Aeris. When I came here as the expedition's priest, there was nothing unusual about me. But I was old and the journey was harsh. By the time I got here, I knew I was dying. I didn't know how much longer I had so I felt there was little risk in what I attempted.

"I did the one thing we are cautioned against doing: I ate the leaves of a Blighted tree. Oh, not in large quantities. In fact, I took a single leaf, dried it out, and ate only the tiniest sliver of it every day. And, though I thought at first it might kill me, and it did make me ill, it didn't kill me. I stopped aging. The debilitating sickness that threatened my health receded and I have been thus ever since. And still, every day, I partake of the smallest portion of a 'poison' leaf."

"And you haven't told anyone about this?"

"No one. Oh, there have been times when I've been tempted. A few generations ago, I fell in love with a girl who developed a virulent disease. I spent many sleepless nights wrestling with the possibility of giving her doses. In the end, I didn't. To this day, I don't know if it was the right decision but I think if I made my discovery known, the consequences could be disastrous. Not only is eating even a small portion of a Blighted leaf dangerous but if news of this 'immortality recipe' reached the cities, think of the impact and abuses."

I considered. I could see how this had been a hard choice for Father Backus. Unregulated, the consumption of Blighted leaves would result in many deaths from people adopting a "more is better" approach. And hundreds, if not thousands, of travelers would arrive here looking for this world's version of The Fountain of Youth. The

Blight would be deforested, the ecosystem ruined. On the other hand, if there was a chance to stay young and healthy longer, I'd want to know about the opportunity and would be willing to take the chance.

I was in no position to sit in judgment of Backus. But I wondered why, after all these years, he had chosen to share the secret with me. Was he that sure that I was a Summoner?

"Why tell me now?"

"Because of who you are and because you may need this knowledge at some point. I'm an old man and, although the leaves have kept me alive and hale for many generations, I have a… premonition… that the end is near. Of late, I've begun to feel my age more keenly. It would be unfortunate for this knowledge to die with me. But there's another reason, something specific to you." Then, with a smile, he added, "But that's a topic for tomorrow's lesson. Once again, we've gone past our allotted time for teaching. Your chores await and I wouldn't want to be accused of keeping you from them."

Dumbfounded, I stared at Backus, teacher turned tormentor. Surely that wasn't it for today - pique my curiosity then end the lesson? Keep me hanging, unfulfilled, until tomorrow? I sat there for a few moments, my expression pleading with him to continue, but he gave every indication that he was done. He wasn't the sort of man to relent, even in the face of doe eyes and a frown. With one hand, he made a shooing gesture. I ground my teeth in frustration.

"Patience, Janelle. It's one of life's most underrated and necessary characteristics."

I departed, muttering a few phrases under my breath that, in the world I came from, would most likely have earned me a rebuke from the nearest adult. Backus either didn't hear them, didn't know what they meant, or wasn't shocked that I used them.

My conversation with the priest lingered in my thoughts for the rest of the morning and into the afternoon as I went about my duties. My daily chores consisted of collecting soiled garments in a wicker basket and carrying them to the Greenswood River (which ran just west of town) where a group of children and older women would scrub them clean. Of all the tasks I had attempted during my brief sojourn in Aeris, this was the only one for which I had exhibited the necessary physical stamina. Even the washing, which at first had appeared innocuous, had proven to be beyond my limited capabilities; my arms had been too sore to continue after less than an hour. As for farming… I had never imagined it could be so arduous. A short time in the fields had left my soft hands so blistered that the healer's ointment had been necessary to make them useful. So my "working day" consisted of a lot of walking back and forth with a heavy basket that I repeatedly loaded and unloaded. Never before had a scholar's life held such appeal.

Later in the day, I had an opportunity to spend time with Samell during our mutual mid-afternoon break. As we sat in the shade of a house munching on nuts, berries, and non-Blight leaves (that tasted like romaine lettuce), I sought his opinion about some of the issues that were bothering me. He was one of the few people in Aeris I trusted and with whom I felt I could be open.

"Do you think I'm a Summoner?"

He chuckled. "That's the third time you've asked me. My answer hasn't changed. No one but a Summoner could have done to that earth reaver what you did. As far as I'm concerned, that's proof. The skeptics weren't out there with us but Esme and me, we know."

It was compelling evidence but I wasn't convinced. It's wasn't hard to believe I had been Summoned. After all, my transition from *there* to *here* fit the definition and it was hard to deny the reality of the situation. Maybe my abilities were just a manifestation in this world or something latent in my own. It wasn't uncommon for people on Earth to claim to have ESP or a "sixth sense." Being a Summoner was like being a wizard and, thus far, outside of killing the earth reaver, I hadn't manifested any powers that would be considered magical.

"If I am, what would that mean to you? Personally."

He appeared surprised by the question and a prolonged period of silence ensued as he considered his response. I didn't press him. I was glad he was taking it seriously and not laughing it off. Finally, he spoke. "First, it means I've been privileged. Few people in their lifetime meet a Summoner. Until your arrival, no one in Aeris had except maybe Father Backus. Second, I feel a sense of responsibility. We owe each other our lives. That binds people. Summoners don't just arrive for no reason and their paths are never easy. Eventually, you'll have access to great powers. In a time of peace and prosperity, you might never need to use them." He stopped abruptly, as if he had more to say but thought better of it.

"But…?" I pressed. I wanted to hear the unvoiced words. I wanted to understand what his "responsibility" meant to him.

"We may have crossed into what I've heard called a 'turbulent era'. There have been whispers about this and what happened with the earth reaver makes me believe them. In all the years since Aeris' settlement, there's never been an earth reaver attack. Not one. Sightings have always been rare. Hunting expeditions from the south have occasionally set out to kill one and bring home the head as a trophy. None have succeeded. Now The Verdant Blight is growing at an unprecedented rate. A new Summoner has come into our midst. And not only has an earth reaver been sighted but it's been slain in combat. Things aren't as they always have been. And, whatever it is that you have to face, I can't let you do it alone."

I was touched by his words. It meant something that at least one of my new companions believed in me strongly enough to make such an offer. However much I hoped it wouldn't come to that, I suspected Samell's words would be put to the test. If the time arrived to leave behind his family, his duties here, and his home, would he still be as resolute?

"What do you think of Father Backus?" he asked.

"He's nicer than I expected. He even has a sense of humor. And he hasn't rapped my hand once with his little pointy stick."

"You're getting favorable treatment. He doesn't want it said that he angered or abused a Summoner." I couldn't tell whether Samell was joking or not.

"How old do you think he is?" I asked, curious whether my friend had noticed the priest's lack of aging.

"Old."

"How old?"

"Can't rightly say. Three generations, maybe? At least as old as the elders, probably older. I guess when you get to be his age, the number of years you've been alive doesn't much matter."

Perhaps that explained how Backus had been able to continue in his position without anyone questioning him. If his aging had been frozen when he had been young, it surely would have been detected but, since he had already been old, the lack of advancing years wasn't as noticeable. I realized that his hairiness was probably more a means of camouflage than evidence of lazy grooming. Presumably, those who had realized the truth about him had decided to turn a blind eye. He was, after all, the chosen representatives of the gods in Aeris. Perhaps, they reasoned, that gave him unusual longevity. They would likely be shocked if they learned what constituted "unusual."

The next morning, I arrived early for my lesson with Father Backus. He opened the door at my eager knock.

"Amazing! A pupil arriving before the appointed time of the lecture. In all my years of teaching - and you know there have been a great many of them - I don't think that's ever happened. Come in, Janelle, and I'll satisfy your burning curiosity before it consumes you."

I doffed my moccasins and sat cross-legged on the floor in front of his chair as was my custom. I tried to contain my impatience but knew I wasn't doing a good job of it. As Backus had advised yesterday, my patience needed improvement.

"You worry that you're not really a Summoner." It wasn't a question.

I confirmed his suspicion. "You say I am. Samell believes I am. Probably more than half the village would agree with you both. But I don't *feel* it. You've said that Summoners have a direct channel to magic that regular people don't have. If that channel's there, I don't know how to find it."

"Putting aside the simple truth that you killed a powerful, dangerous creature comprised of earth magic without touching it, have you ever attempted to use your powers?"

I hadn't. Then again, I didn't know how I would do it. I told him as much.

"I can't help you, I'm afraid. It's either something you're going to have to discover by yourself or, if you need guidance, with the aid of another Summoner. But there's something I can do for you. I believe there's a test that can confirm without question whether you are what I believe you to be."

My heart skipped a beat. If there was a way to take away the uncertainty, to give me clarity… "What do I have to do?"

His face became serious; his eyes locked with mine. "This is no trivial matter, Janelle. What I propose isn't without risk. If you are a Summoner, there's little danger. But if you aren't, and you take this test, it will kill you."

Chapter Seven: The Summoner's Test

Kill me? Whatever price I had been expecting to pay to learn the truth, the possibility of dying was well outside of my comfort zone. My expression revealed my shock to the priest.

"I'll admit it's daunting, which is why you shouldn't be too quick to accept," said Backus. "But the evidence is strongly weighted in favor of your being a Summoner and, if you are, the leaves won't hurt you. At worst, they'll give you a sour stomach. They don't taste very good. I can assure you that from experience, although I only eat a tiny portion each day."

I wished I had his faith but I didn't, yet a part of me needed to know. I couldn't envision going through the next years of my life trapped in a state of uncertainty. Or worse, believing I was something that I wasn't. *Better a direct trip to Hades than lingering forever in the purgatory of not knowing.* Someone had said that to me once. A grandmother, I think.

Although the rational part of my mind could accept the priest's argument, the finality of failing the test made me balk. It was strange, though. Back in the other world, I couldn't recall ever thinking about death seriously - or at least as it applied to me. Death was something that happened to old people or sick people. Here, though, it had been a constant companion: The Verdant Blight, the river, the earth reaver...

"If I'm not... Isn't there something you could give me? Like an antidote?"

"A Blight leaf doesn't kill in the same way that a traditional poison does. It's not like a five-pointed redvein or a purpleberry. The leaf is imbued with latent magic and, if someone with no affinity for magic consumes it, the reaction will cause a rapid, corrosive failure. There's no known way to stop or reverse it. If a Summoner eats the leaf, its magic will be neutralized, absorbed into the body. So it would be like consuming an ordinary tree leaf - no better or worse. Not the tastiest or most nutritious of meals but certainly not fatal."

"The risk makes it frightening." This world might be unreal, but death here wasn't.

"I can appreciate that. It's easy for me to argue that the chances of your failing the test are small; I'm not the one taking it. And my dying at this overripe age would be of little consequence. I've lived the full life of a man four times over and long ago came to peace with my mortality. My continued existence comes at the sufferance of the gods. You, on the other hand, are young. Your life is ahead of you, not behind. I can understand how what I'm proposing might unnerve you. For that reason, I offer this merely as a *possibility*. If you want to proceed, I can help you. If not, we can continue with our lessons of history, culture, and geography. We need not discuss this again. That's entirely up to you. The way of the Summoner is hard enough without me making it harder."

After that, Father Backus began the day's lesson as if he hadn't just placed a millstone around my neck. I absorbed nothing of what he taught over the next several hours. Despite enduring a lengthy discourse about Gilbert the Great, I couldn't have named a single exploit of the legendary hero. Backus' voice was a background drone but I think he understood my mental state. Living three-hundred years gave a man insight into the workings of a person's mind. I suspect Backus may have known what my eventual decision would be even if I didn't.

I was distracted even after I left the priest's abode. Fortunately, my chores didn't require much in the way of thought. Muscle memory took over: load, walk, unload, re-load, walk, unload, repeat. I wished I hadn't been made aware of the test. It would have been easier to continue in a state of ambiguity, not certain one way or another, than to know that the answer was available. It was like the story about the slave offered a choice between two doors. Behind one was salvation and freedom. Behind the other was certain death. An impossible choice but hardly more tolerable than to walk back into slavery knowing what might have been.

"What is it, Janelle?" asked Samell that afternoon as we savored a respite from our respective duties. The shade from a house kept us cool as we sat with our backs against its outer wall. In just a few days, my friend had become attuned enough to my moods to recognize my distraction. I needed to unburden myself to someone. Maybe he could advise me.

"There's a test - a Summoner's test. Backus knows about it. If I take it, it'll let me know for sure that I'm a Summoner."

"That's wonderful!"

If only it was... "If I fail, it'll kill me."

Samell's nonchalant reaction surprised me. He merely shrugged. "Doesn't much matter. You're a Summoner so it won't kill you."

The certainty with which he said those words almost made me believe. Almost. But it wasn't his life. Failure would cost him a friend not his future.

"I wish I had your confidence." I tried not to sound dejected but failed.

"Of course you don't have it. You don't come from here. You don't know our ways, our history, our stories. Everyone who knows your story believes you're a Summoner except you. As for the rest, they'll either come around or they won't. There's really no need to take this test except that *you* need to be convinced. The lack of conviction is why you're scared."

"So it's a Catch-22."

Samell gave me a look of blank incomprehension. Of course he didn't understand the reference. He brushed it aside. "Backus wouldn't have proposed it if he thought there was a chance of losing you. He knows your uniqueness and importance. I'm sure he's prayed about it and sought the gods' advice and they wouldn't steer him wrong."

"I accept that I'm one of The Summoned, that I come from a different world. But Backus has already admitted that being one of The Summoned doesn't require me to be a Summoner. What if I'm just someone picked at random and brought here? What if the only thing special about me is that I'm an outsider?"

"To bring you here, a Summoner gave his life. That's as big a sacrifice as anyone can make. He wouldn't have done that if there wasn't something very special about you. A Summoner can only cast one Summoning. To do it, he would have had to be sure."

Talk about putting pressure on a person… In addition to worrying about whether this test would kill me, I had to live with a heavy burden of expectations. I hadn't even thought about it until Samell spelled it out. I had no idea how a Summoning worked. Did the Summoner who brought me here have a choice or had it been a random trick of fate? Had he acted out of calculation or desperation? Questions heaped on questions with far too few answers.

"What's the test?" asked Samell.

"Eating a leaf."

"From a Verdant Blight tree," he surmised. "I can see why that might worry you. No cure for that poison."

"Thanks for reminding me."

Puzzlement crinkled his features. In Aeris, people rarely (if ever) used sarcasm so its meaning was usually lost on them. "Is Father Backus certain you won't die if you're a Summoner?"

I suppose that was another concern. What if I was a Summoner but the test was faulty? What if Backus' deduction about the Summoner's ability to absorb the leaf's poison wasn't right? It's not as if he'd had a chance to prove that. His assumptions might be logical but that didn't mean they were true.

"He seems sure," I said, doubt dripping from every word.

Samell offered a comforting smile. "I believe you're a Summoner. Every bone in my body tells me that's the case. So much about you is different from every other girl in the village… But if you're that concerned about the test, don't take it. It won't change who or what you are."

I wished it was that simple but I the need to *be sure* was hardwired into my personality, a character flaw since childhood. And, as I realized when recalling an old vampire movie (yet another of my jumbled memories), there was another concern. In it, a man had tried to use a crucifix to drive off a vampire but it hadn't worked. The vampire's explanation: "You have to have faith for this to work on me!" Was magic like that? If I was a Summoner, did I have to *believe* in myself in order to use my powers?

By the time I lay down next to Esme that night, I was mentally exhausted. Samell hadn't spoken to me much at supper or afterward, opting to give me the space he thought I needed. Unfortunately, this wasn't a situation I could think myself out of. It came down to a simple choice: Was I more afraid of dying than not knowing? If so, then I could put the decision off indefinitely. If not…

The house was more active than usual when I awoke the next morning. It wasn't yet light out, although one of the moons shone from its perch high in the sky, and everyone was getting ready for the day. The residents of Aeris normally rose early but this was atypical. As I struggled to shrug off the vestiges of an interrupted sleep, Samell explained. "Yesterday's patrol hasn't come back. Sometimes, like with us when we found you, a patrol is late, but never this late."

"Could they have gotten lost?"

Samell shook his head. "Everyone who goes on patrol knows the surroundings well. Rengen is a long-timer. He's been patrolling for more'n a half-generation, nearly as long as I've been alive. No, this is something else."

He didn't say what that *something* might be. He didn't have to.

"Can you sense anything?" he asked. As if it was that simple.

But when I concentrated, I discovered it *was* that simple. My mind was like an elastic band and all I had to do was stretch it out. I didn't sense any earth reavers - or at least I didn't feel the way I had back in the Blight when one had been stalking me. However, to my surprise, I intercepted the feeling of anxiety that was seeping through the townsfolk. The patrol's disappearance had everyone on edge.

"No earth reavers but I don't know what my range is."

"Good to know there's nothing close to the town. A group of us are going out to search for Rengen and Elena."

"I could go with you. If there's something out there, maybe I could warn you…"

"Stay here," said Samell firmly, slinging his scabbard over his back. "You're too valuable to risk and we don't know what we're dealing with. If you want to help, keep checking the area to see whether there's any danger. If you sense something, alert the elders immediately. They'll get a messenger to us."

The curt dismissal stung, even though I supposed it made sense, but it provoked another memory to resurface. It was of a recent event, perhaps no more than a year or two in the past. I was in high school and had been invited to a party. All my friends would be there. My parents, however, found out and forbade me to go, claiming they had "heard" that alcohol was going to be served (an inevitability considering whose house it was at) and that there would be no parental supervision (also true, which was one of the attractions). So, while everyone I knew at school was enjoying themselves, I was forced to stay alone, sitting in my room, texting with my friends at the party. I had felt humiliated and marginalized even though, in retrospect, I understood the reasons for my parents' decision. My mother, whose image remained as unclear as my history, had said to me: "This isn't to punish you, Janelle. It's for your safety and well-being." That's what Samell was telling me now, although not in so many words. While the intention might not have been to impugn my trustworthiness, that was the result. I was *unworthy* of going on the expedition.

By the time I went to Father Backus' house for my day's training, the search party, which numbered ten (including Samell, Rickard, and Esme), had been gone for several hours. Activity in the village was subdued. Men and women went about their duties but everyone was waiting for word about the missing pair. I did as Samell had requested, occasionally casting with my mind to see if I could pick up indications of a nearby threat. The sense of worry throughout the populace was palpable but I could detect no immediate danger, at least not one similar to the earth reaver.

"I'm a little surprised you're here," said the priest after opening the door to my knock. He stood to one side to let me enter. "I thought they might take you with them."

"According to Samell, I'm 'too valuable to risk.'"

"I'd say he's right but you obviously don't agree."

I didn't answer, preferring instead to stand in sullen silence just inside his doorway.

"You're not ready, Janelle. Seven days of sitting patiently through my lectures and doing chores doesn't make you a trusted member of this community or a valuable part of a search party. Bringing you wouldn't have been wise or practical. Aside from a few sessions of crude practice with Esme, what weapons training do you have? How would you defend yourself if attacked? You're young, new to Aeris, and untried. I don't mean to be cruel but you wouldn't have been an asset. Everyone else in the group knows how to take care of themselves but, through no fault of your own, that's not the case for you. Learn to walk before you try to run."

I desperately wanted to contradict Backus but I couldn't. He was right and that stung as much as Samell's carefully framed rejection. I would have been a liability on the search. So I had been left behind.

Caught in the sudden grip of restless recklessness, I blurted out, "I want to take the test." I think I surprised myself as much as Backus when I said those words, but they were out of my mouth before I could think better of it.

"I'm not sure you should be making that choice in your current frame of mind. Hurt feelings shouldn't provoke a decision of this importance."

"I thought you said it wasn't dangerous? That it was a formality?"

Backus scratched his voluminous beard. "I don't think those were my exact words. I implied that it *shouldn't* be dangerous not that it *couldn't* be. I could be wrong. I have been before, more often than I'd like to admit. This is your choice, your decision, and there's an element of risk. It shouldn't be made in a heated moment, driven by an emotional response."

The impulse that had prompted me to make the declaration was fading, being crowded out by anxiety about the possibility of failure. "If I don't do it now, I may never find the courage again. You and I both know I need certainty. If I pass, I can move forward without being tentative or timid. And if I fail, at least you'll know that I couldn't have fulfilled whatever destiny you think I have."

Backus nodded somberly, as if something in my short speech had convinced him. He shuffled over to a trunk near the back of the room and, after rooting around in it for a few seconds, withdrew the burlap pouch containing his stash of Blight leaves. They were dried and looked similar to the brown oak leaves of my world that covered many lawns in the fall - except they were about twice the size.

Hurry, hurry, hurry, I wordlessly implored him, my resolve wavering. I knew I couldn't afford to contemplate the action I was about to take or I'd back out. *Do it and be done with it. Don't think about it. Just act.*

He handed me a leaf - whole, unbroken, and looking as mundane as any natural detritus. Hard to imagine that this was poison. Harder still to believe that, if Backus was wrong about me, it would be my executioner.

Taking a deep breath, feeling my heart racing, I raised it to lips suddenly dry with fear. My nostrils caught the faint perfume of dirt and mildew. The last moment arrived for me to stop this madness then passed as I put the leaf into my mouth and chewed.

The taste was slightly bitter but not so awful that I wanted to spit it out. The biggest challenge was manufacturing enough spit to moisten it. I gagged once but I don't know whether that was because it tasted like earth or because fear had partially closed my throat. I swallowed once, twice, three times - then it was done. Backus handed me a goblet of liquid that I accepted it, my hand shaking. I downed the contents in one gulp, gasping when I realized that what I had taken for was water was considerably stronger.

I didn't collapse in a paroxysm of agony. My body didn't undergo a transformation that left me feeling physically different. As I stood there, awaiting my death, it gradually dawned on me that nothing was going to happen. Backus was smiling like a proud parent.

The action had been commonplace but its implications were profound. I was a Summoner.

Chapter Eight: The Missing

"What now?" I asked. In the immediate aftermath of passing the test, I wasn't sure how to feel. Confused? Elated? Relieved? All of the above?

"I'll inform the elders. They won't question me when I tell them we've tested you and confirmed without a doubt that you're a Summoner. What happens then will be up to them. It changes nothing, however. You remain a newcomer to this world who's woefully unprepared for much of what it has to offer. You have the ability to control magic but no idea how to access your powers. Like a toddler, you must crawl before you can walk and you'll fall down many times along the way. Trying to do too much now is a greater danger than eating that leaf ever could have been."

It changes nothing. Backus was a wise man but he was wrong about that. It changed everything. It changed how I saw myself. And it would change how many in Aeris perceived me. To this point, I had been a *possible* Summoner. Now, doubt had been removed. I had accomplished what no other person in this village could do and, through that action, had established myself as more than a lost innocent needing protection. Backus had known. Esme had known. Samell especially had known. Now I knew. Soon, everyone else would too.

In retrospect, it seemed foolish to have been so afraid. *It's nothing to be ashamed of*, I chided myself. *I might have died eating that leaf.* But I hadn't and now I was on the other side. I had crossed something mightier than the river that had once separated me from Esme and Samell.

By mid-day, word of my successful testing had spread throughout the village. I could tell by the way people were looking at me. Instead of the fey weakling girl they had been whispering about since my arrival, I was now a Summoner in their midst. They didn't know what to make of it but condescension and pity had been replaced by awe and deference. Whatever information Backus had circulated, its effect had been immediate and substantial.

But the citizens of Aeris had greater concerns today than the sudden elevation of their resident stranger. Yesterday's patrol had still not reappeared and there hadn't been any word from the group of eight sent to look for them. Some of the communal anxiety was relieved a cycle past the sun's zenith when Esme returned to let everyone know that the searchers were all right, although there was still no sign of Rengen and Elena.

She came to talk to me before heading back out. "The town's all abuzz about your passing some kind of test. Good for you. Now maybe everyone will believe what we already know. We may need your help. It's like they've disappeared. We're doubling back, trying every trail they might have used but nothing seems out of the ordinary. There aren't signs that anything bad happened but we haven't found them alive, either. A few of us are wondering if your skills might reveal something we're not privy to. Samell doesn't think you should be exposed to 'the dangers of patrolling,' whatever that means. As a Summoner, you're probably better equipped to deal with them than any of us."

I sincerely doubted that but appreciated the vote of confidence. And if they needed me…

"Three agree with Samell, although not for the same reasons. Rickard thinks you'll slow us down. But if we don't find at least a sign of Rengen and Elena soon, their resistance will go away. If we have to go out again tomorrow, you'll be with us. I'll make sure of it."

I smiled at Esme, happy to have her as an advocate.

"Could you check?" she asked, wiggling her fingers in what I guess she assumed was a "wizardly" way. "See if you can sense anything from here?"

I didn't tell her I had been trying all day and reached out again with my mind. The more often I did this thing, the more natural it felt. I didn't know if I was actually using magic but it wasn't something I had done before coming here. I wondered if this was how clairvoyants and telepaths felt in my world and belatedly realized I had perhaps done them an injustice by dismissing them as charlatans.

The foremost thing I sensed was the overwhelming concern for the lost patrollers. The town's collective grief and anxiety was overpowering and I was about to "disconnect" when I caught a whiff of something else. It was faint, almost too faint to be sure, but it felt disturbingly like what I had experienced during those nights alone in The Verdant Blight. I concentrated, trying to filter out the closer, more immediate sensations, but I lacked the experience to do that, and the distant impression vanished. Had it been my imagination?

"There might be something. I can't be sure and can't pinpoint a direction. But be careful. If what I felt is real - and I only sensed it for a moment - there could be another earth reaver out there, somewhere beyond the village."

Esme thanked me, advised me to be patient, and left to rejoin the others. A part of me wanted to follow her but, for once, I heeded my rational impulses. Eating the Blight leaf had represented enough suicidal impulsivity for one day.

The search group returned just before nightfall when the sky was turning a deep purple. Tonight would be a "darker night" - a time when only one moon traversed the firmament. Knowing little about astronomy, I assumed it was because the other moon was "up" during the day but the residents of Aeris had a long story about why Ire was hiding from Concord (or the other way around). The upshot was that the possibility of continuing the search at night had been rejected. The weary, frustrated searchers returned home to eat a meal and get to bed so they could leave at the earliest possible time in the morning.

Samell was dejected. I sat next to him in silence at the supper table. Rickard had come home and grabbed something to eat before leaving with Lissa to confer with the elders. An exhausted Esme had skipped her meal and gone straight to bed. She lay on the floor in the next room.

"They're dead," he said finally, his voice thick. "I know it. We all do but no one will say it. If they had been able to get home, they would have been here by now. I couldn't stop thinking about our encounter with the earth reaver and what would have happened if you hadn't been with us. Rengen and Elena didn't have you. And, as competent as they are with their weapons, that might not have been enough."

I didn't say anything. During my short time in Aeris, I had met Rengen only once or twice. He was a gregarious man at least twice my age with a wife and two children. Elena, on the other hand, was maybe a year or two older than me and we had spent several evenings together along with Samell and a few of their other friends. In that short time, I had realized there was something between Elena and Samell, although I didn't know whether it was "official" or not. They liked each other and there was a mutual attraction but no one had mentioned them being engaged or intended for one another.

I thought about taking his hand in mine but decided against it, unsure whether such a gesture of simple comfort and support might be misinterpreted or unwelcome.

"Esme said you took the test." His change of subject surprised me.

"It was impulsive but it felt like the right thing to do. Now at least I *know*."

"Not just you. The search patrol is going to ask you to come with us tomorrow. No one would think less of you if you refused."

"Why would I refuse?"

"Because it's too soon." His words echoed Backus'. "Being a Summoner doesn't guarantee that you can access your powers or use them properly. When you killed the earth reaver, you admitted you weren't sure what you were doing or whether you could do it again. You had a crippling headache that prevented you from traveling for the afternoon. Going on the search might not be the best thing for you. There will be expectations of you as a Summoner that you might not be able to meet. And there could also be danger out there."

"Samell, your people took me in when I didn't have anywhere else to go. How can I turn them down if there's something I might be able to do to help? I may not understand what it really means to be a Summoner but I can sense things and maybe that'll make a difference."

"What do you sense now? Esme said you warned her that there might be something in The Verdant Blight."

I had struggled with that all day, trying to rediscover the elusive presence I had so briefly brushed against earlier. No matter how hard I concentrated, there was nothing, making me wonder if it had really been there. Jumping at shadows, running from the wind - was that what I had become? Knowing that I was a Summoner made it all the more important that I be able to validate the impressions of my "sixth sense." In this case, I wasn't sure. I had urged that Esme to be cautious but anyone with an ounce of common sense could have given the same advice. There *might* be more earth reavers in The Verdant Blight. An earth reaver *might* have killed Rengen and Elena. It didn't take a Summoner to make those deductions and there was nothing I could add to them.

"It could have been something. Or nothing," I said. "I'm not sure. It's like if you see a blur of motion far off in the distance out of the corner of your eye. Then you turn to look directly at it and there's nothing. You don't know whether the movement was real or whether you imagined it. That's how it was this afternoon. Before I met you in The Verdant Blight, the presence was near and constant, impossible to miss even if I didn't understand at the time what it represented. If there's something out there and I can get closer, maybe I'll be able to identify it."

"So you're determined to go?"

"If I'm asked, yes."

"Then stick close to me and Esme. We'll keep you safe."

This time I took his hand. Giving it a reassuring squeeze, I said, "I know you will."

So it was that I exited the house in the pre-dawn hours with Samell, Esme, and Rickard. Although my friends' attitude toward me hadn't changed since I had passed the test, Rickard had become less abrasive. He had even smiled at me once or twice this morning as we got ready to join the search patrol. My presence under his roof had elevated his status in the village. There was even scuttlebutt that he might be asked to join the council of elders. It didn't bother me that he might profit from my presence. After all, he had allowed me to shelter in his house (even if that was more because of his children than him).

Cool and impassive, Backus was waiting at the staging area for the patrol.

"Are you coming as well?" I asked, somewhat surprised. This didn't seem like an appropriate activity for a three-hundred year-old man.

He shook his head. "No, no. My days of patrolling are long past. I wouldn't get far with these arthritic knees. I'm here to give you some advice. I don't know what you'll encounter out there today. Maybe nothing. But if the gods will that you have another encounter with an earth reaver, don't be too hasty to interject yourself into the battle. Let those with a skill of arms form the first line of defense. You said yourself that you thought the earth reaver you killed was nearly dead by the time you dispatched it.

"Use magic only as a last resort. And, whatever you do, don't repeat how you attacked the other one. You may have drawn on your own life's essence, which is so dangerous that even experienced Summoners avoid it. You're lucky the headache wasn't permanent and it didn't do more serious damage. If you try it again, there's no telling how long-lasting or debilitating the effects could be. Of necessity, some of your magical training will be trial-and-error, but you don't want to explore something that risky without supervision."

"You're remarkably well informed," I said, a suspicion forming.

"I have an extensive library and spend at least three hours each evening reading."

It was a plausible explanation… so why didn't I think it was the whole truth?

"Don't overtax yourself. If you become careless, the world will have one less Summoner and there are so few left that we can't afford to discard one for little benefit." For the first time I saw the stern taskmaster in Father Backus.

The company numbered ten including me. In addition to Samell, Esme, and Rickard, there were three of Samell's close friends, Judah, Minal, and Stepan; one of the elders' deputies, Anna; Rengen's oldest son, Tomas; and Elena's older sister, Beatrice. Everyone except me was a veteran of numerous patrols and hunts. They knew the road, trails, and forest well. Anna was an expert tracker. She and I were the only new recruits to the search party. The other eight had gone out yesterday.

We departed Aeris on the road headed south, walking in three rows of three abreast with Anna alone in the lead. I was flanked by Esme to my left and Samell to my right. The Verdant Blight rose like a green wall beyond Samell. On the other side of the road was a gently sloping pasture. In the far distance, a group of animals were grazing. From here, they looked like cows but I had learned that this world didn't have cattle. So much for any aspirations I might have had for opening the first MacDonald's.

"What about to the north and west?" I asked, suddenly aware of how big a task it could be to find two people in all this land. Thousands upon thousands of acres…

"We did a sweep in concentric circles around Aeris yesterday morning. Today we're going to head farther south. Their path would have been predictable for the first cycle beyond the city. After that, however, there are a lot of ways they could have gone. We're hoping you and Anna can give us some insight. Otherwise, we'll just follow the common trails.

If someone or something didn't want Rengen and Elena found, it would be easy enough to hide them, dead or alive. This was needle in the haystack territory. Searchers could go out every day for seasons and not find anything if the two had deviated from their normal routine. I wondered how many days the searchers would go before calling it off.

When I was a child, my family owned a cat, Dusty, who we put outside in the evenings and let back in in the mornings to be fed. One day, he didn't come home. I remember standing on the front porch shortly after waking up, barefoot and in a nightgown, calling his name, and not hearing the answering jingle of the bells on his collar. My father suggested he had maybe run off but I spent the entirety of two days scouring the nearby woods for him, calling out his name with increasing desperation. Even all these years later, in a different reality, I could taste the despair. The impossibility of finding him in all those woods... What if he was hurt? What if he had gotten into a fight with a raccoon or a fox? Sometime later, I learned that my father had discovered him run over in the street but hadn't told us, feeling that not knowing offered hope that he might still be alive somewhere. I couldn't see how the search for Rengen and Elena was going to end up better, and "not knowing" in this case didn't offer the possibility of optimism.

I concentrated on the surrounding area and discovered little with my hidden sense that I couldn't otherwise detect. The mass of concern that represented the town's feelings was fast fading into the distance. The Verdant Blight was a silent presence, lifeless except for the vegetation. The eastern plains were home to a variety of small creatures although, this close to the magically poisoned forest, there were fewer than one might expect in a healthy locale. "Nothing yet," I said aloud by way of reporting my findings.

We traveled in silence, footfalls on the hard-packed clay road and the occasional jingle of a weapon or other item being the only sounds. Anna would occasionally stop to look at something just off the highway but she hadn't yet taken the patrol into the woods or fields. My probes were unhelpful, although I learned that my range was less than a full cycle. Once that amount of time had passed, I could no longer sense anything of Aeris.

By the time we stopped for a midday meal of stale bread, warm water, and dried jerky, everyone was disconsolate. It was becoming hot, although a low-hanging deck of clouds kept the sun masked, and the humidity was suffocating. Everyone was sweating profusely; it looked as if we had all just emerged from a swim in the river. It hadn't rained since immediately before my arrival but it looked like the drought might soon break. The clouds to the north were unpromisingly dark. Rarely had I seen more ominous thunderheads.

"Shouldn't we move off the road? Maybe closer to the river. When I go on patrol this far south, I never stay on the road," said sandy-haired Stepan. Samell and Esme voiced their agreement. If we headed directly west from our current position, I estimated we'd arrive at the river close to where I had first encountered my new friends.

"That may be so," said Anna, her voice as tired and weathered as her features. "But there's been no evidence they left the road so either they didn't come south this way in the first place or they stayed on the highway longer than the norm. Maybe they were following something or noticed something unusual."

"I don't sense anything wrong," I said. I was starting to feel inadequate. Maybe Backus and Samell were right; I wasn't ready. Everyone was expecting me to be able to blaze a trail directly to the missing patrollers' position. It didn't work that way. Or maybe it did and I was ignorant about how to do it. Too bad being a Summoner didn't come with a user's guide.

"We continue on the road till we have to turn back. We may not find them but at least we can eliminate this as a direction for future searches."

So the early afternoon found us continuing our southward trek while thunderheads built behind us. The storm didn't appear to be headed in this direction; it was moving west-to-east, north of Aeris. A wayward gust of air blown all the way from the center of the cyclone caused my nape hairs to stand on end. When I paused to stare at the distant, swirling clouds, everyone looked at me curiously, wondering why I had suddenly stopped.

"That's not a normal storm." I don't know how I knew that but I did. The knowledge came in the same way that I had felt the stalking in the Blight. I was too far away to discern anything specific about the storm but it reeked of the arcane.

"Magic?" asked Samell.

I nodded. What else could it be, especially if I was sensitive to it?

"Air reavers, then," said Rickard. "Stands to reason that if their earth cousins are emerging that they would as well." On the road to Aeris, Samell had mentioned fire reavers. Of course, one for each kind of element: earth, air, fire, water.

"That storm is close to Aeris. Might even be grazing it." This was the first thing Tomas had said on the journey.

Anna considered. "North of the village, I think, but worrisome nonetheless. Earth reavers we might expect because of our proximity to The Verdant Blight. It's almost surprising we haven't seen more activity before now. But air reavers?"

She started to say more but I didn't hear her. At that moment, the fullness of my concentration was demanded elsewhere. I became mindful that we had more than distant air reavers to concern us. The malevolent presence I recognized from my time in the forest was creeping back into my awareness. It was approaching, slowly but inexorably, from the south and west, deep in The Verdant Blight. And it was bigger than what I had previously experienced. Much bigger.

"We have a problem," I said, interrupting Anna and trying to stay calm. Panic was easy but it wouldn't do us any good. I was the Summoner. I needed to stay in control.

"An earth reaver?" asked Samell.

"More than one." Maybe a whole army. With every passing second, the manifestation became more forceful. "I don't know how far away but they're south and west of here."

"That's where we met you." Samell pointed in the general direction where my sense told me the danger was massing.

"Air reavers to the north, earth reavers to the southwest. I think we'd best get back to Aeris. Finding our lost patrollers is the least of our concerns right now and, considering what's happening, we can make a good guess what became of them." Anna paused then added. "Now let's make haste before we join them."

Chapter Nine: By the Pricking of My Thumb

The trek back to Aeris was difficult. Not only did I slow the entire patrol because I couldn't match Anna's desired pace but the earth reavers' presence was a constant irritant – an itch I couldn't scratch.

Fortunately, they weren't advancing aggressively. They weren't after us or, if they were, they weren't investing much effort in catching us. Even moving slowly because I could only jog in spurts, we easily outdistanced them. It wasn't clear to me whether they were traveling in a specific direction or merely expanding within a confined area. It would be naïve to believe they wouldn't turn their attention to Aeris at some point, and probably sooner than later. All alone, days away from NewTown, it was vulnerable. The settlement's isolation, a boon for many of the residents over the years, might now prove to be an insurmountable obstacle. Aeris couldn't field a militia and that's what would be needed to defeat the earth reavers if they massed for a coordinated attack.

Anna occasionally asked me for updates and I told her what I was able to. My limited information didn't satisfy her but she did a good job hiding her frustration. She was also annoyed that I was holding everyone back. She couldn't risk splitting the party to send the faster runners ahead because, if it came to a battle, even ten people (including an untrained Summoner) might not be enough. So we crawled north and arrived at Aeris just as the cloud-enhanced premature twilight was falling.

Asking me to accompany him, Rickard headed for the elders' hall. All six of Aeris' rulers were waiting, almost as if they had been expecting us. Father Backus was there as well, looking as somber as ever beneath his bushy beard.

"You didn't find them, then," surmised one of the women - the one who had been the chief speaker on my previous visit.

"No. But it's about more than the missing patrollers," said Rickard.

"The storm," interrupted Backus. "To the north. It isn't a natural manifestation. It's an abomination in the eyes of the gods." He spoke to the assembly but his eyes were fixed on me.

"That's part of it," agreed Rickard. "The young Summoner said as much but that's not all she said." He stood to one side, ceding the floor to me.

I had never been a good public speaker. That realization stirred a recollection of giving an oral report in front of my sixth grade class. Nerves had caused my voice to quake and my hands to tremble. When the teacher had given me a glass of water, I had taken two sips before spilling it all over myself. The snickers of the other children echoed in my memories. This was a smaller audience but I felt even less comfortable, if that was possible. These were important people, not kids who would forget about my words by recess, but the seriousness of the circumstances gave me the measure of courage I needed to speak with conviction.

"There are earth reavers in The Verdant Blight. A lot of them. I can't tell whether they're massing or moving but there are more than just one or two or three. The storm felt similar - magical in nature."

"Are they coming in this direction?" asked the man who resembled Ebenezer Scrooge.

"It's difficult to say. I wasn't able to observe them long enough to figure out what they're doing. For the moment, everything feels normal here." Along the road, the presence had faded the closer we came to Aeris. Now, I couldn't sense it at all. I could still feel the storm although its potency was dissipating. With the urgency dampened, the panic I had experienced while on the patrol seemed like an extreme reaction - the difference between facing a nightmare by the light of day rather than at the moment of waking.

"What say you, Father?" asked another of the women. I remembered her as being more generous with her smiles than her fellows.

Backus' voice was without inflection. "I have faith in Janelle. She is young, inexperienced, and untried but she is a Summoner. As I informed you yesterday, any doubt about that has been removed. Magic calls to magic. If Janelle suspects that magic is at work, you can believe her instincts. We're fortunate to be privy to her insight. Had she not been here, we would have been none the wiser about a danger to our village. Now, we are forewarned. We must turn that knowledge into preparation. To do otherwise would be irresponsible."

"You believe we could be attacked?" The man who looked like Santa was incredulous. His snow-white eyebrows were raised, his blue eyes wide.

Backus remained infuriatingly calm. I found his demeanor strange. He was almost too reserved; I would have expected more urgency. "It's always been a possibility. Our forebears knew that when they came here just as we know it today. Aeris is isolated. The nearest settlement of any size is four days' travel. The nearest city is a half-season's walk. This makes us a target. Admittedly, we never considered a hoard of earth reavers as a foe but, in combat, few are given the luxury of choosing their adversaries."

At his use of the word *combat*, faces fell. He had spoken aloud what none of them wanted to hear. Many of Aeris' citizens were proficient with weapons but this was primarily a farming community.

"We should send for help," said Ebenezer.

Backus shook his head in the negative. "I'm not sure that's wise."

"A fast messenger on a horse could get to NewTown in less than two days and could carry a response back in the same. Surely you don't expect us to be under siege that soon."

"I have no expectations. Janelle can't feel the reavers here so that argues we have some time. How much, I can't say. But sending men south would force them to cross through the heart of the danger. We have no idea how far the area of peril extends but the road moves through the Blight a day south of here and detouring around it by a safe distance would add days to the journey. And consider what our messenger's reception would be. If he's believed, which isn't certain, would NewTown commit a large force of men to our defense when those people might be needed to protect their village? I propose we send out homing birds with messages to NewTown and West Fork but not jeopardize the lives of people who could be put to better use preparing for a possible attack."

"So we prepare for a fight?"

"That would seem to be the prudent course."

"And what can she do?" asked the first woman, pointing a fat index finger at me.

"In battle, not much. She's still new to this world and her craft. She doesn't understand how magic works and that's not something that can be learned in a matter of days. But when it comes to tracking the enemy's approach, she'll be better than the most accomplished scout. You needn't post men in and around The Verdant Blight to watch for earth reavers. If anything comes within a cycle of Aeris, she'll be able to warn us."

"And you, is there anything you can do?" asked Santa.

"Pray."

Despite admonitions from Backus, Lissa, and Samell to get a good night's sleep, I spent most of the dark hours tossing and turning on the floor where my straw pallet had been arranged. Next to me, Esme snored lightly. It was like a slumber party but without the sleeping bags, giggling, and talk of boys.

There were many things to think about, the most obvious being the role I would play if it came to a fight with a swarm of earth reavers. Despite Backus' suggestion that I would be of limited use in any battle, I'm sure most of the village would be expecting me to do more than cower behind the front lines. Still, I wondered if I'd be able to accomplish something beyond taking my lovely little stick and whacking the creatures across their snouts with it. Thinking of those dark, angry faces made me shiver.

Then there was the riddle of Father Backus whose identity might be concealed from much of Aeris' citizenry but was apparently known to the elders. His detachment had been odd. If I didn't know better, I would have assumed he was on drugs tonight. First thing in the morning, I needed to speak to him.

As I lay in a complete darkness facilitated by a cloud cover heavy enough to hide the moons, I released my mind to quest for signs of an enemy's approach. Like tendrils spreading across the ground, my senses slithered away from Aeris, growing thinner and less sure the farther they spread from the village. Nothing. I knew the earth reavers were out there but they were beyond my range, whatever that was. Likewise, the storm had either abated or passed on. For the moment, at least, everything was peaceful. That realization allowed me to drift off into a short, fitful slumber.

The morning dawned gray and rainy, with a persistent drizzle making everything damp. The oppressive humidity made the air thick and prevented even covered areas from drying. As best I could determine, this was a natural weather pattern but that didn't make it more pleasant. Everyone in Aeris went about their business but today's chores weren't the usual ones. Arrows were being fashioned and fletched. Tree branches were being stripped of their bark and shaped into javelins. Swords and knives were being sharpened. The village was taking the possibility of battle seriously. And no patrol was going out today. The search for Rengen and Elena had been abandoned, at least temporarily. There were more immediate concerns that demanded the people's attention.

"You're awake. Good," said Rickard, strolling into the front room where I had been sleeping. His voice was as gruff as ever but there was no trace of animosity in his tone. "Father Backus asked to see you when you're ready. Your time is better spent with him than doing the menial tasks the rest of us are attending to."

Seeing Father Backus wasn't just a good idea, it was a necessity. Less than twenty minutes later - the time it took me to get something to eat and splash water on my face - I was sitting on the priest's floor, gazing up at him as he reclined in his chair. He looked no more or less concerned than he had on any of the other mornings I had visited him. It was almost as if the possibility of an attack didn't concern him.

"Are you going to come clean?" I asked him.

His look of incomprehension made me realize that idiom didn't translate. "Are you going to tell me the truth?"

"What truth do you suppose you deserve?" It was an odd response. I wondered if we were about to engage in word games and riddles. I hoped not. I wasn't in the mood.

"You're a Summoner."

He didn't respond immediately and, in that pause, any doubts I had about my leap of intuition were wiped away. A denial would have been firm and immediate. I didn't congratulate myself on my Sherlock Holmesian powers of deduction. I should have come to this obvious conclusion much earlier.

"I wondered how long it would take you to figure that out. I had intended to tell you eventually but it seems the earth reavers have advanced the timing."

"You're a Summoner," I repeated more firmly.

"Technically, I'm a wizard."

"There's a difference?" I hadn't heard the term yet in this world but it enjoyed commonplace usage where I came from.

"A wizard is a Summoner who's either not formally trained or incapable of practicing meaningful magic. To put it plainly in my case, I'm burned out."

I wondered what it meant for a Summoner to lose his powers and whether it had anything to do with the warning Backus had issued before I left on the patrol: *Use magic only as a last resort.*

"What gave me away?" he asked.

"You knew things that even a very old priest wouldn't know. The self-medication with the leaves was too fantastical…"

"It's true, though. Daily doses have maintained my life far beyond its normal span. But I can only endure them because I'm a wizard. If I wasn't magical, even small amounts, if administered regularly, would be fatal. What can be healing and beneficial to Summoners can kill those without our special body chemistry."

"What happened? What caused you to burn out?" If there was a lesson here - and I'm sure there was one - I was determined to learn it. Never in my life had I been more hungry for knowledge.

"Every magical act, no matter how insignificant, requires energy. It's one of the basic laws of existence that matter and energy can't be created, only transformed. One thing that differentiates a Summoner from a common person is the ability to capture mundane forms of energy and convert them into the volatile, permeable form we call magic. It's neither matter nor energy but something altogether different and it can't spring into being out of nothingness.

"As Summoners, we can draw on two forms of energy for our power. The first is the essence of our being. This is limited and therefore limiting. Drain it and you die. Delve too deeply into it and you can end up a weakling or an invalid. Life's essence doesn't regenerate. Once gone, it never comes back. The other, more common source is emotion.

"Any emotion will do although stronger acts require extreme emotion. Our emotional reserves refill, although slowly. They're a well - deep but finite. Summoners often use what we call 'flash emotions' for minor workings. Let me demonstrate…" So saying, he withdrew a needle from a pincushion he kept under his chair. He then slid from the seat to squat next to me on the floor and, with surprising deftness, jabbed the pad of my left thumb with the instrument.

"Ow!" I shouted, jerking away my hand. No serious damage, just a moment's sting and a single droplet of blood, red like a liquid ruby. I put the injured finger in my mouth and sucked while regarding the priest with an angry glare.

"If you understood how to channel emotion, you could transform your surprise and anger into something productive. It will fade on its own so it needs to be used immediately. Other, deeper feelings can last for years or longer. Plumbing them is dangerous because it undermines your essential character."

He was right. The anger, like the pain, was already diminishing. I had no idea how to harness the emotion so it trickled away without bearing fruit. Had he expected me to do something with it or had the object of the lesson been less aggressive?

Replacing the needle, he continued, "Emotions are like treasures. Some - the most valuable ones - have to be locked away so they can't be lost. Over the years, I've learned there are limits. When you've exhausted your current supply of emotions, you get used to the feeling of emptiness. It becomes comfortable. New emotions are anathema, unwanted and unwelcome. It's not that I don't feel *anything*, but my feelings are shallow, my thoughts and actions grounded in logic. For me, magic is a thing of the past. I daresay I could manage little things - tricks and illusions, mostly. But nothing significant. I haven't been a true practitioner since before I came to Aeris."

It was almost too much to process. I felt like I had been sitting in a class where a teacher had just given all the answers to the next test and I hadn't taken notes.

"So you're saying that..." My voice trailed off as I realized I didn't fully understand *what* he was saying.

His response was patient, exhibiting no exasperation at his pupil's slowness. "Magic is a force. It takes many forms, some recognizable, some not. Naturally occurring magic can be a cranky thing to control because its lack of purity makes for unpredictable results. You need energy to fuel the creation of magic and the Summoner's emotion provides that. This is a gross oversimplification but think of it this way: you have the ability to transform emotional energy into magical energy, and that magical energy can then be used to do something: light a torch, fell a tree, stop a sword, heal a wound, kill an enemy…your imagination provides the limitations. But every 'transaction' drains your emotional wellspring. And if you lose too much, you'll end up a cold shell of a person struggling to hold onto the vestiges of your humanity." Of course, he was speaking of himself. Suddenly, I wasn't sure about this whole "Summoner" thing. Things were always more impressive until you read the fine print.

"How much can you teach me? About changing my emotions into magic, I mean."

He sighed, a gesture more theatrical than genuine. "Very little, I'm afraid. I can't demonstrate it and the process isn't easy to explain. Could you teach me how to listen? No? Magic is just as instinctive. I learned it gradually when I was young. I was never formally tutored and only those closest to me knew my secret. Everything I did was the result of trial-and-error. I never learned the spells or cantrips used by well-schooled Summoners. If I had it to do again, maybe I would seek out a master, but I find it hard to regret my choices. Your path must be different. Instinct may unlock some of your abilities but you'll need to seek the knowledge of someone who's negotiated this road more adroitly than I have."

Do as I say not as I do. His advice was the ultimate in hypocrisy. Maybe it made sense as a future goal but it wasn't helpful in the here-and-now. The growing sense of frustration was difficult to fight down. Too bad I didn't understand *the process* or I could transform it into magic and do something with it.

"Can you control which emotions you…use?"

"I was never able to. My magic was inconsistent. Disciplined Summoners can, though. It allows them to become stronger. If you learn to burn off all your negative emotions - fears, sadness, pain - and leave behind only the precious ones, it could make you a calm, resilient woman. Commoners think of Summoners as clear-headed and intelligent. Not all are the latter but most are the former."

I was about to ask another question when I suddenly felt an unwelcome twinge at the edge of my awareness. My heart dropped into my stomach. The earth reavers were on the move toward Aeris.

Chapter Ten: Something Wicked This Way Comes

As soon as my senses had pinpointed the threat to Aeris, Backus took me to the elders' hall. We were admitted without delay and, although only two members of the council were present - one of the women and Ebenezer (whose actual name was Targen) - my report was given the highest priority.

After that, I spent the day with Esme, Samell, and Esme's friend Alyssa by my side, monitoring the earth reavers' approach as best I could. Their initially faint presence grew more pronounced as the minutes ticked by. An attack wasn't yet imminent but everyone accepted its inevitability. Preparations kicked into overdrive as the citizens prepared for the battle. People died all the time in communities like Aeris but this place had never seen the kind of bloodshed likely to occur if the earth reavers continued their advance.

Shortly after I began my watch, Samell approached me, offering to replace my stick (really just a crudely shaped tree branch) with a finely crafted wooden staff. "I wish I'd had more time to finish it. It's still a little rough. But I hope it'll be useful." He spoke the words almost shyly as he proffered the gift.

I wasn't sure why he was dissatisfied. It was a beautiful item, suitable for use as a tool or a weapon. The six-foot long pole of stained wood was dark, smooth, and hard. One end was capped with an iron spike while the other was blunt and unadorned. Although it wasn't ornamental, the craftsmanship in its creation was evident.

"My first possession in this world," I said with a satisfied smile, feeling its weight and balance as I practiced a couple of the moves Esme had taught me. The air provided a worthy opponent; I doubted I could have landed a blow on a real person. "Well, except for my clothing." The local clothes maker had tailored the blouse and pants I currently wore and a cobbler had replaced Esme's ill-fitting moccasins with larger, more durable footwear.

"I wish I'd been able to give it in less urgent circumstances. And I hope those of us assigned to defend you will make sure you don't have to use it."

Those of us assigned to defend you... My "honor guard," Backus had called it. They were all people I knew and trusted: Samell, Esme, Rickard, and Alyssa. Their primary duty, if an attack occurred, was to ensure that no harm came to me. The priest had been frank about one point: "A fully trained Summoner wouldn't need protection. Quite the opposite: she would protect everyone around her. But the likelihood that you'll be able to contribute is small. And you don't dare repeat what you did in The Verdant Blight." The memory of the headache's intensity convinced me of the wisdom of his words.

It was a long, uncomfortable day with a light mist coating everything. Occasionally, the leaden skies would let loose with a heavy burst of rain, thoroughly soaking everyone and everything. My clothes were sodden and my skin was beginning to prune. I had removed my boots because they provided no protection from the damp. I was encouraged to stay within but the house smelled so strongly of uncured hides and wet fur that it was easier on my nose and stomach to remain outside. For the most part, the citizens of Aeris seemed unaffected by the weather. They went about their business with a crisp orderliness that impressed me.

The cloudy sky brought an early twilight and the blackness of a moonless, starless night quickly descended. Torches and lanterns were lit all around the village. Samell escorted me inside, made me a warm meal that tasted a lot like stew, and encouraged me to get some sleep.

"I don't know if I can," I said, trying to get comfortable on the pallet of damp, smelly straw.

"I could sing you a lullaby."

I smiled at the attempt at humor. Samell so rarely cracked jokes that it was refreshing to hear him try, especially in these circumstances: his girlfriend lost (probably dead), his village readying for battle, and the possibility that his whole way of life would be gone after tomorrow.

As I lay there in the dark, his reassuring presence close by, I found sleep to be hopelessly beyond my grasp. I frequently "checked" on the approach of the earth reavers but, like the proverbial watched pot not boiling, it was difficult to detect changes from minute-to-minute. So I was left alone in my head with my thoughts and worries.

I couldn't help but wonder whether everything that was happening now was connected to my arrival. Or maybe it was the other way around. The emergence of a force of earth reavers, the appearance of air reavers, the first attack on Aeris in ten generations…even the most devout defender of coincidence would have a hard time denying a relationship between those things and the arrival of a new Summoner. But the question remained: were they happening because I was here or was I here because someone (presumably the man or woman who had called me) knew that I would be needed? In the end, perhaps it didn't matter. I was here. The earth reavers were coming. And the routine of many lifetimes was about to be ruptured.

I also wondered how widespread this activity might be. It seemed unlikely that only one remote town would be the target of a swarm of earth reavers. Was this one of many orchestrated attacks or was the world at large immune and unaware? What was happening now in NewTown, West Fork, the other hundreds of villages around the land, and the great cities to the east? The elders had sent messages by birds to the closest habitations but it would be days before responses could be expected, if they came at all.

"I can't sleep," I finally admitted, my voice sounding unnaturally loud in the stillness of the house. Samell and I were the only ones here. Rickard, Lissa, Brin, and Esme were elsewhere, helping with the preparations.

"Scared?" he asked.

"Terrified. We might be facing twenty or thirty or more of those things. You and I both know how hard they are to kill."

"Thanks to that encounter, we know what to expect. We know what they look like, how they attack, where they're dangerous, and where they're vulnerable. Go for the face and neck, not the body."

"Everything here is just so different from what I know…and I can't even remember half of what my old life was like. I only have a vague notion of what my mother and father look like and I don't know whether I have any brothers or sisters. Now, to be here…I'm trying to be brave but…" *Don't cry. Don't cry.* He wouldn't see the tears, of course, but I so wanted to be strong. I *needed* to be strong. At the moment, though, I didn't feel like a Summoner. I felt like the lost girl who had awakened alone and confused in The Verdant Blight.

"I'm not frightened," he said softly. I could tell by the nearness of his voice that he had moved closer to me. "Do you know why?"

I stupidly shook my head then realized he wouldn't see the gesture in the darkness. "Because you're here. A Summoner. No matter how much you downplay your capabilities, just having you here makes us stronger. Without you, this village would die tomorrow. We wouldn't have known what was coming. The earth reavers would have taken us unaware and killed us all. Now, because you came, not only are we prepared but we know what it takes to beat them. Janelle, even without swinging that staff, you've proven your value. I'll defend your life tomorrow with all I have and so will everyone else in Aeris."

Then, unbidden, the tears came.

Eventually, I slept. Like last night's slumber, it was fitful and I'm not sure I was better for it. My guardians took turns watching over me during the night. After Samell, it was Esme. In contrast to her brother's calm, she was a bundle of nerves and wanted to talk. I was almost relieved when shy, quiet Alyssa followed her. Rickard was there when I woke up at dawn's first rays. The storm had blown over during the night and the sun was rising to dry out the morning.

My first probe of the new day confirmed that not only were the earth reavers still there but they were much closer. *How* close was difficult to determine with precision. Part of the problem was that, in this world, the same units were used for time and distance. A "cycle" represented both a fixed fraction of the day and the distance a normal person could travel during that time. So, although the creatures might only be a couple of miles distant, I suspected (based on their recent rate of movement) it would take at least several hours for them to get here. In terms of "cycles," I had no idea what that meant.

"Good morning," said Rickard with a tight smile. "I won't ask if you slept well since you were tossing and turning the whole time I was here. But at least you slept. Where are they now?"

"We have some time but not much. They'll be here before midday."

"We sent scouts out a little while ago. They should be able to give us precise information when they return. Now that the reavers are close, you can worry less about tracking them and more about preparing for what you can do when they get here. I'll be open with you on that account. Some of the townsfolk expect you to singlehandedly save them. I know that's not the case. When it comes to the fight, do what you can. Don't put yourself in danger by trying things you're not equipped for. If I was you, I'd be desperate to prove myself, to fill everyone's expectations. I'm telling you now, that's the quickest way not to survive what's coming. And as for proving yourself, you've already done that. When you came here, no one was more suspicious of you than me. I didn't trust you. But I've watched you day in and day out and, one by one, my doubts have fallen away. You're a credit to Aeris, Janelle. We're proud to have you here with us."

The waterworks threatened again but I managed to hold them back. With a lopsided attempt at a smile, I got up, ate the meager meal someone had left for me, and went in search of Father Backus. I hoped he could be more helpful and less cryptic today than yesterday.

"I wish there was something sage I could tell you," said Backus a short while later. "Like I told you yesterday, using magic isn't something that can be taught. It's something you do. No one instructs you how to breathe. You simply do it. It's ingrained. Same thing for magic. You have to find your own path and, once you do it, replication shouldn't be a problem. Find the trigger. Magic in this world is simple compared to the one I came from."

"The world you came from?"

"Like you, I was one of The Summoned. I wasn't born here although I suppose this is where I'll die. I came from a land called Ayberia, where magic worked with different rules. But that's a story for another time.

"The only advice I can offer is that when you try to do magic, look *inward*. When you encountered the earth reaver in The Verdant Blight, you looked *outward*, toward it, and that nearly killed you. I'm not sure how you did what you did. Using your life's essence, you shouldn't have been able to manipulate it, although its magical nature probably facilitated that. But the control, the dissemination of emotional energy, happens within you. The external manifestation of your power occurs after you've harnessed it within."

I had no idea what he was talking about. It was almost like he was speaking another language. I'm not sure if he thought he was making sense but my baffled look brought him up short. He actually chuckled then, although it was a dry and mirthless laugh. "As I mentioned, it can't be taught. Once you do it, everything I said will make sense. Until then, it will sound like gibberish."

So much for Father Backus being able to help me make a difference in the battle that was rapidly approaching.

"What about you?" I asked. "Will you be on the front lines?"

"Me? I'm an old man. What would you expect me to do?"

"You're a Summoner. Surely that's of some value even if you don't have full use of your powers."

"'Don't have full use...' - that's a kind way to put it, although not accurate. I don't have any powers. That's what I've been trying to tell you, Janelle. I'd be more apt to get in the way than provide a tangible benefit. I'm sorry if that sounds selfish or unhelpful but it's the truth."

He was right. It did sound selfish. But I supposed I wouldn't be in a position to judge him until I had lived three-hundred years and that seemed profoundly unlikely. Right now, I'd settle for three-hundred cycles.

"Can you sense their approach?" I asked, curious about what abilities he might have retained.

"Yes, although not with your clarity. I only became aware of them during the night and, at the moment, they're a hazy blur, although I suspect not far off. The ability to sense things with your mind dims with age, just like your eyesight and hearing. It's inimical to Summoners but not magical in nature. It's like your ability to understand my words as if I was speaking your language. I'm not, of course. I'm speaking the High Common Tongue of Ayberia but you probably hear it as whatever you're fluent in. That's a natural ability."

It made sense. I had given up wondering how Samell could speak perfect English. Now I had an answer.

I didn't spend longer with Backus. Although there wasn't much I could do to prepare Aeris for battle except stay out of the way, it had become strangely claustrophobic in the priest's quarters. I wondered if this was the end of our sessions. If he truly was as decrepit and defenseless as he claimed, he might not survive what was to come. But I found it unlikely that Backus was ready to step meekly into his grave. Despite his protestations, I suspected he was addicted to living and, muted emotions or not, he would find a path to salvation if he had to forge it with a weak store of magic. I didn't believe his protest that he had *no* powers. Whether he was willing to show his hand and use what he had left was another matter.

By the time Samell found me, nearly a cycle later, my nape hairs were standing on end. The earth reavers had advanced so close to

Aeris that they threatened to overwhelm me. It was as if the oppressiveness I had felt in The Verdant Blight had been multiplied fiftyfold. The thrumming produced by the creatures - something apparently only I (and Backus?) could feel - sent waves of trembling through the ground and into my body. My private earthquake. But the citizens of Aeris didn't need my mystical abilities to understand their peril. Shouts from the outer sentries confirmed it: the earth reavers had arrived.

Battle scenarios had been rehearsed many times yesterday and during the morning. Everyone knew where their starting position would be. If we were victorious, this preparation might have proven to be the difference-maker. Archers were on rooftops. Those with swords, pikes, and other hand-to-hand weapons were ringed around the center square, using houses for cover and to break up the ranks of the enemy. Initially, the southwest-facing portion of the defensive line would face the stiffest challenge since that was the direction from which the earth reavers were approaching, but it was expected that once battle was joined, they would spread out and attempt a flanking action. The most vulnerable of Aeris' residents - those too valuable to lose in battle or too infirm to participate, were locked inside houses close to the village center. I was an exception. Although the elders had suggested that I retreat inside, I had refused. So, although my position was behind the front line by about a hundred feet, I was in the open, staff in hand and heart thumping loudly.

With Alyssa and Rickard otherwise engaged, Esme joined Samell and the three of us made our way toward the center square. If a final stand was required, that's where we'd make it. My protectors would have preferred to play a more active role in the battle but they were aware of their importance if the line buckled or collapsed. There were only a handful of secondary defenders to protect Aeris' most vulnerable residents. Samell and Esme might well see their share of combat.

How would I fare in a fight? I didn't know. I could recall having gotten into a few playground scraps -mostly hair-pulling and slapping contests with other girls - but that was a far cry from risking life and limb squaring off against monsters that belonged in a movie or a computer game. True, I had done it already but the incident in The Verdant Blight had been different. I had acted instinctually, not thinking or knowing what I was doing. That attacker had been a random, isolated creature; this was a hoard compelled by a purpose.

It wasn't long before my eyes and ears confirmed what my mind had known was coming. As the archers shouted out intelligence about position and numbers, I saw the tall grasses beyond Aeris' limits begin to bend and sway and part as if under the influence of a strong wind. Then, almost magically, the earth reavers appeared - a wave of ground-hugging horror surging toward the defenders, looking from this distance like a tide of black tar flooding Aeris' outskirts. I knew how they would seem close up - the grotesque offspring of a snake and a giant, hairless rat. There were perhaps fifty (so many!) of the scurrying, undulating creatures. In preparation for the attack, they had arranged themselves in a wedge formation, the head of the arrow pointed directly at the area where the heaviest cluster of citizens was congregated. The reavers showed no indication that they were going to flank the defenders or spread out their attack. This was a brute force strategy, an attempt to overwhelm and punch through.

At that moment, I experienced the terrifying realization that I might be their target. I wasn't sure why the notion first occurred to me at this particular instance. Perhaps they weren't interested in Aeris at all - it was just an impediment to attaining their real goal. Maybe they were here to hunt and destroy the newest Summoner. My blood ran cold as I contemplated how many people might die today because of me. Instead of bringing salvation to this small hamlet, had I lured death and destruction into their midst?

One-hundred feet from the front edge of the wedge, I could hear the half-growls/half-screams the reavers made as they rushed forward.

I was familiar with the cacophony but, magnified as it was by four-dozen voices, it set my nerves on edge. As forcefully as their impressions were on my eyes and ears, however, that was nothing compared to the assault of bile against my mind-sense. My revulsion was immediate and primal - far more overwhelming than it had been in The Verdant Blight.

When the pre-determined signal was given, the archers initiated the battle, raining arrows on the invaders. Some of the missile heads were coated with flaming pitch and some were just plain iron. The wedge moved inexorably forward even as a portion of the missiles found purchase. The timber of the creatures' voices neither wavered nor changed. If they were hurt, they didn't vocalize it. With archers reloading and loosing again, it seemed that nothing could survive the deadly hail. But, in part because of the toughness of their hides, the earth reavers took surprisingly light damage. I'm sure some of them died but it was impossible from my vantage point to determine how many and it didn't look like it was many. The formation remained intact as the creatures closed the final feet separating them from physical contact with their opponents. The arrows stopped when the leading edge of the wedge reached the defenders. Men and women brandishing poles and blades stepped forward to stem the advance. The archers, tossing aside their bows in favor of hand-to-hand weapons, dropped from the rooftops. The bloody close-quarters battle was joined. This was war. This was horror.

Knowing the difficulty of disabling or killing an earth reaver, the defenders coordinated their attacks so three or four could simultaneously strike the same target. While an effective strategy in principal, it left many of the combatants vulnerable to catastrophic counter-attacks. Reavers, impervious to pain, often maimed or killed multiple enemies before succumbing. As the melee intensified on the front line with the initial order devolving into chaos, it became difficult to determine what was happening. For the men and women involved in the hand-to-hand struggle, it was no longer about winning or losing - it was about surviving.

Soon, the combatants were waging a primarily defensive fight and, although this slowed the tide of human casualties, it meant that few of the defenders were taking the risks necessary to dispatch the reavers. If a stalemate developed, I knew the citizens of Aeris would be worn down. Stamina wasn't an issue for the earth reavers. The longer the battle lasted, the greater the potential for them to surge forward and overwhelm us. I was no tactician but I recognized the strategy. I wondered if those coordinating the human combatants saw it as well or whether they were too close to the bloodletting to be aware of the larger picture.

Watching the battle unfold in all its brutality was surreal. For the moment, I existed in a semi-detached state, having difficulty grasping that *this* was actually happening. Monsters. Magic. Carnage. The implausibility of it all came crashing down on me. A part of me hadn't reconciled my "old life" with my new one and now the denial my logical brain had been clinging to was no longer possible. Coping wasn't good enough. I had to engage and, to engage, I had to accept.

Except in a funeral parlor, I'd never seen death (or at least not that I could remember). Now, it held me as close as a lover's embrace. The sight of it, the sounds of it, the smell of it… they were all around me. At the beginning, more than one-hundred able-bodied residents had stood ready to defend the village. Now, familiar voices had been forever silenced. These peaceful, industrious people of Aeris had shown their mettle and were being eviscerated for standing in the way of this malignant wave.

It was only a matter of time before the creatures would poke holes through the now-porous outer defenses and more might flow through than my guardians could handle. I knew from the encounter in The Verdant Blight that one earth reaver would be a challenge for Samell and Esme. Two or three would overwhelm them. There might well be more than that. The battle plan relied on the front line holding, allowing at most a few stragglers through. That wasn't going to happen. In the beginning, there had been fewer reavers than people. Now I suspected the numbers were approaching parity and, considering the creatures' inherent advantages, that meant defeat.

Without a bird's-eye view of the battle, I couldn't tell whether the reavers were still employing their wedge or whether they had spread out to put pressure on the entire front line. It seemed like there was skirmishing around much of the perimeter rather than at one central point although the fighting was still the fiercest there. Then it happened - the first crack. Samell saw it at the same time that I did: an earth reaver coming toward us, *inside* the outer defenses.

None-too-gently, Samell shoved me behind him, putting his body between me and the attacker. Esme's bow sang as she fired a volley of arrows. Her movements were a blur: fit, draw, loose, repeat. I marveled at her economy of motion, her intensity of concentration. If she was frightened, she didn't show it. From our earlier encounter, she had learned about the reaver's vulnerabilities and tailored her aim accordingly. Three of her four missiles became buried in the creature's face but it neither paused nor slowed in its advance. It raced toward us, impossibly fast, its gait a half-scuttle/half-slither.

Samell stepped forward, sword leveled in front. Unlike the previous encounter, he was guarded, leaving the creature no obvious opening to exploit for a critical blow. As he engaged it, seeking to strike soft tissue, its whip-like tongue lashed him, tearing through his leather vest and shredding the flesh beneath. As a reddish stain blossomed across the ruined clothing, he let out a grunt of pain. A feint to the left caused the reaver to react, offering Samell an opportunity. He put everything into his attack, an unblocked, two-handed thrust to the head. It struck with the sound of an ax splitting a log, stopping the creature in its tracks. The earth reaver convulsed, spewed a geyser of ichor as black and viscous as oil, and ceased all movement. But there was no time to celebrate the small victory.

Samell staggered back, his breath coming in great heaves and his face bathed in sweat. The attack had taken a lot out of him. Esme moved to help him then re-directed her attention as another two reavers broke through the line. We weren't the only defenders inside the perimeter but the attacking reavers were ignoring everyone else. Again, I wondered: *Am I the target? Is this all because of me?*

Esme got off two arrows before the reavers were too close for her to continue relying on her bow. She drew her knife and moved to her brother's side. Brother and sister had to give ground to avoid being overwhelmed in the initial attack. The screaming, growling earth reavers were working in concert, attacking almost as if they were a single creature. Their speed and power were too great for the siblings, whose efforts were now purely defensive, warding off blows as they slowly fell back, buying time for me to get away. *But to where?* There was nowhere to go. Delayed by neither pain nor fear, the earth reavers pressed their advantage. Esme took a wound to her left forearm and Samell was hit at least once on a leg. He staggered and nearly went down. His sword dipped, giving the earth reaver an opening.

My reaction, fueled by equal parts panic and adrenaline, was instinctual and instantaneous. Another person might have screamed but I channeled the silent scream inwards. I couldn't allow these two to die protecting me. I could do no less than submit to the same risks that all the men and women around me were enduring. The screams of the injured and dying were deafening, each one an accusation. The hard-packed dirt roads of Aeris ran red with blood. My mind-sense was overwhelmed with the enormity of the violence around me. I felt the hatred of the earth reavers - hatred directed at me. All of it, at me. If I died, perhaps they would retreat. But I didn't intend to accommodate them. Self-sacrifice, no matter how noble, wasn't in my nature.

I lowered my staff and with the thought of striking at the creatures preparing to slay my friends. Time dilated, slowing to a crawl. The sensation was unlike anything I had previously experienced. My thoughts sharpened and the doodles of my imagination became playthings to shape into reality. An impulse, primal and unfettered, was given form as something deep within me was triggered. I didn't understand what was happening but it was a natural function of who (or what) I was. I had heard that in delivery rooms, doctors spanked newborns to start their lungs. Then they would cry out and breathe. Now it was this Summoner's turn to emulate those babies.

Heat and light coalesced, conjured out of the raw emotions that threatened to drown me in a maelstrom of turmoil. A gout of fire spurted from the spiked end of the staff to immolate the reavers attacking Samell and Esme. The siblings were blown backward by the concussion that obliterated the reavers. There was nothing left of the magical creatures but wisps of fetid smoke and small scorch marks on the ground.

Another pair of earth reavers, advancing toward my position, ceased their forward motion. As if recognizing their jeopardy, they turned and fled. Perhaps I should have pursued and destroyed them - I momentarily entertained the possibility and an awakened part of me thrilled at the idea - but winning the immediate struggle seemed sufficient.

An eerie calmness descended even as the headache began to throb. The pain wasn't as debilitating as it had been in The Blight but it was bad enough to disorient me. The plume of fire at the end of my staff sputtered and died as I dropped to one knee. I was dimly aware of Esme and Samell grabbing me, lowering me to the ground. I could smell them - his pungent male scent and her equally strong feminine one. They were saying something. Words in a strange language that I couldn't decipher. Were there others there as well? Had I been more aware, my mind-sense would have told me that the remnants of the earth reaver attack force were in retreat.

My vision swam and I threw up before blacking out.

Chapter Eleven: The Consequences of Breathing

I remembered the hangover. For everything, there was a first time and mine had been the day after Katy Renshaw's slumber party. There were three of us - Katy, me, and a girl whose name I couldn't recall even though it had been only a couple of years ago. We had been celebrating something, probably the end of the school year. Katy found the key to her father's liquor cabinet and we began sampling, with much choking and coughing, a $200 bottle of whiskey. As much fun as the night had been, that's as miserable as the morning after was. Katy, the other girl, and I all made a vow after the worst of the hangover had passed never to do anything that would put us through that again. I had stayed true to that oath…until now.

My head felt muzzy, my stomach rebelled. My mouth tasted as if something had crawled in there to die. My temples throbbed. The sound of my own breathing was unbearable. I didn't dare open my eyes. The paleness of the lids indicated there was daylight and I wasn't ready to face that.

I wasn't in Katy's basement, of course. I was somewhere (I assumed) in Aeris. I wasn't dead or at least I didn't think I was dead. It was getting hard to know. If I had died back in my world, did that make Aeris heaven or hell? And if I died in heaven or hell, where was there to go after that?

"She's awake." The words were whispered, thankfully. Esme's voice? Difficult to say when it was so soft. I sniffed. Esme's scent was unmistakable. She was there. So was Samell. And others I wasn't familiar with. Since when had I been able to identify people by their aromas? Since I had opened myself up to magic, apparently.

I wasn't dead. Neither were Esme, Samell, and the others. I probably could have opened my mind to assess the situation but I didn't feel up to making the attempt and, the last time I had put my poor brain through this trauma, it had taken a while for the ability to return. I guess my first real use of magical power had turned the tide of the battle since I doubted the earth reavers took prisoners.

"How are you feeling, Janelle?" demanded Backus, his voice as loud as a trumpet. I winced and groaned. The man was devoid of sympathy and compassion.

My response comprised a plethora of profane metaphors, suggesting a few rather shocking things he could do with himself.

After a loud "Harrumph!" he excused himself, saying he'd check in on me when I was in a more sociable mood. His exit was punctuated by the bang of a slamming door. I curled up in the fetal position and wished everyone else would follow his example, although more quietly. The presence of other people, watching and waiting, was oppressive.

"Janelle, try eating this." Samell was kneeling by my side, his scent strong and reassuring. He spoke quietly and gently. "Father Backus said it might make you feel better."

I opened one eye, squinting. Before shutting it again, I glimpsed the brownish powder Samell was proffering in a spoon. I couldn't say for certain but it was probably the ground leaves of a Blight tree, Backus' cure-all.

"Did he tell you not to eat it yourself?" I asked. My voice sounded thick and hoarse.

"He did."

No doubt about it, then. I was dubious about its efficacy but willing to try anything. Sitting up - a slow, graceless process - I took the spoon and a mug of water from Samell. The powder was gritty and tasteless and washed down easily. I was grateful for its mildness. My stomach was churning enough that it would have rebelled against most other things attempting to gain entry.

The effect of the Blight leaf powder was immediate and startling. The numbness of the hangover vanished. The sensitivity to light and sound diminished substantially. The cobwebs lifted and I felt, if not entirely myself, a lot more hale and healthy than I had a few moments earlier. In short, I was ready to face the situation, whatever it might be. I opened my eyes.

There were six people there, all watching me: Samell, Esme, Brin, Alyssa, Rickard, and Lissa. I recognized with some surprise that this was the room where I normally slept. Despite not being inside the "protected zone" created by the defenders' perimeter, the house hadn't been destroyed. This room looked no different than it had before the battle.

Samell, Esme, and Rickard had been injured. Samell's bare chest was wrapped in cloth bandages. The cuts on Esme's face and arms made it look like she had clambered through a bramble patch. Rickard appeared to have suffered the most serious wound. He was using crudely made crutches and both legs were heavily bandaged.

Samell was sitting distractingly close, his knees within inches of mine. Only then did I become aware that my mind-sense was functioning - his presence was filling it. Tentatively, I probed beyond my immediate environs. Nothing, or at least no earth reavers.

"What happened?"

"They're gone," said Samell. Then he smiled. "You drove them off!"

Esme elaborated, "As soon as you used magic to kill the ones attacking us, the rest of them ran."

"How long was I out?"

"It's morning," said Samell. "The battle was yesterday."

An afternoon and a night - that was a long time to be incapacitated. Longer, in fact, than when we had been attacked in the forest. But this time so much had been different. And, the headache, although bad, hadn't seemed as crippling.

"How many did we lose?" I didn't want to know the answer but had to face the truth. Battles had casualties.

Rickard answered this question. "Twenty-seven. And three who probably won't live till sunup tomorrow. Another fifteen with bad injuries and many others like me. We gave a good accounting of ourselves, though. Took down nearly half the enemy. Tough to get the exact number. After they die, they melt into the earth."

I winced. Not at the earth reaver death count - that was more impressive than I had expected - but at the number of citizens lost or hurt. It wasn't devastating enough to wipe out the village but it would take years, perhaps even a generation, for Aeris to recover. And that presupposed another attack wasn't imminent. I worried - and I'm sure I wasn't the only one - that this might be the beginning. What if this was the vanguard of a concerted effort? It seemed unlikely that a small force of earth reavers would take this action in a vacuum.

"We lost Anna," reported Samell. "And two of the elders who refused to stay in safety. And Bart and Jeanmar. But it would have been a lot worse without what you did. We knew you were essential before the battle but now that we've seen with our eyes what you can do… There's no doubting your importance."

I spent the morning recuperating. Physically, my recovery came quickly as I had suffered little more than nicks and scratches (inflicted when I was hit by shrapnel from the fire-blasted reavers). Mentally, I knew the struggle would extend over a longer period. As expected, my mind-sense was inaccessible (temporarily, I assumed). My emotions were also scrambled, likely the result of having used magic. If emotion was a Summoner's fuel, I had ignited some. By the time the sun reached its zenith, I was ready to emerge and face the results of yesterday's brutality.

The cleanup was well underway. Houses that had been damaged were being mended with new timbers put into place and roofs re-thatched. The bodies, human and reaver, had been cleared away for burning. A ceremony for the dead would be held on the morrow. The village looked strangely normal for a place that had so recently been a battlefield. There were fewer citizens going about their duties than usual and many had suffered injuries of varying degrees. When they saw me come out of Rickard and Lissa's home, they stopped and cheered. Tears sprang unbidden into my eyes even as I tried to smile. I felt anything but worthy of their praise.

"Is this my fault?" The possibility had haunted me since the attack and it was the first thing I asked Backus once we were alone. Crossing the village to reach his cabin had taken nearly a cycle. There had been so many people who had wanted to talk, so many injured who had asked for a moment. I was no longer the strange girl with limited skills or the potential Summoner seeking shelter. I didn't know which experienced had changed me more - using magic for the first time or experiencing the aftermath of it - seeing the gratitude and friendliness of these people. Aeris was in my debt but was I also the cause of this disaster?

"A strange thing to wonder," mused Backus. His voice and expression were, as always, inscrutable. Sometimes his calm was infuriating. "I can't think why you might believe that. You saved them. You reached down deep and found the trigger. I sensed it when it happened and it gave me a moment's joy. Strange to feel something like that after so many years of deadness."

"Did my presence bring this on them?"

"I won't deny it's a possibility. But I suspect this is just a link in a chain of cause-and-effect. It's possible that the earth reavers came to Aeris with the express purpose of killing you. They may have sensed your arrival, sent one of their kind to monitor you in The Verdant Blight, then attacked in force when circumstances favored them. Or it may be that you were Summoned to save Aeris from an attack that your Summoner foresaw. You'll never know. And it may not matter because it's unlikely this was an isolated event. No earth reaver has attacked a human settlement in recent history and nothing like this has ever been recorded. Past events can no longer be used as predictors of the future. The value of dozens of generations of history has become moot. We're in uncharted territory. Even if you were the target this time, an attack of this magnitude would have been inevitable, and soon.

"The deep lore of the Summoners is hidden from me because I'm not an acknowledged member of their exclusive order. Never took the training, you see. But I have read enough of the Old Tomes to glean an understanding of what the Summoners have feared for generations upon generations. Once, when we were many, we could command and constrain the forces of magic, bending them to our will, keeping them tame. But now we are few, not nearly enough to constrict the wild strains that breed in the dark places. This time was inevitable. As the powers of the Summoners wane, so the enemy becomes emboldened.

"I believe - and this is merely supposition on my part - that you were brought here because your Summoner was weak or dying and, in his wisdom, he recognized that the world's hope lay in attracting someone young, hale, and capable of standing against the wild strains of magic. He sacrificed himself for the greater good. It's something I would like to think I'd do if I was able but, alas, I don't know the spell of Summoning nor am I likely to find someone willing to teach it to me. There are so few Summoners left…"

I knew where this was going and didn't want to think about it too deeply. The implications were uncomfortable. At some point, probably sooner than later, I was going to have to find one of those Summoners. It was obvious that Backus, despite his magical abilities, would never be an adequate teacher. Oh, he could provide some of the basics and offer a few of the "tips" he had learned during his more than two centuries of practice, but he was an amateur. I needed the mentoring of a learned Summoner.

"But on to more practical matters. Let's talk about your headaches."

Let's not and say we did. "Do we have to?" Having finally recovered, the last thing I wanted to do was to go back and relive the experience. "If that's the price I have to pay for using magic, I don't think overuse will ever be a problem."

"You didn't overextend yourself like you did in the Blight?"

"I don't think so. It felt different, like I stayed inside myself. When I attacked the earth reaver in the forest, it was as if my mind left my body. Here, it was different. Once I found the trigger…it's like what you said, like breathing. But afterward, the headaches. How did you cope with them?"

"I didn't."

"What do you mean, you 'didn't'?"

"I didn't have to cope with them because I didn't experience them. And I don't understand why you are. I've never read about a Summoner becoming incapacitated after using magic. I'm wondering if you did permanent damage the first time or whether it could have something to do with the world you came from."

No headaches at all for Backus. I couldn't say whether I found that comforting or confounding. "Is there anything I can do?"

"I don't know. Even a true, trained Summoner might not be able to help with this. Like with any ailment, a diagnosis is needed before a remedy can be prescribed. The only way for that to happen is for you to keep using magic."

"You mean…invite the headaches?"

He nodded. My stomach did a flip-flop at the thought.

"I'm not sure I want to do that."

"You don't really have a choice - not if you plan to live as a Summoner. Even without the need to determine the cause of the headaches, you would need to practice. Not great feats but little things. Things that don't require a lot of emotion. Things that will enable you to manipulate magic with greater ease and gain better control over which emotions to jettison. For accomplished Summoners, this becomes second nature. Unfortunately, I never figured out how to do it so I am as you see me now - a second-rate wizard whose powers are gone.

"I would have liked to participate in the battle. I tried to see if I could help but I could muster so little energy that any effort would have been ineffectual." There was disappointment in those words - one of the rare times I had sensed emotion from the priest.

I had another question. "There's something else. I've noticed that my sense of smell has gotten stronger. With my eyes closed, I can tell who's close by their scent."

"And it started at the time of your magical awakening?"

I nodded.

"That's not uncommon. Never happened for me. Some Summoners have reported a strengthening of one sense or another. Get used to it."

"Now what?"

"Now you spend a day or two recuperating. Then we'll see what it takes to bring on a headache and what we can do to mitigate it."

It was hard to think of a worse prospect for the immediate future.

Two days later, Father Backus decided it was time for me to start probing my limitations. By then, my mind-sense had returned after more than a day's dormancy. It had come back stealthily – one moment it wasn't there, the next it was. I wasn't sure of the exact time of its restoration.

When I saw the priest striding purposefully across the square to where I was hanging wet washing out to dry, I heaved a sigh. Samell, who was working nearby finalizing repairs to one of the damaged houses, shot me a sympathetic look. He, Esme, and Alyssa had become my confidantes. They knew how wary I was of the ordeal that lay across my path.

"Are you ready?" he asked, more out of politeness than out of a concern for what my answer might be.

"Would it make a difference if I said 'no?'"

He offered one of those strange humorless smiles he sometimes used, his eyes remaining cold despite the upturning of his lips under the mountain of snowy whiskers. "You know the answer to that, Janelle."

He was right about that. There was only so long I could procrastinate.

Once we were secluded inside his cabin, he started with a lecture. "Never do with magic what you can do by other means. Oh, there's no doubt you could lift a heavy rock but why use even a small bit of magic when your friend Samell could pick it up? There may be times when circumstances will compel you to do such things but, for the most part, you shouldn't use your powers unless it's for something that can't be accomplished by other means."

Backus suggested that we start with something that would require almost no energy: lighting a torch. It occurred to me that making fire in this world wasn't as easy as in the one from which I came. There were no matches or lighters here. For the most part, torches, lanterns, and cook fires were ignited from existing sources but, on those occasions when there were no flames available, it came down to flint and steel or the torturous-looking process of rubbing two pieces of wood together fast enough to produce an ember. So, the capability of using magic to make fire could have important applications. However, although there was value to my practicing, this was more about whether I could do anything without falling down clutching at the sides of my head.

Lighting the torch was surprisingly easy - an act that felt as commonplace as inhaling. Now that I knew the location of the trigger, it was easy to activate. I had no control over the emotion used to fuel the magic - that would hopefully come later. Emotion became magic and magic became fire, all with a cursory thought. It was satisfying to be able to do even such a simple thing. But, as before, it came with a price.

The headache wasn't as severe as it had been during the Battle of Aeris or in The Verdant Blight, but it wasn't "nothing." I could feel it - a dull ache between the temples. A couple of aspirin would have taken care of it.

Backus scrutinized me like my pediatrician, looking into my eyes and ears, feeling the glands in my throat. I had no idea what he was doing or if it was telling him anything. Finally, with a grunt, he shuffled off to prepare some of his Blight leaf powder, which I washed down with something that tasted a lot like the disgusting cough medicine I had been given as a child. The headache receded to near-imperceptibility.

Backus harrumphed, shook his head, and harrumphed again. "I can't sense anything wrong. I watched you work your magic using my mind-sense and you did it perfectly. Better, actually, than I expected from someone with your lack of experience. The headache must be your body's reaction to using magic. Maybe a residue from how it's used in your world."

"My world doesn't have magic. I've told you that." Backus could be forgetful. I sometimes wondered if he was getting senile. Living for three-hundred years could lead to that, I suppose.

"All worlds have magic, yours included. It may be that the magic is hidden or inaccessible. In the world I come from, magic is served through energy that flows from a place called the Otherverse. If the conduits to the Otherverse were all blocked, magic would still exist but no one would be able to use it. Perhaps it's like that in your world."

I shrugged. Hard to explain to someone who had lived with the *reality* of magic for so long that the only mysticism in my world was associated with trickery. Was it possible that, among all the showmen, illusionists, and charlatans, there were a few real magicians? Considering my current circumstances, I wasn't in a position to scoff.

"Maybe it's a barrier. Something you need to build immunity against."

Great. Exactly what I wanted to hear: the way to overcome the headaches was to subject myself to them over and over again until I became so used to them that they no longer mattered. Then I could label myself The Masochist Summoner.

"Let's push on. Fire and earth are the two easiest elements to work with. Air is mercurial and requires patience to control even in small amounts. Water is the trickiest of all, so let's see what you can do with it. Drip a few drops into my wash basin."

"How am I supposed to get water? Out of thin air?"

The smile made another appearance. "Precisely."

Over the next several hours (or cycles), I learned a few things. First, as long as I didn't try any large magical workings, the headaches were manageable, especially if I accompanied each act with a dose of Blight leaf powder. Second, I couldn't feel any emotions draining away but I was aware of becoming more focused and less anxious. Thirdly, Backus' impassive persistence was irksome. The lack of compassion, the smug smile, and the superior attitude made me understand why he wasn't the most liked man in the settlement. Idly, I wondered how much energy it would take to make him disappear.

Chapter Twelve: Fragments of a Life that Was

I was starting to remember. Maybe magic had opened the doors in my mind or maybe it was a coincidence but my past was returning. Some things were welcome, others weren't. But, although the memories were coming back, they seemed disconnected, almost as if they belonged to another person. It was hard to reconcile *that* Janelle with me. People normally changed so gradually that their evolution was slow, measured, and continuous. For me, there had been a discontinuity in my existence and it was difficult to reconcile my "old" self with my "new" one.

I also had difficulty ascertaining the differences between real memories and dreams. They were jumbled together. I'm pretty sure I hadn't held any long, meaningful conversations with a beagle, but what about kissing a boy? What about holding him tight while dancing at Senior Prom?

The memories came back randomly, not all at once. Sometimes a sight, sound, or smell (especially a smell) would trigger one. The scent of fresh-baked bread had brought back a cavalcade of holiday remembrances at my grandmother's house. Some would come at night as I drifted into that twilight world between wakefulness and full sleep. Others would sneak up on me when I let my mind go blank during the hours of drudgery that marked my daily chores. Some memories returned unnoticed; others electrified my attention with their forcefulness. However, instead of unifying my identity, they were fragmenting it – not what I had expected or hoped for.

I didn't mention any of this to Father Backus. I knew him well enough by now to recognize he would either ignore it or claim that it was "just one of those things" that Summoners had to cope with. I was becoming depressed with how little the priest knew about the subject of magic. Although he had never officially studied it, I would have expected that, over the course of three centuries, he would have accumulated more knowledge than he seemed to have. Was it possible that, in the less than half-season I had lived in Aeris, I had outgrown his teachings?

What I didn't confide in Backus, however, I told to Samell. He was a good sounding board, able to suggest things that put a particular memory in a different light. The jigsaw puzzle metaphor, although often overused, was apt in this case. Only when all the pieces had been put in their proper places would I have a complete picture of who I was (or who I had been).

"You're never going to remember everything," said Samell after one of my frequent outbursts of pique. "Ask me what I had for supper ten days ago and I won't be able to tell you."

"That's a detail. No one remembers those things. But I can't remember big things. Like my mother's name. Or whether the girl I talked to was my sister. Or whether the boy I kissed was my boyfriend." My frustration was difficult to put into words. He hadn't experienced it so he didn't know what it was like: the uniqueness of the amnesiac's reality.

"Did you care about him?" asked Samell, referring to the nameless boyfriend.

Did I care? Or should it be *Had I cared?* "I don't know. If I think hard, I can almost see his face. But I don't feel anything. No sense of loss. No longing to be with him again. And I don't know whether that's because we were never close or because I don't have a full picture of what we might have been to one another."

"How could you have kissed him and not cared about him?"

In Aeris, a kiss was as good as a marriage proposal. This was a more conservative society than the one I was familiar with. The conservativism made sense in a small community. The social fabric was based on a solid family structure. Children didn't grow up and leave Aeris. They got older, married someone else from the town, and had their own children. It was as steady as it was insular. They would view kissing without a pledge as promiscuity and promiscuity was a danger to the stability of this tiny corner of the world. So the idea of kissing or touching or doing something intimate with someone other than a pledged life-mate was difficult to address.

"In the world I came from, kissing doesn't have the... importance... that it has here. Sometimes, friends kiss. It can be... recreational." The widening of Samell's eyes alerted me that I had used a wrong word but I forged ahead. "I went to a dance with this guy. Sometimes after a dance, or even during it, people kiss. They do it because it feels right at the moment or even because everyone else is doing it and they don't want to feel awkward." With a sigh, I stopped trying to explain. I knew that by now my face was red. I had always blushed easily. That was something else I remembered.

"I kissed Elena," admitted Samell in a quiet voice. "We did it where no one could see but it was a promise between the two of us to be together one day even though our parents didn't approve."

That surprised me. Aside from the elders, Father Backus, and now me, everyone in Aeris was on the same social level. There were no divisions, no landowners or nobility. Everyone was the same - peasants, farmers, workers. If two people wanted to be together, why keep them apart? Life here was difficult enough without having to look at the person you loved every day and knowing you could never have her.

Aware that I might be wading into sensitive territory, I phrased my question as delicately as I could manage. "Are there rules in Aeris about who you can marry?"

"Yes. There aren't many but Elena and I, if we'd gotten married, would have broken one of them. You see, we're cousins. My mother and her father are sister and brother. There are strict prohibitions against marrying someone who's such close kin. It has something to do with unfit children. You're encouraged to marry someone of the most distant blood but the only forbidden marriages are those who share a parent or grandparent."

As cruel and arbitrary as it might sound to Samell, I understood the reasoning (and even agreed with it). In a community like this, inbreeding was a danger. Only careful policing and arranging of marriages would prevent the gene pool from becoming too shallow. Elena was dead and that was a tragedy but it had solved a dilemma for Samell.

"I liked kissing her," he said, his faraway look indicating that he was reliving the moment. My memories of my kiss were too vague for it to be more substantial than a moving picture. Had I enjoyed it? I didn't know although I wasn't averse to trying again at some point to find out. "The softness of her lips. The taste of her breath. The smell of her skin and hair."

"Do you miss her?" It was a stupid question but I couldn't think of anything better to say and I knew that a prolonged silence would become awkward.

"Not as much as I thought I would. I suppose it's because of everything that's happened since. No time to mourn the dead. I lost other good friends as well. Esme lost Jeanmar, her intended." I raised an eyebrow at that. I hadn't realized Esme was engaged, especially to someone as dour and introverted as Jeanmar. "But she'll always be special to me."

You always remember your first kiss. That was a saying from the other world. I envied Samell that it was true for him. I even envied his grief. My situation had robbed me not only of a clear, meaningful memory of my first kiss but an understanding of whether I should be sad about losing my partner.

"Are you promised to someone else?"

"No. It was always Elena for me. My parents knew that and, even though they couldn't approve a marriage between us, they thought it would be counterproductive to force an engagement on me. Elena was promised to Hickard. It made for some uncomfortable moments." I didn't know Hickard although I might recognize him by sight. He hadn't been in the search party although there could have been a lot of reasons for that.

"The boy you kissed…do you remember his name?" asked Samell.

"No. Just about the only thing I know about him is that we danced and kissed. It wasn't that long ago." His name was a blank. His features were fuzzy. He was an avatar of maleness in my mind. Maybe that's why I didn't feel anything for him. "It doesn't seem real. Here, you and I talking, that's *real*. Kissing some guy, it's like it happened to someone else." I wondered if we had gone farther than kissing. Something told me the answer was "no." I hoped that was the case.

The conversation with Samell resulted in my thinking about this mystery boy all afternoon as I went through the motions of carrying baskets of wash and hanging the clothing and bedding up to dry. The work was physically demanding (my hands were already toughening up with calluses having formed and hardened on the palms and fingertips) but it left my mind unencumbered. The catalyst for another memory was the prick of a small insect that Esme had called an "ear pincher." Attracted by the scent of my sweat, it alighted on my bare forearm and gave me a kiss as potent as a wasp's sting. I yelped and suddenly another piece fell into place in the jigsaw puzzle of my past.

I was sitting cross-legged and barefoot on a blanket in the middle of what appeared to be a poorly-cut lawn or a meadow. It was a warm, breezy day and I was wearing a summery dress. My unbound hair, teased by the wind, refused to behave so I had pulled it back into a ponytail. I wasn't alone. A guy - the guy - sat close by. Now I knew his name. Jarrod. How could I have forgotten it? How could I have forgotten him?

The day had begun beautifully. A nice little picnic followed by some kissing. This was after the dance. That had been our first kiss. It hadn't been our last. We were an "item" at school - or had been until graduation. Now, with friends scattering to the far winds and becoming occupied by summer jobs, the old social cliques were breaking down. By September, they would be gone as most of us went to college and the few who didn't moved into the permanent workforce.

Jarrod and I had two months together until I left for the West Coast and he headed south to Miami. Or at least I thought we had two months together. He had set a precondition on our continuing relationship that I wasn't aware of and, when he made it clear what it was, I couldn't agree.

"Come on, Janelle. We've been together for over a month and we were friends before that. We've known each other since junior high."

Pressure. My friends had all said it would come but I hadn't believed them. It might be true of their boyfriends but not Jarrod. He was different. He and I... it wasn't all about physicality and hormones. We had a connection. Or so I had thought. An hour ago, I had been happy. Now, I was miserable. I wasn't a prude but this was a step beyond my comfort zone. "I know," I murmured. "I'm not ready." Three words he really didn't want to hear.

The rest of the afternoon progressed predictably, with him spending the better part of the next two hours cajoling and listing reasons why his "solution" made sense. What we had, he argued, needed to "evolve" or it would never survive our autumn separation. I heard the words and my heart broke – I couldn't believe that Jarrod, my sweet, generous Jarrod was just like all the others.

I didn't give in. At first, I seriously considered it – not so much because I wanted it but because it was so important to him. But the more he pushed, the more upset I became about the whole thing. The harder he tried to convince me, the more remote and sullen I became. Eventually, he drove me home. We didn't speak in the car and, when he pulled up in front of my house, we didn't kiss goodbye. I knew then it was over. The next morning, I awoke to a text message from him telling me that he thought we had "run our course" and it was time to "take a break." Two days later, I spotted him with Chloe Wendel.

Looking at the two of them together, I had no doubt she wasn't afflicted by my hang-ups.

I had stopped working as I absorbed the memory. Unlike many of the other chunks of my past, this one came accompanied by a tidal wave of emotion. I felt now what I had felt then. I wanted to cry or throw up or both. Almost without realizing it, I started reaching for my magic. I caught myself before I touched it but was shocked at how easily I could access it. Too easily. For the first time, I recognized the danger. Emotion wasn't just the fuel for magic; it was a catalyst. Instead of staring daggers at someone who insulted me, I might plunge actual blades into them.

I asked Backus about it when I went to his house the next morning for my "lesson". I knew it wasn't a problem for him now but maybe it was an issue he had encountered in his youth.

"Powerful emotions?" he ruminated. "I can see how that might be a problem, at least until you learn how to govern the use of magic. Can't say I remember having issues with it, though. Even as a young man, I was rather... reticent. For a Summoner, though, too much emotion is always preferable to too little. The more you have, the more you can afford to lose. Some of the old lore tomes claim that all the most powerful Summoners were women since they typically have access to greater emotional reserves than men."

It wasn't the most helpful advice he had ever given me. In fact, it was like a lot of what he had been telling me of late - obvious "secrets" I had either figured out on my own or that didn't apply to my situation. He had been a dabbler and his lack of legitimate skill became evident in his lessons. To his credit, Backus was as aware of this as I was but he seemed to be at a loss about how to proceed from here. We both knew where this was headed: I would have to leave Aeris and seek someone who could act as a mentor.

I didn't want to go. I was just starting to feel comfortable in this village, the only home I had known since coming to this world. In Rickard and Lissa, I had found substitute parents. I had friends and was respected. If anyone in Aeris didn't like me, they kept their feelings hidden. The elders, after an initial period of skepticism, had hailed me as the best visitor to Aeris in a generation. I was happy here - or as happy as a confused girl with uncertain memories could be. But I was also keenly aware that I couldn't grow. If I stayed, I would end up like Backus - a second-rate wizard who had spent a life wasting his meager, underdeveloped talents. Maybe I'd marry and have children, but that wasn't the reason a Summoner had spent his life bringing me here.

What were the ramifications if I left? Aeris would be undefended if another wave of earth reavers attacked. No one talked much about it but killing half their number meant there were more than two dozen from that group left with possibly others in reserve. Were they regrouping? Would it be better for the village if I stayed or left? If I was their target, would they spare Aeris if I was elsewhere? Or would it remain in their cross-hairs, a lone human habitation in The Verdant Blight and a place where they had suffered a defeat?

As evening approached, a storm front crawled across the sky toward Aeris and its environs. The roiling black clouds reminded me of the air reaver squall from before the attack but this one seemed to be completely natural, at least insofar as my senses could detect. The village became a hive of activity as citizens prepared for the imminent combination of rain, hail, winds, and lightning. I watched with a detached curiosity, opening my senses to the immensity of the front as it swept in from the northwest.

This was different in some indefinable way from the frequent summer thunderstorms in my world. It seemed raw and more untamed. The lightning was brighter, the thunder louder, and the winds howled with the force of a hurricane. When the rains arrived, mixed with hail the size of a golf ball, they did so in sheets, a deluge the likes of which I had never before seen. Calling this a "thunderstorm" was an insult to its majesty, power, and ferocity. It was nature unleashed. I wondered if this world's incipient magic had something to do with this although my sixth sense detected nothing unusual.

I was hunkered down with Samell and his family in their home. Like a mantra, Rickard repeatedly mentioned that the house was sturdy enough to withstand the storm, almost as if the reiteration would make it so. Everyone except Lissa was uneasy. She merely sat in her chair and knitted. Reading her, I could tell the calm wasn't an act; she was genuinely unperturbed by the explosion of nature's rage going on outside.

"Do these storms come often?" I asked Samell. I had to bend close to his ear to be heard over the tumult of nearly constant thunder and the torrent of rain and hail assaulting the roof. Since my arrival, there had been periods of precipitation but this was the first time I had experienced anything like this.

"Once or twice a year, usually around this time. Backus explained why but you'd have to ask him if you want the specifics. This one's a little more energetic than usual."

Aside from a few leaky roofs and other minor damage, Aeris escaped the wrath of the storm relatively unscathed. By the time I lay down to sleep that night, the thunder was still booming but, as it receded, it had the hollow, almost gentle quality of a danger that was past. For me, however, the storm was but a prelude to the true ordeal.

The remembrance that came to me that night, swift and violent as a thief, slipped into my mind at the precise moment when waking became sleep. Its veracity was difficult to determine. Was it a genuine memory pulled from behind the lingering haze in my mind or was it a nightmare masquerading as something legitimate?

The distant thunder rumbling beyond Aeris transported me into the recollection.

I was on some kind of hill. I had been running. My heart was beating twice its normal rate. My breath was coming in great, heaving sobs. My face was wet from tears. Someone or something was coming after me. My life was collapsing around me. Everything I had considered solid and sacred had been despoiled in one night. And now this...

Lightning searing the sky. The smell of ozone. A scream in the distance and an explosion of thunder so loud that it shook the ground. Rain pouring from the clouds, camouflaging the tears that still flowed.

I had been betrayed and the betrayal had led me to do something so rash, so stupid... I had never been good at reining in strong emotion and this time, it had gotten the better of me. So I had lashed out and run, putting myself in harm's way.

Jarrod, my Jarrod, and my sister. Images of those two that nothing would ever wipe away. Chloe Wendel had been bad enough but now this... That was the root source of the pain I now felt, but it didn't explain the guilt or the fear. Something else was happening. Something monstrous. Another bolt of lightning, another clap of thunder - this one so loud I could feel it in my bones.

I wasn't alone out here on this hill. I had seen him oh-so-briefly by the lightning's strobe-like flash. He was approaching from the southeast, ascending the hill toward my position, his gait unhurried. I never should have fired that gun. I never should have run out of the house like that. I never should have come here. A series of horrible mistakes culminating in this moment.

More lightning, more thunder then a flash so loud that I was sure I must have been struck. A white-hot, searing pain...

I woke up screaming.

Chapter Thirteen: The One-Handed Tinker

I awakened to the soft sunlight of an early dawn. For the briefest of moments, I was wrapped in a gossamer blanket of contentment. I lay in Samell's arms; I could feel the warmth of his body and smell his unique scent. It took only a moment, however, to remember *why* he was holding me and what had led to our being so close. After the nightmare, I had been hysterical, inconsolable. Sobs, tears, piteous moans... Only Samell's strong, comforting arms wrapping me in a bear's hug had stopped the shaking. And only his constant, reassuring presence had allowed me to fall back asleep. Strangely, despite the trauma, my subsequent rest had been deep and undisturbed. My body felt restored. My mind...that was a different matter.

Integrating my newest memories into the patchwork of my past was a tricky and uncertain process. The preeminent question was whether my vision had been an accurate remembrance of a fragment of my life or whether it was the fabrication of a fevered and fatigued subconscious. Had it been a nightmare, a memory, or some twisted combination of both? Even if I was to accept that it was an unvarnished recollection, there were many unanswered questions. Although I now knew that I had a sister (something I had previously suspected), what had happened at the house between us? How did Jarrod - my ex-boyfriend turned her lover - fit into this? And who was my stalker? The concussion that had ended the dream/memory likely represented the moment of my transition to this world, but what to make of the disturbing events preceding it?

"You okay?" asked Samell, aware that I was awake and disentangling his body from mine. The closeness became remote; the sense of loss was palpable.

I tried without success to smile. "Better this morning. I had a vision of something that happened right before I came here. I thought that somehow regaining my past would make me whole. Now, I'm not sure." The implications, if true, might reveal a very different Janelle from the one I wanted to find. Could I have changed that much in such a short time?

"Whatever happened to you, whatever you may have done before you came here, is of no matter. You told me once that in your old world you were 'just another girl' who did 'ordinary things.' Here, in Aeris, you aren't 'just another girl' doing 'ordinary things.' You are a Summoner. Your past is immaterial. Maybe that's why you can't remember it clearly, because it doesn't matter. Because you're no longer the same person you once were."

Deep thoughts for a farmer. I almost said it aloud but decided not to. Sarcasm wasn't widely used or understood here and my words might be misconstrued. Instead, I said, "You may be right. But it's not that simple. You have...continuity...in your head. It might be easier if I couldn't remember *anything* before I came here - if it was all a blank. But remembering some things...it's frustrating. And the memory or nightmare or whatever it was last night, was terrifying. It opens the possibility that I may have done something terrible before I came here or that something bad was going to happen to me. I can recall those moments but not the ones that came before and understanding requires a wider picture - one I can't get until I remember more."

"And you're not sure if you want to."

Now he understood. Ever since I had arrived naked and defenseless in The Verdant Blight, one of my goals had been regaining my sense of identity. Did I need the memories of my old self to achieve that? "I'm starting to think I might not like who I was."

"That's a good thing, isn't it? It shows growth. Whatever the case, you can start over here. Dwelling on the past isn't positive in the best of circumstances and if your past distresses you, make new memories with us."

Now I managed a smile, although a sad one. If I didn't find out, it would always be a scab - something to pick at and worry over. Was I really two different people? Had I been 'born again' and not in a religious sense? "Can I like myself now if it turns out that I did horrible things before I came here?" That was my fear. And *horrible* truly meant that.

"Why not? I like you fine just as you are now. And asking these questions makes me like you even more. If it didn't matter to you, that would concern me." He squeezed my hand for reassurance. "I'm glad I met you, Janelle, and I know everyone else in Aeris would say the same thing. However much you struggle with your past, don't lose sight of who you have become. Most people are anchored by their past but not you."

As the days of a seemingly endless summer passed, a sense of normalcy returned to Aeris, yet things weren't precisely as they had been. There were too many fresh graves for that to be the case and, even after all the damage had been repaired, the memory of the battle hung over everything like a gray cloud on a sunny day. For those who had lost someone close, the grief hadn't aged enough to have receded. For the others, one of the great cornerstones of their lives had been sundered - the village was no longer the bastion of safety and security they had believed it to be. And everyone wondered, although few voiced the concern, whether the earth reavers might return.

As a Summoner, I could have abdicated my responsibilities as a washer girl. Samell said that if I wanted to, I could join the Council of Elders - a possibility I immediately dismissed. Even if they wanted me (rather than grudgingly accepting me), it would bind me to Aeris. Much as a part of me wanted to stay, I knew this was merely a way station. Every morning when I woke up, I felt closer to the day of my departure.

One reason I was delaying the inevitable was because I knew that my leaving would plunge the village into a state of near-panic. While it was flattering to be acknowledged as the Savior of Aeris, it also placed a mantle of responsibility over my shoulders that, in my current fragile state, I wasn't ready for. Rightly or wrongly, the men and women of this hamlet saw me as their defense against a future attack. If I left...when I left... I would take that surety with me.

How long had I been in this world? It was difficult to be sure. Days here weren't the same length as they were where I was from. Seasons were different. I had arrived in summer - or "Warmth" as it was called here - and the daytime high temperatures hadn't varied much in the intervening days. But the nights were cooler, leading me to believe we might not be far from "Fading", this world's analog for autumn. By my reckoning, I had been here four or five weeks of my old life's time. This nameless world didn't have weeks or months - only days, seasons, years, and generations.

"How long until you leave Aeris?" asked Backus conversationally one morning. He spoke as if it was a foregone conclusion, not a momentous decision that required consideration and discussion. His casual tone took me aback.

When I didn't respond, he pressed, "We both know you've reached the limits of what you can learn here. I wish that wasn't the case. I wish I could be a suitable mentor but my deficiencies have constrained what I can teach you. I know my limitations and I suspect that, by now, you recognize them as well. I can tell you're becoming frustrated by my 'lessons'. And, as much as I *personally* would like you to stay here and act as Aeris' protector, that wouldn't be fair to you, the world in general, and the Summoner who brought you here. He didn't intend for you to remain in one obscure village. More importantly, many untrained Summoners exceed their reach and perish. Magic isn't something to be trifled with."

"Do you think the earth reavers will attack again?" I might not have been capable of great feats but I knew I could make a difference if there was another battle.

"If you remain here, yes. I suspect you draw them like iron to a lodestone. If you go elsewhere, possibly not. As we've discussed, it's not clear whether *you* were the earth reavers' objective or whether it was eliminating a human habitation in an area they wanted to claim as their own. It's possible that Aeris will be safer with you gone."

"And it's possible that they'll need me if there's another attack."

"Janelle, I'm not a soothsayer. I can't see the future or read the signs. It's a risk either way. What's clear to me is that the fate of this village is a small thing compared to your need to become conversant with the ways of a Summoner. You may think what you did against the earth reavers was impressive and in a way it was, but it was crude magic and used far more energy than was necessary. You need to understand how to budget your emotions - how to control and sort them - and how to manage the headaches. Trial and error can only get you so far and it's more likely to get you killed than make you into a master Summoner."

"That's not very helpful." I know it sounded petulant but I couldn't help it.

"It's the best I can offer. Generations of life may not have made me powerful but I'd like to think they have imparted wisdom and perspective. So when are you planning to leave? I can understand your trepidation but this isn't a decision that can be put off indefinitely. Procrastinating won't make it go away."

That single word - "procrastinating" - triggered another memory, my first substantive one since the nightmare.

My mother and I were arguing about some important school assignment. Due in less than two weeks, it was mandatory for high school graduation but I hadn't started it yet. My mother, thanks to a heads-up from my spiteful sister, had learned of my dereliction. Her sermon was predictable - a long diatribe about how I would never amount to anything if I didn't become more focused, how someone of my intelligence and talents was wasting "God's gifts", and so on... I had heard it all before. This time, however, I didn't listen meekly. I snapped back, using language my mother had never before heard come out of my mouth. After I was finished, red-faced and a little embarrassed that I had lost control, my ashen mother turned and left my room, shutting the door quietly behind her. I think I would have preferred for her to have slammed it. At that moment, I knew things would never be the same. Vanquishing a parent in such a cruel manner would have consequences, and not just a firm talking-to by my father after he got home from work. Something fundamental in my life had changed.

"Janelle? Are you all right?"

I blinked twice in rapid succession, slipping back into the present. The uneasy feeling relaxed its grip and the knot in my stomach untied. Repairing the fabric of my memory was becoming a traumatic experience. How many people had I *hurt*? Was this new life a chance at redemption?

"Just another memory," I murmured. "One at a time, piece by piece."

"The past is overrated," said Backus, echoing Samell's thesis. I got the impression he was trying to comfort me in his own unsentimental way. "If you get to be my age, you won't remember most of it. You remember a few incidents - moments of importance one way or another - but most of it is forgotten and you don't realize what's missing or worry about it. Whole decades vanish, claimed by the passage of time. Most of my 'active' memories are from the last few years. It's different when you're young, though. You have so few years to look back on that any deterioration is substantial. I'd like to tell you that I can empathize but the truth is that I remember less of my adolescence than you do."

I departed his house that morning without answering his question about when I would leave because I didn't know. He was right, but if the newest memory was an indicator of my past behavior, procrastination might be an enduring trait. It also wasn't just about leaving - it was about having a destination. I felt certain that Backus had one in mind. Maybe he knew, or thought he knew, where I could find a trained Summoner.

As I walked across the village toward my spot for the day's chores, I noticed a large group of people congregating near Healer Drabek's cottage. Between twenty and thirty people were milling around as if in anticipation of something. I approached Samell, who was standing there with two of his friends, Octavius and Matrick.

Octavius saw me first and waved in greeting. My arrival didn't excite much interest, which was unusual. As something of a local celebrity, people normally noticed my comings and goings.

"What's happening?" I asked.

"A tinker arrived from NewTown a little while ago. He was attacked on the road a few cycles from here."

"An earth reaver?"

"That was my first thought but he said it was flying and buzzed like an angry insect. It cut off one of his hands, killed the horses pulling his wagon, and destroyed the wagon. He said the wreckage looked like he had been hit by a whirlwind."

"An air reaver?"

Samell shrugged. "We can assume. No one really knows. No one around here has seen an air reaver."

Until recently, no one had seen an earth reaver, either.

"I have to leave. Leave Aeris, I mean." This news made it more important, advanced the timing from "sometime" to "imminent."

"I know. I'm surprised you've stayed this long. We all knew this was coming and, as I told you before, I'll be by your side when you decide to go. I've talked to Esme about it and she'll come as well. And a few of the others. You'll need good people around you, people you can trust and who know the ways of this world better than you do."

I was grateful for his words. I knew he'd previously agreed to be one of my companions but, when he had made the statement, my departure had been a possibility not a certainty. Now that it was tangible and approaching, I was relieved that his support hadn't wavered. I needed people with me; this wasn't something I could accomplish on my own.

"Can I talk to the tinker?" If we were going south, which seemed likely based on my limited understanding of the local geography, I needed to get an idea of what we could be facing and where the danger might lie.

"After the healer has mended him. He was probably given a sleeping draught. From what I saw, it wasn't a clean wound and he may have a touch of fever."

"I have to get started on my chores." I was already late. Such was the way with procrastinators. "If he's able to talk, have someone fetch me."

Although I spent the rest of the day in a state of expectation, no one came with an invitation to visit the tinker. When I arrived home for supper, I learned that he was unconscious. His injuries had been mended to the best of Drabek's abilities but the fever had become serious. The healer was using potions to keep him in a deep sleep in the hope that his body would be able to fight off the infection. With no antibiotics, that was the best they could hope for. I suspected that a trained Summoner might be able to cure him but, unsure and untried, I wasn't about to make an attempt that could result in killing a man who might be able to survive on his own.

Two days later, the recovering patient sent word that he was willing to receive visitors. When I entered the side chamber of the healer's cottage where he was convalescing, I was surprised by his appearance. I had expected to see a sickly, older man near to death's door but the tinker was young - perhaps only four or five years older than me - and in good shape and good spirits. His left arm was heavily bandaged where it ended below the elbow. His swarthy skin, or at least what I could see of it under his bushy black beard and mustache, was a healthy color, showing none of the pallor one might expect from someone near death's door.

"So this is a Summoner!" he said by way of greeting. His voice was a bass rumble, surprisingly deep for one with such a lean form.

"Prettiest one I've ever seen!" His sapphire eyes sparkled with mischief.

"Likely the only one you've ever seen," grumped Father Backus, who had joined me for this visit. Like most of the villagers, he knew the tinker from his numerous past visits. He was one of several itinerant merchants who visited Aeris regularly. "This is Janelle."

"Name's Gabriel. I'd offer my hand but I'm afraid I misplaced it." His tone was playful but I sensed it was a front for deeper feelings. Distress? Anger? Anxiety?

"Can you tell me what happened?"

"Not much to tell, is there? I left West Fork like usual for my twice-a-year trip north. Had some good trinkets this time along and some exotic seeds. Things went about as expected in NewTown. Spent several days there trading and visiting friends, then set off for Aeris about five or six days ago. Hard to keep track of time. There were rumors in NewTown about strange goings-on to the north but no one knew anything firm and I wasn't going to let innuendo keep me from a good profit.

"The attack came on the second day out of NewTown on a part of the road almost no one travels. I wasn't paying much attention - just letting the horses pull the wagon. They knew the way. I was dozing when all of a sudden there was a loud buzzing like a hive of killwings and the wagon was struck by what felt like a whirlwind. I lost the hand as I was falling. Something clipped me and sheared it off. Killed the horses too. Made another pass and smashed what was left of the wagon into tiny pieces.

"I know what you're going to ask next: What was it? Wish I could say. It happened so fast I never got a good look at it. I can tell you this much - it was big and had wings. Bigger than the biggest bird I've ever seen and black as the night. It brought the wind with it. That wasn't anything natural. I've been all around the world and I've never met with something like that.

"Anyways, I found a wad of clean cloth and bandaged up the arm as best I could and made the rest of the trip on foot. I kept expecting the thing to come back but it didn't. The one night I spent out there after the attack... let me tell you, I didn't expect to still be alive come morning. It's only by the providence of the gods that I'm here today." He turned to Backus. "Isn't that right, Father?"

"It is indeed, my son," said the priest, his tone solemn and pious. "Tell me, Gabriel, do you have any thoughts about what the creature might have been?"

"At the time, I wondered if it could be an air reaver. I know that sounds crazy but, while I was recovering, the healer told me earth reavers had attacked here recently and it no longer seemed impossible. Never heard tell of anyone meeting one before. Or maybe it's just that no one survived an encounter to tell others about it. Either way, guess that makes me lucky."

Backus nodded. "When you were in NewTown, did you hear anything about the potential danger to Aeris? We sent messages by bird to NewTown and West Fork informing them of our situation."

"Like I said, there were rumors. One innkeeper I know said if he was me, he'd steer clear of the northern road this year, but he couldn't say why. Said a messenger got a day north and turned back because he didn't like the 'feel' of things. I doubt any of the birds made it through, though. Mayor Galbreth would have sent men if there was a threat. Even though Aeris is independent, he's always viewed it as NewTown's northern outpost."

We spent a little longer with Gabriel but he didn't have more to say except that he wanted to get back on the road as quickly as possible. He was worried about how he was going to "rebuild" now that he'd lost his horses, wagon, and goods. As a tinker, his life was on the road although he had a small cottage in West Fork that he shared with a few others. He assumed he'd have to hire himself out to one of his "brothers" for a time - at least until he made enough to buy a new wagon and team.

As we were leaving, I paused to ask Healer Drabek about Gabriel's condition. "He's got a strong constitution. It was touch-and-go when he got here but, as soon as the fever broke, I knew he'd be okay."

"When will he be able to travel?" I asked.

Drabek was surprised by the question. "The man's just lost a hand. That's not like losing a fingernail. It's going to take a while before…"

"When will the danger be past of the wound reopening? Of the infection returning?"

"There's more to his recovery than a healed wound and clean blood."

"I understand but I'm not sure he will. Do you think he has the temperament to wait around in Aeris while his body gets used to having only one hand? He's itching to get back on the road." *And I need a guide - someone who knows the terrain beyond Aeris' immediate environs.*

Drabek was quiet for so long I thought he wasn't going to give me an answer. Finally, reluctantly, he said, "Ten days. At a minimum."

"He leaves in three days. Do what's needed to get him ready."

Chapter Fourteen: The Long Road Beckons

There were six of us. Although the elders had advocated for a larger force, Backus had advised that a small company would be more mobile and better able to avoid an attack. I also hadn't liked the thought of bringing too many of Aeris' healthy fighters with me. If another offensive came, they would need every bowman and sword-arm available. So, in addition to myself, Samell, and Esme, the group included Esme's friend Alyssa, and Samell's compatriots Stepan and Octavius. Gabriel was accompanying us as a guide (after all, we were going his way) but it was unclear how long he would remain. I'm sure the consideration of traveling with a Summoner as protection was an inducement.

Aside from Gabriel, who I didn't know, I felt comfortable with my choice of companions. Outside of Samell and Esme, I knew Alyssa the best, having spent time with her doing chores. She was a shy, sweet girl of Esme's age with short blond hair and piercing blue eyes. The seeming fragility of her thin form was belied by her stamina and tenacity. She was adept with almost any weapon - nearly as good as Esme with a bow and superior to any of the other party members with a stave. Given time, I hoped she could offer me lessons.

Sandy-haired Stepan was the oldest of the group, three years my senior. A natural-born leader, he had to curb those tendencies on this trip, acknowledging that I was in charge. He was good-natured about the "demotion," however, not taking offense at playing the follower's role. Like almost everyone in Aeris, he was in excellent physical shape. His conventional good looks made him one of the village's most eligible bachelors. I knew of at least three girls who would have said yes to a proposal but Stepan hadn't made a decision where a wife was concerned. I wondered if going on this trip was a way to put it off.

Although not as good as Samell with a blade, he was competent and would be an asset in a fight.

I knew Octavius the least. Although he and Samell were friends, I hadn't spent much time with him so it surprised me when he lobbied hard to join the group. With Samell playing his advocate, I couldn't refuse him. He was short but muscular and the only one among us capable of using a two-handed sword. His black skin and square jaw betrayed an ancestry beyond the immediate environs. (Samell said his forebears likely came from the deep south.) He never talked of his past but he had apparently arrived in Aeris as an orphan and had been reared by the man and woman he called "father" and "mother." Without knowing him, I felt a kinship. Both of us lacked blood connections to our past - something everyone else in Aeris took for granted.

Our path, as identified by Father Backus on a map in his cottage, would take us on The North-South Road through NewTown and as far as West Fork, where we could re-provision. From there, we would head southwest, skirting The Rank Marsh - and careful not to venture into its environs lest the pockets of sucking sand and inhospitable fauna prove troublesome - and heading toward The Southern Peaks. Backus' "understanding" was that the reclusive Summoner Bergeron lived in the foothills.

"He's not the most accommodating of hosts," the priest had warned. "By all accounts, he prizes his isolation and discourages visits. However, he may react differently when he discovers you're a Summoner. There are so few magic practitioners left that they rarely reject one of their own. Of course, it's possible that Bergeron was the one who summoned you. In that case, you'll find a corpse and you'll have to go all the way east to the cities to find another."

As for more specific directions, Backus had been unhelpful. "I've never visited him personally nor do I know anyone who has. As I said, he's a recluse. Wouldn't serve his purposes if his house was marked on every traveler's map, would it? When you get close, you should be able to send out magical feelers. They'll lead you to him… if he's still there."

Gabriel hadn't been able to offer much in the way of help. "Everyone in West Fork knows *of* Bergeron but I doubt you'll find anyone who's met him. He's four or five days west of the town over some rough terrain. The direct path leads through The Rank Marsh, which is home to some creatures almost as unsavory as earth reavers, and it's said that trolls roam the high passes of The Southern Peaks. Not exactly inviting country."

I wasn't pleased about the ambiguity of the journey's route. My hope, and it was admittedly a nebulous one, was that we could find a guide in West Fork who might (for a few coins) take us into The Southern Peaks. The elders of Aeris had provided a generous allowance for that purpose. As Rickard, their newest member, had suggested, "Your status as a Summoner will result in a lot of bowing and scraping but little in the way of meaningful help. Gold coins from the cities, however, will serve you when it comes to procuring aid." Gabriel's eyes had widened when he had seen how much had been entrusted to us.

The warm morning sun beat down on us as we wended our way south on the hard-packed dirt road, which was actually little more than a wide trail. Little consideration had been given to riding. Horses were scarce in Aeris and I didn't want to deprive the village of one of their resources. Plus, I didn't know how to ride, my last experience on a mount having been ten years ago on a pony at a birthday party. I could think of few things less dignified than a mighty Summoner falling off her faithful steed or hobbling around with sore buttocks. Walking would take longer but it was preferable. And we didn't have to worry about feeding and watering the horses.

The scents of the road enveloped me - from the fragrance of small wildflowers thriving so close to the Blight to the sweat of my companions. Once awakened, the sensitivity of my sense of smell had not abated. If anything, it had become more acute. If I closed my eyes,

I would be able to pinpoint the location of each member of the group by his or her scent.

A cycle out of Aeris, I was already wistful. I hadn't realized how important the concept of a "home" had become until it was behind me. Now, I was a wanderer. There was no telling if or when I would return to Aeris. I suspected that if I ever saw the village again, it would be as a visitor. There was something sad about that. Although three of my closest friends were with me on the road, I missed Lissa's kind, knowing smile, Brin's youthful enthusiasm, Rickard's gruff manner, and even Backus' inscrutability.

"Something wrong?" asked Samell, dropping back to walk beside me. Gabriel was leading the way, followed by Esme and Alyssa then Stepan, with Octavius bringing up the rear.

My lips quirked upward at his perceptiveness. Sometimes it was almost scary how well he understood me considering that we hadn't known each other for very long.

"I don't like goodbyes." I guessed it was true although I couldn't recall any specific memories to confirm it. Maybe it was just *this* goodbye I didn't like.

"Father Backus was sorry to see you go. He never shows regret but there was some this morning. My guess is that he'll miss your morning sessions. By now you must be the second-most pious person in all of Aeris."

"I guess I know the basics about the gods. There are four of them, right? Sovereign the sun, the moons Concord and Ire, and Vasto the void. I'm afraid Backus' theological teachings were lacking."

"What were you doing all those mornings? We assumed he was giving you a detailed history of religion and indoctrinating you into the inner workings of the priesthood."

A priest alone with an 18-year old girl… Where I came from, it would have incited gossip but in Aeris, no one would even consider the salacious possibilities of such daily meetings. Was this almost charming naiveté a characteristic of this world or merely the result of Aeris' isolation?

It wasn't my secret to tell but, on the other hand, how could I keep something important from Samell? "How much do you know about Father Backus' past?" I asked.

"His past? You mean that he's lived for a very long time and never seems to age? Everyone knows that. A gift from the gods."

I suppose that's one way to see it. "It's a bit more complicated than that. Do you know there are two kinds of people who can use magic?"

Samell nodded. "Summoners and wild-wizards. Everyone knows that."

"Backus is what you call a 'wild-wizard'. He was brought here about ten generations ago but never learned his skills from another Summoner. Now, his magic is mostly burnt out, although there's enough left for him to prolong his life."

Samell was thunderstruck. "Father Backus…a wild-wizard? Are you sure?"

I nodded. "My sessions with him weren't about the gods. They were about learning how to use magic. He taught, or tried to teach, some techniques. But his limitations were obvious and he knew that if I didn't go on this trip, I'd end up like him."

Samell was quiet for a while as he absorbed what I had told him. I was content to wait for him to speak.

"Why tell me? Why now?"

"Because I trust you. Because I think it's something you have a right to know. But it's not my secret to tell and, as long as we were in Aeris, I didn't feel it was my place."

"So, by telling me now… You don't think we're going back to Aeris, do you?"

I phrased my response carefully. "I'm probably not going back. Or, if I do, it won't be for long. My immediate goal is to find another Summoner. Beyond that, I don't know, but if Backus is right, the earth reavers' attack may just be the first offensive in something much larger."

"And the rest of us…?"

"That will be up to you. I hope at least some of you might want to stay with me for a while but I can understand if you want to go back to Aeris. It's your home and it may need defending."

Samell smiled. "You still don't understand our ways, Janelle. Those of us with you, except Gabriel, are pledged to you and your cause. We're your coterie. Aeris is no longer our 'home.' We're with you until you dismiss us. I thought you knew that."

The revelation surprised me. I hadn't realized… I had assumed my companions from Aeris were with me as guides and possibly protectors for the immediate journey. I had underestimated the depth of loyalty associated with their commitment, giving up everything - a town, a lifestyle, families, future marriages and children - to accompany someone they barely knew. Along with the flood of warmth and gratitude, this spawned a twinge of anxiety. The responsibility was enormous and I wasn't sure I could live up to it. It was much to ask from someone untried.

"None of us did this on a whim. We're with you because we believe in you. We think you're important - important enough to give our lives if necessary. The only way we'll go back to Aeris is if you go back there."

I spent the rest of the morning traveling in silence, processing what Samell had told me, coming to grips with what the other five had surrendered to be here. Had I been aware of this before leaving Aeris, would it have made a difference? If I was honest, the answer was no. I needed them. Alone, I never would have undertaken this journey. Being by myself in this wild country was a frightening proposition. I still remembered my first days in The Verdant Blight.

The others chatted among themselves, gossiping about things of little consequence, almost as if they were on a day trip rather than a long, uncertain quest. I marveled that they could be so calm, so matter-of-fact about it. When we stopped for a rest and to eat a light meal of traveler's rations (nuts, dried berries, cured meat, and lukewarm water), Esme approached me.

"Are you okay, Janelle? Did Samell say something to upset you? He does that without realizing it. He's not always the best with words. Sometimes when he tries to say something, it comes out almost the opposite of what he means."

"No. I'm just thinking. The enormity of what we're doing is sinking in. It's madness, believing we can find one of the few people in the whole world who can answer my questions."

"Summoners can do the impossible." She said it with such earnestness that I almost believed her.

"What about you? Won't you miss Aeris?"

"Of course I will. I lived my whole life there. But Alyssa's with me and it softens the blow to have my oldest and dearest friend along. We're all with you to do what we can to keep Aeris safe. This isn't about abandoning our home; it's about saving it, if that makes any sense."

It did.

By mid-afternoon, the road slipped into the fringes of The Verdant Blight. The great, green forest which had been a constant presence to the right crept closer until we were under the canopy. I guessed this was the general area where I had first met Samell and Esme, although that had been to the west. There was a several-mile gap between the river and the road, although I had been told that the two generally paralleled each other all the way to NewTown, where they diverged.

My normal senses found the Blight to be as strange as on my previous visit. Other than us, nothing moved. Nothing lived. The plants were healthy but there were no buzzing insects, no burrowing animals. I reached out with my mind-sense but found nothing. No earth reavers or air reavers. I could feel the forest's magic but there was nothing inherently malevolent about it. It wouldn't harm me and, assuming my companions were careful, it wouldn't harm them either.

As the afternoon wore on, I became restless. My legs and feet were growing sore. Although I was in a lot better shape physically than I had been upon my arrival, six weeks (or however long it had been) wasn't enough time to turn a pampered high school girl into a toned athlete. To keep my mind on something other than my aching muscles, I broached a subject with Samell that I had wanted to discuss with him: religion.

Before coming to this world, I hadn't been a believer in a higher power. Actually, that wasn't strictly true. I hadn't given it much thought. For me, the concept of an omnipotent deity who would engage in personal relationships with his creations seemed less realistic than Santa Claus. But could there have been something out there, something to have set all these things in motion, something to have seeded the universe…? Someone had once told me that children and adolescents never give god much consideration. They either accepted or didn't accept what others told them. Questioning and pondering came later in life. Now it was time for me to start that questioning and pondering.

Going through what I had endured, it was hard not to acknowledge that there might be a higher purpose. Although I had accepted the reality of my current situation, I didn't understand *where* "here" was or *why* I had been chosen. Maybe it was all random. Or maybe I had died in my world so I could be reborn here in a purgatory I would escape only by finding salvation or redemption.

Backus had taught me the basics about religion in this world. Beliefs were closer to what the Greeks and Romans had once accepted than what I was accustomed to. There were four gods: Sovereign, the sun; the two moons, Ire and Concord; and the blackness of the void, Vasto. These celestial objects weren't merely representations of the gods, they *were* the gods. In the world I came from, faith demanded acceptance of the unseen. Here, the objects of worship weren't invisible.

"Do you believe in the gods?" I asked Samell, breaking the companionable silence as we walked side-by-side.

"That's a strange question," he said. "They're all around us. Sovereign's eye watches even now." He glanced skyward although the leaves and branches obscured direct sunlight. "How could I not believe in them?"

Science had taught me that suns, like all stars, were superheated balls of gas. But no one in this world would understand what that meant. Was it possible that the astronomical truths of my world might not be the same here? How different were the fundamentals? And if I argued against them, would I become like Galileo?

"I've never seen you praying or worshipping." No churches, either, at least in Aeris. And, although Father Backus was a priest, I hadn't observed him doing much ministering.

"Do they do that a lot in your world?"

When I was a little girl, it had felt strange being one of the few people in the neighborhood not to go to church on Sunday mornings. It was like a club I had been excluded from because my parents were "lapsed Christians" who preferred sleeping in. Then, as I got older, I discovered that I was envied by many of my church-going friends because I didn't have to endure the boredom of a weekly service.

"Yes," I said. "At least some of them do."

"Things may be different in the cities," said Samell. "But out here, living in the open, we just accept that the gods are watching and listening to us. And if we need something and have led lives they approve of, they may consider granting a request if we ask for it."

"Do you choose one god over the others?"

Samell shook his head, amused by my ignorance. "How would that make sense? They are all there. What would be the point of ignoring one or preferring another? True, 'prayers' might be targeted depending on the request. You wouldn't ask Vasto for a sunny day or Sovereign for a clear night. Each has their own domain and we venerate them equally. Apparently, Father Backus spent more time teaching you about magic than theology."

I couldn't debate him about that.

"Look, I don't know what the gods are like where you come from or what kind of relationships your people have with them but if you have any questions about our gods, just ask. After all, they're *your* gods as well, now. Whether you want to believe in them or not, they're always there. You can't hide from them. So, even though we don't talk about them often, we're aware of them." He glanced skyward again. "It's hard not to be."

I didn't know what to think. The sun was just a ball of gas, wasn't it? And those two moons at night, they were just rocks in space, orbiting the planet? When did astronomy become so complicated?

By the time the late afternoon sky started deepening into twilight, we had covered about a quarter of the distance from Aeris to NewTown, which put us on target since the plan was for us to arrive before nightfall on the fourth day if the weather held and we were able to maintain a strong pace. We set up camp a short distance off the road under the trees. My mind-sight confirmed there were no dangers in the immediate vicinity. No nothing, in fact. Except for the thriving vegetation, we were the only living creatures nearby.

Gabriel decided not to light a fire. When I asked him about it, he said, "Don't really need it, do we? It's a warm night. Even in the coldest hours, we won't need more than a light blanket. And there ain't a worry about things sneaking up on us in the dark, what with you being a Summoner and all. Besides, I don't like burning Blight wood. If the trees are poisonous, I'd rather not inhale the smoke."

I guess the toxicity of Blight wood could be an issue, although I had been under the impression that most of the wood burned in Aeris for cook fires was taken from trees that grew in or near the Blight. It was strange to think that something that wouldn't affect me could be fatal to my companions. But that wasn't unique to this world. I remembered an incident in elementary school where one of my classmates went into anaphylactic shock after eating a brownie with bits of peanuts in it. If not for the quick actions of our teacher, she might have died. Dangerous to her but not to me. The brownie, as I recall, had been delicious.

The night passed without incident although I didn't sleep well. Lying on the hard ground didn't agree with my back or sore muscles any more than it had during my first couple of nights after being Summoned. And the rich, pungent smells of the forest were difficult to ignore. Some, like the top layer of loam, were comforting. Others reeked of decay and disuse. Although I was left out of the watch rotation, I was probably awake longer than anyone else. When the crisp, clear dawn arrived, I greeted it sandy-eyed and tired. During the morning's walk, I was uncommunicative. Samell made several overtures but my monosyllabic responses convinced him to find another conversation partner.

Around mid-day, the road emerged from the forest. According to Gabriel, the Blight hadn't yet overtaken the southernmost reaches of the great woods. A quick check with my mind-sense confirmed the presence of insect and animal life. "Ten years ago, the Blight was just a small part of the forest, far to the north and west. An oddity for most, a place to visit for the curious, and certainly not a danger. We used to call this part 'Greenswood.' A year from now, there won't be anything left of Greenswood. Sad. The great fear in NewTown is that the Blight will spread all the way south to The Long Orchard. Seems unlikely but no one ever thought the Blight would eat up Greenswood the way it has."

Travel was monotonous. During nearly two days on the road, we had encountered no other souls. Apparently, no one was heading north toward Aeris. Gabriel asserted this was normal for the time of year, that there was little congress between villages during the warmer months. The forest receded from the road, giving way to the vast plains that represented so much of the local geography. We had stopped for an afternoon break, with my calves urging that this would be a good place to rest for the night, when our guide announced, "It happened around here. I've been looking for signs of the wreckage of my wagon and the bodies of the horses but I haven't seen anything. Someone or something must have cleared it away."

A cursory probe of the surroundings revealed nothing unusual but I decided to search more deeply. Sitting cross-legged, I closed my eyes and let my mind roam. Then, almost instinctively, I reached for my magic.

Immediately, my mind's vision sharpened and expanded. Things that had been blurred snapped into focus. I became aware of every bug, every creature crawling through the tall grass or burrowing beneath the ground, every bird in the air. I was like a child whose poor vision was suddenly corrected by putting on a pair of glasses. I almost gasped aloud at the clarity.

And there it was, well beyond the range of my unaugmented senses. Somewhere to the east, perhaps as far away as fifty miles, it was meandering. Even at this distance, its magical nature called out to me like a beacon. An eerie calm accompanied a chilling realization: if I could sense the air reaver, the reverse would also be true. And if it detected my gaze being directed at it, there seemed little doubt it would turn its attention toward our small band. As Backus had said, it was the iron and I was the lodestone.

Chapter Fifteen: Ill Wind

"It's coming." No sense hiding the inevitable. "It's coming because it knows I'm here and I'm its target." In effect, that answered the question about the earth reavers and Aeris. They had attacked because I had been there. I may have saved the town but I had also put it in danger. They were better off now that I was gone but my companions were in danger.

What I said next, I didn't want to say. It terrified me. But if these six people stayed with me through the inevitable confrontation and any of them died because of that, I knew I wouldn't get another restful night for the remainder of my life. "I think it would be best if we split up. I can stay here, wait for it. The rest of you can head directly for NewTown and wait there for me. I'll follow when I'm able."

"I can tell you ain't no tactician," said Gabriel. "That's probably the dumbest plan I've ever heard. It's more likely to get us all killed than save even one."

I didn't know whether to be embarrassed, relieved, or angry. "If we split up, it will come for me and leave the rest of you alone. And I should be strong enough to beat it." I didn't know that, of course. The air reaver was likely to be a bigger challenge than the earth reavers. Victory wasn't a given.

"Hogwash," said Gabriel. "You've got no idea whether we'd be safe if we left you. You weren't anywhere near here when I was traveling north and that didn't save me or my horses. It might come for us first - easy prey - then move on to you. Or, if it killed you, we might be next. The way I see it, we fight it together. Maybe in the end, you're the one who kills it, but we stand a better chance seven-against-one with a Summoner than in any other configuration."

"She thinks it will be her fault if one of us dies," said Esme, making an accurate estimation of my concerns.

"And she'll be right." Gabriel's tone was harsh. "But that's the nature of leadership. Deciding who lives and who dies. It's a lesson she's got to learn. Like it or not, she's a Summoner and that makes her a leader. If she lives long enough, people around her are going to die. The objective here is to kill that thing and that means coming up with the best battle plan. You don't retreat before the enemy has been engaged, especially when you've got a numbers advantage."

I stared shamefacedly at the ground, feeling like a little girl who had just been scolded by a teacher for a wrong answer. He was right, of course, and that made it all the more galling. Splitting up was a stupid plan. I'm sure they all knew it. Only Gabriel, the outsider, had exhibited the forthrightness to openly object, to call it what it was.

"You're going to need our help, Janelle," said Samell, his voice gentle but no less insistent. "If not during the fight then after it. We've seen what happens to you after you use magic."

Wordlessly, I nodded. Of course the headache would come. I had no idea whether the exercises I had done with Backus would make it bearable but it would be there, lying in wait. It was notable, however, that I had felt no pain after using magic to amplify my mind-sense. Maybe there was a clue in that to avoiding the headaches. I wished Backus was around to discuss it with.

The plan was that there was no plan. We would continue our southward journey as a single group with me monitoring the air reaver's approach. Gabriel was hopeful we might outpace it but I harbored no such illusion. My use of magic had acted like a beacon and it would come for me. Based on the tinker's description, it would take more than arrows and blades to stop the creature. However, without seeing it, it was difficult to assess what kind of magic would be useful. In addition to my affinity for procrastination, I had always been drawn to improvisation. I could only hope that skill would be an asset.

The sense of being hunted lent an eerie aura of déjà vu to this segment of the trip. If I relied on my unamplified sense, there was nothing to cause concern but when I used a magical filter, I could see the entity moving toward us at a pace that not even a galloping horse would outrun. "It will reach us within a cycle after sunset regardless of whether we stop for the night or keep going. I don't think we'll be able to evade it."

"Can't run, can't hide, so we fight. Unfortunately, I'm not going to be much help with only one hand," remarked Gabriel. "Best I can do is stab at it with a knife and, against that thing, that ain't going to do much." He looked mournfully at his bandaged appendage.

"Ire and Concord kissed two nights ago, so they'll be separating. Ire should be up before the sun sets so at least we won't have to fight in full darkness. But we won't see it until it's nearly on us," said Samell.

The decision of how to proceed was mine. Like it or not, ready for it or not, I was the leader. "We'll keep moving until dusk then we'll stop and get ready." I couldn't think of anything else to do. We were too far from Aeris or NewTown to seek sanctuary or hope for aid. Whatever happened, it would be up to the seven of us and, if we perished, no one would know what had happened.

The remainder of the daylight hours crawled by as we made our way southward, chased by an invisible presence that only I could detect. It was an unusually warm and humid day and we were all drenched in sweat by the time we decided to stop as the last of the sun's rays bathed the world in their glow, creating impossibly long, distorted shadows. The air reaver was perhaps ten miles away, moving unerringly toward us at a speed that would bring it into contact in a half-cycle. We had that long to prepare ourselves.

Low in the eastern sky, rising up to replace the sun's glare with its fainter, silvery presence, was Ire. This battle would be fought under her pale gaze. By the time Concord rose, the end would be written. I didn't know whether those orbs in the sky were asteroids caught in this planet's orbit or the heavenly manifestations of some greater beings but, whatever the case, it wasn't going to matter tonight.

It was decided that the three Aeris men, all of whom were proficient in hand-to-hand combat, would be in the front. Esme and Alyssa, expert archers, would be behind them with me. Gabriel, who wasn't physically able to fight except in dire circumstances, would be in the far back. Our concern was that a flying creature could make such a formation useless. This wasn't like battling the earth reavers. It could come at us from any direction with such speed that we might not have time to adjust.

By now, it was close enough that I could "see" it without magical amplification. It felt similar to the earth reavers, radiating the same malignancy and vitriol, but stronger. I wondered about its solo presence. Was it like the first earth reaver I had encountered, a scout sent out to seek its quarry, or was this something different? And to what degree did the reavers interact? Surely, it wasn't a coincidence that earth reavers and air reavers had emerged from their reclusive existences at the same time. Was there coordination in their activities? More questions for an experienced Summoner.

"Do you have your powder?" Samell's voice startled me with its closeness. Despite the strength of his unique scent, I hadn't realized he was standing immediately behind me.

"In my satchel." I gestured toward the sack I had been carrying, which was now in a pile with the rest of our non-combat items, ready to be retrieved when the fight was over. "You know what to do?"

He nodded. "A pinch under your tongue and another in each nostril. Then, when you're able to drink, a mixture of it in water."

"Be careful with it. It may help me but it could harm you."

He smiled. "I know, Janelle. I've lived here my entire life. I'm well aware of how dangerous Blight leaves are."

I held back a chuckle. Of course he knew. Only someone new to this world might have thought otherwise. It would have been like someone telling me to avoid shiny three-leaved plants.

Through the long hour after sunset, I tracked the approach of the air reaver, which was coming directly toward us, showing no sign of deviation. As it closed to within 500 feet, my other senses began to note its approach. Although the light was too faint to see it at this distance, I could hear the distant buzz of a hornet's nest and a stiff, foul-smelling breeze stirred the air. With every passing second, as it closed the distance, the sound grew louder and the wind stronger.

"That's it," muttered Gabriel. "That's the thing that attacked me and destroyed my wagon."

Then, in a literal whirlwind of chaos, it began.

The air reaver plunged from the sky, its blackish shape blotting out the face of Ire as it dove toward us, a deadly silhouette. Esme and Alyssa, both possessed of incredible reflexes, were able to get off one arrow apiece before it was on us. One was tossed aside by the wild currents of air cocooning the creature. The other pierced its outer defenses only to clank harmlessly against a shell-like exoskeleton with a sound akin to stone striking metal. The two women ducked and rolled, tossing aside bows and drawing blades as the attacker slashed through the air where, only a second before, their heads had been.

It was big and had wings. Bigger than the biggest bird I've ever seen and black as the night. That's how Gabriel had described the air reaver from his bed in Aeris and now, face-to-face with it, I had to agree. The moonlight made it difficult to discern anything clearly but it looked like the largest bat I had ever witnessed - the impossible wingspan must have been at least eight feet. Its eyes, the only things visible in an otherwise black body, glowed with a reddish intensity. It stank of feces and dead things and the winds emanating from its body were as fetid as carrion.

The creature's assault on the women brought it low enough to give Samell, Octavius, and Stepan a chance to lash out at it before it climbed again. Gabriel, meanwhile, was scampering away off the road and into the tall grass. The three men's weapons made contact - solid blows, delivered with force - and all were turned away with the same metallic clang that had ended the arrow's progress. Even Octavius' large, two-handed blade didn't find purchase. It was as if the creature's hide was impervious to iron. The reaver's buzz was maddening; its tornadic cloak threatened to knock us off our feet.

Emotions surged through me. I tried to corral them then gave up. This wasn't the time for experimentation, not with seven lives hanging in the balance. The magic would use what it needed, even if it denuded me of those emotions. There could be value in that. Take away the terror and calm would remain.

Relying on what had worked during the earth reaver battle, I called fire. It came with ease, pouring eagerly from the end of my staff and circumscribing a reddish-orange arc that ended when it struck the creature, which was executing a mid-air pivot. The fire washed over it like water over a rock, showing no discernible mark. A manifest failure, the attack achieved two things: it illuminated the air reaver well enough for me to make out its obsidian features and it alerted the creature to the location of its quarry. A sudden surge of fear parched my mouth.

The misbegotten thing corkscrewed into the air then dove for us again, coming at the three men from the side. They spun to engage it but weren't fast enough. It was as if they were in slow motion while it moved at full speed. It spat or threw something at Octavius - I couldn't see what it was in the dim light. The strong man tried to dodge but was unable to fully avoid the missile. He went down with a scream. Pain, surprise, anger? I couldn't tell. Stepan and Samell lunged at the reaver from opposite sides as it buzzed past them, starting its run at me. Their attacks, although well-aimed, glanced off the creature's natural armor just as their previous ones had. Meanwhile, still in shock at the ineffectiveness of my fire attack, I was unsure how to proceed. I had used my lone combat-tried weapon. In desperation, I thought amorphously of safety and a shield and was rewarded by a mild concussion as the reaver crashed into an invisible barrier it couldn't penetrate.

Then, as it struggled to regain its equilibrium and my companions took the break as an opportunity to rally, inspiration arrived in the form of a memory from tenth grade chemistry class. A metallic hide might be able to deflect iron and shrug off fire but what about acid? As was its wont when magic flowed through me, thought became reality; the orange-red flower at the end of my staff turned green and a spray of corrosive liquid rained on the air reaver. For a moment, with time slowing to a crawl, it seemed as if this tactic would fail. Then, without preamble, the buzzing stopped, the creature's wind died, and a desiccated corpse dropped to the ground like a drone with its fuel supply cut.

It smelled of sulfur – the powerful stench of rotten eggs. My hypersensitive nostrils felt as if they were under assault. But that wasn't the only aftereffect. The expected headache struck without mercy, sweeping away awareness and thought in a wave of white-hot, debilitating agony. It was worse this time than ever before. Far, far worse.

I woke up choking, the stench of dry leaves filling my nose as something warm and unpleasant was poured down my throat. The headache was diminished but not gone; it had been reduced from a white-hot intensity to a dull throb - a discomfort I could endure, at least in the short term. My mind-sense was unreachable, as had previously been the case after using magic. The only thing I could smell was the leaves - powerful, pungent, and…

I leaned over and threw up. The contents of my stomach emptied, followed by bile, then dry heaves. After that, I felt better (or at least no longer nauseous), but the headache remained.

I then realized I had been lying with my head resting on Samell's legs. I had vomited on them. He took it all in stride. "Nothing a good soak won't fix." It was too dark to see his expression but the words were spoken gently.

I sat up groggily, the recent past coming into focus along with my vision. The others were all there, even Octavius, who I had feared might be dead. They were looking at me with concern - all except Gabriel, whose expression was a cross between fear and awe. I realized that, while the others had seen me "perform" during the attack on Aeris, this was the first time he had seen magic. I could sympathize. I had done it and I could scarcely believe.

"It's dead?" I didn't need to ask.

"It's dead," confirmed Samell. "We assume it was an air reaver. We took a look at it but it's difficult to say. Whatever you did to it pretty thoroughly destroyed it and when we poked at it with sticks, they started smoking and dissolving. So we figured better to leave it alone. We moved down the road and set up camp here."

I glanced upward. Ire had traversed more than half the sky and Concord was chasing her. Much of the night gone... "How long?"

"Between two and three cycles. This was worse than the others. You were really gone. I wasn't sure you were coming back."

It was maddening and frustrating. All the exercises I had done with Backus had proven useless. I guess I shouldn't have been surprised. Those had been minor experiments done in controlled circumstances. This had been a massive expenditure of energy, far greater than anything I had tried while "testing" my tolerance with the priest. I hoped Bergeron would have some answers. I wasn't sure how much longer I could continue using magic if this was the result every time. I liked to think I had a high tolerance for pain, but this... And what if I had an aneurism or a stroke?

"At least it worked," I said.

"A good thing it did," said Gabriel from his spot across the campfire. "Without your magic, I don't think we would have beaten it."

"Are there more out there?" asked Esme.

I shook my head. "There weren't when that one attacked. Now? I don't know. After I use magic, my mind-sense goes numb for a while."

"Let's hope we're alone for now. Arrows and blades didn't do a thing against it." Stepan tried hard to keep despair from his words. I knew he was thinking the same thing the others were - if a force of several dozen air reavers attacked Aeris or anywhere else, the result would be devastation.

"It's not that we can't kill them," I said. "I used magic to generate my attacks but, in the end, the earth reavers were killed by fire and the air reaver by acid. They have vulnerabilities. It's just a matter of figuring out what they are and using them." Fire would be easy enough to manufacture but I wasn't sure about acid. Perhaps there was some other corrosive agent.

"Maybe that was the only one," suggested Alyssa.

"No," said Samell. "Remember the storm before the earth reaver attack? The one that bypassed Aeris? Janelle said that was caused by air reavers. We need to assume there are more of them out there although we don't know where and what their intentions are. This one might have been watching or guarding the road."

"For now, we have to hope there ain't no others around here," said Gabriel. "We're still a couple of days from NewTown."

"How are you?" I asked Octavius. He had been sitting quietly between Alyssa and Stepan, a pained expression distorting his rugged features.

"I'll live." His voice was strained. "I'm not going to lie. It hurts. A lot. But I don't think it's fatal and whatever that thing spat or threw at me wasn't envenomed." He stood and peeled back his leather jerkin to reveal a patch of raw flesh that covered his chest from nipple to nipple and all the way down to his navel. By the firelight's ruddy glow, it appeared angry. I couldn't tell whether the skin was blistered, badly scraped, or a combination of the two. "Don't suppose there's anything your magic can do for it?"

There probably was. Backus had said that some Summoners developed into skilled healers. But my knowledge of human anatomy was limited to what I could remember from high school biology, which wasn't much. If I tried, I would be more likely to harm than help. "Sorry. I wish I could but it's a lot easier to destroy something with magic than to mend it. I might make it worse."

"Thought so. I'll make do with the salves."

With the headache lingering, the nausea was creeping back. Samell must have noticed this. "Why don't you get some more sleep. It's still a couple of cycles until dawn and we don't have to leave at first light if you're not ready.

I smiled wanly. Before again lying down, I took a long, deep draught from one of the water skins. It was a smart decision because, when I vomited several minutes later, at least there was something in my stomach to come up.

I felt much better, although not 100%, when I awoke in the morning. My stomach was settled and the headache had diminished to a distant, barely noticeable throbbing - the kind that made itself manifest only when I thought about it. My mind-sense remained unreachable. I worried, as I had on the previous occasions, that it might not return. Without it, my value to the party would be greatly diminished and it would be exponentially more difficult to use magic.

Gabriel assured me that if we made good time - meaning that if Octavius' injury didn't slow us, there were no more reaver attacks, and the weather held - we would reach NewTown before nightfall tomorrow. That meant spending one more night in the open. None of us were thrilled with the idea but there was no help for it. Night travel wasn't a sane option, especially with only one of us having any familiarity with the terrain. We were farther from Aeris than any of our number had been except the tinker.

We traveled most of the day in silence, the companionable chatter of the earlier journey having been set aside in the wake of the attack. Even though we had survived and, all things considered, suffered little damage (although I wasn't sure Octavius would agree with that assessment), we had been forcefully reminded of our mortality and the gravity of our mission. What had begun in the spirit of a great adventure had become serious business. I wondered if any of my companions were regretting their decision to leave behind Aeris. Samell and Esme showed no qualms and Gabriel had little choice, but the others...? I couldn't read Alyssa, Stepan, or Octavius. If the last of those three was having second thoughts, I couldn't blame him.

The lack of conversation provided me with an opportunity to consider my Swiss cheese memories but, no matter how hard I pressed, I couldn't fill in the gaps. Too much was still missing. Although it was true that my picture today of who I had been was fuller than when I had awakened in The Verdant Blight, it was by no means complete. Many of my memories were isolated, detached. And so much of my knowledge was frustratingly incomplete. I knew who the 18th President of the United States was (Grant) but didn't know the date on which I had left. And I didn't know what had happened with my sister, my ex-boyfriend, and the gun. Or who had been following me.

We stopped at sunset, still having seen no other human activity on the road. It was as if we were all alone out here on a trail in the middle of nowhere. The night was balmy but we made a fire anyway, more for light than warmth. There didn't seem to be an argument against making one. If there were things out here hunting us, the fire wouldn't be what attracted them. Octavius and I were exempted from watch duties but the rest agreed to take single cycle turns. With the last vestiges of the headache gone, it was easy to fall asleep. To my surprise, I slept through the night, not stirring until the sun was once again peeking above the horizon.

Hopefully, we would reach NewTown today. Although I didn't crave luxury, an indoor bed would be welcome and it would be nice to talk to different people and explore a new village. Thus far, outside of the wilds and forests, all I knew of this world was Aeris and, by my companions' estimation (although only Gabriel had first-hand knowledge), it was a different community. NewTown, situated closer to the "Great Town" of West Fork and some of the more fully settled lands, was certain to be more cosmopolitan. According to the tinker, it had shops, a tavern (that doubled as an inn), and a hall for prayer and worship. The population was more than double that of Aeris' three-hundred souls.

There was less tension within the group now that we were more than a full day removed from the attack. Conversation resumed with only Octavius remaining largely silent. Despite a liberal application of some kind of medicinal salve, he was in a great deal of pain. Having gotten a look at his injury in good light, I could understand his discomfort. The redness hinted at infection. I was hopeful NewTown's healer, described by Gabriel as a "miracle-worker", could do something. I had already decided that, no matter how much he protested, I would leave him in NewTown to recuperate. He was in no condition to travel and, if it came to a battle, he was more likely to be an encumbrance than an asset.

"How are you feeling?" Even though I had assured Samell I was fully recovered from my ordeal, he persisted in checking on a regular basis.

"Really, I'm fine. It's nice to know someone's worried about me, though."

"We're all here for you. Well, all of us except Gabriel, that is. I just wish we had proven our worth better in that battle. We're supposed to be protecting you, not the other way around. With us here, you shouldn't have to use your magic."

I almost admitted that I was scared to use it again. I remembered Pavlov and his dogs. If the headaches continued, I could envision getting to a point where I'd rather die than use magic because I'd do anything to avoid the subsequent pain. I was putting a lot of faith in Bergeron, that he would have a solution. But the possibility existed that he would be as unhelpful as Backus. What if these headaches were how my body reacted to using magic? What if there was no remedy? Considering that possibility made my temples throb.

"There are times when it can't be helped," I said. "Hopefully next time it will be different." *Next time*. It was a depressing thought. But that was reality. Even though there might not be another air reaver in the vicinity, none of us were under the illusion that this was our lone encounter with one. Somewhere, some time, there would be another. Perhaps more than just one.

"We'll be better prepared at least. It's comforting to know that the reavers can be defeated if we understand their weaknesses."

"Will they believe us? In NewTown, I mean. When we tell people that Aeris was attacked by a band of earth reavers and we fought an air reaver on the road, will they accept our stories or will they think we're lying or deluded?" I could imagine walking into a police station in my old world and telling people I had seen a monster.

"Some will," said Gabriel, who had been eavesdropping on our conversation. "Some won't. Reavers ain't the sort of thing we see every day but they're not unheard of. And there are books in the faith that predict a great war against 'the elementals'. There are the skeptics, of course, who have to see something to believe it. But they know me there and many will listen when I tell them what I saw and show them what happened to me.

"As to what they can do, that's another question. NewTown is too small to have a militia to mobilize. Outside of drilling and sending out regular patrols - which they already do - and improving communications with West Fork, how else do you prepare for something that may never happen? How do you convince an entire town to change their way of life without concrete proof that they could be annihilated if they don't?"

I understood his point. Believing was one thing. They might accept our words but until a reaver was sighted in the vicinity of NewTown, the attacks we participated in would be events that happened elsewhere. Recognizing that bad things were happening somewhere didn't translate into an immediate danger. In my world, if there was a major spike in the murder rate in Chicago, people in St.

Louis didn't worry that crime would increase in their city. They voiced sympathy for how bad things were to the northeast and changed their travel plans accordingly.

It was late afternoon when we first saw the smoke - a distant haze of grayish white that I initially mistook for a low-hanging cloud. As we drew closer, it became evident that it was being fed by plumes from the vicinity of NewTown.

"That's strange." There was a note of alarm in Gabriel's voice. "Looks like bonfires but it's too early in the year for them. They don't have them till after the harvests have been brought in."

I reached for my mind-sense but, as had been the case since the battle, it was quiescent. When Samell glanced at me, I shook my head.

"Is it NewTown?" I asked.

"Either that or very close to it. And another thing. We're close enough that there should be at least a few travelers on this road. There are some isolated farms to the west and people who live there are always going back and forth to the village."

I didn't need to say what all of us were thinking. If one purpose of our journey had been to warn the towns to the south about reaver activity, we may have arrived too late.

Chapter Sixteen: Pyre

We had arrived too late. The scene of devastation that greeted us when we reached the top of the hill left us stunned into speechlessness. The closer we had gotten, the more apparent it had become that something was *very* wrong at NewTown. There was far too much smoke for just a few fires. The air reeked of it and it didn't just smell like burned wood. Cooked flesh had a specific odor and it was there, impinging on my oversensitive nostrils and bringing waves of nausea as forceful as those caused by the headaches. The actuality of what had happened exceeded even our most dark imaginings.

There was nothing left. NewTown had been reduced to blackened timbers and ash. The conflagration that had consumed the town had left no building untouched. The ruins were still smoldering but this had happened long enough in the past that there were no longer any flames. It was shocking how little remained of the town. As for the residents…there was no evidence of survivors. Although it was possible that some of the people of NewTown had fled, nothing was alive in or around the village's remains.

I couldn't say how long we stood there, dumbfounded, with the sun gradually sinking toward the horizon in the west, its twilight glow bathing NewTown in a hellish red-orange. My mind-sense hadn't yet returned but, if I had been able to use it, I doubted it would have identified a living human in the nearby environs.

Whatever had happened here hadn't been the result of a natural fire getting out of control. Putting aside the natural respect and caution with which villagers in this world approached fire, it never would have taken out the entire town. There were natural firebreaks designed to prevent such a disaster. A few buildings might have burned but the fire should have been contained. To destroy over one-hundred structures, there had to have been at least a dozen (and possibly many more) individual blazes.

"Fire reavers," breathed Esme, her voice breaking. We all looked at her. "Has to be. Nothing else could have done this."

No one tried to contradict her. We'd already encountered earth reavers and air reavers. Was it much of a stretch to believe that another kind of creature could also have emerged?

Gabriel's observation was ominous. "If it was, there ain't going to be survivors." Like me, he had been holding out a hope that a majority of NewTown's citizens had escaped, perhaps heading for West Fork. "If fire reavers are anything like what we fought, these people wouldn't have stood a chance, especially if they were unprepared. A sneak attack at night..." He shuddered.

"It probably happened around the same time we were attacked. I wonder if there's a connection?" Samell didn't expect an answer and I didn't have one to give him. Coincidence seemed an unlikely explanation. Earth reavers attacking Aeris... An air reaver guarding The North-South Road... Fire reavers attacking NewTown... There couldn't *not* be a connection.

"What now?" asked Alyssa. I deferred to Gabriel. I might be the putative leader of this band but he was the one who knew the territory.

"South to West Fork. There's really no choice unless we want to go back to Aeris."

"And hope what happened here hasn't happened at West Fork as well." Octavius voiced a concern the rest of us were trying not to consider. It was as real a possibility as another attack on Aeris. It all depended on what the reavers wanted. Finding Bergeron had become all the more important.

"Should we go down there to...be sure?" asked Samell.

I gazed at the smoking ruin of NewTown. It was getting dark. Our initial hope had been to spend the night in the town's now non-existent inn. If we were going to explore the ruins and hunt for survivors, it would be better to wait until morning. A search in the gloaming wouldn't be productive and it didn't feel right to move on without at least making an attempt.

"Let's go back up the road a ways. I don't want to spend the night this close to the town. Tomorrow morning, we can go down there before heading to West Fork." Based on the primer given by Gabriel before we had departed, it would take about five days to travel from NewTown to West Fork. We didn't have enough provisions. Water wouldn't be a problem. Even with the river diverging from the road to the south, there were plenty of clean springs and brooks. Food, on the other hand, would have to be harvested or caught. Stepan assured me that wouldn't be a problem. All the men and women of Aeris were expert hunters.

The night passed uneventfully and in silence with all of us deep in thought about the horror we would witness up close tomorrow. As devastating as this was to me, I could only imagine its impact on the others. Although they had never been to NewTown, it had been a pillar of their local geography. I had never been to London or Paris but I knew their importance to the world where I had been born. For Samell, Esme, Octavius, Alyssa, and Stepan, the sands were shifting under their feet. Things they had taken for granted were no longer stable. The older, more hardened Gabriel was hard to read. No doubt this was difficult for him but I suspected he might be in a better position to absorb what was happening than the "innocent" Aeris residents.

Sleep used the unremitting stench of smoke to trigger another memory.

The fire had started in the basement. A short circuit, they would later say, misreading the cause. It was the dead of night when the smoke detector went off. Chaos ensued as the members of my family scrambled to get out of the house before everything went up in flames. We escaped unharmed - me, my sister, and my parents. I stood on the front lawn, shivering in my nightgown while waiting for the firemen to arrive. The house was eerily dark with a faint reddish glow emanating from the small basement windows. It didn't take long for the flames to start their greedy progression through the rest of the house.

I watched not with fear or sadness but with intense curiosity. And not a hint of regret.

The firetrucks arrived. Men poured from them and with practiced ease connected hoses and went about the business of quelling the blaze. My family gazed on apprehensively. My perspective was more detached. Powerful streams of water drenched the house, doing as much damage as the flames. Ten minutes after the firemen had arrived, the fire was under control. Another five minutes and it was out. It was hard to say whether the house could be salvaged. At a minimum, it would need extensive repairs. That didn't bother me nor did the recognition that all the things in my bedroom would be damaged or lost. I didn't care much about things. I never had. People in general were too obsessed about them. Experiences mattered more to me.

A few of the neighbors had gathered to watch, most dressed in night robes or wearing light jackets over pajamas. But there was someone else there, a shadowy figure standing across the street near our neighbor's hedges. Outside of the streetlight's pool of light, he appeared almost ghostly. For the first time that night, I felt a shiver of apprehension. A noise behind me, as something in the house collapsed, caused me to turn away. When I looked back, he was no longer there.

I awoke, shaking and shuddering as I absorbed the memory and its implications, horrified by what I had learned about myself and making the obvious connection between the figure and the one who had pursued me during my last night in that world. How many years separated those two memories? More than five, less than ten?

"Janelle?" Samell was there, his strong arms around me, cradling me like a child who had been shocked awake by a blast of thunder. It seemed like two of us had been in this position before, not that I minded the comforting. In some ways, the memories were worse than the headaches although the pain was emotional and psychological rather than physical. I wondered which was worse.

"Another memory," I said. I was surprised how tremulous my voice was. "The more I learn about myself, the more I wished I didn't know."

"And I told you that it doesn't matter who you were. That's another person in another world. All that matters is who you are. The other Janelle - the one whose memories give you nightmares - she's dead. You're a new person. You've been given a chance to start anew. Do you know how many people would give their souls for that opportunity?"

I wished it was that simple but of course it wasn't. It would have been so much easier if I could have absorbed all of the memories in one dump rather than incorporating them piecemeal.

I lay back down, curled up between his spread legs, my head resting against his chest. His smell was stronger than that of burnt NewTown and that allowed me to doze off quickly. When I awoke in the morning, I was lying on the ground with a small sack pillowing my head. Samell, who was nearby talking to his sister, smiled at me reassuringly when he saw that I was up. We didn't speak of the night. There was no need to.

The trip to NewTown was grim with the gray sky echoing our mood. This time, instead of stopping on the hill overlooking what had once been an active, prosperous town, we followed the road all the way to where it became what had been the village's main thoroughfare. The remains had by now cooled but the lack of heat didn't make things easier.

The fires had burned hot enough that little of what remained was recognizable. Numerous bone fragments hinted at a horrific death toll but it was impossible to gauge the body count. The crudely built houses had vanished altogether, consumed by flames. The more stout buildings had fared better with blackened skeletons of their architecture remaining in some cases. Dishes, mugs, knives, and various farming implements were mostly intact. Our boots stirred up clouds of ash everywhere we walked; in some places, it was three inches deep. I couldn't shake the feeling that I was walking through an unmarked cemetery. Every moment in NewTown convinced us there was nothing to be found. Even the memories were gone, stolen along with the people who had experienced them. I had never felt such a profound sense of loss. I didn't need my missing mind-sense to know that my companions were equally affected. It was impossible to express the profound sense of devastation that settled in my breast. After spending more than an hour among the ruins, we headed for the southern entrance to the town where The North-South Road resumed its trek. I wanted to put NewTown behind me as far and as fast as I could, yet I knew it would remain with me to the end of my days, wherever and whenever that would be.

A steady rain started soon after we had put a few hills and valleys between us and the destroyed town. It wasn't hard enough to halt travel but it turned the poorly repaired road into mud and made progress slow and unpleasant. We kept an eye out for survivors or signs of survivors but there were none. The fields to the east and west were barren with no indication that anyone had passed through them recently. By the time we stopped for the night, everyone was sodden and, with the clouds continuing to leak moisture, there was little we could do to keep dry. Because it was too wet to get a spark to catch, we went without a fire. I could have used magic for that but it was warm enough that it wasn't needed and, considering what had destroyed NewTown, flames weren't apt to lift our spirits.

Still and silent, the ghosts of NewTown haunted us that night. I closed my eyes and saw in my imagination what must have happened. For once, I wished for the memories but they stayed away, forcing me to face the more immediate reality. None of us got much sleep so, as we set out the next morning, we were dragging. If there was one good thing about the new day, it was that my mind-sense had returned. It brought with it good news and bad news. On the one hand, I could find no signs of survivors, even when I cast a wide net. On the other hand, there were no reavers nearby, either. It was safe to journey, at least for the time being.

The rain had stopped but, owing to the muddy conditions, travel was messy. The road here was wider than to the north and showed signs of regular use but we hadn't seen anyone. I wondered how well-used the road was and whether the lack of traffic was a sign that something could be wrong to the south. I put the question to Gabriel.

"I've often gone from NewTown to Aeris and not met anyone. It's not a popular trip and the road's not much more than a wide path. Most merchants don't make enough profit and, outside of merchants, there's no reason to head up north. Occasionally, you'll get an adventurous sort who wants to see the world and once in a while someone will go there for a fresh start but, for the most part, Aeris is isolated. NewTown, on the other hand, is part of the confederation of southwestern towns. It's not as big as West Fork or the other places to the south and east of here but it's still important. There's usually a steady trickle of people going back and forth between NewTown and the other villages. It's possible to go a day without encountering another soul but more than that and there's reason for concern."

With all of us wrapped in our own thoughts, the conversation that had flowed so freely in the early days of the journey slowed to a drip. And then I noticed something. Despite the majestic trees of a new forest to the right of the road, the only sounds were those we were making. No insects. No birds.

"It's blighted," said Samell when I mentioned it. "How or why, I don't know, but this part of The Long Orchard is infected by the same condition that's poisoned the forest all around Aeris."

"This is new. Can't say I noticed one way or another the last time or two I passed by here but I'm sure it ain't been like this for long," said Gabriel.

My unwillingness to accept coincidence as an explanation for anything compelled me to add, "It must have something to do with the reavers. All of this is connected somehow." Strands in a web, but where was the spider? Maybe Bergeron could explain... At that point, I realized I was developing unreasonable expectations about what the Summoner could tell us. If he could answer half my questions, I should consider myself lucky.

Octavius' condition concerned me. Although he wasn't complaining, I knew he was in a great deal of discomfort and the chest injury hadn't improved. In fact, it might have gotten worse. There was nothing any of us could do for him. I had been hoping to hand him over to the care of NewTown's healer but, with that option removed, there was little choice but for him to continue on with us to West Fork. When I asked him if he could make it, he laughed it off but I could tell from the pain in his eyes that it would be difficult.

By nightfall, the normal sounds of the forest had returned but other travelers had not materialized. We were all anxious about what might lie ahead but, due to the lack of sleep the night before, exhaustion overcame apprehension. I did a lot of tossing and turning and probably never got more than an hour of unbroken rest but I wasn't conscious of dreaming or uncovering additional memories. The next morning, as we were about to get underway, a wagon appeared a little way down the road, heading in our direction. Almost as one, the seven of us heaved a collective sigh of relief.

There were four people in the wagon in addition to the driver and the man sitting beside him. I imagined it was cramped inside; it wasn't a large vehicle. The two horses pulling it looked beleaguered. Gabriel motioned us to go to the side of the road and keep our hands away from our weapons. He then moved toward the newcomers and hailed them. It appeared they were acquainted.

The wagon slowed to a stop as Gabriel approached. He and the driver engaged in a short discussion then he waved for me to join him. The finely dressed man sitting next to the driver rose and offered a curt bow as I reached Gabriel's side. The driver, an older, unshaven fellow whose expression hovered between contempt and skepticism, gave me a long look then turned to Gabriel.

"You're claiming she's a Summoner?" He was incredulous. In his position, I might have reacted similarly but I couldn't help but be insulted by his dismissal. The other man continued to watch me with a speculative gaze. He was more open to possibilities than his companion. The men in the wagon didn't move. I could sense apprehension radiating from them. They were ready to fight if circumstances required it. I sincerely hoped it wouldn't come to that.

"I'm not sure I would have believed it if I hadn't seen it with my own eyes," confessed Gabriel. "But that's beside the point. I assume you're on a routine drop to NewTown?"

The well-dressed man nodded. "Unlike you, we don't go all the way up to Aeris. Not much profit in that, is there? What about you, Gabriel? Why are you traveling the road like a vagabond in the company of north-folk and this young 'Summoner', as you call her?"

"NewTown has been destroyed."

That got the undivided attention of both men.

"What do you mean by that?" demanded the driver, looking like he was ready to come down from the wagon and punch Gabriel.

"Peace, Galen," said the other man, although his face was as bleak. To Gabriel, he said, "Perhaps you could elaborate?"

"Burnt to a cinder," said Gabriel. "We just left there yestermorn. All that's left is ashes and bits of bone and it doesn't look like anyone survived. Had to have been done deliberately. Can't see something like that happening accidentally."

"And your Summoner wasn't able to do anything?"

I held my tongue, curbing my impulsivity. I knew this was a tenuous situation. The last thing we wanted was a fight. *Let Gabriel handle this. He knows these people and how to talk to them.* I directed my eyes groundward so they wouldn't see the anger there.

"She can't raise the dead and we didn't get there until long after it was over. We encountered…something else…on the road between

NewTown and Aeris and she got rid of it. And she fought alongside the villagers up north when their town was invaded by a swarm of…creatures." I noticed how Gabriel avoided making references to "earth reavers" or "air reavers." Presumably, that would be like someone in my world claiming their house had been burglarized by leprechauns. NewTown's destruction was undeniable but it might take some convincing to make people believe it had been burned to the ground by fire reavers, especially if there were no survivors to confirm that version of events.

"It's not that I doubt you, Gabriel," said the well-dressed man. "But if things are as you say, we have to see them for ourselves. Although I can't fathom what you might gain from adjusting the truth."

"Are things well in West Fork? No signs of danger?"

"No more so than usual. The landowners are threatening to withhold their militias if the chief elder doesn't relent on his latest tax but, other than that, everything is calm. Certainly no monsters lurking in The Infinite Green, if that's what you're wondering."

"Marlek, we need to get word of this to the council as quickly as possible."

"I agree. But my men and I need to make a firsthand assessment of the situation. If you were in my position, would you just take the word of another merchant about something like this? If it is as you say, we'll lose maybe two days. And if everyone in NewTown is dead, it will hardly matter. Two days doesn't mean anything to the dead."

But it might mean everything to the living in West Fork if the fire reavers are headed there next. That's what I would have said but Gabriel was silent. He bade Marlek a curt goodbye and the wagon continued on its way.

"We'll see them again tomorrow. They'll be at NewTown before nightfall today and will head back to West Fork tomorrow. It's frustrating, I know, but I understand. Itinerant merchants and tinkers are suspicious by nature and we've just woven a tale that's impossible to accept without proof. We'll need other firsthand accounts to bolster ours when we present our story to the leaders."

We continued on our way southward, the weather brightening as the day wore on. As the heat beat down on us and dried out our clothing and packs, yesterday's soaking became a memory. But, with the rations having dried up, our stomachs were rumbling. We camped early to give Esme and Stepan an opportunity to catch a few small animals which they expertly skinned and cooked over a fire. The others wolfed down their portions but I picked at mine. Even having lived in Aeris for a while, I wasn't used to meat this stringy and gamey. It smelled almost rancid and that made it difficult for me to force it down. None of the others seemed to mind and I gave my uneaten portion to Samell, who eagerly accepted it. In return, he gave me the last of his nuts and dried fruits. No matter how much water I quaffed, however, I couldn't quite wash away the taste. I knew I would need to acclimate. A picky eater wouldn't survive on a quest.

The third day out of NewTown dawned bright and clear. We had been traveling for about an hour when we saw another wagon approaching. This one looked much like Marlek's, although there were only four men aboard. Gabriel's conversation with them was more cordial but the result was much the same. Despite their shock at hearing his news, they felt it was necessary for them to visit the village before reporting its fate to the West Fork officials. The offered Gabriel a lift but he declined, preferring to remain with our group. I was grateful for that. Even though the route to West Fork was straightforward (just follow the road...), I felt better having someone familiar with the terrain acting as our guide.

As evening approached, Gabriel informed us that we were about a third of the way between NewTown and West Fork. I asked him if he was surprised we had only seen two wagons thus far.

"Not really. This time of year, ain't much trading going on and without goods to trade, why go to NewTown? This road sees a lot more traffic as the weather cools down. Once the harvests come in, there are plenty of goods to trade. Not this year, though. Or likely ever again. People round these parts are superstitious. They won't want to rebuild in a place that was destroyed like that. Aeris will become cut-off but they're self-sufficient enough that it won't hurt their fortunes if no one ever visits." *If Aeris survives.* It wasn't hard to imagine what had happened to NewTown happening to Aeris. In fact, if I hadn't been there, it might have happened already. And there was no telling if or when the earth reavers would try again.

Around the time we were contemplating stopping for the night, Marlek's wagon overtook us on a southward trajectory. The wagon was moving briskly, the horses at a canter. The merchant ordered his driver to pull over when he saw us. As before, the others in his party remained out of sight.

"You weren't exaggerating," Marlek said once Gabriel and I approached within speaking distance. "Never seen a thing like that before and hope I never see another as long as I live and breathe. I was skeptical about everything you claimed, but now… I can't say what did that to NewTown but I'm more likely to believe a fire reaver than an accident. I've got an expert tracker with me. He did a circuit around the entire town and said that if one or two got away, it was a lot. Most of those people, maybe *all* of those people, died there, burned up in fire and not able to get away. We're not going to get back to West Fork and find a band of refugees camped outside.

"We're headed back. We'll tell the council and chief elder what's happened so he can make policy. If they doubt us, which they well might, you and Berick will be along in the next few days to confirm our story. I'd offer you a lift but we don't have the room." He seemed almost apologetic about that.

"I'll get there. Just a little slower. And, without meaning offense, I'd rather travel with a Summoner. I've already seen what she can do in a fight and, as good as your men might be, I'm more likely to live through an encounter with her by my side than with you there."

Marlek didn't look pleased with Gabriel's assertion but he didn't argue. Instead, he offered a curt farewell before telling the driver to make haste. Within minutes, they had disappeared down the long, straight road, leaving only a cloud of dust behind them.

"An attack on Aeris. An attack on NewTown. Why do I get the feeling West Fork is next?" muttered Gabriel. To me, it was more of a *when* than an *if*. The salient question was whether it would happen before or after we arrived.

Chapter Seventeen: West Fork

Gazing out the window in the middle of the night, I couldn't see much outside of the small pool of light created by the dim streetlight across the road. By day, I would have seen all the familiar sights: the bushes and trees, the crumbling rock wall separating our property from our next door neighbor's, Mr. Donvan's broken-down car parked in his driveway in the same place it had been for as long as I could remember... Night hid so many things but it revealed others.

I couldn't sleep. Insomnia had only become a recent companion but since it had first come calling, it had been a reliable visitor. I was tired all the time now. Tired, frustrated, angry. The targets for my ire were diverse: my parents, my sister, my friends, my teachers. They all had it in for me. Things had gotten worse since the fire and, now that we were back in the repaired house, it was unbearable. I hated this room. I hated this window. I hated this view.

I knew something was wrong with me. Instinctively, logically, I recognized that my thinking was off. The lack of sleep was a symptom, not a cause. The now-familiar rage was building inside me and, like last time, I would have to find an outlet or I'd end up going mad.

For a brief, dizzying instant, the view outside the window changed. Or appeared to change. I was suddenly looking somewhere else, a benighted forest with stunted trees unlike those in my front yard. I blinked my eyes and it was gone. Of course, it had never really been there in the first place. I was starting to see things. This hadn't been the first time and it wouldn't be the last. Time to Google a few of my symptoms and figure out what was wrong with me.

I froze. He was there. A shadow among the shadows, just outside the streetlight's reach. I sensed him more than saw him. The same figure who had been lurking around me for months now, always at the periphery of my vision. No one else noticed him - just me. Maybe he was as elusive and illusory as the forest I had glimpsed. Or maybe he wasn't. Which was the more frightening possibility?

I awoke. It took me a few disorienting seconds to realize I was lying on a bed in one of West Fork's three inns. Another dream. Another memory. Another tantalizing fragment of my past. Not as devastating as some of the other recent ones but no less disturbing. Now, with that memory in place, I recognized the forest I had glimpsed in the vision. The Verdant Blight. The place where I had arrived. There were implications to that but I wasn't sure what they were. How deeply had I been connected to this world before I arrived? And who was the figure who had featured in three of my recovered remembrances?

Esme, who was sharing the cramped bed with me, stirred, her sleep disturbed by my wakefulness. I was grateful to be here, sleeping somewhere other than on the hard ground alongside the long, dusty road but there was something about the nonchalant mood of this great town that made me uneasy. It seemed *wrong* that there should be such ordinariness in a place less than 200 miles from the mass funeral pyre of NewTown. It had taken us a week to travel here from that site of devastation and the images of the burnt village still plagued my darker dreams.

We had reached West Fork late yesterday afternoon. Despite being exhausted, we had headed immediately for the council chambers. Although four groups of travelers had preceded us with news of NewTown's destruction, we had expected our arrival to have been anticipated since we had been the first to come upon the ruins, but we had been turned away, informed that the elders had adjourned for the day. They were aware of the situation and would gladly hear our testimony tomorrow. To me, that was an alarmingly casual attitude for a town whose own future might be in jeopardy. Even Gabriel, who was familiar with the town and the way it worked, had been surprised by the lack of urgency. "It's not that they don't believe what they've heard but, not having actually seen NewTown, it's hard to grasp the horror of what happened." The explanation lacked conviction, however.

West Fork was an impressive place, at least in comparison to Aeris and what I had seen of NewTown. More a small city than a village, its streets were set up on a grid with one set of roads running north-south and another set running east-west. The town hall had been established in the exact center with all the important buildings clustered around it. Residences were farther out, with the most opulent, sometimes two and three-story houses, closer to the town hall while farms were on the outskirts of habitation. A marketplace with about a two-dozen permanent stalls was situated north of the houses but not as far out as the farms. According to Gabriel, about two-thousand souls called West Fork their permanent home while another several hundred passed through it daily. It lay at the crossroads of The Great Southern Road, which led to dozens of small farming communities in the rich plains to the south, and The Western Highway, which took travelers to the major villages and cities to the east. The North-South Road, which we had used to come here, terminated at West Fork but it was infrequently traveled since its only destinations were NewTown, Aeris, and the wilds beyond.

The place where we were staying was called The Lantern's Comfort. It was a grandiose name for a greasy, dirty place. No one else seemed bothered by the lack of hygiene but I was used to Holiday Inns and Radissons. Gabriel, who wasn't staying here with us, had negotiated the rates which Samell had paid from the handsome assortment of coins given to us by the elders of Aeris. There were two rooms, each as shabby as the other. One was for Esme, Alyssa, and me, and the other housed Samell and Stepan. Octavius had left with Gabriel to go in search of a healer. Since each room had only a single bed - actually little more than a thin straw mattress on a rickety wooden frame - Esme and I shared while Alyssa slept on the floor.

Still, even as cramped and uncomfortable as it was, it was vastly superior than sleeping out-of-doors.

Unable to fall back asleep, I rose, slipped on my boots and wandered downstairs and outside. Both moons were up, bathing the village in a soft white light. I gazed at the two placid orbs and wondered, if only for a moment, if there really might be gods up there. If there were, how had they stayed their hands while the population of NewTown had been roasted? That had always been my central problem with religion, how a supposedly "good" god could allow so much evil and suffering to happen under his watch. Priests and ministers babbled about it being a test or the result of humans being given free will but that all sounded like a rationalization. The reality, as I saw it, was that if there was a god, he was amoral and uncaring. Bad things happened because he couldn't be motivated to do anything about them. They were part of the natural order and, as such, were beneath his notice. I didn't believe in a caring, loving god. If there was such an entity, I envisioned him as being so far above us on an evolutionary scale that he would be less concerned about our well-being than we were about ants in the field. But that's not how the people of my world believed and that's not how the citizens of these villages believed. They were invested in the four gods of Sovereign, Concord, Ire, and Vasto.

"Not sleepy?" It was Samell. I hadn't noticed him when I had exited the building.

"No. Another memory." *My past, refusing to let me go. Filling in the blanks slowly and in the most inconvenient manner possible.* "You?"

"Stepan snores. Very loudly. I didn't notice on the road but I certainly did in the room."

I chuckled. I had realized it on the road, which is one reason I had always set up my pallet as far from his as possible.

"What now? What if they don't listen to us?"

He was silent for a moment, considering his answer. "It's out of our control. We tell them what we know, what we saw. It's up to them to decide what action to take. They're sending a delegation north tomorrow - first to NewTown then all the way up to Aeris. At least that means they're taking the situation seriously."

"But they may not have much time!"

"Do you sense an attack? Are you seeing something?"

"No." I checked regularly, using magic to amplify my range. There was nothing specific. A few oddities to the northwest at the fringes of what I could identify. More likely some of the unsavory things said to inhabit The Rank Marsh than a massing of earth, air, or fire reavers. "But those fire reavers are still out there somewhere. Just because I can't find them doesn't mean they're not preparing to strike at West Fork."

"It also doesn't mean they *are* planning to strike at West Fork. We don't know what their goals and motivations are. To us, it seems random and brutal. To them, probably not. Our duty is to find Bergeron and learn what we can from him. The sooner we do that, the better our chances will be to figure out what's going on and whether we can stop it."

I hung my head. He was right of course, but I shouldn't have needed him to tell me. My leadership qualities were sorely lacking in some areas.

"Hey," he said, taking a step closer to me and draping an arm companionably over my shoulder. "Don't get down on yourself about this. You've adapted remarkably well. In less than a season, you've gone from being a naked girl I fished out of the river to a poised young woman with enough magical power to offer us a chance against whatever's threatening us. You don't have to do everything and, more importantly, you don't have to consider it a failure whenever you aren't able to."

"You can be my conscience," I said, forcing a smile that I didn't feel in my heart. But I knew he was right about that as well.

"No, I wouldn't be good at that. But I'll be your shadow."

Shortly after dawn the next morning, Gabriel arrived to escort us to the town hall, informing us that Octavius wouldn't be joining us. "The healer is concerned about the nature of his injuries. Claims not to have seen anything like it before. Looks like a burn but isn't healing like one. So it's safe to say that Octavius won't be joining you when you head out to The Southern Peaks." That left me with four companions and an as-yet undetermined guide. After making our presentation to the elders, hiring someone to take us to Bergeron would be the next task.

The town hall was designed to impress. Built from giant blocks of polished granite while every other structure was constructed from timber, it was easily the tallest and strongest building in West Fork, towering seventy or eighty feet high. However, although I understood this to be an extraordinary feat of engineering for a culture with the limitations of this one, it didn't create the sense of wonder in me that it did in my companions.

Samell noticed my lack of a reaction. "You've seen something like this before?"

"If I could take you to New York City, you'd never recover from the shock. Nearly every building there is bigger and taller than this one and there are some that are, without exaggeration, twenty times as high." The strange things I could remember...

He raised an eyebrow. "Someday, when we have some time, I'd like to hear more about the world you come from, or at least what you remember about it. It sounds like a magical place."

Magical - exactly what it wasn't. There was no magic there. Or was there? It was a question I might never be able to answer and I wasn't sure it was relevant, but some of my fragmented memories caused me to wonder.

Our audience with the town elders didn't inspire confidence that anything was going to be done. They listened to Gabriel's account of our travels and asked a few questions. After being informed that I was a newly arrived Summoner, they showed a little interest but, when I was unwilling to "prove myself" by showing them a parlor trick or two (mainly because I wanted to avoid the headache not because I was shy about using magic), they dismissed me as a charlatan. After spending five minutes with them, I was convinced that no matter what we did or said, it wasn't going to matter. They didn't care what had or hadn't happed at NewTown. They were concerned about West Fork and, to their thinking, the only relevance was that they had lost a trading partner - and not a very important one. They weren't curious about what had destroyed NewTown and couldn't conceive that it might pose a threat to them. Had I validated my legitimacy to their satisfaction, no doubt they would have congratulated me, wished me well, and provided no tangible aid whatsoever.

After exiting the building, I muttered a few choice phrases that caused Gabriel's eyebrows to lift. "I didn't think you knew words like those!" His mock indignation lightened my darkening mood.

"That was a waste of time," I said.

"Not necessarily. You have to understand how these politicians work. They say one thing in public and do another behind the scenes. I guarantee they're worried but can't show it. They have to act like either nothing really happened or, if something happened, it wasn't as bad as we're saying. Public confidence cannot be allowed to waver. Fear could cause civil unrest, undermine their authority, and potentially hurt trade. And they can't acknowledge you without proof of who you are because, as much as they might want to believe you, if it turned out you were a fraud, they would look like fools. And there's nothing a leader hates more than seeming like a fool."

"Are the rulers in the great cities like those men? So venal and calculating? They're not at all like the elders in Aeris," said Samell. Like me, the experience had soured him. In fact, the same could be said of all my companions except Gabriel.

"Oh no, the leaders in cities are much more *political* than those men. At least with these elders, you can speak plainly. With kings and queens, you have to understand diplomacy and courtliness."

"So what's next for you?"

"Rebuilding my fledgling empire, such as it is...or was. I don't relish starting again and with only one hand, but there's no help for it. I'm glad to be alive and grateful to you. Without your help, I doubt I would have made it back from Aeris. Best of luck on the rest of your journey."

I spent some time wandering the streets of West Fork in Samell and Esme's company. We saw things through different eyes. To them, this was a large, spacious place - far more cosmopolitan and sophisticated than their village of birth. To me, it was cramped and squalid. Even the gentry's houses seemed small and inadequate compared to the middle-class homes where I came from. The town smelled of urine and feces - the result of inadequate (or non-existent) sanitation. Open privy pits were scattered all around the village and people could be seen doing their business from the roads. I had to remind myself that this was normal here and that my prejudices were unreasonable. Like Dorothy, I wasn't in Kansas anymore (not that I had ever been there, at least that I recalled).

"How are we going to find a guide?" asked Samell, voicing my unspoken question.

"Maybe the innkeeper will suggest someone." It was a vague hope but the only one I had.

"Try the marketplace," suggested Esme. "They sell everything there. Clothing, jewelry, food, women...why not information?"

The marketplace was an open-air park where about two-dozen merchants and vendors had set up stalls to hawk their wares. Located north of the main town, this spot - about the size of a quarter football field - was one of the most frequently visited places in West Fork and, as a result, it was crowded, noisy, and (especially for someone with an enhanced sense of smell) malodorous.

I had barely set foot into the place when I was accosted by a seedy-looking man with a hooked nose and an artificial smile. He was carrying a long, thin stake upon which were skewered a half-dozen roasted animals. The scrawny things, which looked a little like ill-fed squirrels, were charred in places but the spices they had been marinated in smelled tasty. Against my will, my stomach rumbled. It had been a while since my inadequate morning meal.

The greasy vendor, noting that my eyes were fixed on his wares, sensed a possible customer. "Miss looks hungry," he said. "My habishoms will fill your belly, no?"

I had no idea what a 'habishom' was but the scent was weakening my resolve not to spend anything in the marketplace. Our money was for necessities not frivolities.

"No," said Samell. "And those don't look like any habishoms I've seen."

"They are specially bred for cooking," the vendor argued defensively, pouting excessively to show that he was hurt at being challenged.

"Miss looks famished. They will make her feel good."

I pulled Samell aside. Putting my mouth next to his ear so he could hear me over the marketplace din, I asked, "What is a habishom?"

"It's a rotund rodent that spends most of the day rooting around for grubs in fields and gardens. They're usually fat and sedate but surprisingly difficult to catch. My mother cooks them once in a while. These look more like dwarf rats."

I started at that. Regardless of how good the man's wares might smell, I recoiled at the thought of eating them. The vendor caught my look of disgust and made one last appeal. "These are not normal habishoms. They are…ahem…filigree habishoms."

"They're dwarf rats," said Samell in a tone that brooked no disagreement.

The aggrieved vendor looked shocked. "No! I would never sell rats. They are filigree habishoms."

Samell took my hand and steered me away from the rat salesman. At that moment, I realized the exchanged had not gone unnoticed. We were being watched. A tall, dark-skinned man sitting in an apparently empty stall fixed us with an unwavering gaze. I drew Samell's attention to him. "Who do you suppose that is."

"A soothsayer," said Samell. "You can tell by the necklace. We had one visit Aeris a few years ago."

The jewelry in question appeared to be a collection of uncut gems - rubies, emeralds, sapphires, diamonds, and other exotic stones I didn't recognize - strung together by some form of cordage. It wasn't pretty but it was noticeable. Back in my world, I suspected it would have gemologists salivating.

There was something magnetic about his stare and it drew me in his direction despite Samell's cautioning against it. The soothsayer regarded me calmly; there was nothing menacing in his demeanor. He sat placidly behind an empty table, his back ramrod straight and his face devoid of emotion. His pate was bare and it was difficult to discern his age from his features, although I estimated him to be more than twice as old as me.

Once I had closed to within a half-dozen feet, he rose unhurriedly and executed a formal bow. "Greetings, Summoner."

His salutation caused a ripple of shock. I glanced toward Samell but he didn't seem surprised.

"Don't be alarmed," said the man. "I am Marluk. My sight allows me to see things others may miss."

I extended a hand, which he took after a moment's hesitation, as if unsure what was expected of him. "My name is Janelle. This is Samell." I was about to introduce Esme but then realized she had vanished into the crowd, headed off on her own marketplace adventure.

"You're a soothsayer?"

"Some call me that. I prefer the term 'visionary.' It's a better description of who I am. I know why you are in West Fork, where you are bound, and why you have come to this world. I don't claim to have all the answers you crave but I may be able to give perspective and possibly some aid on your quest. If this interests you, I invite you to visit my abode this evening. I can promise you a good meal and open talk. We have entered an era, Summoner, when no person of conscience can afford to stand by idly. What happened at NewTown is only the beginning."

Chapter Eighteen: The Princess and the Guide

I don't know what I had been expecting but Marluk's home surprised me. Maybe I had thought there would be skulls, bones, beads, pins, and such, but his two-room hovel was as plain and unadorned as any of the other peasants' dwellings I had visited in NewTown. Houses here, like in Aeris, were shelters not places in which lives were built. In the world I came from, homes were central to the social order. Here, where property was primarily communal, they were incidental.

There were no chairs. The four of us - myself, Samell, Esme, and our host - sat cross-legged on the hard-packed dirt floor in a circle. We ate in silence, sipping a tasty broth and wolfing down a vegetarian dish that had been liberally seasoned with exotic spices not unlike those used in the marketplace by the rat seller. It was accompanied by a drink that reminded me of a fermented cider - sweet but slightly tangy. Whatever else he might be, Marluk was a good cook. Then, with our bellies filled and our thirst quenched, it was time for talk.

"Summoner, it is an honor to welcome you to my house," said Marluk, repeating the greeting he had offered when we arrived earlier in the evening. "I have awaited your coming."

"You knew?"

"The signs were there for anyone who understands how to read them. But the old ways are mostly forgotten across the civilized portions of this great land. That's part of the reason why we're in such dire circumstances. Men have lost their way and Summoners have forgotten their role. So we seek for our salvation in those not born of our world."

I suppressed a sigh. I supposed it would have been too much to expect Marluk to be a plain speaker. Self-identified mystics loved riddles. Backus was like that and I guessed the same would be true of Bergeron, if I ever met him. I absently wondered whether, if I was lucky enough to grow old (something I seriously doubted), I would become like that.

"You don't understand me," he said, reading my expression. "Forgive me. I keep my own counsel too often. Let me start from the beginning, at least insofar as there is a beginning. What do you know about the history of Summoners?"

"Not much." Actually, *nothing* would be closer to the truth. Backus had taught me a lot about the gods, a little about the history of Aeris and its place in the world, and almost nothing about Summoners beyond what I needed to know to use my powers.

"I don't pretend to be an expert but, in my land across the great angry sea, all children study history, especially those that, like me, share a privileged upbringing. Summoners have been around for as long as the Unmagical. Their original purpose, as determined by the Quartet, was to act as caretakers for men. The word for *Summoner* in my language is the same as the word for *Servant*. You see, although the gods turn their eyes toward us every day, their day-to-day cares are celestial. A thousand-thousand years for us is like a day for them. So they created Summoners and gave them magic to protect and nurture the rest of their creations.

"Magic - and I'm sure you know this - comes from the transformation of the raw energy of emotion. But emotion is not a clean source. It's a living thing, fed from our passions and desires. Thus, it would be foolish to think of magic as merely a fuel to be harnessed and dismissed. It is, after a fashion, alive. It must be tamed. It must be controlled. And, above all, it must be *managed*. What many Summoners fail to realize is that not every act of magic uses all of the energy. There is always a residue and, when released, it is absorbed by the elements. And that's where the problems begin.

"Once, there were many Summoners - perhaps as many as one for every one hundred people. They lived all over the world, marrying and inter-marrying, passing their abilities to offspring, and doing their duty to Summon another when their mortal coil was at its end. During that age, they controlled the magic. They found ways to siphon off the excess and use it for the good of all people. But, over time, their numbers dwindled. They became less social. And they began to neglect the Excess.

"A Summoner named Alberto, who lived ten hundred years ago, saw the danger. He warned that magic, like any living thing, had the potential for sentience. He coined terms for thinking creatures born of magic. You may have heard of them: reavers and daemons. He explained how magic, brewing in the cauldron of elemental power, would give genesis to these things - animate, puissant expressions of their nature. This is now happening. Excess has reached a saturation point and living, thinking beings are forming from it. But they are malignant in nature, twisted and warped by the way they have grown and developed. And there are far too few Summoners for the threat to be contained or managed. They pose a mortal danger to this world. Extinction is their goal - extinction of every being not of their nature. Plant life is already being subjugated; animal life is being exterminated."

Marluk's tale was so extreme that it might easily have been dismissed as the raving of a madman, but the evidence all around - the reavers, the Verdant Blight, NewTown - confirmed the most outlandish of his statements. Deep down, I suspected this was a man I should listen to and whose words I should take to heart.

"You said you knew I was coming, and you identified me in the marketplace."

Marluk nodded, making a steeple with his index fingers under his chin. At that moment, he looked every inch the mystic. "I have been gifted with sight. I suspect it's not that different from your magical senses although my abilities come from a deep commune with the land and its creatures. I don't know who Summoned you, but the Summoning was felt throughout the world and its ripples died near here. It was then that I knew you must come to West Fork eventually, seeking the only Summoner in the west, Bergeron. I heard the rumors of your arrival last night, little rumblings spoken by the most notorious gossip-mongers, and I knew when I saw you this afternoon who you were. There is something foreign about you. You hide it well and those without attuned eyes might miss it but I can tell you aren't from this world. Only Summoners travel so far."

Even Backus with his great years and experience as a self-trained Summoner didn't know as much as Marluk about the ways of magic and those who used it. A suspicion formed in my mind. "How old are you?" My mother had once said it was impolite to ask a woman that question but she hadn't said anything about a man.

He smiled but deflected the question. "Underneath all the seeming normality in West Fork, there's an undercurrent of uneasiness. What really happened in NewTown? That's what they're whispering. No one can fathom the complete destruction of a village."

"But you can?"

"I can," he said. "I have no desire to see it and I can read in your eyes that to stay away is the right decision. There's nothing we can do about NewTown now. It's gone. But the forces brought to bear against it remain. They fester. And they won't rest. Aeris is too small to be worth their time or effort except for completeness. That makes West Fork the next logical target. And I doubt we will fare better than our neighbors to the north despite our greater numbers and quasi-preparedness. Do you know what caused the destruction?"

Samell cleared his throat before answering in my stead. "We think they were fire reavers but we never saw them. Earth reavers attacked Aeris. Janelle helped drive them back. We were attacked on the road by an air reaver. She killed it. We didn't see what happened at NewTown but it's not hard to guess."

"They are moving in concert. We probably have less time than we hope for or need."

"What about water?" I asked suddenly. Fire, air, earth, water - there were four elements.

"That's the question, isn't it?" replied Marluk. "But maybe we're too far from the seas to know the answer. Or maybe, as I read somewhere, the water reavers went extinct long ago. Reavers have been around for many, many generations but it's only now, with their numbers swelling, that they're becoming aggressive. That, and something else. Something intelligent acting as a guiding force."

"A daemon?" whispered Samell.

"A daemon. And if that's the case, we have much to fear."

I didn't know what a "daemon" was but, since they were pronouncing the word a lot like "demon", I could make a few assumptions. Reavers and daemons? What had I gotten myself into? Not that I'd had much choice in the matter. Had any of this been the result of my free will? Until I recovered my full memories, I wouldn't know the answer to that.

"We need a guide to reach Summoner Bergeron. Can you take us?"

Marluk appeared surprised by the request. "I'm not good on the road," he said. The regret in his voice was genuine. "I think you'd find me more of a hindrance than an asset. But I should be able to find someone with the requisite knowledge of the western countryside to get you there. I doubt anyone around here knows exactly where the Summoner lives but we all have a general idea. He's a recluse and doesn't welcome visitors but I'm sure he's as aware as I am that the rules of the past no longer apply.

"While you're seeking him out, I can remain your eyes and ears in West Fork. I have some influence, although not as much as I might like to have, but I may be able to convince some of the less skeptical men and women of means that the threat is real. Publicly, the elders deny any danger. Privately, I believe they think differently."

His words echoed Gabriel's. "Someone else said something similar, that they had to present an unconcerned charade of calmness to keep from starting a panic."

"Whoever told you that knows the pulse of this town. I may be able to nudge them not to change their 'official' stance but to institute covert preparations. Who can say whether anything would make any difference if an army of fire reavers descends on us? West Fork might be able to raise an emergency militia of 400 souls but I doubt that would be sufficient to stave off destruction…unless a trained Summoner stood with us. And that's why it's imperative for you to reach your goal as quickly as possible and for me to do whatever I can to aid you. To that end, although I can't provide you with a guide, I can offer you a companion: my only daughter, Ramila."

My first inclination was to refuse. The last thing I wanted was someone else to be responsible for. But then I realized how ungrateful that would be and, in truth, I needed all the help I could get. My current companions were resourceful and well-meaning but they were as overwhelmed by the circumstances as I was. I expressed my thanks.

"She is strong with a blade and bow, knowledgeable in flora and poultices and, perhaps most important to your purpose, possessed of some of my…talents. I have not yet spoken to her but I have no doubt she will readily agree. As a princess in exile, she understands duty and will know where her responsibility in this matter lies."

A princess? I supposed it could be a figure of speech but that wasn't how it sounded. Marluk was obviously more than just an obscure soothsayer living in a simple shack in a remote village. But, from the way he had pointedly avoided my question about his age, I suspected that probing him about his history would be fruitless. By the end of the night's conversation, despite repeated efforts on my part, I discovered that to be true. Marluk was willing to talk openly about a great many subjects but his own story wasn't among them.

As we parted for the evening, he promised, "Ramila will come to your inn tomorrow morning. She will bring with her someone willing to guide you to the Summoner. Should you need me, seek me here or in the marketplace. If I'm not in either place, ask after me. I am known and someone will be able to locate me."

On the way back to the inn, Samell asked the obvious question, "Can we trust him?"

Could we? Everything about Marluk seemed sincere but the man's unwillingness to discuss his past made me wary. Then again, I was notoriously close-mouthed about my own history. The soothsayer's secrets might have nothing whatsoever to do with our current situation.

"I don't think we have a choice. I mean, we have to trust some people. We need allies. Besides, thus far our enemies have used straightforward methods to eliminate us. Acquiring agents and laying traps doesn't seem to be their style."

"You're assuming our only enemies are the reavers."

He had a point, but following that path led to paranoia. "I think he's sincere. Secretive but sincere. A little like Backus in that he may be hiding things from us but we probably don't need to know what he's hiding and his desire to help is genuine."

Samell grinned his infectious grin. "That's how I felt but I wanted to make sure I wasn't deluding myself. Something about Marluk inspires trust."

Samell, ever the optimist. And me, the pessimist. I guessed we made a good team.

I was up early the next morning, having gotten a poor night's sleep more as a result of Esme's tossing and turning than because of any nightmares or resurrected memories. Sandy-eyed and scowling, I splashed some cloudy, lukewarm water from a basin on my face, slipped my boots onto my blistered feet, and headed for the inn's common room. Esme and Alyssa were still asleep and the men hadn't stirred from their room yet. The sun was in the process of rising but a thick fog was making it difficult.

The common room, where people from all across West Fork gathered in the evenings for a pint of their favorite alcoholic brew, a hunk of stale bread, and a drunken song, was almost eerie in its early-morning emptiness. The establishment's barman was nowhere to be seen and the dozen tables were cleaned and empty - all except one, that is. Sitting there, waiting patiently was a dark-skinned woman who could only be Ramila. Her companion was familiar and the ghost of a smile creased my features when I saw him.

"Gabriel!" I exclaimed.

"Seems you can't get rid of me," he said. "I thought of offering yesterday once I realized it was going to be near-impossible to restart tinkering without an inventory but I didn't know if you'd want me around. Then when Marluk put out the word…"

I heard the tinker's explanation but my attention was riveted on the girl. Ramila was perhaps the most gorgeous woman I had ever laid eyes on. Without makeup, she could rival the airbrushed images of Hollywood stars. Her deep brown eyes were almond-shaped. Her full lips were the color of ripe plums. And her straight black hair hung loosely over her shoulders. She regarded me with a quizzical but not hostile expression.

"I'm Ramila," she said. Her father's voice had a slight accent. Hers didn't. Of course, I wasn't sure what that meant since I was apparently hearing a magical translation. None of the people around me were speaking the actual words I was hearing. If I thought about that too much, it would blow my mind.

"Janelle," I said, extending my hand. She looked at it as if uncertain how to respond. Gabriel helped out by clasping his hand in mine and shaking heartily. After seeing that, Ramila followed suit. Her grasp was firm and her skin cool and dry.

"Has your father told you what we intend to do?"

"He's told me some, and what he hasn't told me, I've guessed."

"You want to join us?"

"You're a new Summoner seeking to find your footing. I can help. Not with finding Bergeron - that's Gabriel's duty - but there are times when you may find my…insight…helpful. Not to mention my blade." So saying, she reached behind and unsheathed a curved short sword that had been strapped to her back. The speed and fluidity with which she drew it was surprising - one moment, her hands were empty and the next, they were brandishing a beautifully crafted (not to mention deadly) katana.

"She's a feisty one," opined Gabriel, eying the sword. "Much as I respect the weapons skills of your current companions, Ramila is of a different caliber. They're farmers who dabble in hunting. She's a fighter who dabbles in soothsaying."

"You're father said you're a princess." Unsure how to raise the subject subtly, I opted to approach the matter in a straightforward fashion.

"As he reckons it, I am. That has more to do with my bloodline than my upbringing. In the lands my father comes from, he's named a prince. As his daughter, I'm a princess, although if I returned to claim my birthright, they'd probably take my head before placing a crown on it." As interested as I was to hear the rest of the story, she mimicked her father's reticence and didn't elaborate. Perhaps it would come out when she got to know me better.

The three of us sat and talked for a short while, our voices lowered conspiratorially. Although I hadn't initially been sure how Ramila would fit into our group, after only a brief conversation I was convinced she would be an asset. Like her father, she exuded an almost hypnotic charisma. She was smart, humble (despite the "princess" title), and possessed a dry wit. She was guarded but not in a way that made her unapproachable. I was certain my male companions would fall hopelessly in love with her and, although I wasn't bothered about Stepan, thinking of Ramila with Samell didn't please me.

"When do you plan to leave?" asked Gabriel soon after the inn's owner strolled through the common room, gave us a curt nod, and went about the business of getting the place ready for the day's trade.

"I can't think of a reason to delay. Quite the contrary, in fact." The fire reavers, representing the barrel of a cocked pistol pointed at West Fork, made a compelling case for haste. Time wasn't an ally. "Are you ready?"

"Mostly. I'll need to buy provisions - food and so forth - for the journey. It will probably take a week to reach Bergeron, assuming we can find him without having to look for too long, but it would be best to plan for a longer trip in case the unexpected happens." By *the unexpected,* he was alluding to the possibility that we might not be able to find the Summoner at all or, if we found him, he might prove unwilling to help us. I hadn't given either of those possibilities much consideration, not because they weren't realistic but because I didn't have a path forward in the event of a dead end. Yet I had known for a while that I was putting too much importance on one man's helpfulness and knowledge.

"I'll rouse the others. Let's meet back here in a half-cycle and we can get started."

Chapter Nineteen: The Westerlands

We were being followed. I hadn't been certain at first but, now that we were more than a half day out of West Fork, across the road and headed due west, the pursuit was unmistakable. The question, of course, was who was following us and, perhaps more importantly, *why*.

The others weren't aware of the situation. Our trailer was keeping his distance, well out of sight and hearing, but my mind-sense had easily detected him during one of my periodic "sweeps" for nearby dangers. I checked on him periodically but he wasn't closing the distance. When we stopped for a short break, he stopped. I couldn't determine intent but I didn't *feel* anything overtly hostile. It was puzzling. I wondered whether the elders of West Fork were having us followed or whether this might be someone sent by Marluk. Neither of those possibilities seemed likely because I couldn't think of any reason for us to be tracked. I wondered whether Ramila, with her "gifts", sensed him as well but, if she did, she gave no indication of it. Her expression was serene and unchanging, a friendly inscrutability. I wondered if she would ever give any of us a peek beneath her cordial façade.

Crossing the Fork South River proved to be a challenge. Due to unusually high rain amounts in this area during the past two seasons, the ford was washed out and, although not impassable, it would have required swimming - a prospect that didn't excite any of us. So we wandered along the banks headed southward. Our mysterious pursuer matched our pace and course. Whoever he was, he was experienced.

"If we don't find a crossing point soon, do you want to backtrack?" asked Gabriel. "We could head a little north and try our luck with the Fork West River. The only danger is that would put us on the outskirts of The Rank Marsh and, although we're going to have to skim along it closer to the mountains, I'd like to avoid it as much as possible."

I didn't say anything. I didn't want to backtrack. That would mean the loss of at least a half-day. Fortunately, circumstances didn't force the decision. Not long after Gabriel had raised the possibility of turning back, we came to a shallow segment of the river where the current was gentle. It didn't offer a dry crossing but at least we wouldn't get wet above the waist.

As I was about to step into the water, I noticed two odd things simultaneously. The first was the river's smell: a faint odor of rotten eggs. It was so subtle that I doubted any of the others noticed it. The other was that our follower was no longer directly behind us. Somehow, while I hadn't been paying attention, he had crossed the river and was waiting for us to catch up, although his position was about a mile upstream.

"It stinks," I said, wrinkling my nose and pointing at the water.

"I smell it as well," said Ramila who, like me, was holding back from entering.

Gabriel made a show of inhaling. "Don't smell anything. But it wouldn't surprise me if you two do. This here river is a tributary of the Fork West, which runs through The Rank Marsh. Who knows what it picks up there. This far away, I imagine it's safe. Just don't drink it if you're worried, although folks from West Fork bathe in it."

"We're being followed."

That pronouncement stopped everyone. When I realized what they thought that meant, I hastily amended my words. "Not anything dangerous. One man, I think. He's been trailing us since West Fork."

"I wondered if he would come," said Ramila quietly, almost to herself. Then, louder and with more assurance, she added, "He means no harm. He has sworn a vow to keep me safe and this is his way of honoring it even though he promised my father he wouldn't come *with* me."

I was relieved and annoyed in equal parts. I didn't mind that Ramila had secrets but if they interfered with what I was trying to do...

"Who is he?" I asked.

"Willem. A captain of the West Fork Watch. He...is courting me. He wants to marry me but my father doesn't approve. No doubt one of the reasons I was sent on this mission was to separate me from Willem."

Wonderful. Now I was caught in the middle of a romantic drama. If we had been closer to town, I would have taken Ramila back to Marluk and let them work out the situation. But I couldn't afford to lose what would amount to two days, not with West Fork's future so uncertain. This would be up to me to resolve. One thing was certain - I couldn't have this man dogging our footsteps all the way into the Westerlands. Not only that but, by himself, no matter how capable he might be, he represented easy prey for a reaver.

"Go get him," I said to Ramila. She was surprised, although I couldn't decide whether her reaction resulted from the command itself or the steel in my voice. She wasn't used to being told what to do. "Bring him back here." When she hesitated, I added, "*Or I will.*" The remnants of my earlier sunny disposition were in tatters.

After crossing the river, we waited, munching on this world's answer to trail mix and engaging in small talk.

"Are you going to send him back?" asked Samell, his voice low enough that the others couldn't hear.

I didn't know. I wanted to get a measure of him, to see if he seemed like the kind of person who would be good in a crisis. I said as much.

"Ramila will be more comfortable with him along and more biddable. If you send him away, she may resent you and there's no guarantee he'll go anyway."

"And conspire to defy Marluk? Our most influential ally thus far?"

"If Marluk is a true soothsayer, he knew this would happen. In fact, he may have manipulated it into happening. Maybe this is his way of determining the man's worth. If you decide to admit this Willem into our company, I doubt he'll fault you for it. If he had wanted to keep the captain away from Ramila, he would have found a more sure way to do it."

Samell's words made sense. Marluk was no ordinary man. Even without supernatural foresight, an insight into human nature would have shown him Willem's likely path. He hadn't blocked it. I wondered if that had occurred to Ramila. Of course, without understanding the whole story, it was impossible to know how accurate Samell's assessment might be.

It didn't take long for Ramila to re-appear, now striding alongside a tall, lanky man who was wearing a vest of chain-link mail and black leather pants. Even at a distance, I could tell that Willem was an imposing presence. He had a full, well-maintained beard and his long, ebony hair was pulled back into a single ponytail that trailed halfway down his back. His eyes were deep blue and his fair complexion had been darkened to bronze by sun exposure. A huge broadsword was strapped to his back and daggers were sheathed on the outside of both boots. Although it was difficult to say for sure, I guessed he was probably several years older than Gabriel, making him the eldest member of our group by a fair amount. I wondered if that was going to be a problem. How was he going to feel about taking orders from a girl who was more than a decade his junior?

When he got close enough, I was able to see that what I had mistaken for a scowl was a more serene expression. Despite his warlike appearance, he exuded an almost ethereal calm. He greeted me with a smile that touched not only his lips but his eyes. As I shook his rough, calloused hand, I instinctively knew why someone as young and beautiful as Ramila might be attracted to him. I wondered how Marluk saw Willem - as potentially worthy of his daughter or an interloper?

"Willem is a wanderer who only recently settled in West Fork. He has seen nearly as much of the world as my father, although different parts of it. He doesn't speak the Common Tongue well, however, so he won't join in many conversations. When he's with people who speak his language, he talks a lot. Most of the time, he's not the strong, silent type. Strong - yes. Silent - no."

Having caught the gist of her words, Willem chuckled. It was a deep, pleasant sound.

"Welcome to our company," I said, making a stab at being hospitable. Expressions of surprise all around greeted my pronouncement. For a moment, I thought I had made a terrible gaffe then I realized what had happened. It was easy to forget how magic influenced my ability to communicate.

"You speak my native language?" asked Willem, his voice a bass rumble.

Apparently, I did. Or at least that's what everyone heard. How to explain this…?

"A Summoner's gift. We understand all languages." The problem for me wasn't knowing what I was saying but in what language I was saying it. I could see how that might become confusing.

"I'm not surprised," mused Samell. "I thought it was odd how easily you picked up our language and there were a few times when it appeared as if the way your mouth formed words didn't match what you were saying."

"It makes communication less difficult," said Ramila. The way everyone looked at her, I suspected she was trying another language. For me, the words were translated into English without inflection so I couldn't be sure.

"It certainly does."

She nodded with satisfaction, as if I had passed a test. "Then, since you have a better understanding of Willem than even I, you can translate when he finds it difficult to express himself."

"You're here against Marluk's wishes?" I asked.

"Maybe. Maybe not. He's a difficult man to figure out, that Marluk. He says I'm not worthy of Ramila, that she was born to be with someone of noble birth, not a rootless wanderer. But I'm wondering if all of this is some kind of test of my worth. He doesn't seem like a man who cares about class. For a mystic, he's practical. And it would be practical to want his daughter bonded to someone who could use his hands and defend what's his. That's me."

"I've seen you around," said Gabriel. "Friends of mine spoke well of you so it's good to have you along. I have a suspicion that, where we're going, we'll be able to use another sword arm."

That didn't inspire confidence. It was worth remembering, I suppose, that a river wasn't likely to be the most formidable obstacle on the path to Bergeron.

For the rest of the day, the trek took us across plains where the brush grew nearly to my shoulders. It was slow going as some of the seemingly innocuous grasses had leaves as sharp as blades. These had to be cut away to proceed. Gabriel had brought a scimitar designed for this but Ramila and Willem grumbled about dulling and nicking their blades for such a mundane purpose. My companions from Aeris had no such compunctions since their weapons were of a cruder sort to begin with and could easily be re-sharpened with a whetstone.

When it came time to camp, we cleared a sizable swath of grass, set up a fire for cooking, light, and warmth, and determined a guard rotation. No one deemed this an especially dangerous place to spend the night and a quick scan with my mind-sense confirmed this. After the sun set, the air temperature dropped precipitously, an indication that the warmer part of the year was coming to a close. We needed the fire, which burned hot and gave off a lot of smoke. It had to be fed constantly because, although there was abundant food for its sustenance, it consumed the grass and brambles greedily.

"Feels a little like Aeris during the Fading season. At harvest's end, we'd light bonfires in the cleared fields and spend all night gathered around them, singing songs and toasting the year's yield. I wonder if they'll be doing that this year." Samell's tone was wistful. It sounded to me like he was describing what the pagans used to do on Halloween.

"I've seen some strange Fading customs in my travels," said Willem. His words were halting, making me think he was speaking in what Ramila had called the 'Common Tongue.' "But almost everyone across the world celebrates the harvest. Some with fire. Some with much drink. Some with other pleasures." He didn't go into details about the latter for which I was grateful.

My time sleeping on a bed in West Fork hadn't softened me. I had spent enough nights on the ground since leaving Aeris that the hard, unyielding surface no longer affected my sleep. The day's travels had left me exhausted and I drifted off almost immediately. Since I hadn't been assigned watch duties - one of the perks of being a Summoner - I slept the whole night through, uninterrupted by nightmares or memories. Such a span of peace was unusual for me. When I woke, the rest of the party was getting ready to travel. The fire had been stamped out and pouches and packs were being re-tied.

Day two of the journey had us turn from a westerly course to one south of west. Gabriel's intention was for us to skirt The Rank Marsh's southern boundaries then swing back to the north after we were past it. The most direct route to our goal - following the river to the pass into The Southern Peaks mountain range - would have taken us through the heart of the swamp, something Gabriel wasn't willing to chance.

"There's two issues with that place, both of which have to be considered. The first is the lack of firm, safe ground. It's a quagmire with plenty of places to trap the legs and pull you under. Travelers have been lost in The Rank Marsh because they stepped in the wrong place and there ain't no road or path to mark where the safe ground is. Some time back, an expedition went into The Rank to blaze a trail. Ain't no one heard from them since.

"Then there are the rumors of *a thing* that lives in the bogs. At one time, I might have dismissed those as fantasies but, after what I've seen in the past weeks... Anything that lives in The Rank Marsh ain't human and, at least based on the legends and tales, the swamp-creature dines on more than just a man's flesh. For obvious reasons, that ain't something we'd like to meet so, whether it exists in reality or just in stories, it's better to stay away and not find out than get into a situation where we wish we didn't know the truth."

As far as I was concerned, those were ample reasons to avoid The Rank Marsh, even if it added (as Gabriel estimated) two days to our trip. As urgent as circumstances were, there were some chances not worth taking. Reavers weren't the only dangers in the wilderness.

"What do you think of him?" asked Samell later in the morning, referring to Willem. He and I were in the rear of our column with Gabriel and Willem leading the way, hacking and slashing their way through the thick, tall grasses. Stepan was paired with Ramila in the second row with Alyssa and Esme immediately in front of us.

"I feel more confident with him in our party but I wonder why Marluk didn't simply send him along. The things we don't know concern me. It may be none of my business and it may not be relevant to our mission but that's not an assumption I feel comfortable making."

"I understand. But it's good to have a seasoned traveler and fighter. I think things might have been different on the road to NewTown if Ramila and Willem had been with us when we encountered the air reaver. That battle exposed us as...not being adequate to be your defenders. Those two may make up for what the rest of us lack." For the first time, I realized how much the fight with the air reaver had shaken his confidence. I had been so absorbed with my own failings during the combat that I hadn't had time to consider my companions' reactions. Before the battle, they had believed they could protect me. Now they knew differently.

"I won't deny that Ramila and Willem will be helpful in a fight if it comes to that. But there's a lot more to what we're doing than swordplay. I need people around me I can trust. Without you and the others from Aeris, I would have been alone and lost. I don't know this world, its customs, its geography… By myself, I wouldn't have beaten the air reaver. Don't underestimate your contribution. I *need* you, Samell. All of you from Aeris who gave up your futures to travel with me, but you most of all." I hadn't meant to get that personal but the words spilled out and I couldn't take them back. Surely by now he knew how much I relied on him, how much I *had* relied on him since the day he and Esme saved me from the river.

Samell appeared thunderstruck by the admission. "Thank you. I… that means a lot to me."

Then, unbidden and unwanted, another memory crept up from the recesses of my mind to ambush me.

Jarrod's warm breath caressed my neck as he nibbled on my earlobe, his soft voice whispering, "That means a lot to me, that you don't want us to end."

It was the day before graduation and everything between us was going so well. My boyfriend. My first boyfriend. I hadn't said it out loud but I repeated the word over and over in my mind. We had kissed. He had said he wanted to spend the summer with me. I was too flustered to say anything.

"Seventy-two days until I leave for college. There's a lot we can do in seventy-two days," he said.

Chloe Wendel wouldn't be thrilled about this development. Nor would my sister. I didn't know what Megan's hang-up was about Jarrod. Hardly a day went by when she didn't tell me to "dump the loser" or that I should find someone more like me, whatever that meant. Chloe's motives, on the other hand, were transparent. She wanted Jarrod for herself. Then, with a flash of inspiration, I wondered if Megan was after the same thing. Only then did I attribute meaning to all the looks she and Jarrod had given one another. In trying to get me to break with Jarrod, was my sister looking after my best interests or her own? After all, she and I had never been close and only someone who didn't know us would describe our relationship as "friendly."

My mood disturbed, I gently disentangled myself from Jarrod's embrace. He appeared annoyed. My inner voice warned me: Finally getting somewhere and now you're pulling back. Always pulling back. He's not going to wait around forever. You know what he wants. You know what they all want. Chloe wouldn't make him wait.

"What's wrong?" he asked.

"What do you think of my sister?"

"Megan? She's hot."

Wrong answer. What guy tells his girlfriend that he thinks her sister is hot (even if it was true)? But that was Jarrod. He wasn't known for filtering his speech. Perhaps recognizing his blunder, he hastily added, "But you're hotter."

I smiled but the smile was as shallow as his tact. The worm of doubt had begun to gnaw into my thoughts. And now, as I pulled myself free of the memory's grip, I knew how this would all turn out. The dreamy bliss of a summer with Jarrod would collapse. He would go to Chloe and Megan. And I would end up here after some sort of ugly confrontation.

"Another message from Janelle-who-was?" asked Samell as I again became aware of my current surroundings. The two of us had stopped while the remainder of our group continued forward. They were some two-hundred feet ahead.

"She picks the most unpredictable times to assert herself."

"Was it something I said?"

"Actually, it was. Associations can trigger memories. Words. Sights. Smells." Pieces coming together. So much still unknown. I didn't feel like talking about it now, though - not even with Samell. Absorbing memories always left me feeling drained and distant. "Let's hurry to catch up with the others."

The rest of the day passed uneventfully as we trudged across monotonously similar territory for hour after hour. Progress was slow because of all the razor grass and brambles that had to be cleared away. We were leaving an obvious trail but no one was following us. The view was the same in every direction - a unbroken plain of browning, shoulder high vegetation. At least there was plenty of small animal and insect life. The Blight hadn't stretched out its arm this far.

The day was pleasantly warm but the sun's angle in the sky was more obviously lower than it had been earlier in the season. As the glowing orb began its final approach toward the horizon, we stopped to make camp for the night. A significant area had to be cleared away to allow room for a fire and everyone to lie down comfortably. As with the previous night, there was abundant material to feed the flames but nothing substantial. It was necessary to constantly feed the blaze to keep it from sputtering and dying.

I caught the scent soon after we had stopped - a distant, fetid tang carried on a wayward breeze. It was similar to what I had smelled in the river but with hints of carrion to enrich the stench. My mind-sense identified hints of a strange, non-human life but at this distance, it was hard to pinpoint.

"How far are we from The Rank Marsh?" I asked as we sat around the fire and gazed into the deepening darkness. The air was definitely chilly; I was grateful for the warmth of the flames, which popped and crackled happily as Esme and Willem took turns dumping bundles of straw, razor grass, and "pricklers" onto them.

"Reckon about two cycles," said Gabriel, chewing on a chunk of jerky. "Assuming the weather holds, we should get there by midday."

"I don't like the way it smells."

His answering chuckle was short and mirthless. "If you don't like it now, you *definitely* won't like it tomorrow." *Something to look forward to.*

Once I had finished eating, I curled up in a ball and drifted off to sleep, my head pillowed on my provisions sack and a threadbare blanket draped over my upper body to help the fire ward off the chill. It was amazing how cold it got out in the open once the sun had set.

Memories didn't chase me that night but something else did - something that made me starkly afraid of what might happen on the morrow when we passed close to The Rank Marsh.

Chapter Twenty: The Presence in the Rank

With every passing minute, the stench grew stronger and, with it, the unease that plagued my mind-sense. There was something out there in The Rank Marsh, something whose nature ran contrary to the natural laws. It was ugly and perverted, the twisted result of dwelling too long surrounded by stagnation and decay. I didn't know what it was but I was sure I didn't want to encounter it up close. And it knew I was here.

Last night as I had slept, its mind had stretched out to mine, perhaps sensing that I was different from the usual humans that skirted its realm. I had recoiled from it but not before we each took the measure of the other - me frightened, it hungry. I could sense its terrible need. It wanted to devour me in ways I couldn't begin to understand. It didn't just want my body. It wanted so much more.

I considered asking Gabriel to detour around the marsh altogether, but it wouldn't matter. The creature wouldn't be constrained by the physical boundaries men had put on the swamp. Like any animal, it could venture outside its territory if it sensed prey. The swamp was its lair but that didn't mean it wouldn't pursue me even if I avoided it by a wide margin. Short of turning back, there was no safe route. Somewhere, the fire reavers were massing for their next attack. I couldn't sense them but I *knew* this. Time wasn't my ally. I had to push forward even though the dweller in the marsh had my scent.

Samell had been watching me with concern all morning. He knew everything wasn't right (not exactly a unique situation on this journey). He had gotten to know me well enough since my arrival to read my moods and he recognized this wasn't the byproduct of a nightmare or a bad memory. I motioned for everyone to stop. They had to know. They had to understand that they were approaching danger.

"Gabriel's rumors about The Rank Marsh are correct. There's something out there. Something ugly and dangerous. Something that's hunting me now. We have two choices: forge ahead knowing it will probably catch us or turn back for West Fork and hope it will give up the chase."

"If we head directly south from here…" began Gabriel.

I cut him off. "It lives in the marsh but it can leave. I sense its relentlessness. It won't give up. Taking a more southerly route will merely prolong the journey not prevent an encounter."

"How far away is it?" asked Willem. "The Rank Marsh is a big place. If it's up by The Long Orchard, we may be well to the west before it makes it this far south."

The strange thing was that, although my mind could sense its presence, I couldn't pinpoint its location. North and west of our present position, that was all. There was no sense of distance. It was almost as if it wasn't physically rooted to this world.

"I don't know. It's somewhere in the swamp but, beyond that, I can't tell. If it's not between us and where we're going, it soon will be."

"Gabriel, may I make a suggestion?" asked Willem.

Our one-armed guide nodded, obviously feeling out of his depth.

Willem bent close to Ramila and spoke quietly to her in his native language. I knew what she was going to say before she translated. "Willem suggests that we head directly for the marsh. These grasses and brambles are taking too long to cut through. As we get close to the swamplands, the underbrush will thin out and, as long as we don't go too far in, the soft ground won't slow us. That should enable us to move more quickly without having to worry about being sucked under."

Although the thought of willingly approaching The Rank Marsh sounded counter-intuitive, I couldn't deny the logic of Willem's proposal. At this point, speed was the most important thing and I didn't think it was substantially more dangerous to skirt the swamp for an extra day.

Willem turned to me. The ease with which he spoke told me that he was using his language. "In my land, we have heard of creatures like these. They live deep in places where men don't venture. We call them soul-rippers. They rarely bother with people but legends say they crave Summoners and those with magic and second sight. While you are undoubtedly their target, Ramila may also be in danger. I don't know if we'll be able to defend you against this thing but we'll certainly try."

I turned to Gabriel. "If we follow Willem's suggestion, how long until we reach the mountains?"

He considered. "Two, maybe three days around the marsh then another day crossing the plains. So figure about four days if nothing slows us down."

"Any counter-opinions?" I asked.

No one said anything. They didn't know the terrain. They were relying on Gabriel's knowledge of the area, Willem's experience, and my mind-sense. They would do what I decided. I was the leader and if I chose wrong, I could get us all killed. Or maybe just me. Willem could be right. Perhaps the soul-ripper, if that's what it was, didn't care about my defenders.

"Then let's do it," I said and, without another word, our new course was established.

The day passed by under a cloud of gloom and the weather reflected our mood with darkening skies in advance of a persistent drizzle that started in the early afternoon. It made travel miserable but didn't slow us down. I continued monitoring the soul-ripper but, aside from the constancy of its presence, I couldn't read much. If it was moving closer, I couldn't tell. Nothing else of interest was in the immediate vicinity - no reavers and no other followers from West Fork.

We reached the edges of the swamp in the mid-afternoon and, as Willem had predicted, travel became easier. The razor grasses thinned out as the ground became soggy and we were able to double our pace. The smell was overpowering - that peculiar stench unique to bogs of decomposing vegetation and the gasses given off by the decaying process. My heightened sense of smell made it difficult to keep down the contents of my stomach.

The overcast sky necessitated an early stop as none of us wanted to venture on past darkness in this terrain. It was obvious that a fire was going to be difficult with the pervasive dampness and lack of fuel conspiring against it but we needed the warmth. Hypothermia was a legitimate concern in these conditions. Not only were we all soaked through but the temperature was dropping precipitously. This was the coldest I had experienced since coming to this world. Underneath the animal hide cloak I had donned, I was starting to shiver. It was time to make use of my magic. Something simple that hopefully wouldn't precipitate a headache.

I knew how to make fire. That was one of the first lessons Backus had taught me. The issue wasn't kindling the flame but keeping it going without demanding my constant attention. I considered the problem while the others made camp and, when I had arrived at a possible solution, I asked them to clear an area for the fire and caused it to spring to life. No one showed any surprise. With the exception of Ramila and Willem, they had all seen me use magic and the two newcomers had accepted my legitimacy without question.

The flames were duller and ruddier than those of a normal fire because they were fed not by air and wood but by the earth underneath them. This fire used clay and mud for its fuel; it would char them and turn them to ash the way a normal fire would do with sticks and brush. It would burn until I commanded it to stop, reaching ever deeper into the earth as the layers above it were consumed. It was self-perpetuating, requiring nothing of me to remain lit and, although it was dimmer than a regular fire, it gave off as much (or possibly even a little more) heat. And my head was fine. I felt a flush of satisfaction at what I had accomplished. Even the longest journeys started with a few small steps.

We gathered around, letting the warmth from the reddish-brown flames wash over us. I slipped off my boots to let my pruned toes dry out. Samell, sitting to my left and rubbing his hands briskly together, said, "It's a nice fire. I guess having a Summoner along is good for something." His lips quirked upward as he took my left hand in his right and squeezed.

I smiled. It was so rare that the serious young man cracked a joke that it would have been rude not to react. The physical contact, however, caused my heart to flutter. It was as unexpected as it was welcome.

"What else can you do?" asked Esme, digging into her pack to get some trail food. The rest of us followed suit.

It was a good question; I wished I knew the answer. "That's why we're on this trip, and the real question might not be what I can do but what I can do without being incapacitated by a headache. I'm no good to anyone if I'm unconscious or overcome by pain." Making fires was one thing. Fighting reavers, daemons, and soul-rippers was another.

"Did you speak to my father about these headaches?" asked Ramila.

I thought back to the night I had spent in Marluk's company. "I don't think it ever came up."

"A pity. He's wise in the lore of plants and healing and may have been able to suggest something. With headaches, there are many remedies. When one doesn't work, another might."

At the moment, I was pinning all my hopes on Bergeron. If he wasn't able to solve the problem… I doubted that a soothsayer would be able to cure an affliction where a wild wizard and trained Summoner had both failed.

"Could you make the trail food taste any better?" asked Alyssa with a giggle, spitting a seed into the fire, where it flared briefly.

I smiled but couldn't help but wonder about the question. Could I? Could I give taste to the bland food? Could I transform dirt into something edible? It was obvious to envision how magic could be useful in battles but what about its more esoteric implications? So much to learn, so many areas to explore...

Wrapped in cloaks and blankets dried and warmed by the fire, we hunkered down for the night with Ramila and Willem taking first watch. I lay in cocoon of silence broken only by the crackling of the flames as they drew sustenance from the ground. A chorus of snores soon joined the fire's peculiar melody. With my mind, I reached out tentatively toward the blackness of The Rank only to draw back when I sensed the *presence*. It was out there, somewhere, watching. If it didn't know where we were, I didn't want to call attention to our location by seeking it openly. Did it even have a physical essence or did it lurk in some non-material plane?

Sleep resisted me, pushing me away every time I got close. The smell was part of the problem; my mind was unusually restless. As I lay quietly, I picked up snippets of the whispered conversation between Ramila and Willem. I felt like an eavesdropper but, my curiosity piqued and my ability to understand unimpeded by a language barrier, I listened anyway.

Most of what they were saying didn't relate to the expedition, at least at first - the kinds of inconsequential things close friends would say when they had hours ahead of them and wanted to fill up the darkness with the comfortable sound of each other's voices. Then they spoke about Marluk's motivations; both were sure this was a test of some sort - that he was probing to learn how devoted Willem was to Ramila. Then the conversation turned to me.

"She's not what I expected. Or at least not what I supposed when my father told me I would be accompanying her."

"How so?"

"She's...soft." As soon as she uttered the word, I felt a flush of anger. *Soft?* Would she still think that if she had seen me in Aeris or on the road to West Fork? "I expected someone battle-hardened. A natural leader whose voice would get things done."

"You misread her," said Willem. "Remember, she is not of this world. Her former life still clings to her like a shawl. But there is steel in her. I'm surprised that someone with your talents would take such a superficial view. Look deeper, my love. See her for what she truly is. It may surprise you."

His words calmed the irritation that Ramila's comment had instigated.

"I don't mean to disparage her," said Ramila. "But she seems more like a pampered princess than someone fit for the hardships that lie ahead."

"Ahhhh. I see where this comes from! I noticed the resemblance to Delphine as well, but they're very different people. Don't let your dislike for your cousin color your feelings about Janelle. Delphine is a 'pampered princess' unfit for most any kind of hardship. I knew that about her after spending only a few minutes with her."

"I would never..."

"Not consciously, perhaps, but you have a tendency to judge harshly and delay reversing your opinions when warranted. However similar their faces and forms, Janelle and Delphine aren't related. They couldn't be. They aren't from the same world."

Although the conversation gave me new insight into Ramila and what she thought about me, I tuned it out when they began talking about intimate things no outsider had the right to overhear. Soon they were cuddled together, kissing and embracing. I closed my eyes tight and wished for something to take my mind away from the present - either a memory or a dream. It didn't take long for the smell of the swamp to grant my wish.

I was 13 years old. It was my second day at "Camp Harmony", a traditional ordeal foisted on all eighth graders at my school since time immemorial. School policy decreed that, during the third week of September, all students in the science/social studies/English classes of

Gilbert, McElroy, and Swiezicky would make the long trip to the New Jersey Pine Barrens where they would spend a week without television, cell phones, and all the other comforts of home. This was deemed by someone in authority to be an "educational experience" and it took an act of God (or a parent's refusal to sign the permission slip) to get out of it. Needless to say, neither God nor my parents were in sympathy with my desire to stay home.

It wasn't all bad, though. There were six students to a cabin (plus one adult supervisor) and, for the most part, we were given autonomy about how to spend our non-structured time. We had one two-hour class each morning, one two-hour class each afternoon, and a "group activity" after dinner. Two of my best middle school friends were with me during the Camp Harmony week: Chloe Wendel and BethAnn Avery. BethAnn preferred to spend her free time in self-imposed solitary confinement. She sat on her bunk in the unheated cabin wearing an oversized cardigan and reading Jane Austen. Chloe and I chose the outdoors (primarily because it smelled less like must and mildew). We both liked sneaking beyond the "allowed areas" and roaming out into the wilds. Truthfully, the act of disobedience was more exhilarating than the fresh air. Rule #1 was "Don't go outside the marked areas" so, of course, that's immediately where we headed.

Camp Harmony was situated in a part of the Pine Barrens dominated by a large cedar swamp. The characteristic smell of a bog hung in the air. It wasn't exactly unpleasant as long as I didn't breathe too deeply. The swamp itself was only dangerous if you didn't pay attention. The trees rose from hummocks covered by moss and, while there were areas of quagmire, they weren't likely to suck in anything more significant than a loosely-tied boot. The water was deep enough in the rust-colored lakes to drown in but only if you were stupid enough to swim out too far. I wasn't about to get wet in 55-degree water. The biggest concern was a twisted ankle. There were countless places where a person could misstep.

This afternoon, I was on a pitcher plant expedition. Pitcher plants were small carnivorous plants that grew in cool, swampy areas. They were also endangered. One of my teachers, the irrepressible woodsman Mr. Parker, had seen a large one this morning and, following his admittedly vague directions, I went looking. I was driven more by morbid curiosity than anything else - I wanted to see one of these insect-devouring vegetables for myself. I suspected it wouldn't live up to its reputation, but how else was I going to kill the two hours between my afternoon class and dinner?

Chloe had fallen so far behind me that I could no longer see her. She moved slowly in the swamp, overly concerned (even on the dry paths) about getting her shoes muddy. She had lacked the foresight to come prepared with a pair of boots like everyone else. So, for all intents and purposes, I was alone. It was just me, the chirping birds, the small animals rustling through the reeds... and the peculiar man squatting by a dead stump directly ahead.

He looked beyond odd in his ill-fitting clothing and I felt a prickling of dread. He was stooped, wizened, and very dirty. He peered at me through squinty eyes. I recognized immediately what he was - a "Piney", one of the civilization-averse, inbred denizens of the deeper Pine Barrens who were whispered about around campfires, usually in association with kidnapping, rape, and the Jersey Devil. My mother's admonition not to talk to strangers echoed in my brain. People didn't get stranger than this.

"You're late!" he muttered, almost to himself. Then, after sizing me up again with an indiscreet stare - an act that sent a shiver up my spine - he spat, "Too young! Too young! Not yet ripe! I've come to the wrong time!"

I stood rooted to the spot, mouth agape, unable to either advance or flee. Somewhere behind me I heard Chloe shout a curse word - apparently she had misstepped.

The man continued to look at me, running a tongue over toothless gums, as he scratched at the stubble on his chin with long fingernails.

I could tell he was wrestling with a decision. Kill me and dismember me or just kill me?

"Come with me, girl! Come with me or I'll just have to find you again."

He stared at me with an intensity that bored into my soul. Strangely, though, there didn't seem to be any malevolence there. Instead, perhaps…desperation?

I found enough strength to break the paralysis and get my limbs moving. I began backing away from him. Initially, he didn't move, opting to continue watching me. Then we he realized he might lose me, he started forward. His movement provided me with the impetus I needed; I turned and fled at full speed, heedless of the uneven ground and the squelching mud. I only stopped when I nearly ran headlong into Chloe.

Out-of-breath, I tried to tell her to run but, when I glanced behind me, there was no one there. My friend regarded me with a mixture of bemusement and surprise before smiling and saying, "Met the Jersey Devil, didya?"

Then I woke up.

The night was still cold and cloudy. The fire burned healthily. But time had moved on. Ramila and Willem were asleep, lying close together across the camp from where I was, the fingers of his left hand entwined with those of her right. Samell and Esme were to my immediate right and left, the former snoring lightly and the latter curled into a ball. Gabriel stood guard alone, his back to me as he gazed into the darkness of The Rank.

I tried to go back to sleep but to no avail. My mind was active, reliving the new memory and fitting it into place in my fragmented past. Suspicion was beginning to dawn. Was this the same stranger who had watched me from the street outside my house? The same man who had pursued me on the night when I had been brought to this land? I didn't know. Perhaps there were other lost memories that would provide more clues. But I was almost certain that this person, or these people, didn't come from my world. They had been sent to watch or stalk me. And if it was possible for them to cross over, could I also go back? Perhaps I wasn't as trapped as I had previously believed.

Chapter Twenty-One: The First Day of Fading

"It's the first day of Fading," announced Samell conversationally as we started the day's journey. The proclamation didn't surprise me. The chilly gloom of the swamp seemed suitably Halloween-ish. *The first day of autumn.* It put me in mind of pumpkins, ghosts, and ghouls. This world might not have the first of those (at least not that I'd seen so far) but I wasn't so sure about the other two.

Fading: the time when life, light, and vitality all dimmed as the angle of the sun dropped lower in the sky. Fields were harvested and homes were prepared for the season of Ice. I wondered how cold it would get here and hoped I might live long enough to find out. Back in my old world, autumn had been my favorite season. I loved the colors, the rich smell of wood fires on cool nights, and the general feeling that things were going into hibernation. "Fading" was an apt description. I wondered whether the leaves here would change color or drop. So far, I hadn't seen signs of it but it had been over a week since I'd been around a forest.

I was grateful for the cloak I had brought with me. Although made from the hides of small animals, it had been brushed with some kind of resin that made it water-resistant. It had kept me from being soaked yesterday and today, as we walked through a thick fog, it deflected the worst of the chill.

"How long until Aeris' harvest?" I asked.

"Not long," replied Samell. "It varies from year-to-year depending on the weather. This year has been warm so far so the harvest will be later. I'm not sure whether there will be a festival, not after losing so many people and with the danger not past. They may be content to strip the fields of their yield and start getting this ready for the cold weather. Plus, they'll have to send wagons out farther this year to get cords of unblighted wood. The more the Blight spreads, the harder it is to get wood for building and burning. Once everything is blighted,

Aeris may die. You can't survive Ice in this part of the world without a healthy supply of wood for every house and the smoke from blighted wood can kill."

Not me. But I understood his worry. Only the fringes of The Verdant Blight still contained untainted wood. In another few years, that might all be gone. Then what? Even if The Long Orchard remained viable, it was too far away to supply every house in Aeris for an entire cold season. The men and women folk of Aeris would have to relocate. It was a depressing prospect and aggressive reaver patrols could hasten its occurrence.

Meanwhile, *it* was still out there. Unchanged, at least insofar as I could tell, from yesterday. Were we walking into a trap? It seemed a very real possibility but I had no idea what the trap might entail. My mind conjured up hoards of the dead rising up from the fens. Probably the result of having seen too many zombie movies in my previous life.

Although the razor grass no longer impeded our progress, the fog slowed us down. It wasn't so thick that we couldn't see each other but since we didn't want to inadvertently wander deeper into the swamp, we had to pay attention to the solidness of our footing. The softer the mud got, the greater the risk that we were going off track. In this pea soup, it was impossible to tell for sure that we were headed in the right direction, although Gabriel assured us that we were.

As the day wore on, the fog first lightened then retreated. To the left and behind, the grasslands stretched to the horizon. Ahead and to the right, the swamp, with its reeds, cattails, and stunted trees, dominated. Gabriel was doing a good job keeping us skirting the edge of the wetlands. He maintained a course that didn't take us back into the tall grass but never allowed our boots to sink more than an inch into the muck. Chloe Wendel, my once-friend turned romantic rival, wouldn't have been pleased with how filthy her $200 shoes would have gotten.

For me, traversing the bog's southern reaches was more mentally draining than physically demanding. By now, I was used to walking long distances. My leg and butt muscles had toughened up to the point where I could keep moving for hours on end without soreness. But a combination of the almost overpowering stench and the looming presence made it difficult to maintain my forward momentum. My stomach rebelled against any food. Even the cool, clear water we carried in our skins caused it to churn.

Although the heaviest of the fog had evaporated by the time the sun reached its zenith, a residual mist remained, layering everything in a ghostly white. It made the trek surreal, a journey through a sinister, ethereal realm.

Dusk found us camping alongside The Rank for the second night. I started a fire then sat and stared into its depths as the others busied themselves getting things ready for the night.

"What's wrong?" asked Samell, crouching next to me. The mother hen worried about her vulnerable chick.

"Everything about this place. I can feel that thing in my head. It's out there and it never goes away."

"We'll protect you." He meant it. I could hear the determination in his voice - a resolve not to fail the way he had on the road to West Fork. It caused me to smile. But he didn't know what he was talking about any more than I did, and chances were good that swords and knives might not work. The more I contemplated the creature, the more certain I was that it didn't have a physical form, at least not at the moment. Was it stalking us or waiting for us to spring a trap?

"What's that?" There was a faint tremble in Esme's voice. Her finger pointed to the north, toward the heart of The Rank. At first, I didn't see anything, then it caught my attention - a faint, flickering light, greenish in color and hovering about ten feet above the ground. I couldn't be sure how far away it was but it wasn't close. My mind-sense indicated nothing beyond the omnipresent soul-ripper.

"Will o' the wisp," I said, putting the best name I could to what we were seeing. Apparently, the term translated because Gabriel nodded grimly.

"Aye. Those things are common around swamps. Many a traveler's gone to his death, sucked into the mud when he thought he was following a torch to a fellow journeyman."

"Are they dangerous?" Esme's eyes were fixed on the distant light.

"Only if you follow them. Don't rightly know if they're even living. One of my friends suggested they're like glow-lichen in a cave. They exist and give off light but they're not alive like you and me."

"They're creepy. It's like they're watching me."

I woke once during the night, shocked out of a light slumber by a sense of wrongness. I sat bolt upright - an action that caught the attention of Willem, who was standing sole watch. I motioned to him that I was okay although I was trembling under my cloak. Out over the swamp, a half-dozen will o' the wisps were twinkling wildly while, up in the sky, both moons were making their nightly excursions from horizon-to-horizon, although the mists softened and blurred their waxing faces. Still, there was enough illumination to bathe everything in a pale light that leeched color.

Something had changed about the soul-ripper. I could tell this immediately. Its presence was stronger and more forceful. It didn't feel *closer*, exactly, but it had begun to act. Esme's comment about being watched made me wonder whether the will o' the wisps might be the soul-ripper's eyes. Regardless, I knew our time was almost up. I doubted we'd get through another day without an encounter. I only hoped it would wait until after dawn.

Morning seemingly took forever to arrive and I was awake for every agonizing second. I was the first to rise and was pacing agitatedly by the time the others began to stir. Ramila, who had last watch, observed me with a look of concern. If she had enhanced senses, she would be as aware as I was that all was not well. The soul-ripper now had achieved at least a partial physical form and it wasn't far away - perhaps no more than a few miles. Right where the will o' the wisps had been.

Before we set off, our course now headed in a northwesterly direction, I let everyone know that I expected an attack to come during the day. As it turned out, we didn't have long to wait.

"It's coming," I said. Less than an hour after we started our day's trek, the massive presence began moving to intercept us. Its speed was such that I knew we only had a few minutes to prepare. That was enough time to arrange ourselves in the defensive position we had practiced, with Gabriel and me, the two most vulnerable members of the party, in the center of a tight circle. Ramila, Willem, and Samell faced toward the swamp with Esme, Alyssa, and Stepan behind me. We waited in tense silence, our every sense focused on detecting our adversary.

The soul-ripper did little to hide its approach. It appeared like a greenish mist drifting toward us across the bogs as if driven by a great wind, with dozens of will o' the wisps twinkling inside. Its stink, that of rotting carcasses left out in the sun too long, was so overpowering that several of my companions lost their meager breakfasts. Compelled by necessity, I contrived a way to use magic to block my ability to smell. In a less stressful situation, I might have been full of self-congratulation for such an innovative trick. To my mind-sense, the creature was like a building tidal wave, its approach swift, ominous, and undeniable; the devastation it would unleash was certain. It could not be turned back or thrust aside. We would have to stand against it and hope we didn't go under.

It was not entirely amorphous and psychic, however. Weapons needed a target to strike at and the soul-ripper accommodated. Something massive and unrecognizable emerged from under the mud. Encased in the filth of the swamp, it was impossible to figure out precisely what its form might be, although it was slick and scaly and evidenced numerous tentacles. I suspected that, if sluiced clean of the mud and detritus, it might resemble a squid or octopus in form if not in size. With the will o' the wisps dancing above it, it surged toward us and the battle was joined. The quiet of the befogged morning erupted into the cacophony of men struggling to survive. All the sounds were ours, however; the creature made no noise.

Esme, Alyssa, and Stepan went to work with their bows, sending arrow after arrow on high parabolic courses that ensured none of us would inadvertently be struck. The target was large enough that precision wasn't necessary. Whether the arrows penetrated the creature's hide was impossible to tell; the fog was too thick for us to see. It seemed uninjured (or at least unaffected). Willem, Ramila, and Samell, each brandishing a blade of differing quality and engineering, engaged the soul-ripper in close combat, their weapons flashing as it lashed out them with an impossible number of tentacles. Ten, twenty, thirty…the air was thick with them snapping and flailing. I took a step back to avoid having my cheek ripped open by one's lash.

Ramila went down almost immediately, a tentacle wrapping around her calf and jerking her off her feet. She kept her grip on her katana and was able to use it to free her leg. Willem leapt to her aid, but no sooner had he chopped off one of the tentacles seeking to re-ensnare her than a half-dozen replaced it. Some were being used as whips, cracking as they attempted to deliver nasty blows while others sought to entangle arms, legs, weapons - pretty much anything that was exposed. There were so many of them that not all could be defended against. Some found purchase, often leaving behind ugly, slimy-coated welts as they withdrew. Ramila's face was bleeding and Willem had an ugly gash on his bare left forearm.

I assessed the situation as best I could but, with no background in combat tactics, I had to rely on common sense. I didn't think any attack on the tentacles would represent the best use of my abilities. Even if I created a massive scythe to shear through dozens of them, that wouldn't be enough and I suspected the ensuing headache would disable me. No, any attack I attempted had to be against the creature's broad, partially buried body. A bolt of pure magical force, undiminished by a transformation into a more common form of energy, directed at the creature might be enough to drive it away.

Killing it seemed unlikely; even an obliteration of its physical form wouldn't accomplish that.

I hadn't previously attempted this kind of brute-force attack where stamina was more important than skill. I knew I had to act fast. My three companions on the front line were hard pressed. Only Willem remained standing. Ramila and Samell were fighting from the ground - her in a sitting position and him on his back. Although Willem's sword swipes were methodical, obviously the result of long hours of training and practice, Ramila and Samell were swinging desperately at everything and anything. Their blows were effective but clumsy and it was obvious that such spastic action would quickly sap their endurance. In their current vulnerable positions, it wouldn't take much for a tentacle to deliver a fatal hit. Meanwhile, the three archers, having exhausted their supplies of arrows, had drawn daggers and were moving to help their comrades. Next to me Gabriel ground his teeth in frustration but there was little that he could do with one arm except make himself a target.

Everything in front of me was a side-show, a distraction: Willem's professional fighting, Ramila and Samell's frantic attacks, and the largely ineffective efforts of the other three. They couldn't win. They were overmatched. So it was time for me to see if I could once again provide a decisive edge. I knew that if I failed, we might all die. There was no middle ground here, no hope that some of us might escape. Fear clawed at my throat threatening to choke me. I forced it down as best I could. I knew it would soon be gone; the first emotion consumed by magic was always the one closest to the surface.

I cleared my mind as best I could and let instinct take over. Using magic was more about *feeling* than *thinking*. The experience was visceral, not intellectual. As I opened myself up to the eldritch forces, I could feel emotions falling away like shorn wool from a sheep. The potency built quickly and, when it reached the point where I could no longer contain it, I let the dam holding it back burst. A blast of raw magical power arced from my outstretched palm to strike the mud-encrusted behemoth squarely in the center of its form. The energy, a white-blue color so bright that it seared afterimages into my retina, crackled like an electrical storm and dissipated the fog within yards of its passage. By all rights, it should have obliterated its target. The power unleashed exceeded by an order of magnitude anything I had previously attempted. It drained me physically and mentally and rearranged my entire emotional composition. There should have been nothing left of the soul-ripper. But it was seemingly unaffected. It absorbed the attack without difficulty and continued to press my companions. If anything, it became stronger. Then, perhaps sensing that I had done my worst, it came for me.

Its assault wasn't physical. It rode the magical onslaught back to its source, slamming into my mind like a sledgehammer, seeking a mass violation to sate its unbridled lust. It forged an instant psychic link, intending to use that to dominate me and feed on my thoughts. However, just as I hadn't been prepared for its method of attack, it wasn't prepared for what it encountered in that instant of vulnerability when it opened itself up to devour me.

Pain! An agony to dwarf anything I had previously experienced, a consuming sensation that blotted out all reasoning. A headache as massive as the magical feat I had attempted. In these unique circumstances, it became a weapon. Instead of feeding on an open, unarmored mind, the soul-ripper was forced to absorb wave after wave of searing anguish. It was as defenseless as I was and far less prepared.

My consciousness splintered into a million jagged pieces, pulling the soul-ripper along with it into an oblivion that was anything but peaceful.

The next thing I knew, I was floating. My body, so small and fragile in its undeveloped form, was encased in a warm fluid that soothed every pore of my being. My senses were active, my nerves alive. For a while, the only thing I could hear was the thrumming of a heart - so close, so loud, so immediate. The tranquility was as profound as it was transitory.

I knew little. My mind couldn't grasp even the simplest of concepts. Then I felt everything around me shifting. I was being forced. Something was pushing me. Pause...wait...wait...move. Over and over again - inch by inch, inexorable, unstoppable. It was painful, traumatic. It seemed to take forever. The heartbeat receded. Anguish burned in my chest - a sensation that was as unfamiliar as the panic that was settling over me.

Then I heard the voices - startlingly loud and clear. The harshness of cold air, hands on my body. I couldn't see - my eyes were clamped shut. I couldn't process all the noise around me. I wanted to cry, to scream but the pain in my chest wouldn't allow it. Not a word, not a sound, not a breath. I wanted back the warmth, the comfort of the heartbeat, the safety of where I had been. I craved what had been before now.

"It's a girl." Words whose meaning I didn't know at the time but would learn later. Then, after a moment's pause: "She's not breathing." No concern. Hands on my chest, my butt being spanked. The burning in my chest was now more insistent.

"Nothing, doctor."

"Cut the cord. Get me the respirator."

Everything fading away. Heaviness. The surcease I wanted, descending. Death, so soon after birth.

When next awareness tickled me, I was lying somewhere. Cold, discarded. If I could have moved, I would have shivered and curled into a ball but my muscles were flaccid. There was no life in my body. How was it that this glimmer of consciousness remained?

"You must live, little one." The voice was grating and repulsive. "Your death is written but it isn't today. The universe isn't done with you yet. I'm not done with you yet." Then, like a flash of lightning, life rushed into my body. Warmth flooded my limbs and a wail escaped my lips. Just like that - born not dead.

"Doctor!" A shout of surprise and relief.

Then the memory was over and I was falling back into the present, choking as something bitter was poured down my throat.

"Thank the Four!" Samell's voice vibrated with relief.

"I thought for sure we'd lost her this time. Guess Death isn't ready to invite her in just yet." Gabriel's words were flippant but his tone betrayed his concern, inadvertently echoing what the unknown man with the unpleasant voice had said.

The way I felt at the moment, however, I wish Death had been a little more forthcoming with the invitation.

Chapter Twenty-Two: Stricken

I was awake but I didn't want anyone else to know it. There were times (and this was one of them) when I needed a few moments' waking peace. As soon as I stirred, they would be all around me, buzzing like bees. Was I all right? How did I feel? Was I up to traveling?

Good questions but I didn't have the answers now. The headache was gone and that was a blessing. Even the residual throbbing had vacated my mind, leaving behind a numbness not unlike what I got the morning after taking a narcotic. My continued existence was evidence that we had survived the encounter with the soul-ripper, although I wouldn't know the cost until I opened my eyes. My mind-sense was dead but that wasn't a surprise. It would return (or not) in time. I felt two things: an unnatural calm and an entirely natural weariness. Both were byproducts of what I had done. How much emotion had I drained and how much of my stamina had I robbed? I was no longer whole and I wondered whether I could ever become so again. More than ever, I was acutely aware of my need for training and understanding. How close had I come to killing myself? Something Backus had said came back to me: "When it comes to using magic, it's not the things you know that will destroy you; it's the things you don't know." At the moment, it seemed like I didn't know a lot.

The people around me were talking quietly, almost whispering. I concentrated to identify the voices: Samell, Esme, Ramila, Gabriel. At least those four were alive and, because I could understand them, it meant that my magical ability to translate was intact.

"We could carry her," said Samell. He sounded as exhausted as I felt.

"We need a litter," said Ramila. "When Willem returns, he and I will search out the materials."

"What if she doesn't wake up?" Alyssa's voice spoke for the first time, pregnant with anxiety.

No one spoke for a long moment and, when the silence had become uncomfortable, Samell filled it. "We continue the search for Bergeron. Janelle isn't dead. Maybe he can find a way to bring her back from wherever she's gone."

"If there's anything left of her mind," said Ramila. "None of you felt what happened the way I did. The concussion of it. She drove off the soul-ripper, but at what cost?"

At what cost? That was something only wakefulness and activity would tell me. Time to end the suspense for them; continuing to play possum would be cruel. With infinite reluctance, I opened my eyes, squinting against what appeared to be a morning's light, and struggled into a sitting position. The world swam as a wave of nausea washed over me.

The moment they realized I had rejoined the world of consciousness, six of my companions (minus Willem who, as Ramila had indicated, was away from camp) rushed to my side. I was relieved to see that all of them had survived and none appeared to have suffered a major injury, although Ramila's face was a mass of cuts and bruises.

The expected questions came immediately.

Samell: "Are you all right?"

Esme: "How do you feel?"

Gabriel: "Are you up to traveling?"

The next half-hour was spent with me reassuring the others that I was able-bodied and of sound mind (although I wobbled a little the first time I stood and had to return to a sitting position until the dizziness retreated) while they filled me in on what had happened during the day-plus I had been unconscious. Willem returned mid-way through this conversation, having completed scouting the immediate environs.

I learned that, at the moment I fell, the soul-ripper had fled. No one was certain whether it had died or not but the tentacles and body had vanished under the muck, the greenish mist had dissipated as if torn apart by a strong wind, and the will o' the wisps had winked out. Gabriel and Samell believed the creature had perished but Willem and Ramila weren't sure. Regardless, after its attempt to feed on my tortured mind, it hadn't returned to harass the party. After caring for their injuries, which had been mostly minor, their only issue had been what do with me.

Nothing they had tried had provoked a reaction from me. In the end, they had force-fed me a warm liquid infused with herbs gathered from the swamp that Ramila claimed had healing properties. Then Willem had slung me over his shoulder and carried me like a sack of potatoes until we were far enough from the swamp that everyone felt safe. And there they had remained for most of yesterday and all of today, dithering over how they should proceed: continue the search for Bergeron with me in an insensate state or turn back and see whether the healers in West Fork could tend to me.

"I don't have my mind-sense, so we'll have to search without it." I wasn't sure how much it would have helped anyway. If a Summoner wanted to be unseen by a mind-sense probe, magic could accommodate. It was just another form of invisibility, probably not much different from the trick Backus had taught me of blending with the background to foil detection.

We didn't set out immediately. Willem said he was going to do a little more scouting and the rest of the group decided to wait for his return. It was a feint to give me additional time to recover and I was grateful for it. Although I felt fine when sitting, my legs turned to jelly when I stood up and I wasn't sure how far I could walk in my current condition. I also felt dissociated from everyone around me, almost as if I was watching through someone else's eyes. It was...*strange*. I didn't know whether this was the result of channeling so much magic or an aftereffect of being mentally attacked.

Then there was the memory I had experienced while unconscious, apparently of my birth, something no person should be able to recall.

So why had I been able to? And had that memory been there before, when my past had been a whole tapestry in my mind, before I had come to this world? Or was it a new "addition"? Perhaps the most salient question was whether it was real, a fabrication of my tormented mind, or something else.

By the time Willem returned from his "reconnaissance", I was able to stand on my own and move slowly. Samell hovered nearby, a worried expression creasing his features, ready to swoop in and steady me if I appeared ready to collapse. I gave him a wan smile of thanks but never needed his gallant aid. After we had been walking for the better part of an hour, my gait was more stable. I no longer felt like my legs might give way with each step.

We were traveling off to the northwest of the swamp. Looking over my shoulder, I could see a distant mist hanging near the horizon. If that fog concealed the soul-ripper, there was no way to know at the moment. We were back on the plains, although the vegetation here wasn't as savage as it was to the east. The nastiest of the plants, like the razor grass, was less vicious and it didn't take nearly as long to hack our way through them. To the west, I could see the rises of The Southern Peaks reaching skyward. That's where we were headed although what we were going to do once we got there was anyone's guess.

The closer we came to the mountains, the more impressed I was by their size. As an East Coast girl, I didn't have experience with this kind of range. Oh, there were "mountains" in the East but nothing like the Rockies, which I had seen a few times during trips. And the Rockies, as majestic as I remembered them to be, were dwarfed by The Southern Peaks. I wondered if this is what the Himalayas looked like. Even at this distance, I could tell that the tops were snow covered.

"Let's hope we don't have to do any climbing," said Samell, his eyes following my gaze. "I've heard once you go up a ways, it's difficult to breathe."

Gabriel harrumphed. "He's not supposed to be *in* the mountains. Even a Summoner would have problems building a house up there and I doubt he's holed up in a cave. No, he's likely in the foothills. But there are a lot of foothills and unless your powers" - he wiggled his fingers in what I assume was intended to be a pantomime of a magical gesture - "give us a clue where to look then we may be looking for a very long time."

I didn't say anything. Without my mind-sense, I wouldn't be able to provide much in the way of scouting help. We'd have to rely on Willem's tracking - something he appeared to be adept at. It was amazing to consider how valuable an asset he had become when he hadn't initially been intended as part of our company.

We made camp for the night in small grove of stunted (but unblighted) trees. Considering how recently the temperatures had been balmy and summer-like, the nights were remarkably chilly with our ever-so-slow progression in elevation enhancing the cooling. At least the fire burned with sufficient vigor to keep us comfortable. We were just drifting off to sleep when we were startled into remembering how much we had come to rely on my ability to sense dangers from afar.

At first, I didn't know what was happening. Jolted out of the twilight between wakefulness and slumber, I at first thought the chaos around me was part of a dream. It took a few moments to discern the reality. Willem, who had been standing first watch, was facing something in the darkness, sword drawn, while Ramila and Samell had assumed places to his left and right. The inimitable half-growl/half-scream of an earth reaver told me what they were up against. Black on black, the darkness camouflaged it but there was enough firelight for my companions to discern its shape. Samell and Ramila had taken up purely defensive positions. Willem was the aggressor. Samell's previous encounters with reavers had given him an understanding of their weaknesses that he exploited, using quick, well-timed thrusts then jumping back out of the way of the whiplashing tongue.

I didn't doubt that the three would be able to defeat a single member of the undulating species but there could be more out there and killing one would wear down their stamina. I hoped I might be able to put a quick end to the encounter without compromising my health. I knew enough by now to estimate how much magic I could control without inviting a headache. As long as I didn't push my limits, I would be okay. Maybe a little bolt of fire... It had worked in Aeris. No reason why a similar (but more controlled and limited) display couldn't help now.

I reached for the magic...and couldn't find it. Panicked, I tried again with equally dismal results. The ability that had allowed me to refine emotions into malleable magical energy was gone or, at the very least, beyond my grasp. Ever since I had first become aware of this skill, it had been reliably accessible, even in the wake of a headache...until now. My mouth went dry with fear - not fear that the reaver was going to kill us, but fear of what this meant for me, our group, and everything else.

Displaying a dogged persistence born of desperation, I kept trying and kept failing. Like my mind-sense, my magic had deserted me. I was still standing there, ashen faced and stricken, when Samell came to my side and Willem and Ramila scouted to see if there were other reavers nearby. The others had taken up positions around the camp's perimeter, straining to penetrate the darkness with their vision and identify any dangers that might be lurking out there. Our ears detected only the normal sounds of the as-yet moonless night.

Shaken, I sat down hard. I hadn't felt this inadequate since the early days when I had been naked in The Verdant Blight. In this world, in the absence of a full catalog of memories, magic had come to define me and now it wasn't there. Had lost it? Was it gone for good, corrupted beyond repair? Or was this a temporary aberration caused either by my pushing too close to my limits or having my mind invaded by an outside presence? Something had disturbed whatever internal mechanism allowed me to access powers available to Summoners.

"It was only the one," said Samell, misunderstanding the foundation of my current state. "Willem will make sure there are no others but this doesn't appear to be a member of a larger pack." His voice was firm, confident. Had my own crisis not been so acute, it would have cheered me. More than anything, my companions needed to win a battle without magical interference. They had gotten that but not because I had used restraint.

"I've lost my magic." The words sounded distant and forlorn, the wail of a helpless child.

"Like the other times?"

"No. This hasn't happened before. The headaches have always wiped away my mind-sense for a while but the magic has been there. But not now."

"I'm sure it will come back." His tone conveyed sympathy but no real concern. He was convinced that things would right themselves. But he couldn't feel the emptiness gnawing at me. Something was wrong. An inner instinct told me that this wasn't normal. I felt sure that if Backus was here, his face would wear that expression of worry and consternation it donned only when he was faced with a serious dilemma.

For the next half-hour as Willem and Stepan did a thorough check of the vicinity, I sat with Samell. Sensing that what I needed more than words was a gentle presence, he put an arm around me and allowed me to rest my head on his shoulder. For the first time in a long while, I realized how thoroughly exhausted I was. It wasn't just the good, wholesome tiredness that came from doing a hard day's work. This was deeper and more pervasive. It went to the soul.

"All clear. Whether that one was just a stray or some sort of advance scout, we can't know," said Willem upon his return, enunciating each word carefully to make sure he was using the right ones. "We'll double the watch but I think we'll be okay for the night."

Despite all the dark thoughts haunting me, I fell asleep almost immediately and my night's rest was uninterrupted. I woke shortly after dawn when Esme lightly shook me by the shoulders. "Time to get up. Gabriel wants to start moving. He wants to get as far away from that" - she pointed at the remnants of the earth reaver, lying just beyond the camp's clearing - "as we can. Get into the foothills before night, search a little, and camp there. He thinks Bergeron will have built his home close to the river so that's where we'll start."

It was as good a plan as any. I just wished I could be more enthusiastic about it. My slumber had cured the outward signs of fatigue but I was soul-sick. Without access to my magic, I felt worse than useless. When we had set out on this quest a few days ago, I had felt certain that finding Bergeron would be *the solution*. Now, so much that had seemed possible in West Fork had become a vapor dream. Yet all these good people stayed with me, believed in me. However deep my personal doubts might be, I couldn't burden them with those.

The closer we got to the mountains, the more aware I became of how immense they were. Looking up at them from even miles away was dizzying. By mid-day, the peaks had eclipsed the sun. Traveling in those long shadows and with our elevation climbing, it was becoming increasingly chilly. Even my cloak wasn't equal to the task of keeping me warm. Back home, I would have opted for a lined leather jacket or even a winter coat. Here, I had to make due. I was far from the closest L.L. Bean.

Gabriel's path, which had brought us directly west, gradually turned to the north as the terrain became rockier. By the time he called for a halt to the day's journey, I could hear the distant roar of a river even though I couldn't see it.

"We may have to cross it eventually," he said in answer to my question about whether it would block our way. "Not sure how we're going to do it since I doubt there's a fording point anywhere near here. This far west, it's deep and rough. Maybe Bergeron set up his home south of the river. Worst case, I suppose you could always use your magic and fly us to the other side."

My response was a wan smile. Everyone knew I didn't have my mind-sense. Only Samell knew the full depth of what I had lost during the battle with the soul-ripper.

"I don't want to get too close to the river on our first night in the area. We don't know what animals might be lurking nearby and the terrain is getting unfriendly. Bad things happen on riverbanks in the dark, especially near game trails. Better to stop here and start fresh after daybreak. We'll have good sun in the morning."

As the others were busying themselves setting up camp, Samell said something to Esme before approaching me. "Walk a little ways with me."

For a moment, I thought he was going to take my hand but he kept his distance. I fought down a sudden and altogether unexpected pang of disappointment. As we strolled a little way from the newly cultivated fire, I could feel eyes on us. Some, like Alyssa and Stepan, were no doubt wondering what we might have to say to one another that excluded the rest of the group. Others, like Willem, wanted to make sure we didn't stray too far in an area where the threats hadn't yet been catalogued.

"You think you failed," said Samell when we were out of earshot of the others. "We all feel it - a sense of despair that's never been there with you, not even after the attack on Aeris or the horror at NewTown."

I nodded. *Failure*. It weighed on me like a millstone.

"The problem with having power and authority - not that I'd really know - is that those who have it can easily be overwhelmed by a mistake."

"When you make a mistake, the day's hunt goes poorly or a section of the crops wither. When I make a mistake, an entire village might pay the price. We both know that what happened at NewTown isn't going to be isolated. The reavers aren't going to stop there." I paused before saying the next words. They were harsh but needed to be spoken. "It may have already happened at Aeris."

It was his turn to nod. "It may have. We're too far away to know and communication between West Fork and Aeris has never been robust. But don't you think there's a little arrogance in what you're saying? That you and *you alone* represent the difference between salvation and extinction? If you had been at NewTown, we don't know that you could have saved them. More likely, you would have been overwhelmed and killed. Thinking of yourself as a tool devalues you as a person. There's more to you than just the ability to use magic. I've known that since I helped you out of the river, before we suspected you were a Summoner.

"The magic is gone now but it will probably come back. And if it doesn't, we'll cope without it. You aren't defined by your powers, Janelle, any more than you are by your memories. But you think you are."

My response was tinged with bitterness. I knew he was only trying to be kind and pragmatic but he couldn't see the situation from my perspective. "It's easy for you to say that. My memory, like my identity, is fragmented. In becoming a Summoner, I found something to cling to - something that made it less important to remember who I was. If I've lost that, I don't have anything."

"If your magic is gone, and I don't for a moment believe it is, then you're just like the rest of us - people standing against whatever is trying to tear apart our world. You still have your voice and your intelligence. You've survived an experience none of us could imagine and did so with grace and calm. With or without magic, you're still our leader and we'll follow you. We don't do that out of obligation but friendship and affection."

After saying that, he touched my shoulder in a gentle sign of support then returned to the others. I followed in his wake, disturbed as much by what he had said as by the vehemence with which I had resisted his counsel.

Samell's words stayed with me through the late afternoon and into the evening. His rebuke stung and, even though it had been delivered with more tact than I could have managed, its accuracy was undeniable. It forced me to admit that my current mood was caused in no small part by self-pity - not the most admirable of qualities. It was counterproductive to mourn what I had lost. The goal was to move forward with what I had and, if possible, recover my magic. To that end, I had to find Bergeron. The objective hadn't changed even if the need for finding the Summoner was greater than it had ever been.

Our campfire discussions focused on strategies for locating a hermit. No one knew our quarry's exact location. Rumors suggested that he had erected a small, well camouflaged fortress somewhere in the foothills. Gabriel believed it was close to the river since such a location provided obvious advantages.

"The big question is whether he'll permit himself to be found," said our guide. "If he wants to stay hidden, does he have the power to block attempts to locate him?" The question was directed at me but I didn't have a good answer. I was little more capable of evaluating Bergeron's talents and limits than any of our group.

"Possibly. One of the reasons we're looking for him is to find out things about the limitations of a Summoner's powers. It's hard for me to imagine what he might be able to do after having studied and practiced magic-use for decades."

"Could you do it?" asked Esme. "Hide yourself, I mean."

Right now, I couldn't do anything. But I didn't say that. "I can understand a way it might be done but it would require constant concentration and, even then, it would be imperfect. We have to assume that, if Bergeron doesn't want to be found, we won't be able to find him. We have to hope he's aware of how serious the situation is and is willing to reach out to us."

It wasn't the best plan. Everyone knew that. But, especially with my powers curtailed, there wasn't anything more we could do. We knew Bergeron had lived out here for countless years and no one had found him. Of course, it didn't seem like many people had gone looking for him.

Once it came time to lie down for the night, I had regained a semblance of equilibrium. Samell's pep talk had driven back some of the negativity ingrained in my personality. The distant sound of the river and the gentle light of one of the moons lulled me to sleep. When I awakened the next morning, I was immediately aware of three things: my magic was still gone, my mind-sense had returned, and our situation was dire.

Chapter Twenty-Three: Smoke Signals

We weren't in imminent peril but the danger was large, apparent, and growing. To the northwest, deep within The Southern Peaks, a cluster of earth reavers was massing. It wasn't big enough to qualify as an army but it dwarfed the force that had attacked Aeris. At the moment, the reavers weren't moving but, when they decided to act, there were likely enough to overrun West Fork, if that was their goal. If, instead, they went north to Aeris, the village would have no chance. Even if I was there with my magic intact, I doubted I could make much of a difference.

The others needed to know. Our previous sense of urgency was nothing compared to what it needed to be.

"I can see again," I whispered to Samell.

"And the other thing?"

I shook my head in the negative. It was odd that my magical abilities hadn't returned with my mind-sense but all I could do was accept what had been given back to me. At the very least, it made us less vulnerable, or at least more aware of how precarious our situation was.

In addition to the reavers, I was conscious of a distant, nebulous apparition somewhere in The Rank Marsh. I assumed it to be the soul-ripper or its remnants. Its puissance diminished, it wouldn't be a danger unless we wandered deep into the marsh's waters. Over time, it might redevelop into a threat but, at the moment, it could safely be ignored. As for Bergeron...my mind-sense detected no evidence of his presence.

"How many?" asked Willem after I finished briefing my companions.

"It doesn't work like that. She can't count individuals," said Ramila.

I nodded my agreement. "I can feel strength and that hints at numbers. It's a large group, much larger than the one that attacked Aeris. As to how many? At least a hundred, maybe more. If I was closer, I'd be able to make a better guess but they're pretty far away." *Just not far enough.*

"And you're sure they're *earth* reavers?" asked Gabriel

"I know their signatures by now. It's like recognizing a smell or taste."

"They may be planning to strike at Aeris again!" Stepan's voice was tinged with alarm.

"It's possible," I conceded. "Or they could be mounting an attack on West Fork. Or planning something altogether different. There's no way to guess their intentions until they move. If they come east, there's no way the eight of us can stop them. We need to find Bergeron." Would even his magic be enough?

"We need to warn West Fork," said Gabriel. "They can send a rider to Aeris. It doesn't matter whether the reavers are moving or not. They're a cocked arrow pointing at our villages and a warning needs to be issued. The more time they have to prepare, the better the chance they might survive."

I didn't say anything but I knew he was right, although "survival" in this case probably meant "evacuation". It would be irresponsible not to send immediate word to West Fork. I couldn't control what the leaders did with the information but they needed to have it. Still, finding Bergeron was of equal, if not greater, importance. We were going to have to split the party.

"I'll go," said Gabriel. "I'm of no further use here. I've guided you as far as I can. Bergeron's exact location is as much a mystery to me as you."

As brave as the offer was, I wasn't about to send a one-armed man through the wilds back to West Fork on his own. The way looked safe at the moment, but that was *here* and *now*. There was no telling what it might be like in another day, and there were normal animals that could put an end to his trip as easily as a reaver or a soul-ripper. Eventually, maybe Gabriel would learn to fight one-handed but he was only weeks away from having lost the limb and, despite his grit and resolve, he wouldn't be able to effectively defend himself.

The optimum choice to accompany Gabriel was Willem. In a fight, he was worth at least two of the rest of us, possibly more. But, perhaps selfishly, I wanted him with me. His advice was as valuable as his sword-arm. He was also a seasoned traveler, although not in this part of the world, and a calming influence on the mercurial Ramila. The next best option was Stepan. Although he didn't know the terrain, he was capable with both sword and bow and had shown himself to be a reliable companion. I also suspected that he wouldn't be averse to returning to West Fork to see how his injured friend Octavius was recuperating.

Persuading everyone that Stepan and Gabriel should travel to West Fork while the remaining six of us continued our search for Bergeron required more diplomacy than I had anticipated. Gabriel argued that he could go alone and didn't need a "keeper". He admitted that, although he couldn't fight, he was an experienced enough outdoorsman that he could avoid or run away from any danger. I countered that his message was crucial and we couldn't risk him being eaten by a bear along the way. He *had* to reach West Fork. For his part, Stepan was reluctant to leave me because he saw that as an abandonment of his duty. He relented only after a lengthy private conversation with Samell. I don't know what was said between the two of them but Stepan dropped his objections and pledged to see the tinker back to the village.

By mid-morning, Gabriel and Stepan had vanished into the scrub and grass to the east while the rest of us were hiking northward toward the sound of the river. We topped a gentle rise and stared into the belly of a canyon. There, perhaps one-hundred feet down, was the raging torrent of the Fork West River, filling the gorge from side to side and churning with a violence that reminded me of white water rapid rides.

"If it comes to it, crossing *that* isn't going to be easy," muttered Willem. *Not easy* was an understatement; *impossible* was a better word. If we needed to continue our search north, we would have to backtrack along the river until we found a crossing point.

We headed toward the higher ground, picking our way westward along terrain that was increasingly unforgiving. I was looking with my mind and eyes but wasn't sure what might constitute a clue. I doubted we were just going to stumble across a classically built castle out in the open with a well-manicured path leading to the doorway. It was likely to be hidden, either by magical or mundane means (or perhaps both) so we were looking for traces of its existence - little discrepancies that might mark its location. Unfortunately, when it came to the outdoorsmanship, ineptitude was one of my defining characteristics. For eighteen years, I had been an indoor girl. Two months wasn't enough to correct a lifetime's ignorance.

We stopped to rest and eat around the time that the sun dipped behind the tallest mountain peak. The temperature plummeted by about ten degrees in a matter of minutes. The afternoon's search was as abbreviated as it was fruitless. We were forced to stop and make camp nearly two hours before the sun would have set on the plains. Stoking a fire proved challenging. Fuel was scarce and the stiff wind gusting down from the mountains made it difficult to keep the flames from blowing out. When Willem asked me to repeat what I had done near the swamp with the earth-fed fire, I was forced to confess.

Esme, Alyssa, and Willem made no response to my revelation. Ramila, however, wasn't as restrained. "This changes things," she muttered. "Doesn't make much sense looking for Bergeron if we don't have a Summoner anymore. We *all* should have gone back to West Fork with Gabriel instead of stumbling around looking for someone we probably wouldn't find if we had an army and a century."

I wanted to contradict her but a deep-rooted sense of self-recrimination wouldn't allow me. Surprisingly, however, I had no shortage of defenders.

"Janelle's magic will likely return, just like her special sense did," said Esme. "We've seen how scrambled she becomes after using magic and what she did to the soul-ripper was bigger than anything she's done before."

"It's more important now than ever to find Bergeron," interjected Samell. "If something has happened to Janelle's magic, who better to investigate it than a Summoner? And, regardless of whether he can help her or not, we need him to fight against the reavers."

Willem's tone was solemn. "We pledged our service to Janelle to undertake this journey. I see no reason why that should change now. To question her decisions is to undermine her authority. She is the leader. We can make suggestions but, in the end, we must follow her direction." He spoke in his native tongue, necessitating Ramila's translation. The rebuke was a blow to her pride; a nasty glance in my direction showed where she placed the blame.

There was little talk around the campfire that night. Willem was gone much of the time cutting up brush to feed the flames and my revelation had put everyone else in an introspective mood, myself included. Samell sat silently by my side, offering silent encouragement by his presence. Ramila wouldn't look at me. I couldn't tell whether she was more upset by my revelation or Willem's anger at her response. Whatever harmony we had shared during the early stages of this journey was gone.

Still weary from my experience, I lay down before anyone else. Sleep was elusive, however. The presence of so many earth reavers at the edge of my awareness nagged at me like a sore tooth - just uncomfortable enough to keep me awake and impossible to banish from my consciousness. Was it growing bigger and deeper? Was there more potency there than when I had first noticed it? Or was that my imagination, stoked by fear and worry.

With those thoughts dancing in my mind, I knew I was in for a rough rest even before I finally crossed the threshold into slumber.

There, in the blackness of the night, another memory forced my acknowledgment.

I was a pyromaniac, or at least that's what they told me. Whether or not it was true, it was a label I couldn't remove because it had been attached by people in authority. Sometime after the fire had burned down our house, the investigators had figured out it had been intentionally set. It hadn't taken a crack team of detectives to speculate who the culprit was. Ignoring the possibility of an intruder (since there were no signs of forced entry), that left my parents, me, and my sister. The one who liked to play with matches and owned a half-dozen propane lighters (even though I didn't smoke) got the blame. The crime had been so inept, it was almost like I had wanted to be caught. To me, the clumsiness of the act was more disturbing than the fire-setting. I was smarter than that. Why had I acted so recklessly and with so little regard for the consequences?

There had been "conventional" punishments, of course. Groundings, deprivation of possessions like my cellphone, and so forth. A lot of yelling and screaming and threatening. My mother told me she wished I had never been born. And I had been forced to see a shrink. It was a court-mandated order so even if my parents had disagreed (which they hadn't), it wouldn't have mattered. Dr. Graham was going to be a part of my life for at least the next two years, maybe longer. According to the judge, we were together to "determine what prompted this criminal act and ensure that nothing like it happens again."

Dr. Graham was nice and patient, adopting an attentive paternal demeanor in our three-times-per-week sessions. It also helped that he was easy on the eyes. At 29, just about double my fourteen years, he was too old to be seriously considered as a romantic interest (older guys not being my "thing"), but his good looks were such that I looked forward to my hourly blocks with him more than I might otherwise have. Whether we were "making progress"...that was in the eye of the beholder.

I thought the whole thing was a waste of time. I didn't have a compulsion for an encore but no one believed me when I said that. My parents searched my room for fire starters every time I left the house. Dr. Graham didn't pressure me on my pyromania; he asked questions to get me talking but most were about my upbringing and my feelings and had nothing to do with the night that had landed me in this situation. Until today, that was. During this afternoon's situation, he had finally confronted the reason the two of us were spending so much time together.

"Do you know why you did it, Janelle?"

He didn't have to say what "it" was. We both knew. At least he didn't insult me by asking if I had done it. I gave him the same stock answer I had given everyone else: No, I didn't know. It had been impulsive. I had wanted to lash out and destroy something and fire had seemed the surest way to get it done. The moment I realized what I had done, I wished I could take it back. (That was a lie.) It had been the biggest mistake of my life. (Probably true but only because I got caught.) I would never consider doing something like that again. (Although who knew what the future might hold?)

He listened to my rote explanation with his usual attentiveness. When I was done, he leaned forward, rested his elbows on his desk, and brought his hands together so his steepled fingers rested against his mustached upper lip.

"You know, the Native Americans once lit huge bonfires. They used them to create smoke signals, a form of long-distance communication that predated the telegraph or telephone." I was surprised that he was talking down to me. One of the things I liked about Dr. Graham is that he accepted my intelligence and treated me with respect. Of course I knew about smoke signals. Every kid learned about them in elementary school. What was his point?

"The fire you lit was your way of sending out smoke signals, Janelle. A bit extreme, I admit, but burning down your house was a way of communicating with people who weren't hearing you. I don't

believe you're remorseful about what happened and I don't think the fire got out of control. I think you knew what you were doing and achieved the result you wanted. Smoke signals - the way to get the attention of a mother and father who otherwise didn't know you existed."

The memory faded as I woke up, momentarily disoriented and thinking I was in my old bed in my rebuilt room. Then, as my eyes focused on my surroundings, I remembered where I was. The night had passed. The fire was a mass of cooling embers and the first rays of dawn were peeking through the low clouds clogging the eastern horizon.

Perhaps these memories could be useful for more than making me despise my previous self. Having retrieved this small chunk of my past, I was struck by a sudden inspiration about what could be done in the search for Bergeron. If my younger self could use "smoke signals" to force her parents to pay attention to her, could my present-day self use the same tactic to catch the notice of a Summoner?

When Willem noticed that I was awake, he came over to me. "We're going to have to find a crossing point today. I thought about this during the night. If I came out here looking for seclusion, I'd build my home along the northern bank. The river provides a natural barrier to anyone traveling from West Fork, unless they're foolish enough to hazard the swamp. Living on the southern bank would make him more accessible to civilization."

I nodded my acquiescence. His logic was impeccable. Of course, it made sense for Bergeron to make his lodging as isolated as possible. The river and swamp were imposing impediments and he would use them to their best advantage. With a guardian like the soul-ripper and an impassible gorge, the Summoner would be safely protected from any West Fork-based intrusion unless a party wanted to detour to the far north, head west then come back south again - an inconvenient and time-consuming route.

We spent a few morning hours continuing our search for traces that someone might be living in the foothills near the river but, like the day before, there was nothing. Or, if there was something, we weren't looking in the right place for the right thing. That was the frustrating part, figuring out what could be meaningful. Around mid-morning, I called a halt and asked Willem what he suggested. He told everyone what he had mentioned to me earlier: we needed to follow the river eastward and hope there was a crossing point before it entered The Rank Marsh. He believed there would be one but didn't know how long it would take to find it. "With a swift current like this, we need a ford where we can wade across with the water no higher than our waists. Swimming isn't an option."

Despite a general sense of dejection and frustration, no one grumbled and we set our course back in the direction from which we had come, keeping the river on our left. It didn't take long for the waterway to come even with the banks but the muddy flow was sufficiently deep and rough to discourage a crossing.

"River's high and the current's fast," said Willem. "Either a lot of snow melt or unseasonably heavy rains in the mountains. Fortunately, The Rank Marsh will absorb most of the flooding so there won't be problems at West Fork."

My attention was captured by the change in ground cover. As we descended from the foothills, the grasses and other vegetation became more plentiful. Most of the scrub was dry enough to feed an ember. Impatient and unconvinced that we were going to find a crossing point without a lot more walking and wasted time (and even that was no guarantee of locating Bergeron), I decided that now was as good a time as any to put my plan into action. I called a halt and had everyone gather around me so I could outline my intentions.

Initial curiosity turned to shock as my companions realized what I was proposing.

"You're planning to light the fields on fire?" Ramila was incredulous.

"It's dangerous," warned Willem. He paused then added, "*Very dangerous.*"

Even Samell was dubious. "A raging fire so close to his home might get the Summoner's attention but it could so easily get out of hand. Once you set something like that, you can't control it and, regardless of where we retreat to, a gust of wind could put us in its path. I wouldn't be as concerned if you still had your magic."

If I still had my magic, I wouldn't have to consider hazardous things like this. But, to my thinking, there wasn't much choice. We could wait and hope my magic returned. We could hike a long distance around the river and maybe get lucky and find something on the northern bank. All of that would take time and, in that time, the mass of earth reavers would be getting closer to taking whatever action they were planning. Patience, often a valuable ally, was our enemy. Time was the enemy's weapon. Why didn't the others see this?

"I don't like it any more than you do. But we don't have the luxury of being careful. There are a lot more earth reavers out there than there were at Aeris. They're going to come down out of the mountains and strike somewhere and, no matter how well-prepared West Fork might be, they're not going to survive it. Not without Summoners."

"Perhaps not with them, either." The voice, surprisingly loud and authoritative, came from behind me. I whirled around to confront the stranger who, despite my fully functional mind-sense, had come upon us without my knowing.

"And please don't set fire to these grasses. Lightning does it often enough and the blazes are exhausting to contain. I have no desire to expend unnecessary magic extinguishing a man-made inferno. Dramatic, desperate action isn't necessary to get my attention even in dramatic, desperate times.

"My name is Bergeron. I believe you're looking for me.

Chapter Twenty-Four: The Man in the Mountain

For an old guy who had lived in isolation for who knew how many years, Bergeron looked pretty hot. His skin was swarthy (darker even than Ramila's) and he had a stubble-free bald pate that shone in the sunlight. His close-cut salt-and-pepper beard and mustache were impeccably groomed, not obscuring the well-defined bone structure of his lower face. His eyes, nestled under furry brows, were a deep chocolate color and conveyed empathy and perhaps a little pain. Tall and slender in his dark, heavy robes, he resembled a monk or priest. I couldn't guess at his age. He looked like he was in his mid-fifties but, with Summoners, appearances could deceive.

His home, as Willem had supposed, was on the north side of the river, but deeper into the mountains than we had expected. His magic, employed effortlessly, had allowed us to cross the water and ascend a dangerous precipice with little peril. I realized that we could have searched for weeks and never found this place. The entrance was a slit in a rock face barely wide enough for a person to squeeze through. To all appearances, it was a natural fissure, but it concealed a living space more worthy of a noble than a hermit: a spacious, multiple room apartment carved directly into the side of a mountain, hollowed out with such smoothness and precision that it could only have been accomplished by magic. An army of construction workers with pick-axes would have taken decades to cut through this much stone and the results wouldn't have been as aesthetically pleasing. Although Bergeron used torches and lanterns for light, some of the rooms' floors emitted a natural phosphorescence - a gentle white light that was warm and soothing not harsh like the fluorescent bulbs from my old world.

After his surprise introduction, Bergeron had said little, promising only that there would be "time enough to talk about all manner of things once we're away from the prying eyes and ears of the outside world." He had led us in silence to his abode and offered us seats around a large wooden table in a circular chamber that was as big as the common room in the inn in West Fork. He had then played the role of the perfect host, providing each of us with goblets of a fruity beverage and setting out platters heaped high with a variety of cheeses and cured meats.

It was hard to reconcile this image of Bergeron with what I had been expecting - a grizzled introvert living in isolation who would only reluctantly admit us when he recognized the immediacy of our peril. Instead, the Summoner was urbane and polite. There was no sense of wariness about him and he welcomed us without reluctance. Like all unexpected things, it made me suspicious.

Once we had eaten our fill which, especially in Willem's case, represented a substantial portion of the foodstuffs provided by our host, Bergeron cleared the table and sat in a chair at its head. When he spoke, he didn't bother with small talk or the niceties of chit-chat, instead cutting immediately to the heart of the matter at hand.

"I've known of your presence for some time now." He spoke to us all but his gaze was fixed on me. "I've been expecting you and was becoming concerned. It took you longer to come within my sphere of influence than I anticipated. Not only that but our enemy is moving faster than I thought possible."

"You've been tracking us?" I asked.

"Not specifically. My attention of late has largely been focused on the growing mass of reavers that has been sprouting in The Southern Peaks. Most worrisome. I first became aware of your party when I sensed a disturbance in The Rank Marsh that lead to the dissolution of its supernatural guardian. However, the lack of any magical signature caused me to dismiss you as those I was waiting for. This morning, I noticed that you were here and decided to creep in for a closer look. Only then did I recognize Janelle as a Summoner - a fact apparent only in close proximity."

"My magic isn't working." It was a clumsy way to phrase it but an accurate assessment of my predicament. "It hasn't been since the battle with the soul-ripper."

"I can see that. It's been blocked. To be more precise, you have blocked it."

"Me?"

He nodded. "Perhaps not consciously but your present circumstances are your own doing. It's most curious, a rare ability. Not something I could do no matter how hard I tried."

I stared at him dumbfounded. "How do I get it back?"

"I may be able to help, although I don't pretend to be an expert at this sort of thing. Summoners who live in isolation are rarely good at probing the minds of others. My guess is that your brain blocked the magic as a form of automatic defense. To keep you from burning yourself out, it shut the valve off, so to speak. To restore your abilities, you have to open the valve."

After completing his explanation, Bergeron looked into my eyes, catching and holding me with his gaze. At first it was comforting but, after a short while, I felt something like panic welling from within. The stare, which had initially seemed curious, had become piercing. I couldn't break it, not even to blink, although I desperately wanted to. He held me powerless, those eyes boring into me. Then I felt it, almost like a physical sensation, and he released me. I gasped for air, only just realizing I had been holding my breath.

"That should do it," he said with a smile. A cold, hard smile that didn't touch the eyes I had initially mistaken as being gentle.

He was right, though. I knew it immediately. My magic was accessible. I was whole again: Janelle the Summoner. I wasn't sure how to feel about Bergeron at this moment. He had restored me but, in doing so, he had displayed a ruthlessness that made me uncomfortable. I felt violated, as if his mind had gone places where it had no right to be.

The others were looking at me expectantly so, for their benefit, I said, "It's back."

"Want to try a trick? Light a candle or something?" offered the Summoner.

"No need. Will it happen again?"

Bergeron shrugged. "Hard to say. If you never push yourself again, probably not. But I've never heard of a Summoner who doesn't push him or herself from time-to-time, and we may be entering a volatile period when that's a daily requirement. So the likelihood is that this will happen again. You'll need to learn how to remedy it yourself, which will be an interesting trick. In order to break the block, I needed magic. The block prevents you from accessing magic, so you can see the dilemma."

My heart sank. I didn't want to face that stare again but, worse, it meant that if Bergeron wasn't around, I could become trapped away from my magic.

"Let me think about it later. I'm sure there's a simple solution. For now, there are plenty of other things to talk about. I gather you're here to learn and you've brought some friends as guides and protectors. I can tell by looking at you that you're not from this world. Not surprising. I don't think a Summoner has been born here in a dozen generations. We're all from other worlds, myself included, although I've been here for so long that I think of myself as a native."

"Father Backus in Aeris said you might be able to teach me a few things about being a Summoner. He also believes you might have some insight into why I get debilitating headaches every time I access magic."

"Backus?" Bergeron barked a laugh. "Is that old fool still alive? I guess it shouldn't surprise me." His voice became momentarily wistful. "What a Summoner he would have made if he'd had the discipline to curb his excesses and study…"

"He can't use magic."

"Burned himself out, I guess. Can't say I'm surprised. At any rate, I can tell you the location of every known Summoner across the land but wild wizards like Backus remain elusive - there may be quite a few and we'll have to root them out and rally them to our cause. That won't be easy. There's a reason why they rejected becoming a Summoner in the first place. But magic, even untamed and uncontrolled, will be needed for what's to come."

"Can you help Janelle?" asked Samell.

"Perhaps. Headaches, you say?"

I nodded.

"Not a common symptom. In fact, most uncommon. I think I read about a Summoner many centuries ago who suffered something similar. It's probably related to the blocks your mind creates. Another defense mechanism, perhaps? Given enough time, I have no doubt we'd be able to identify and correct the problem." He paused, somewhat theatrically I thought, before adding: "But time may be one thing we don't have much of. Before we delve more deeply into the specifics of your condition, which is better done when the two of us are alone, there's one subject we need to address with everyone present."

"The reavers." Willem's voice was flat, without inflection, but I knew Bergeron would catch his accent.

"Yes, the reavers," acknowledged the Summoner. "You're not from around here, are you? From your features, I'd guess you come from quite a distance away, perhaps from the southeast. Erenton?"

Willem's face quirked into a mirthless smile. "Somewhere close to there. I've spent a lot of my adult life on the road. Most recently, I settled in West Fork."

"Which explains your participation in Janelle's expedition. But not yours, Princess." He fixed his unblinking stare on Ramila.

She was obviously startled by his knowledge. It showed in both her expression and her inability to form an immediately reply.

Bergeron extended a slender finger toward the silver necklace she wore. I had seen it before but never given it much thought. For the first time, I noticed a distinctive charm dangling from the end. It looked like a "+" sign inside an ellipse. "Only true royalty or a daring imposter would wear that sigil. It's more likely you're the former than the latter. But it begs the question of why you're here, probably as far from home as your warrior companion."

I wondered if Bergeron was flaunting his superior erudition, proving to us that he was a master of observation and deduction. There was no reason for him to mention Willem's foreign birth and Ramila's heritage beyond establishing his perspicacity. I had never liked show-offs.

Ramila quickly recovered her composure. "My father and I had to leave our home some time ago. There were…issues…with a cousin on my mother's side. We live in West Fork. When we learned that a new Summoner had arrived, we offered our help."

"Who is your father?"

"Marluk. Marluk the Peacemaker."

"Ah. That explains much." To him, perhaps, but not to me. Now I wondered even more about the hidden past neither Ramila nor her father had seen fit to entrust me with. "You are most welcome in my humble abode, Princess. As are all your companions. Now, to the matter at hand. How much do you know about the reavers?"

"Several weeks ago, a force of about fifty earth reavers attacked Aeris. We were able to kill some and drive off the rest."

Bergeron's left eyebrow lifted. "Really? I wasn't aware of that. It must have happened outside of my range or before I was paying close attention. Go on."

"On our way south, we encountered a lone air reaver, possibly a scout. I couldn't detect any others. Then we came to the ruins of NewTown. Although the attackers were gone by the time we got there, the evidence pointed to a sudden, violent attack by creatures of fire. On our way to locate you, I became aware of a large group of earth reavers, perhaps the beginnings of an army, massing in the mountains."

"So you sent two of your party back to West Fork to warn them. A shrewd decision."

I started, once again surprised by his awareness.

"Don't be so astonished. I told you I've been mindful of your party since you spectacularly dispatched The Rank Guardian."

I wondered if his senses were strong enough to have tracked Gabriel and Stepan on their return journey. "Did they make it?"

"I can't say for sure. My sight doesn't extend all the way to West Fork. But by the time I lost them, they were still hale. I suspect they'll arrive intact. Whether anyone other than Marluk will pay attention to what they have to say is another matter. There are many disbelievers. Apocalyptic talk is rarely taken seriously regardless of the evidence."

"If they saw what happened at NewTown, they'd believe," said Esme bitterly. Those were the first words she had spoken to the Summoner since introducing herself outside.

"True, my dear. Disbelief will doom them if they don't shake it off or have someone shake it off for them." His eyes fixed on me. It was evident who he had in mind for that task.

"So what now? What's our next step?" asked Samell.

"Prepare for war."

"War?"

"War," affirmed Bergeron. "The legion being amassed by the earth reavers can serve no purpose other than the eradication of sentient life in this part of the continent. The specifics of their plan are largely irrelevant. West Fork may be their first target but it won't be their last. NewTown is already gone and Aeris isn't likely to survive long after West Fork falls. Human habitations are relatively isolated in The Western Wilds and will be easy pickings. After that…they could go east or south but they won't stop. There's a single-mindedness to those creatures. I'm surprised they retreated at Aeris. That's concerning because it indicates an awareness and intelligence. Reavers have always been beings of instinct and hunger, born of magic but with little in the way of brain capacity. I wouldn't have expected them to organize much less have a genocidal strategy."

"Why now? Does it have something to do with me?" It wasn't lost on me that the sudden aggressiveness of the reavers had coincided with my arrival. And, even if there wasn't a direct cause, I wondered whether some people might make the connection and assign blame to me.

"An important question. I suspect 'I don't know' isn't going to satisfy any of you, so let's speculate. Without question, a daemon is involved. Reavers are inherently malignant but tend to reside in out-of-the-way places where they can congregate and feel safe. Earth reavers are typically buried well underground. Fire reavers love volcanoes. Air reavers prefer mountain tops and clouds. Water reavers call the depths of the oceans home. Only a daemon can roust them and, while there have been no confirmed signs of a living daemon for generations upon generations, there now may be multiples of them. Our immediate concern is an earth daemon but, judging by the activities of the other reavers, it's reasonable to assume there are also active air and fire daemons as well. It's too soon to say whether there's coordination or simply opportunism at work."

"Why haven't we seen any water reavers?" That had been nagging at me for a while now.

"There are a couple of possibilities," said Bergeron. "It could be that there's no water daemon. Or, since we're landlocked here, it might be that there aren't any around. It may be different in the distant south or east, near the coast. In fact, the harbor towns and cities may have more to fear from water reavers than the other three varieties."

"How many earth reavers are there in the mountains?" asked Willem.

"At the moment, hundreds. But there are more coming. Many more. I don't know the number the daemon has access to but, assuming he can mass all the earth reavers in this part of the world, his army will be in the thousands. Possibly the ten thousands."

My heart plummeted at that. Considering how difficult it was to bring down *one* of those... Thousands? Was this world doomed?

"How do we stop them?" breathed Esme, her eyes wide. I could almost see her thoughts: remembering Aeris, remembering NewTown.

"The best we can hope for here, in the west, is to slow them down. It's not realistic to believe we can save West Fork. It's too small a settlement to be able to assemble a decent militia and too remote for help to come from any place with enough men. If we can delay the reavers, an evacuation might be possible. That presupposes the elders are sensible enough to heed the warnings." Bergeron's tone implied that he was skeptical.

"The real battle will be in the east. There's enough manpower out there to build an army large enough to counter whatever force the earth daemon assembles."

"But...thousands of those things...they're so hard to kill." Esme was struggling with the image of a wave of earth reavers flooding across the world. A flash of a memory impinged on my consciousness: a swarm of beetles fanning out over a decaying tree trunk, turning the ground into a metallic, moving carpet. It would be like that, only on a much larger scale.

"Hard to kill? No doubt," agreed the Summoner. "But not impossible. Enough stout soldiers with sharp weapons...it can be done. Earth reavers lack the innate skill to apply their nature to anything more than brute-force attacks. Of all the reavers, they're the least dangerous and the easiest to defeat. The daemon, on the other hand, is a real danger."

"What if we killed it?" I asked.

"That would be a quick and efficient way to end the threat. Without the daemon, they would retreat back to the safety of their underground burrows. But killing a daemon is no easy thing. Even a lone Summoner would be hard pressed in such a battle. They are magic incarnate so victory requires turning their nature against them."

The conversation continued for some time after that with Willem, the most tactically astute of our group, taking an active role. Much of the information he solicited related to things I had already learned from either Backus or Marluk. My mind drifted as Willem proposed various strategies, most of which were dismissed by Bergeron as inadequate or ill-advised. Even if the combined armies of all the cities of the east were able to drive back the earth reavers and their daemon, there were still three other elemental powers to be considered, and all of them were stronger.

As he patiently answered Willem's questions and debated options with him, Bergeron's eyes frequently sought mine. He was assessing how well I was absorbing the information. Finally, noticing that we were beginning to droop from a combination of despair and weariness, he motioned for us to follow him. He led us to a spartan chamber, bare except for a series of straw mattresses laid out on the floor.

"Sleep now," he advised. "What lies ahead will require a clear mind and rested body. You may be taxed to the brink. Replenish yourselves while you have the chance." Turning to me, he added, "All except you, Janelle. Come with me. It's time you learn what it *really* means to be a Summoner."

Chapter Twenty-Five: The Mysteries of the Mind

It was easy to forget that Bergeron's home was buried under a mountain. Putting aside the lack of windows, it replicated in nearly every way a traditional, free-standing mansion. He had taken great pains to ensure that the floors, walls, and ceiling were smooth and flat. Most rooms had wooden doors - more a decorative than functional touch for someone living alone. Part of me marveled that magic could have accomplished the crafting of such a domicile.

"Impressed?" asked Bergeron conversationally, noticing the interest I was showing in the architecture.

"I didn't think…I can't imagine how you did all this."

"It took a while. Years, in fact. I started out with a small cave and gradually widened it into a series of rooms. Every so-often, I do a little more work when I grow bored with reading and study. There are always new tricks to practice. Mastering magic is a combination of book-work and application. Unfortunately, you will have little time for either. Summoners of my era were bred as scholars. Now we'll have to learn to be warriors. Either that, or pass on the mantle to others like you, who arrive as blank slates and can be taught from the beginning how to use their powers for battle. I'm afraid that the epoch of The War Summoner is upon us."

"Do you know who brought me here?"

"I do. In many ways, he was the most powerful of us all and possibly the oldest. I couldn't say how long he had been around. From the old days, I suspect, when Summoners weren't as rare as they are today. They say that over the years, he had thirty wives and none at the same time. All of those were before I came here. We Summoners can use magic to prolong our lives to incredible spans but mortality eventually overtakes even the greatest of us. Sometimes our bodies give out and sometimes we lose the will to continue. Unending life seems like an amazing boon until you start to experience it. Longevity leads to boredom and monotony and, with no one to share the passage of days with, it can be very lonely. Not something you need to be concerned about, at least for now."

And if all the reavers attack, maybe not something I'll ever have to worry about.

Our stroll through the halls and rooms of Bergeron's rambling home terminated in a small chamber that served as his office. Books and scrolls were everywhere and the comforting scent of old paper hung in the air. The hallmark neatness of the rest of the mansion wasn't evident in this mess of jumbled clutter. Two lanterns hanging on poles illuminated the small space. I noticed they weren't giving off smoke and the flames weren't flickering. My companion motioned for me to sit across a small table from him. He cleared it by sweeping his arm across its surface and unceremoniously dumping sheaves of paper and a heavy leather-bound tome onto the floor.

"Even though it was so very long ago, I still remember what it was like waking up in this world, a stranger pulled away from all that was comfortable and familiar. Where I came from, I had been pampered and bowed to, but there hadn't been any meaning in all that genuflecting. Here, my life has purpose but it took decades for me to understand that. I had the luxury of time to come into my powers and hone them. Your circumstances are different."

"You're not from Earth, are you?"

"Is that what your birth-world is called? Earth? No, I come from Urs, a small island-nation not unlike this one in climate and magical selectivity. A loremaster would be able to explain things better, but my understanding is that the planes of existence are constantly shifting and a Summoning draws from the closest one at the time when it happens. When there are clusters of Summonings, newcomers may arrive from the same world - there are historical records of that happening.

"Place of origin matters less than how quickly a Summoner acclimates. As you've experienced, the process is traumatic. Over the years, our ranks have thinned because some would-be Summoners haven't done well with the transition and have therefore been unable to call a replacement. Most are fine but if one out of ten goes insane or dies unexpectedly, there are long-term implications. The situation is made worse because there are so few natural-born Summoners. Most of those with a latent magical talent don't discover their abilities or, if they do, they avoid having them officially acknowledged."

"How many of you are there?"

"Including you, there are eight recognized Summoners. No one has a count of wild wizards since many do their best to avoid detection for fear of being 'conscripted.' Loremaster Lawrence, the Summoner who brought you here, believed there were around a dozen of them. He devoted the last years of his life to locating them and pleading with them to be accepted into our fraternity. He had only one success."

"Eight doesn't sound like a good number to stand against an army of reavers and daemons."

Bergeron didn't sugar-coat his response. "It's pathetic and inadequate and speaks to our failure over the years. I can offer no excuse for the position we find ourselves in. After all, it's supposedly our duty to use magic responsibly and safeguard this world from its abuse and side-effects. We have always suspected this day would come but complacency allowed us to believe it would be in the far future, perhaps not even in our lifetimes, and certainly not something to worry about at the moment. How quickly the future has arrived." He shook his head, a gesture of regret. *Theatrical or genuine?* I couldn't decide. Although Bergeron seemed to be opening up to me, I wasn't convinced of his sincerity. Something about him didn't inspire trust. Respect, yes, but not trust.

"What are we going to do?"

"First, we have to convince the citizens of West Fork to abandon their town and flee eastward. That won't be easy. Not only are people reluctant to leave behind their land and property but The Western Highway is dangerous even for large groups of travelers. Once, the

High King in Erenton kept the road patrolled but that was before infighting among his heirs fractured the kingdom into a half-dozen competing fiefdoms, all of which are more concerned about skirmishing with their neighbors than maintaining trade with the sparsely populated west.

"After evacuating West Fork, our next step will be to convene a Conference of Summoners, something that hasn't been done in several generations. We need to gather all of the Summoners - and as many of the wild wizards as possible - into one place to plan for the oncoming storm. I fear this is something that should have been done years ago but we'll have to make the best out of a bad situation. With Lawrence gone, we'll have to rely on Loremaster Alexander to lead us. He's a good man - pragmatic and wise - but not as widely venerated as Lawrence was."

"What about Aeris?" In the grand scheme of things, it was a small place, hardly worth mentioning when the fate of hundreds of thousands lay in the balance, but my fondness for the small hamlet was genuine. Those people had welcomed me and given me a temporary home in a foreign land.

"Messengers will be sent to all the outlying villages including Aeris and the settlements in The Far Hills. But I warn you, Janelle, there's a possibility that Aeris has already suffered the same fate as NewTown. And even if it still stands today, it may have been razed by the time the messengers reach there. Its isolation won't protect it from an attack, especially since the reavers have tried once and failed. They'll return in greater numbers."

"I care about those people."

"I know you do. I cared about the family that took me in when I arrived. But you'll learn, as I did, that *duty* must override *affection*. It's a harsh truth but a truth nonetheless."

"When you arrived here, were your memories intact?" It was time to start investigating the things that were impeding my abilities.

"Mostly. Time blurs all things, of course. This many years later, I remember my old life like a dream, but the Summoning didn't damage my memories. I assume it's different for you?"

I nodded. "My life before I came here…it's a jumble, a puzzle with many missing pieces. I remember some of the strangest things - books I've read, movies I've seen, historical trivia - but many of the important events in my life are blanks. And individual memories return at random. Sometimes they come to me at night, sometimes when I'm on the road."

"It's not uncommon but, taking into consideration your headaches and the block your mind created to protect you from overusing your magic, there's something unusual at work here. Have you noticed anything else odd?"

"Since I started using magic, my sense of smell is stronger."

"Those who use magic often gain an enhancement to one sense or another. In my case, it's hearing. I've discovered that it's more often a nuisance than an asset but I doubt that's related to any unique condition you may be experiencing."

I hesitated. Should I tell him about the strange figure or figures that haunted my past? I didn't trust Bergeron, at least not fully. There was something about him that inspired unease. But I had come to understand my powers and limitations, and to alleviate the condition causing my headaches. At some point, I was going to have to take a leap of faith, or what was the point of being here?

So I told him everything. The man who had shadowed me on the night of my Summoning. The lurker across the street from my house. The strange person who had approached me at Camp Harmony. The doctor who had brought me back to life as a baby.

My account disturbed Bergeron. I could see it by the way his face clouded and his brow furrowed. "Were these all the same person?" He asked.

"Yes. No. Maybe." The truth was that I didn't know. The memories weren't crystal clear and, in all but one case, the face (or faces) had been too far away to discern.

"I don't like the sound of this. We need to discuss it with Loremaster Alexander. He may know what this portends but it appears likely that someone or *something* attempted to make contact with you prior to your Summoning. I've never heard of such a thing before. I didn't think it was possible."

"Someone or something from *here*? Visiting my world?" The possibility was startling, as were the implications. Could I get back home? If things went bad here, was there a way back? I'll admit it wasn't the most admirable thought but it was the first thing that came to mind.

"I can't think of another explanation. The lore of the Summoning makes it clear that persons of power can be pulled across the plane to this world via the ritual. It stands to reason that it may be possible to travel in reverse. Perhaps the gate swings in both directions. Alexander will know more. If anyone has researched this sort of thing, it's him.

"I can anticipate your next question, Janelle," he said with a rueful smile. "In your situation, it would be mine as well. Alas, I've been here far too long for it to be relevant. I don't know if this means you can return to your old world. But consider this: if it was possible, would you want to?"

Would you want to? Another question I didn't know the answer to. Did I have a life worth going back to? My memories were too fragmentary for me to decide, although the isolated one from the final night didn't offer cause for optimism. But had I come from a bad situation to a doomed world?

"I have other things to worry about now." It was a fair answer. I'd make the decision if and when it became available to me. That wasn't now. "What about the headaches?"

"I'll need to look into your mind again. Last time, I sensed reluctance on your part. This incursion would be even more…intense."

The last thing I wanted was once again to be pinned down by his glare, to feel his mind pushing its way into mine. I suspected he had tried to be gentle last time but the sensation had still been profoundly unpleasant. Enduring something more "intense"…I didn't know if I could manage that.

"You're asking a lot."

"I'm asking nothing," he responded, his tone matter-of-fact. "I would gain nothing from this; it would be to address *your* problem. It's your decision. If you determine the touch of mind-to-mind is too intimate, I won't do it. I'm not going to force you, Janelle. That isn't the way of Summoners."

His words were reasonable but we both knew I didn't really have a choice, at least not if I wanted to access the full spectrum of my powers. Becoming disabled after a magical act might be feasible in a peaceful world but not in one where I might be called upon repeatedly in battle. I had to allow him to do this even if it unnerved and nauseated me.

"Do it," I muttered through clenched teeth.

He rose from his seat and walked around the table to stand over me. "Try not to resist. I know it's unnatural but I won't do anything to hurt you. If you push back, however, I might have to apply more pressure than either of us would prefer. Relax your mind."

He placed an index finger under my chin to tilt my head up so I was looking directly into his eyes. I absently noted how warm his flesh was - warm and soft, that of a man who had never done any labor with his hands. Not at all like Samell's. Then, as those dark eyes bored into me, I became lost. I could feel the pressure, pushing past my defenses and surging into the depths of my thoughts and memories. I concentrated on remaining calm and pliant, allowing the intruder to accomplish what he needed to do to fix whatever was defective. I was successful until his efforts triggered the very thing he was supposed to be remedying.

As soon as I felt the first stirrings of a headache - the dull throbbing beginning deep in my brain - I reacted with a vehemence that hurled Bergeron from my mind. He staggered and would have fallen if he hadn't grabbed the table for support. I exhaled deeply and blinked several times in rapid succession.

"I'm sorry," I managed. "I started to feel a headache."

"Quite understandable." Bergeron's voice was unsteady. "I'm not sure what to say or how to proceed."

"Then you didn't fix it?" My voice was thick with disappointment. Had I undergone that ordeal for no purpose?

"I'll admit that most of my knowledge of the mind's workings comes from books. It's been generations since I explored a real person but your pathways are like none I've encountered or read about. It's almost as if they have been intentionally manipulated to limit your magical abilities. The headaches are burned into your brain; I don't think they can be removed without doing serious damage. And your reaction when I accidentally triggered a headache…that kind of mental power could be a terrifying weapon if you could learn to control it. It's tied into your magic but somehow separate."

"My magic is gone again." My awareness of it had vanished the moment I expelled Bergeron from my mind. I groped for it to find only a vacuum.

"Not surprising. I suspect I triggered the same thing the soul-ripper did, although thankfully with less devastating results. If necessary, I can reset it the way I did earlier but it would be better if we could explore finding a way for you to do it. It's not good for you to have to rely on another Summoner."

We spent the remainder of the night wrestling with this problem. Bergeron did something with his magic to wipe away our weariness and keep us as alert as if we had experienced a full night's rest. "It's a trick," he explained. "Don't rely on it too much. Used sparingly, it replaces sleep. Overused, it will enflame the brain and can lead to insanity. Even Summoners need sleep - we just don't need as much of it as other people."

Despite persisting past the point of frustration, I couldn't get the hang of what he wanted me to do. "Look into your mind," he kept saying but no matter how I tried to contort my brain, I couldn't reach the "deeper plane of consciousness" where he wanted me to go. Too bad I didn't know transcendental meditation. We gave up around dawn without having made discernible progress.

"You're going to have to keep trying. This is something you need to do on your own. Maybe there's a trick to it. I don't know. Now, before I restore your magic, there's something else we have to discuss. What do you know about Summoning?"

"Only what Backus told me. When a Summoner is dying, he casts a massive spell that pulls across someone from another plane. The spell kills the Summoner. Backus called Summoning 'the last and greatest act of any practitioner of magic.'"

"A crude and not entirely accurate description. Summoning is more of a ritual than a spell, although the terms are largely interchangeable. It's an act that causes power to cascade through the Summoner, building to intense levels and transforming all available emotion into magic. The resulting maelstrom pulls another living being across the barrier between planes in what we call 'the lodestone effect'. The forces involved devastate the Summoner, leaving behind an emotionally bereft and physically decimated husk. I have never heard of anyone surviving a Summoning and, if it could be done, I don't think anyone would want to. But the Summoner doesn't have to be dying to invoke the ritual. It can be done at any time although only suicidal Summoners would do it before they feel the end approaching."

"How do you learn it? Is there a book? Backus said that only after I learn the spell will I truly be a Summoner."

Bergeron smiled one of his cold smiles. "It's more complicated than that but he's correct that one of the salient differences between wild wizards and Summoners is our understanding of the ritual. It's not learned from a book or scroll. To the best of my knowledge, it hasn't been written down or, if it once was, the text has long since been lost. The capability to Summon is *implanted* - given directly from one Summoner to another through a mind-to-mind connection."

I knew what was coming next…

"If you'll permit me, I'll undo the block and place knowledge of the Summoning ritual in your mind."

"You want to go back in *again*?"

"There's no other way."

"How do you know I won't throw you out?"

"I don't. In fact, I think there may be a danger to me. If I push too hard in the wrong spot, you could rip open a corridor to my mind to render me a gibbering idiot. But I'm willing to chance it because the world needs you for the coming struggle."

When he put it like that, how could I refuse?

Things went smoother this time. Maybe it had something to do with knowing what to expect or perhaps my mind was becoming receptive to his. Whatever the case, the discomfort wasn't as acute and the intrusion wasn't as intimate. It went quickly enough that, when he withdrew, I was surprised. I blinked once to break his gaze and was immediately aware that my magical abilities had returned. And there was something else, something buried deep, an itch I couldn't quite scratch.

"You'll get used to it. It feels odd at first but, over time, your mind will assimilate it."

"How do I access it?"

"Concentrate on it. At least that's what I plan to do when the time comes. The only ones who can say for sure are dead but since there are no records of failed Summonings, it can't be that difficult. Once triggered, it probably runs by itself. There's a caution in that - if you start the process, you can't stop it.

"Now, return to your companions and sleep a little. Your mind is bruised after all the incursions. When you're done resting, you can find me here and we'll start planning our war."

Chapter Twenty-Six: Hobson's Choice

It was frightening to be awakened in the middle of the night by an unfamiliar noise. I lay in my bed, hyperaware of my surroundings, my eyes open staring into the darkness and my heart beating at twice its normal rate.

It was a hot August night and our air conditioning wasn't working. It had been so warm inside that, before going to bed, I had opened my windows wide. The sound had come from somewhere outside. I remained immobile, breathing shallowly under the thin layer of sweat-drenched sheets.

Then I heard it again - a scrabbling against the side of the house like what one might expect from a rat trying to climb the siding. I wondered if my sister and parents could hear it but I doubted that - their windows were on the front of the house while mine was on the back. Whatever was out there was protected from being seen from the street.

By the light of day, this might not be so terrifying but, in the pitch black while shaking off the effects of a dream, I was more scared than I could remember being.

"Janelle." It was clear, precise, and unmistakable. A raspy voice had whispered my name. When I didn't respond, it was repeated, this time louder and more demanding. Whoever was speaking didn't like being ignored.

"Come downstairs. I have something for you."

I resisted the urge to burrow under the sheets.

"I know you're awake. I know many things about you. Don't make me come inside. You wouldn't like that. You wouldn't like another fire, would you?"

If there was one threat to spur me into action, that was it. I slipped out of bed, put on a cotton robe to cover my near-nakedness, and padded on bare feet over to the window. Looking out was pointless. The unlit backyard was a Stygian crypt.

"Come down here. Don't wake anyone." The voice was louder, coming from directly under my window. I squinted but it was useless. Even dark-adapted eyes needed some light and there was none out there. So I did the only thing I could think of - I crept through the upstairs hallway, avoiding the board that creaked, and descended the stairs. I turned the deadbolt lock in the back door slowly to muffle the unnaturally loud click it made then flipped on the outside light before exiting.

He approached me cautiously, almost as if he was as wary of me as I was of him. Then, with a shock of recognition, I knew who he was: the man from Camp Harmony. The one who had said, "Come with me, girl! Come with me or I'll just have to find you again." It made no sense. That had been three years ago!

"I'm not going to hurt you," he said as he approached. The circumstances argued that those words might not be entirely truthful.

I found my voice, "What do you want?" Like him, I was whispering. Perhaps I should have been screaming at the top of my lungs but his threat and the unnerving sense that he could make good on it kept me quiet. I would have backed up but the aluminum door was behind me.

"To prepare you for what is to come. None of this will make sense to you now, nor should it. But in another time, another place…Only I can give you the tools you will need to endure your ordeal."

By now, he had approached within touching distance. He smelled…odd. I had been around many unclean old men before and their scent was the same: a cologne of dried sweat and urine spiced with a hint of mold or mildew. With this stranger, it was different, a little like a musty attic or basement mingled with singed hair. The closer he got, the stronger the odor of burnt flesh became.

He was dressed in what appeared to be a sweatshirt and ill-fitting jeans. His feet, like mine, were bare. The hood was up, hiding his features. The light, affixed to the side of the house up and behind him, allowed his face to disappear into backlit shadows. A voice in my mind shouted for me to run but some power held me paralyzed, powerless to move. Strangely, however, the fear drained away. At the moment I should have been the most terrified, I was almost calm.

Slowly, he reached out with both hands and gripped my head. His warm, supple fingers caressed my cheeks and temple almost lovingly. Then everything went blank. There was a moment of pain but it was gone as quickly as it had come.

When I recovered, I was squatting at his feet. I had wet myself but it didn't matter.

"This memory will be hidden from you until the time when you need it. There are other things as well, things that must be. When you remember these words, seek out Alexander. He holds the key."

Then I forgot. Until now.

I woke to find myself alone in the sleeping chamber. Alone except for Samell, that is. He was watching me the way he often did, with a serious, wistful expression.

"That wasn't a long sleep," he said when my eyes opened. "How do you feel?"

Not refreshed but not tired. But this nap hadn't been about banishing fatigue; it had been about recovery this particular memory. A memory that changed everything. I wondered whether Bergeron had known. He had to be told.

"Find the others and stay with them," I told Samell. When he started to object, I cut him off. "I have to tell Bergeron what I just remembered. I don't know if he can make sense of it but it changes my mission here." *There might be a way for me to go home.* But I didn't say that aloud. I didn't want him to hear it because he might misinterpret it.

The rest of the group was in the feeding chamber, consuming whatever foodstuffs Bergeron had set out for their morning meal. The Summoner was where I had left him, poring over maps. He glanced up when I entered. Seeing in my face that I had something to say, he put aside an atlas and gave me his undivided attention.

I related the details of my new memory to him. Throughout my account, his features remained impassive. After I was done, a full minute of silence ensued before he made a remark. "It seems I have a lot to learn about the lore of Summoners. And here I thought I was a scholar."

His reaction angered me. I had just revealed a disconcerting snippet from my past and all he could think of was how it affected *him*.

"If there was any doubt that you need to see Alexander, this removes it. I assume, although I can't be certain, that your visitor was Lawrence. It's too bad you can't give a better description. Clothing isn't helpful since he would have had to come across naked. And the scent is probably a result of the transition. I recall stinking like I had walked through an ash pit. This changes very little about our immediate goal, however, but it opens some intriguing long-term possibilities. And it indicates that, for whatever reason, Summoners were tinkering with you long before you were brought over. How and why are the obvious questions and I don't think we're going to be able to answer them until we get to Erenton.

"Now," he continued without pause. "It's time to send your companions on their way back to West Fork. You, of course, will remain with me."

Bergeron's declaration startled me but, on consideration, I decided that it made sense. As much as my companions' presence would provide a sense of security, they weren't needed. There was nothing here for them to do. I would be getting a crash course in magic from Bergeron then helping him with whatever he intended to do against the reavers. The best course of action for the others was to return to West Fork and add their voices to those of Gabriel and Stepan. At the very least, Willem and Ramila should have enough clout to get the elders' attention. I would miss them all, of course, especially Samell. I was surprised to realize how much I had come to rely on him and how lonely things would be when he was gone.

When I told the others about the decision, I received mixed reactions. Willem said nothing but nodded as if he had expected this. Ramila also thought it was sensible. The three from Aeris protested, however, with Samell being the most forceful.

"Janelle, I came with you to be your guide, protector, and friend. I can't be any of those things in West Fork if you're still here," he said. Esme and Alyssa voiced their agreement.

"If there was any purpose to your staying, I'd welcome it, but Bergeron and I are going to be secluded and keeping you here doing nothing wouldn't benefit anyone. When we left Aeris, you agreed to come with me to help me reach Bergeron. We're here. Now we have to move forward with a new plan. Once I'm done here, I'll come to West Fork and join you. But for now, there's nothing you can do here and a great deal that might be accomplished if you return to West Fork. The town has to be made ready. I'm not sure what Bergeron and I can do against a force of reavers that large but I assume his goal will be to slow them down. They'll come eventually and in greater numbers than West Fork is prepared for."

"And if they attack here when there's no one to defend you?" Samell wasn't giving up easily.

"As much as it pains for me to admit it, I don't think a small group of armed guardians is going to make much of a difference if the reavers come in force. And if only a small number comes, I'm sure Bergeron can take care of them."

Samell wasn't happy but he conceded the logic of my arguments and, when he agreed to go, Esme and Alyssa capitulated as well. I felt bad because I knew how I would feel in their circumstances. I would fight tooth-and-nail to stay.

Bergeron didn't emerge to say goodbye but I accompanied them outside. It was a nice autumnal day - cool, crisp, and sunny. So much different from the heat and humidity that had dogged us when we left

Aeris. How long ago had that been? Only a few weeks but it seemed like so much longer. The more days I spent in this world, the more remote my old life seemed. Given a chance, would I really want to go back?

I had never been good at farewells and this was the first time I had been faced by one of significance in this land. Leaving Aeris had been different since Samell and Esme had remained by my side. Now, however, I was sending my two closest friends away. Necessity demanded this. It was the right thing to do. But that didn't make it any easier.

"Be careful, Janelle," said Esme. "You don't know him. I know he's a Summoner and you need what he can give you but don't trust him too much. There's something about him...it's hard to put into words." She shrugged helplessly.

"I know. I've felt it as well. I think it comes from using magic." *Specifically, from losing emotion as a result of using magic.* "I'll be careful. Don't worry."

Willem shook my hand without a word. He nodded, as if confirming something to himself, then stepped back.

Alyssa said only, "We'll miss you. Join us as soon as you can."

Ramila was equally brief, "When you get to West Fork, seek out my father and you'll find us. Until then, try to stay alive. We're going to need you."

That left Samell. He stepped close to me, closer than any of the others had. "I don't feel good about leaving you. I promised...but you're right. You have to stay with Bergeron and it's pointless for me to loiter here waiting to get killed by an army of reavers. Whatever happens, know that I'll be waiting for you." He paused but instead of saying more, leaned into me until his lips brushed my cheek.

"Goodbye," I whispered, my voice husky. "We'll meet again. I'll find you in West Fork...or wherever. Look for me before the hour grows dark."

That was all there was to say. I stood outside and watched them leave – kept watching until they vanished behind a boulder that blocked my view to the south. I kept the tears at bay but one or two slipped out, especially when Samell turned back and our eyes connected across a great distance. I wondered if any of us would be able to keep the promises we had made at the parting. Suddenly, this world seemed to be an inhospitable place.

Bergeron was waiting inside for me, continuing to study his maps. He pointed out several salient geographical features and I realized this was the first time I had seen a representation of this world on paper. "This map was drawn by Matthias, the most reputable map-maker in recent years. His travels took him all over the land, from sea to mountain, from the icy wastes in the north to the steaming jungles in the south."

He pointed to a spot deep in The Southern Peaks. "That's where they are. Use your mind. Tell me what you see."

I concentrated and was shocked by how much stronger the host had gotten since the last time I had checked. It hardly required any concentration to pinpoint their location. Equally importantly, they were no longer concentrated in a single, tight area as before. They had begun to spread out, infesting an ever-increasing range of the mountains.

"There are so many…" I was hardly aware of speaking aloud.

"Tens of thousands, drawn to that location by the power of the daemon. The force is nearly complete. It will sweep out from there and overrun the west. They are assembling faster than I would have thought possible. Instead of having weeks, we have a day or two at most. Your companions won't have reached West Fork by the time the reavers begin their march."

"Then the town is doomed." I felt sick to my stomach.

Bergeron nodded. "The reavers move quickly and don't tire. They will crush West Fork and kill anyone trying to escape. Within two weeks, every living creature in the west will have been eradicated.

And there's nothing anyone can do about it…except perhaps you and me."

The statement was audacious. He thought there was something the two of us could do against such a hoard? Was he mad? I again cast my mind into the mountains to see if I had missed something but nothing there gave me reason to hope.

"There is a way, or at least something we can do to make a difference. There's much danger in it, though. I can't guarantee either of us will survive. In fact, the odds are against it."

I digested his pronouncement and realized that the possibility of death didn't frighten me the way it once had. "If we do nothing, are we more likely to survive?"

"No. But you might live a little longer. You might be able to steal a few more days or weeks with your friends."

There wasn't really a choice but I hadn't expected there to be. "What do you need me to do?" And, just like that, my future - and possibly my death - was set.

"When it comes to your involvement, we have to keep in mind your limitations. Much as I'd like you to be able to engage fully, the headaches and your blockage will limit the amount of magic you can wield. We have to husband your resources, using them sparingly and only when absolutely necessary. So your function will be to watch and be ready. If I need you, I'll call for you. If you see something happening that I'm not aware of, like a physical attack when I'm otherwise occupied, you may have to handle that. I don't have a script for how this is going to progress. Our goal is less to defeat the army than it is to delay and disorient them. Once we make our presence known, they'll come for us and, because they're creatures of magic and earth, our location under a mountain isn't going to provide protection."

"What *exactly* are you going to do?"

"Element-based magic has its strengths and weaknesses. There are synergies and counters. Earth is vulnerable to water, which can wear it down and disperse it. I propose to use my abilities to divert a mountain tributary into the area where the reavers are massing. If we're lucky, it will kill a few but it will sow discord and chaos and force them to regroup. It will also make the daemon aware that it's being watched and hunted."

"Do we want to confront the daemon?"

"*Want??* The last thing I can imagine is *wanting* to confront a daemon. This is a matter of necessity. Stopping the reavers, or at least severely retarding their progress, requires that we negate their leader."

"How do you kill a daemon?"

"How indeed… Most physical attacks will be countered and magic won't be effective against a creature of eldritch puissance. There are a few things I can try but, in the end, it may come down to a last act of desperation. If I fall, Janelle, you mustn't attempt to fight the creature on your own. You lack the knowledge and skill to be able to overcome it and your internal inhibitions will prevent you from being able to stand against its full might. If the worst happens, flee to the east. Find the other Summoners and tell them of my fate. Don't stop at West Fork. Don't stop for anything."

Those were the words of a man who didn't expect to survive this day. Out there in the mountains was a tsunami of earth and magic preparing to crash down on the west. And if Bergeron was the only thing standing between that wave of disaster and its victims, I could understand his fatalism. As for me…never before had I felt so inadequate to the task set before me.

"When?" I asked, hoping we could at least wait long enough to give my companions a few more hours, not that such a meager amount of time was likely to make a difference.

"Waiting gains us nothing and gives them everything. The sooner we strike, the better our slim chances will be." He gripped my hand in what was intended to be a gesture of solidarity. Then it was time to begin.

Chapter Twenty-Seven: Summoner's Gambit

"Concentrate, Janelle. Try to align your mind's vision with mine. Sense what I sense. Experience what I experience. That link will be critical once we begin. You need to understand what I'm doing when I'm doing it, not just rely on seeing the results."

We had moved to a different chamber of Bergeron's home, a cylindrical room with a concave floor. It was empty and nearly dark, with only a lantern hanging in a nearby hallway to provide scant illumination. We sat barefoot and cross-legged on the cold stone. "We'll be facing creatures of the earth. The more intimate contact we have with their element, the better we'll be able to sense their actions." I was grateful that he didn't suggest I strip naked and lie on the ground.

"When you use magic, you have to learn to rely less on your natural senses, which aren't attuned to your abilities, and more on your mind. Many lesser Summoners fashion self-imposed constraints based on what they can see, hear, feel, taste, and smell. Greatness and access to power comes through overcoming those limitations. If you can *think* of something, magic can make it real. Your imagination should be your only barrier. Now, pay attention."

I did my best to follow the mental trail he blazed but it was difficult. I wasn't used to abandoning my physical body and relying on my mind-sense as my sole means of connection. Although being disembodied was a strange sensation, there was something freeing about the experience. I was a presence, soaring unconstrained through the ether, able to go anywhere on a whim without being concerned about physical impediments or time constraints. There was so much more to the mind-sense than I had previously realized. It wasn't merely a means to "see" beyond the range of my eyes' vision. It opened a window on an entirely different plane of existence.

Could I accomplish this unchaperoned? That was a dubious proposition. I felt inadequate to the task - transforming my understanding of magic from concrete to abstract wasn't something I could do on the spot. I wasn't sure whether I would ever be able to change my thinking to accommodate it.

You will be able to. It will take practice but it will come. The voice was as clear in my head as if I had originated the thought.

Bergeron acknowledged my surprise. *The link between us will remain anchored for as long as both of us are alive. It will allow us to communicate without the encumbrance of words. It will allow you to "see" what I do.*

He seemed to take it for granted that I would meekly accept this...link...without question or objection. But the idea that he was again inside my head, reading my thoughts, didn't sit well with me. I was by nature a private person and to have lost even the most basic privacy was anathema. And if he could read my thoughts, why couldn't I read his?

I can understand your qualms and, if we survive what is to come, we can argue about the ethics of this later. As for reading my thoughts, they're available to you. You only have to learn how to find them. The gateway to my mind is open; you only need step through. That also takes practice. You need to understand the workings of magic if you intend to replicate or adapt them. Some instruction can only come through action and we don't have time to start with small things.

"You set this up while you were in my mind?" I spoke the words out loud, an act that restored my awareness of my body. The sense of dissociation was profound – a part of me was with Bergeron's consciousness, deep in The Southern Peaks launching an attack, while another piece sat placidly beside him in his underground manse. The impression was a little like how it felt when memories were re-integrated.

His reply was verbal. "Yes. Because you need it and because you would have objected if I had asked you. You'll learn that dire circumstances often force us to abandon the morally upright choice in exchange for the expedient one. We don't have time to argue the *rightness* or *wrongness* of what I did. Discussion is for later."

I was about to say something to rebut him when the part of my mind linked with his recognized that he was approaching a critical juncture. Best not to distract him now. He was right – the time for discussion was later, assuming we survived.

Bergeron focused on a tributary of one of the many rivers winding through The Southern Peaks. I could feel the potency engendered by so many millions of gallons of water – the power to give life or destroy it. At the point where the roiling stream passed closest to the reavers' gathering, he unleashed a tightly focused burst of magic that collapsed the left riverbank, diverting the water flow into the canyon area where the creatures were massing. I marveled at the economy and simplicity of Bergeron's process, knowing I couldn't have done the same thing with such little effort over a great distance. So little emotion expended to accomplish such an imposing task...

That's because you constrain yourself. Distance is a physical barrier; your mind doesn't recognize it. As for the amount of magic I used...that comes from training. Summoners have a tendency to use more than they need. The excess is not only wasteful but it results in the creation and propagation of magic-based species like reavers and daemons. When you drive home a spike, hitting it with all your might will do the job but the same thing can be achieved with less effort if you strike just hard enough.

"And now?"

"We wait. It won't be long. You'll know as soon as the daemon takes notice of us."

Joined with his mind-sense, I observed the results of his magic. Chaos cascaded through the ranks of the reavers as the water poured from the mountain above them, an impromptu waterfall that inundated them, churning them under. The order that had defined their gathering disintegrated as they fled for higher, drier ground. Some certainly died, torn apart by the flood, but that number wasn't significant. What was a hundred compared to twenty-thousand? And any sense of satisfaction I might have experienced at the success of Bergeron's tactic was short-lived. A heavy, baleful influence turned its attention toward me and I felt my heart go cold as it locked on my presence. It was trying to look into my mind but, unlike Bergeron, it didn't have a pathway. The feeling was similar to what I had experienced when I had first encountered an earth reaver, only magnified a hundredfold.

"The daemon has found us," said Bergeron, his voice suddenly hoarse. I could tell he was under strain. "It will come. Now we gird for battle."

Everything started shaking at once – a quaking so violent that I thought for sure it would bring millions of tons of earth and rock down on us. Vibrations throbbed deep in the mountain. The floor shuddered so badly that if I hadn't been sitting, I would have lost my footing. Then, with the sound of thunder, a fissure big enough to admit a car opened in the wall. Through that opening stepped our adversary.

In the dim light, it was difficult for my eyes to distinguish much in the way of detail but the gross features were evident. The daemon's form was a grotesque parody of a human's, although bigger (at least 7 feet in height) and bulkier. Standing upright on legs as thick as tree trunks, its eyeless head was like a boulder and its long arms ended with sharp, prehensile claws. It appeared to be made out of rock and was accompanied by a nearly overpowering smell of dirt – not the clean, cool loam of topsoil but the decaying rot of a compost heap. It adopted an aggressive stance, towering over us as it prepared to strike.

My mind-sense revealed more. The daemon was a source of unalloyed power. I was unable to tell whether it could use the magic the way Bergeron and I could but that energy formed the essence of its composition, like water for the human body. Recognizing this gave me an inkling of how it could be defeated: the magical equivalent of dehydration. Drain a person of water and they died. Drain a daemon of magic and the same might be true. But how to do that…? I hadn't a clue.

As we rose to confront it, Bergeron motioned me to stand behind him, near the room's entryway.

"Summoner." The bass rumble shook the chamber, the voice of such a deep timber that it was felt as much as heard. "How fitting that one of your kind should be the first of my victims." Hatred dripped from every word; the daemon's desire wasn't simply to vanquish but to annihilate. There would be no compromising, no asking for or giving of quarter.

Bergeron was steeling himself either to attack or defend. I couldn't tell which but I could feel his tension. He was preparing something.

"A second Summoner?" The daemon noticed me despite Bergeron's attempts to keep me hidden from it. The initial puzzlement was replaced by something else (satisfaction?) when it next spoke. "Are you the one who has been promised?"

I didn't have time to ponder what *that* meant because Bergeron chose the moment to act.

There was no massive frontal assault or explosive display of magical prowess, although I hadn't expected either. The Summoner's first attacks were the equivalent of jabs: quick moves that tested the daemon's resilience against various forms of offensive weaponry like water and magic. Nothing was successful. If our opponent was aware of Bergeron's thrusts, it gave no indication. Through the link I shared with Bergeron, I sensed resignation. He hadn't expected such basic tactics to bear fruit but he had been obligated to try.

The daemon's retaliatory onslaught was one of brute force. Delivered magically, the blow didn't require physical contact, although the creature took a step forward to intimidate (as if its bulk wasn't menacing enough). It slammed its clawed appendages together; the resulting shock wave drove Bergeron and me to our knees, with my companion absorbing the worst of the attack. After it had passed – and it seemed to take a long time doing so - he was slow to recover.

My eyes told me little but my mind-sense indicated that he had been seriously injured, all parts of his body traumatized.

His riposte was more violent than his initial blows – a complex weaving of water and magic that, although imbued with the crushing force of a wave, was ultimately no more effective than his opening gambit. It might have penetrated the daemon's protection but any damage it did was insignificant, no more devastating than a bee sting. The creature made a sound that might have been a bark of laughter before launching its counterattack.

This strike was different in nature, an assault on Bergeron using every mote of dust and dirt in the vicinity as a superheated projectile. He was hastily able to fashion a crude shield to deflect the missiles but was taken unawares by either the nature or the ferocity of the daemon's tactics. The only headway he was making was to prove that no Summoner, even a trained veteran, could stand toe-to-toe against a daemon. Its weaknesses, if any, were concealed.

I watched helplessly, knowing there was nothing I could do. Anything I tried would be pointless – a drop of water in a lake. At this point, I doubted that retreat would be an option. After our adversary disposed of Bergeron, what chance would I have? It wasn't likely to allow me to run away.

A flurry of lightning-fast attacks by Bergeron – expressions of power so elegant that I marveled at their proficiency – left the daemon unfazed. It was effectively immune to magic and it didn't seem to share the reavers' weakness for water.

The creature lunged, surprisingly agile for something so hulking, and raked with its talons. Bergeron partially dodged - enough at least to keep his head from being demolished - but the impact wrenched a cry of pain from his lips as the flesh of his left shoulder and arm was shredded and the bones shattered.

Panic rose like bile in my throat. Paralyzed by a paroxysm of indecision, I remained rooted to the spot.

"Whatever...happens...don't interfere." For Bergeron, every labored word was an effort. Had I been in that much pain, I don't think I could have spoken. As I observed with my mind, he began the working of something colossal – an undertaking he was only partially in control of. It blossomed from deep within his subconscious where it had been implanted for this moment. I understood what he was doing.

Casting a Summoning was an instinctual process but Bergeron wasn't going about it in the traditional way. Instead, he was attempting to manipulate it to work in a manner that hadn't been intended. I hoped he could finish before the daemon realized what he was attempting.

Going into this confrontation, Bergeron had known what I had belatedly recognized: the way to neutralize a daemon was to drain the magic that comprised its essence. He had figured out a way to do that – or at least a way that *might* accomplish it. The question was whether he could implement his plan.

There was so much intricacy involved in the Summoning that it was difficult to follow. The undertaking required massive amounts of energy but Bergeron wasn't generating any magic. He was holding back, intentionally starving the process of the "fuel" it needed to trigger, forcing it to locate an alternative source. Glowing like a beacon, the daemon was impossible to miss.

The creature sensed its danger immediately, but that was already too late. Once unleashed, the Summoning couldn't be stopped. It devoured the daemon's magic to initiate the process then recoiled on Bergeron to siphon off the rest of what it needed. A Summoning demanded two kinds of energy to function – magic and the life's essence of the Summoner. To kill the daemon, Bergeron was sacrificing himself and there was nothing I could do to stop it or save him. This had to happen. There was no other way.

The daemon's death was strangely anticlimactic, similar as it was to that of the reavers. After raging and struggling for a few seconds, clawing at the air and uttering incoherent roars, it simply collapsed into a pile of steaming debris. So enraptured was I by the magical storm surrounding me that I barely noticed. The Summoning had taken over. With the daemon drained, Bergeron was now feeding it magic in addition to his fading life force and it was nearing its climax.

There was a moment's wrenching when time seemed to skip a groove, a flash of light that lit up the darkness like an exploding sun, and the odor of burned flesh and hair. Then it was done. I was left in silence near the ruined corpse of our adversary and the dying body of the man I had hoped would be my mentor.

I was amazed that Bergeron was still alive. The lantern in the corridor had gone out, plunging everything into blackness, but I could hear his labored breathing and my mind-sense told me that a spark of life (although no more than a spark) remained. Stunned and made dizzy by all I had experienced, I couldn't get to my feet, so I crawled across the floor toward him.

"Janelle, are you here?" The voice, a tortured whisper, sounded like the sound coming from someone with a trach tube. I groped for Bergeron's ice-cold hand and, when I found it, grasped it hard.

"I'm here." The words sounded unnaturally loud in the silence.

"Find my successor. You'll need each other. There will be more daemons and we can't afford to sacrifice a Summoner for each of them. Now get away from here. Go fast. The daemon's arrival destabilized this mountain and it will come crashing down once I'm gone. Flee or be buried with me."

Those were the last words he spoke, at least in my hearing.

Epilogue: Alone Again

There was no doubt about it: I was going to have to spend the night out here in the foothills of The Southern Peaks. Alone. For the first time since my early days in The Verdant Blight, I was by myself. My companions had a day's start and by now were approaching The Rank Marsh's southern fringes. Regardless of how fast I traveled, I wouldn't be able to catch them but my goal was to be not far behind when they entered West Fork. At least I wasn't being chased.

Bergeron was dead and, as he had warned, the caves comprising his home had collapsed in a mini-earthquake only moments after I escaped into the warm afternoon's air. My mind-sense no longer showed a massing of earth reavers in the mountains. They had scattered – in part because of the flooding and in part because their leader had been exterminated. The snake had lost its head and the tail was flailing about.

I was still amped up on adrenaline and fear. The two went hand-in-hand and had kept me going for much of the day. Remnants of the dizziness and vertigo lingered as well. The more I considered the events of the day and the extraordinary feat Bergeron had engineered, the more astonished I was that I had survived. Had this been his plan all along? Surely he had suspected from the beginning that no conventional magical attack would have damaged the daemon. The Summoning had been his contingency. He might have hoped to endure it, believing that with the daemon providing the magic, there could have been a path to survival. I suppose that made me his legacy...me and the new Summoner.

He had tasked me with finding him/her. I had no idea how to do that. Once again, I needed help. I would go first to West Fork. The villagers had to be made to understand how dire their situation was. One dead earth daemon didn't end the threat. In fact, it might introduce greater peril. All the other elemental forces – reavers and daemons alike – would know the means by which Bergeron had triumphed and would act to ensure his success wasn't repeated. The advantage of surprise could no longer be counted on to tip the scales.

After West Fork, my path would take me to find Loremaster Alexander. That had been Loremaster Lawrence's command. The advice of my Summoner and the man who had visited me in the world of my birth. It would be foolish to ignore it. Bergeron had pointed me to the southeast, to a city called Erenton, once the capitol of a great nation. Perhaps I would find the answers Bergeron hadn't been able (or willing) to provide. At the very least, I could expect to meet allies and perhaps become part of a coalition dedicated to the survival of humanity in the face of an implacable enemy. An enemy that my kind, Summoners, had been instrumental in creating through their own negligence.

There were other words to be considered as well – ones not spoken by Lawrence or Bergeron. *Are you the one who has been promised?* That hadn't been an idle or random pronouncement. There had been a purpose and meaning. It hinted at something dark. I needed to know what it meant.

For now, it was time to make camp, break out a portion of the meager traveler's rations I had left, and settle down for what was bound to be a long and taxing night. Physically, no one and *nothing* was hunting me, but the ghosts around here might visit me in my sleep.

Though I might again be alone, I wasn't the same frightened girl who had fled from the earth reaver in The Verdant Blight. I had discovered unsuspected powers, met faithful friends, and won at least a few fights against a malevolent enemy. Maybe Samell was right – when I thought of him, I wanted nothing more than to hear his voice – and the "old Janelle" was irrelevant. All that mattered was who I was today, who I had become during my brief time spent with Bergeron. I was Janelle the Summoner. I would dedicate my life to saving this world in the hope that I would either find a home here or uncover a way back to the place I had left behind.

* * *

Janelle and her companions will return in *The Elusive Strain Book 2: The Malignant Elements*, in which she will pursue the charge given to her by Bergeron, travel to new lands, and uncover an unsettling truth about her past.

Made in the USA
San Bernardino, CA
16 August 2018